Edited by Jack Dann & Gardner Dozois

UNICORNS!
MAGICATS!
BESTIARY!
MERMAIDS!
SORCERERS!
DEMONS!
DOGTALES!
SEASERPENTS!
DINOSAURS!
LITTLE PEOPLE!
MAGICATS II
UNICORNS II
DRAGONS!
INVADERS!
HORSES!
ANGELS!
HACKERS
TIMEGATES
CLONES
IMMORTALS
NANOTECH
ARMAGEDDONS

Edited by Terri Windling

FAERY!

ARMAGEDDONS

EDITED BY
JACK DANN & GARDNER DOZOIS

ACE BOOKS, NEW YORK

Care has been taken to trace ownership and obtain permission, if necessary, for the stories included in this book. If any errors have occurred, they will be corrected in subsequent printings if notification is sent to the publisher.

ARMAGEDDONS

An Ace Book / published by arrangement with
the editors

PRINTING HISTORY
Ace edition / November 1999

All rights reserved.
Copyright © 1999 by Jack Dann & Gardner Dozois.
Cover art by Phil Heffernan.
This book may not be reproduced in whole or in part,
by mimeograph or any other means, without permission.
For information address: The Berkley Publishing Group,
a division of Penguin Putnam Inc.,
375 Hudson Street, New York, New York 10014.

The Penguin Putnam Inc. World Wide Web site address is
http://www.penguinputnam.com

Check out the ACE Science Fiction & Fantasy newsletter
and much more on the Internet at Club PPI!

ISBN: 0-441-00675-2

ACE®
Ace Books are published
by The Berkley Publishing Group,
a division of Penguin Putnam Inc.,
375 Hudson Street, New York, New York 10014.
ACE and the "A" design are trademarks
belonging to Penguin Putnam Inc.

PRINTED IN THE UNITED STATES OF AMERICA

10 9 8 7 6 5 4 3 2 1

Acknowledgment is made
for permission to reprint the following material:

"Fermi and Frost," by Frederik Pohl. Copyright © 1984 by Davis Publications, Inc. First published in *Isaac Asimov's Science Fiction Magazine*, January 1985. Reprinted by permission of the author.

"A Desperate Calculus," by Gregory Benford. Copyright © 1995 by Abbenford Associates. First published (as by "Sterling Blake") in *New Legends* (Tor). Reprinted by permission of the author.

"Evolution," by Nancy Kress. Copyright © 1998 by Nancy Kress. First published in *Asimov's Science Fiction*, October 1995. Reprinted by permission of the author.

"A Message to the King of Brobdingnag," by Richard Cowper. Copyright © 1984 by Colin Murry. First published in *The Magazine of Fantasy and Science Fiction*, May 1984. Reprinted by permission of the author and the author's agent, Georges Borchardt, Inc.

". . . The World, as We Know't," by Howard Waldrop. Copyright © 1982 by Flight Unlimited, Inc. First published in *Shayol* #6, Winter 1982. Reprinted by permission of the author.

"The Peacemaker," by Gardner Dozois. Copyright © 1983 by Gardner Dozois. First published in *Isaac Asimov's Science Fiction Magazine*, August 1983. Reprinted by permission of the author.

"The Screwfly Solution," by Raccoona Sheldon. Copyright © 1977 by Alice B. Sheldon. First published in *Analog Science Fact/Science Fiction*, June 1977. Reprinted by permission of the author's estate and the agents for the estate, Virginia Kidd.

"A Pail of Air," by Fritz Leiber. Copyright © 1951 by Galaxy Publishing Corporation. First published in *Galaxy*, December 1951. Reprinted by permission of the author's estate and the agents for that estate.

"The Great Nebraska Sea," by Allan Danzig. Copyright © 1963 by Galaxy Publishing Corporation. First published in *Galaxy*, August 1963. Grateful acknowledgment is made for this story.

CONTENTS

PREFACE

Throughout most of human history, the end of the world was something that was brought about by God (or the gods, depending on who you were and where and when you were living), something determined by invisible forces that moved beyond the secular realm, something that was out of the hands of mortal man. The most commonly used word for the end of the world, "Armageddon," maintains this religious connotation to this day, although its use has been broadened to cover world-ending catastrophes in general as well as the specific event prophesied in the Christian Bible. So if you thought of the world coming to an end, you thought of it as something brought about by divine Powers —God sending a flood, or a pestilence, or plunging the world into cleansing fire.

It wasn't until the nineteenth century that the idea that the world could end by secular means—by random means related to the blind shuffling and interaction of cosmic forces, rather than by the direct will of God, began to penetrate into popular perception, spread by books and stories, such as H. G. Wells's "The Star," Mary Shelley's *The Last Man,* Edgar Allan Poe's "The Conversation of Eros and Charmion," and Arthur Conan Doyle's *The Poison Belt.* Wells also helped to establish in the popular mind two other ways that the world could end: by invasion, hostile aliens bent on exterminating the human race as casually as we would exterminate insects or vermin infesting a house (in *The War of the Worlds*); and by unending global warfare that would at least destroy much of civilization, even if it did not eradicate every human being on Earth (in *The Time Machine, The Shape of Things to Come,* and elsewhere).

This last idea was particularly potent, as it established the concept that *we* could bring about the end of the world (or at least the end of civilization) ourselves, by our own human efforts, without recourse either to blind cosmic accidents— such as a collision with a comet— or to the wrath of God (a lesson driven painfully home by the subsequent horrors of World War I).

By the time your editors came along, part of the post—World War II Baby Boom generation, the awesome shadow of the Atomic Bomb had risen over the world, and it was well understood that we humans could, if we chose, launch a war that would quite probably destroy not only civilization, but the human race as well, and possibly even all life on Earth.

Throughout the '50s, what most people worried about when they worried about the end of the world coming was the Bomb. Later, in the '60s and '70s, the idea of environmental destruction came along, a way that we could kill the human race (and perhaps all life on Earth) without even meaning to, as an accidental byproduct of the "progress" of our technological civilization. People then worried about pollution, overpopulation, DDT, *as well as* the Bomb. (But, if asked, most people would probably have been hard-pressed to come up with any other way that the world could end.)

What simple times those were! Now, from the perspective of the end of the '90s, just about to hurtle past the millennium and into the next century, we can think of dozens of new ways for the world to come to an end, for global Armageddon to come, ways that very few people would have even thought of twenty years ago, let alone *worried* about. Dozens of new ways that now are in the forefront of the public mind, and which probably cause as much dread and sleepless nights as worrying about the bomb ever did.

Few people twenty years ago, for instance, spent much time worrying that a giant asteroid might smash into the Earth and wipe us out at a stroke (although this was a scenario that scientists have known about for generations). But now, thanks in part to widespread and well-publicized speculation that such an asteroid strike might have been what killed off the dinosaurs, everyone knows (and worries) about this possibility; two separate big-budget movies about asteroids striking the Earth, *Deep Impact* and *Armageddon* were released in 1998—and now even people who didn't know about this scenario before are probably worrying about it! An increased sophistication in the earth sciences and a better understanding of geological forces has shown us that there's no place on Earth where you are safe from earthquakes and volcanic eruptions (this knowledge has been transferred to the public mind by films such as *Volcano* and *Dante's Peak*. One volcanic explosion that took place in New Mexico a million years ago, for instance, not only vaporized a 27,000-foot-tall mountain, but left behind a hole in the ground 12 miles across and 3,500 feet deep, and was powerful enough to throw debris as far away as Nebraska. A volcanic eruption of similar force taking place today, even in an area as relatively unpopulated as the American Southwest, would kill hundreds of thousands of people. Earthquakes on the scale of the one that struck the Mississippi Valley in the eighteenth century would kill millions, and we now know that tsunamis on a really massive scale, far greater than anything thought possible forty years ago (as vividly portrayed in *Deep Impact*), are not only possible but have happened with dismaying frequency over the millennia, leaving their marks on the geologic record.

In addition to the old worries about pollution, we now have to worry about global warming (the melting of the Antarctic icecap would flood large areas of the world) and the ever growing hole in the ozone layer that is letting in ever more dangerous levels of ultraviolet radiation (and the latest issue of *Discover* magazine warns us that the atmosphere itself may be shrinking). Some stubborn scientists hold out against the idea of global warming and instead warn that a new Ice Age is possible, one that could reach full glaciation with frightening speed, dozens of years instead of hundreds of thousands, grinding much of our civilization to powder in the process.

But wait! There's more! We know now that a nearby (as stellar distances go) supernova could spray the Earth with enough hard radiation to endanger or destroy terrestrial life . . . and, in fact, a minor, low-intensity version of this happened in 1998, knocking out several communications satellites. For that matter, our own sun has been acting suspiciously, not conforming to current neutrino-emission models. Could this be a prelude to the sun going nova, or emitting an immensely powerful solar flare? And if none of those things gets us, recent evidence has shown that the center of our own Milky Way galaxy is dominated by a massive black hole that not only may periodically emit killing bursts of radiation, but which will eventually swallow up everything else in our galaxy, including *us*. That is, if another galaxy doesn't smash into ours first in a cosmic collision of unimaginable proportions, something that we can see happening elsewhere in the universe. And then there're the esoteric possibilities for doom, involving things such as the release of quantum energy from the structure of the vacuum itself . . .

Nor have any of the *older* possibilities gone away: The Four Horsemen of the Apocalypse remain always ready to ride; starvation on a global scale is an ever more plausible possibility, as population continues to climb and resources shrink; disease, the threat of some world-girdling pandemic or plague, is a specter we always have to live with, perhaps more potent than ever in these days of jet travel between continents, when someone exposed in Africa or South America to a rare virus that's never before made it out of the jungle can be in New York City or London a few hours later (to say nothing of deliberate biological warfare or terrorism, or the fact that overuse of antibiotics is quickly rendering most of them ineffective, or that the potential for a biological-research accident that could have devastating effects has never been greater). Nor has war vanished as a threat to the survival of the human race, in spite of the end of the Cold War. In fact, it seems likely that not only will there continue to be wars in the next century, but that they will be fought with horrifying high-tech weapons more strange than anything that is currently possible for us to imagine. (Nanomechanisms, for instance, that gobble everything they touch, turning the world to "gray goo," is only one of the possibilities, and probably less radical than many of the weapons that will be developed by the time the century turns again—if anyone survives to see it, that is!)

It's no wonder, with all these dooms (and scores of others) hanging over our heads, that we're all getting a little nervous as the dawn of the new millennium—a time-marker of great supernatural significance, historically always a time of panic about the end of the world—approaches.

Since you're worrying about all this anyway, as millennium fever grows more intense (wait! We didn't even *mention* the Y2K problem!), we thought you might be interested in reading about some of the ways the end of the world might come, perhaps giving you some new stuff to worry about (great for those conversations at the office the next day), or at the very least providing some entertainment and distraction for you as you wait for us all to check out. If you're going to worry about the end of the world anyway, then you might as well let the world's most imaginative dreamers and prognosticators, the science fiction writers you'll find in the pages that follow, show you some really imaginative (and frightening) scenarios for cosmic Armageddons that *might* happen . . . and also, some of the glimmerings of hope that may persist even if worse *does* come to worst.

If, as we suspect, the world *doesn't* come to an end with the turning of the millennium, then you'll have had the fun of reading some of the best science fiction stories our weary old world has yet produced.

Maybe you better read *fast*, though—just in case!

(Fans of end-of-the-world scenarios will find more, of varying sorts, in the Ace anthologies *Future War, Nanotech, Hackers, Invaders!, Isaac Asimov's War,* and *Isaac Asimov's Earth.*)

FERMI AND FROST

Frederik Pohl

One of the most plausible ways for the world to end is that we end it ourselves, either by the irreversible damage to the ecosystem caused by modern industry, or deliberately, by plunging the world into global nuclear war. Entire generations have grown up in the terrible shadow of the Bomb since the end of World War II. And at times, such as the tense days of the Cuban Missile Crisis, we did come within a hair-breadth of someone actually pushing the Button and starting World War III, and perhaps dooming the human race to extinction. Here in the post–Cold War era, we like to congratulate ourselves that we're beyond the threat of atomic Armageddon; but, alas, with new countries like India and Pakistan joining the nuclear arms club, this smug self-congratulation may turn out to be premature; it may even be that a nuclear war is more likely now, with nuclear arms capability being scattered among so many nations, than it was in the old balance-of-terror days of one-on one confrontation between two opposing superpowers.

It's hard to find a more powerful evocation of what it might be like if the Button ever does get pushed than the harrowing and immensely sad story that follows, one that, alas, is not really dated in any significant way in spite of being fourteen years old, and one that we'd better pray won't prove to be prophetic, for all our sakes.

A seminal figure whose career spans almost the entire development of modern SF, Frederik Pohl has been one of the genre's major shaping forces—as writer, editor, agent, and anthologist—for more than fifty years. He was the founder of the Star *series, SF's first continuing anthology series, and was the editor of the* Galaxy *group of magazines from 1960 to 1969 (during which time* Galaxy's *sister magazine,* Worlds of If, *won three consecutive Best Professional Magazine Hugos). As a writer, he has several times won Nebula and Hugo Awards, as well as the American Book Award and the*

French Prix Apollo. His many books include several written in collaboration with the late C. M. Kornbluth—including The Space Merchants, Wolfbane, *and* Gladiator-at-Law— *and many solo novels, including* Gateway, Man Plus, Beyond the Blue Event Horizon, The Coming of the Quantum Cats, *and* Mining the Oort. *Among his many collections are* The Gold at the Starbow's End, In the Problem Pit, *and* The Best of Frederik Pohl. *He also wrote a nonfiction book in collaboration with Isaac Asimov,* Our Angry Earth, *which takes a hard-eyed look at the various ways that we continue to destroy the ecosystem of the only planet we've got. His most recent books are the novels* O Pioneer!, The Siege of Eternity, *and* The Far Shore of Time.

On Timothy Clary's ninth birthday he got no cake. He spent all of it in a bay of the TWA terminal at John F. Kennedy airport in New York, sleeping fitfully, crying now and then from exhaustion or fear. All he had to eat was stale Danish pastries from the buffet wagon and not many of them, and he was fearfully embarrassed because he had wet his pants. Three times. Getting to the toilets over the packed refugee bodies was just about impossible. There were twenty-eight hundred people in a space designed for a fraction that many, and all of them with the same idea. Get away! Climb the highest mountain! Drop yourself splat, spang, right in the middle of the widest desert! Run! Hide!—

And pray. Pray as hard as you can, because even the occasional planeload of refugees that managed to fight their way aboard and even take off had no sure hope of refuge when they got wherever the plane was going. Families parted. Mothers pushed their screaming children aboard a jet and melted back into the crowd before screaming, more quietly, themselves.

Because there had been no launch order yet, or none that the public had heard about anyway, there might still be time for escape. A little time. Time enough for the TWA terminal, and every other airport terminal everywhere, to jam up with terrified lemmings. There was no doubt that the missiles were poised to fly. The attempted Cuban coup had escalated wildly, and one nuclear sub had attacked another with a nuclear charge. That, everyone agreed, was the signal. The next event would be the final one.

Timothy knew little of this, but there would have been nothing he could have done about it—except perhaps cry, or have nightmares, or wet himself, and young Timothy was doing all of those anyway. He did not know where his father was. He didn't know where his mother was, either, except that she had gone somewhere to try to call his father; but then there had been a surge that could not be resisted when three 747s at once had announced boarding, and Timothy had been carried far from where he had been left. Worse than that. Wet as he was, with a cold already, he was beginning to be very sick. The young woman who had brought him the Danish pastries put a worried hand to his forehead and drew it away helplessly. The boy needed a doctor. But so did a hundred others, elderly heart patients and hungry babies and at least two women close to childbirth.

If the terror had passed and the frantic negotiations had succeeded, Timothy might have found his parents again in time to grow up and marry and give them grandchildren. If one side or the other had been able to preempt, and destroy the other, and save itself, Timothy forty years later might have been a graying, cynical colonel in the American military government of Leningrad. (Or body servant to a Russian one in Detroit.) Or if his mother had pushed just a little harder earlier on, he might have wound up in the plane of refugees that reached Pittsburgh just in time to become plasma. Or if the girl who was watching him had become just a little more scared, and a little more brave, and somehow managed to get him through the throng to the improvised clinics in the main terminal, he might have been given medicine, and found somebody to protect him, and take him to a refuge, and live. . . .

But that is in fact what did happen!

Because Harry Malibert was on his way to a British Interplanetary Society seminar in Portsmouth, he was already sipping Beefeater Martinis in the terminal's Ambassador Club when the unnoticed TV at the bar suddenly made everybody notice it.

Those silly nuclear-attack communications systems that the

radio stations tested out every now and then, and nobody paid
any attention to any more—why, this time it was real! They
were serious! Because it was winter and snowing heavily
Malibert's flight had been delayed anyway. Before its resched-
uled departure time came, all flights had been embargoed.
Nothing would leave Kennedy until some official somewhere
decided to let them go.

Almost at once the terminal began to fill with would-be
refugees. The Ambassador Club did not fill at once. For three
hours the ground-crew stew at the desk resolutely turned away
everyone who rang the bell who could not produce the little red
card of admission; but when the food and drink in the main
terminals began to run out the Chief of Operations summarily
opened the club to everyone. It didn't help relieve the conges-
tion outside, it only added to what was within. Almost at once
a volunteer doctors' committee seized most of the club to treat
the ill and injured from the thickening crowds, and people like
Harry Malibert found themselves pushed into the bar area. It
was one of the Operations staff, commandeering a gin and tonic
at the bar for the sake of the calories more than the booze, who
recognized him. "You're Harry Malibert. I heard you lecture
once, at Northwestern."

Malibert nodded. Usually when someone said that to him he
answered politely, "I hope you enjoyed it," but this time it did
not seem appropriate to be normally polite. Or normal at all.

"You showed slides of Arecibo," the man said dreamily.
"You said that radio telescope could send a message as far as
the Great Nebula in Andromeda, two million light-years
away—if only there was another radio telescope as good as
that one there to receive it."

"You remember very well," said Malibert, surprised.

"You made a big impression, Dr. Malibert." The man
glanced at his watch, debated, took another sip of his drink.
"It really sounded wonderful, using the big telescopes to listen
for messages from alien civilizations somewhere in space—
maybe hearing some, maybe making contact, maybe not being
alone in the universe any more. You made me wonder why we
hadn't seen some of these people already, or anyway heard
from them—but maybe," he finished, glancing bitterly at the
ranked and guarded aircraft outside, "maybe now we know
why."

Malibert watched him go, and his heart was leaden. The thing he had given his professional career to—SETI, the Search for Extra-Terrestrial Intelligence—no longer seemed to matter. If the bombs went off, as everyone said they must, then that was ended for a good long time, at least—

Gabble of voices at the end of the bar, Malibert turned, leaned over the mahogany, peered. The *Please Stand By* slide had vanished, and a young black woman with pomaded hair, voice trembling, was delivering a news bulletin:

"—the president has confirmed that a nuclear attack has begun against the United States. Missiles have been detected over the Arctic, and they are incoming. Everyone is ordered to seek shelter and remain there pending instructions—"

Yes. It was ended, thought Malibert, at least for a good long time.

The surprising thing was that the news that it had begun changed nothing. There were no screams, no hysteria. The order to seek shelter meant nothing at John F. Kennedy Airport, where there was no shelter any better than the building they were in. And that, no doubt, was not too good. Malibert remembered clearly the strange aerodynamic shape of the terminal's roof. Any blast anywhere nearby would tear that off and send it sailing over the bay to the Rockaways, and probably a lot of the people inside with it.

But there was nowhere else to go.

There were still camera crews at work, heaven knew why. The television set was showing crowds in Times Square and Newark, a clot of automobiles stagnating on the George Washington Bridge, their drivers abandoning them and running for the Jersey shore. A hundred people were peering around each other's heads to catch glimpses of the screen, but all that anyone said was to call out when he recognized a building or a street.

Orders rang out: "You people will have to move back! We need the room! Look, some of you, give us a hand with these patients." Well, that seemed useful, at least. Malibert volunteered at once and was given the care of a young boy, teeth chattering, hot with fever. "He's had tetracycline," said the doctor who turned to boy over to him. "Clean him up if you can, will you? He ought to be all right if—"

If any of them were, thought Malibert, not requiring her to finish the sentence. How did you clean a young boy up? The question answered itself when Malibert found the boy's trousers soggy and the smell told him what the moisture was. Carefully he laid the child on a leather love seat and removed the pants and sopping undershorts. Naturally the boy had not come with a change of clothes. Malibert solved that with a pair of his own jockey shorts out of his briefcase—far too big for the child, of course, but since they were meant to fit tightly and elastically they stayed in place when Malibert pulled them up to the waist. Then he found paper towels and pressed the blue jeans as dry as he could. It was not very dry. He grimaced, laid them over a bar stool and sat on them for a while, drying them with body heat. They were only faintly wet ten minutes later when he put them back on the child—

San Francisco, the television said, has ceased to transmit.

Malibert saw the Operations man working his way toward him and shook his head. "It's begun," Malibert said, and the man looked around. He put his face close to Malibert's.

"I can get you out of here," he whispered. "There's an Icelandic DC-8 loading right now. No announcement. They'd be rushed if they did. There's room for you, Dr. Malibert."

It was like an electric shock. Malibert trembled. Without knowing why he did it, he said, "Can I put the boy on instead?"

The Operations man looked annoyed. "Take him with you, of course," he said. "I didn't know you had a son."

"I don't," said Malibert. But not out loud. And when they were in the jet he held the boy in his lap as tenderly as though he were his own.

If there was no panic in the Ambassador Club at Kennedy there was plenty of it everywhere else in the world. What everyone in the superpower cities knew was that their lives were at stake. Whatever they did might be in vain, and yet they had to do something. Anything! Run, hide, dig, brace, stow . . . pray. The city people tried to desert the metropolises for the open safety of the country, and the farmers and the exurbanites sought the stronger, safer buildings of the cities.

And the missiles fell.

The bombs that had seared Hiroshima and Nagasaki were struck matches compared to the hydrogen-fusion flares that ended eighty million lives in those first hours. Firestorms fountained above a hundred cities. Winds of three hundred kilometers an hour pulled in cars and debris and people, and they all became ash that rose to the sky. Splatters of melted rock and dust sprayed into the air.

The sky darkened.

Then it grew darker still.

When the Icelandic jet landed at Keflavik Airport Malibert carried the boy down the passage to the little stand marked *Immigration*. The line was long, for most of the passengers had no passports at all, and the immigration woman was very tired of making out temporary entrance permits by the time Malibert reached her. "He's my son," Malibert lied. "My wife has his passport, but I don't know where my wife is."

She nodded wearily. She pursed her lips, looked toward the door beyond which her superior sat sweating and initialing reports, then shrugged and let them through. Malibert took the boy to a door marked *Snirting,* which seemed to be the Icelandic word for toilets, and was relieved to see that at least Timothy was able to stand by himself while he urinated, although his eyes stayed half closed. His head was very hot. Malibert prayed for a doctor in Reykjavik.

In the bus the English-speaking tour guide in charge of them—she had nothing else to do, for her tour would never arrive—sat on the arm of a first-row seat with a microphone in her hand and chattered vivaciously to the refugees. "Chicago? Ya, is gone, Chicago. And Detroit and Pittis-burrug—is bad. New York? Certainly New York too!" she said severely, and the big tears rolling down her cheek made Timothy cry too.

Malibert hugged him. "Don't worry, Timmy," he said. "No one would bother bombing Reykjavik." And no one would have. But when the bus was ten miles farther along there was a sudden glow in the clouds ahead of them that made them squint. Someone in the USSR had decided that it was time for neatening up loose threads. That someone, whoever remained in whatever remained of their central missile control, had realized that no one had taken out that supremely, insultingly dangerous bastion of the imperialist American interests in the North Atlantic, the United States airbase at Keflavik.

Unfortunately, by then EMP and attrition had compromised

the accuracy of their aim. Malibert had been right. No one
would have bothered bombing Reykjavik—on purpose—but a
forty-mile miss did the job anyway, and Reykjavik ceased to
exist.

They had to make a wide detour inland to avoid the fires and
the radiation. And as the sun rose on their first day in Iceland,
Malibert, drowsing over the boy's bed after the Icelandic nurse
had shot him full of antibiotics, saw the daybreak in awful,
sky-drenching red.

It was worth seeing, for in the days to come there was no
daybreak at all.

The worst was the darkness, but at first that did not seem
urgent. What was urgent was rain. A trillion trillion dust
particles nucleated water vapor. Drops formed. Rain fell—
torrents of rain; sheets and cascades of rain. The rivers swelled.
The Mississippi overflowed, and the Ganges, and the Yellow.
The High Dam at Aswan spilled water over its lip, then
crumbled. The rains came where rains came never. The Sahara
knew flash floods. The Flaming Mountains at the edge of the
Gobi flamed no more; a ten-year supply of rain came down in
a week and rinsed the dusty slopes bare.

And the darkness stayed.

The human race lives always eighty days from starvation.
That is the sum of stored food, globe wide. It met the nuclear
winter with no more and no less.

The missiles went off on the 11th of June. If the world's
larders had been equally distributed, on the 30th of August the
last mouthful would have been eaten. The starvation deaths
would have begun and ended in the next six weeks; exit the
human race.

The larders were not equally distributed. The Northern
Hemisphere was caught on one foot, fields sown, crops not yet
grown. Nothing did grow there. The seedlings poked up
through the dark earth for sunlight, found none, died. Sunlight
was shaded out by the dense clouds of dust exploded out of the
ground by the H-bombs. It was the Cretaceous repeated;
extinction was in the air.

There were mountains of stored food in the rich countries of
North America and Europe, of course, but they melted swiftly.
The rich countries had much stored wealth in the form of their

livestock. Every steer was a million calories of protein and fat. When it was slaughtered, it saved thousands of other calories of grain and roughage for every day lopped off its life in feed. The cattle and pigs and sheep—even the goats and horses; even the pet bunnies and chicks; even the very kittens and hamsters— they all died quickly and were eaten, to eke out the stores of canned foods and root vegetables and grain. There was no rationing of the slaughtered meat. It had to be eaten before it spoiled.

Of course, even in the rich countries the supplies were not equally distributed. The herds and the grain elevators were not located on Times Square or in the Loop. It took troops to convoy corn from Iowa to Boston and Dallas and Philadelphia. Before long, it took killing. Then it could not be done at all.

So the cities starved first. As the convoys of soldiers made the changeover from seizing food for the cities to seizing food for themselves, the riots began, and the next wave of mass death. These casualties didn't usually die of hunger. They died of someone else's.

It didn't take long. By the end of "summer" the frozen remnants of the cities were all the same. A few thousand skinny, freezing desperadoes survived in each, sitting guard over their troves of canned and dried and frozen foodstuffs.

Every river in the world was running sludgy with mud to its mouth, as the last of the trees and grasses died and relaxed their grip on the soil. Every rain washed dirt away. As the winter dark deepened the rains turned to snow. The Flaming Mountains were sheeted in ice now, ghostly, glassy fingers uplifted to the gloom. Men could walk across the Thames at London now, the few men who were left. And across the Hudson, across the Whangpoo, across the Missouri between the two Kansas Cities. Avalanches rumbled down on what was left of Denver. In the stands of dead timber grubs flourished. The starved predators scratched them out and devoured them. Some of the predators were human. The last of the Hawaiians were finally grateful for their termites.

A Western human being—comfortably pudgy on a diet of 2800 calories a day, resolutely jogging to keep the flab away or mournfully conscience-stricken at the thickening thighs and the waistbands that won't quite close—can survive for forty-five days without food. By then the fat is gone. Protein reabsorption

of the muscles is well along. The plump housewife or busi-
nessman is a starving scarecrow. Still, even then care and
nursing can still restore health.

Then it gets worse.

Dissolution attacks the nervous system. Blindness begins.
The flesh of the gums recedes, and the teeth fall out. Apathy
becomes pain, then agony, then coma.

Then death. Death for almost every person on Earth. . . .

For forty days and forty nights the rain fell, and so did the
temperature. Iceland froze over.

To Harry Malibert's astonishment and dawning relief, Iceland was well equipped to do that. It was one of the few places
on Earth that could be submerged in snow and ice and still
survive.

There is a ridge of volcanoes that goes almost around the
Earth. The part that lies between America and Europe is called
the Mid-Atlantic Ridge, and most of it is under water. Here
and there, like boils erupting along a forearm, volcanic islands
poke up above the surface. Iceland is one of them. It was
because Iceland was volcanic that it could survive when most
places died of freezing, but it was also because it had been cold
in the first place.

The survival authorities put Malibert to work as soon as they
found out who he was. There was no job opening for a radio
astronomer interested in contacting far-off (and very likely
non-existent) alien races. There was, however, plenty of work
for persons with scientific training, especially if they had the
engineering skills of a man who had run Arecibo for two years.
When Malibert was not nursing Timothy Clary through the
slow and silent convalescence from his pneumonia, he was
calculating heat losses and pumping rates for the piped
geothermal water.

Iceland filled itself with enclosed space. It heated the spaces
with water from the boiling underground springs.

Of heat it had plenty. Getting the heat from the geyser fields
to the enclosed spaces was harder. The hot water was as hot as
ever, since it did not depend at all on sunlight for its calories,
but it took a lot more of it to keep out a -30°C chill than a +5°C
one. It wasn't just to keep the surviving people warm that they
needed energy. It was to grow food.

Iceland had always had a lot of geothermal greenhouses. The flowering ornamentals were ripped out and food plants put in their place. There was no sunlight to make the vegetables and grains grow, so the geothermal power-generating plants were put on max output. Solar-spectrum incandescents flooded the trays with photons. Not just in the old greenhouses. Gymnasia, churches, schools—they all began to grow food under the glaring lights. There was other food, too, metric tons of protein baaing and starving in the hills. The herds of sheep were captured and slaughtered and dressed—and put outside again, to freeze until needed. The animals that froze to death on the slopes were bulldozed into heaps of a hundred, and left where they were. Geodetic maps were carefully marked to show the location of each heap.

It was, after all, a blessing that Reykjavik had been nuked. That meant half a million fewer people for the island's resources to feed.

When Malibert was not calculating load factors, he was out in the desperate cold, urging on the workers. Sweating navvies tried to muscle shrunken fittings together in icy foxholes that their body heat kept filling with icewater. They listened patiently as Malibert tried to give orders—his few words of Icelandic were almost useless, but even the navvies sometimes spoke tourist-English. They checked their radiation monitors, looked up at the storms overhead, returned to their work and prayed. Even Malibert almost prayed when one day, trying to locate the course of the buried coastal road, he looked out on the sea ice and saw a gray-white ice hummock that was not an ice hummock. It was just at the limits of visibility, dim on the fringe of the road crew's work lights, and it moved. "A polar bear!" he whispered to the head of the work crew, and everyone stopped while the beast shambled out of sight.

From then on they carried rifles.

When Malibert was not (incompetent) technical advisor to the task of keeping Iceland warm or (almost incompetent, but learning) substitute father to Timothy Clary, he was trying desperately to calculate survival chances. Not just for them; for the entire human race. With all the desperate flurry of survival work, the Icelanders spared time to think of the future. A study team was created, physicists from the University of Reykjavik,

the surviving Supply officer from the Keflavik airbase, a
meteorologist on work-study from the University of Leyden to
learn about North Atlantic air masses. They met in the gasthuis
where Malibert lived with the boy, and usually Timmy sat
silent next to Malibert while they talked. What they wanted was
to know how long the dust cloud would persist. Some day the
particles would finish dropping from the sky, and then the
world could be reborn—if enough survived to parent a new
race, anyway. But when? They could not tell. They did not
know how long, how cold, how killing the nuclear winter
would be. "We don't know the megatonnage," said Malibert,
"we don't know what atmospheric changes have taken place,
we don't know the rate of insolation. We only know it will be
bad."

"It is already bad," grumbled Thorsid Magnesson, Director
of Public Safety. (Once that office had had something to do
with catching criminals, when the major threat to safety was
crime.)

"It will get worse," said Malibert, and it did. The cold
deepened. The reports from the rest of the world dwindled.
They plotted maps to show what they knew to show. One set of
missile maps, to show where the strikes had been—within a
week that no longer mattered, because the deaths from cold
already began to outweigh those from blast. They plotted
isotherm maps, based on the scattered weather reports that
came in—maps that had to be changed every day, as the
freezing line marched toward the Equator. Finally the maps
were irrelevant. The whole world was cold then. They plotted
fatality maps—the percentages of deaths in each area, as they
could infer them from the reports they received, but those maps
soon became too frightening to plot.

The British Isles died first, not because they were nuked but
because they were not. There were too many people alive there.
Britain never owned more than a four-day supply of food.
When the ships stopped coming they starved. So did Japan. A
little later, so did Bermuda and Hawaii and Canada's off-shore
provinces; and then it was the continents' turn.

And Timmy Clary listened to every word.

The boy didn't talk much. He never asked after his parents,
not after the first few days. He did not hope for good news, and
did not want bad. The boy's infection was cured, but the boy

himself was not. He ate half of what a hungry child should devour. He ate that only when Malibert coaxed him.

The only thing that made Timmy look alive was the rare times when Malibert could talk to him about space. There were many in Iceland who knew about Harry Malibert and SETI, and a few who cared about it almost as much as Malibert himself. When time permitted they would get together, Malibert and his groupies. There was Lars the postman (now pick-and-shovel ice excavator, since there was no mail), Ingar the waitress from the Loftleider Hotel (now stitching heavy drapes to help insulate dwelling walls), Elda the English teacher (now practical nurse, frostbite cases a specialty). There were others, but those three were always there when they could get away. They were Harry Malibert fans who had read his books and dreamed with him of radio messages from weird aliens from Aldebaran, or worldships that could carry million-person populations across the galaxy, on voyages of a hundred thousand years. Timmy listened, and drew sketches of the worldships. Malibert supplied him with dimensions. "I talked to Gerry Webb," he said, "and he'd worked it out in detail. It is a matter of rotation rates and strength of materials. To provide the proper simulated gravity for the people in the ships, the shape has to be a cylinder and it has to spin—sixteen kilometers is what the diameter must be. Then the cylinder must be long enough to provide space, but not so long that the dynamics of spin cause it to wobble or bend—perhaps sixty kilometers long. One part to live in. One part to store fuel. And at the end, a reaction chamber where hydrogen fusion thrusts the ship across the Galaxy."

"Hydrogen bombs," said the boy. "Harry? Why don't the bombs wreck the worldship?"

"It's engineering," said Malibert honestly, "and I don't know the details. Gerry was going to give his paper at the Portsmouth meeting; it was one reason I was going." But, of course, there would never be a British Interplanetary Society meeting in Portsmouth now, ever again.

Elda said uneasily, "It is time for lunch soon. Timmy? Will you eat some soup if I make it?" And did make it, whether the boy promised or not. Elda's husband had worked at Keflavik in the PX, an accountant; unfortunately he had been putting in overtime there when the follow-up missile did what the miss had failed to do, and so Elda had no husband left, not enough even to bury.

Even with the earth's hot water pumped full velocity through the straining pipes it was not warm in the gasthuis. She wrapped the boy in blankets and sat near him while he dutifully spooned up the soup. Lars and Ingar sat holding hands and watching the boy eat. "To hear a voice from another star," Lars said suddenly, "that would have been fine."

"There are no voices," said Ingar bitterly. "Not even ours now. We have the answer to the Fermi paradox."

And when the boy paused in his eating to ask what that was, Harry Malibert explained it as carefully as he could:

"It is named after Enrico Fermi, a scientist. He said, 'We know that there are many millions of stars like our sun. Our sun has planets, therefore it is reasonable to assume that some of the other stars do also. One of our planets has living things on it. Us, for instance, as well as trees and germs and horses. Since there are so many stars, it seems almost certain that some of them, at least, have also living things. People. People as smart as we are—or smarter. People who can build spaceships, or send radio messages to other stars, as we can.' Do you understand so far, Timmy?" The boy nodded, frowning, but— Malibert was delighted to see—kept on eating his soup. "Then, the question Fermi asked was, 'Why haven't some of them come to see us?' "

"Like in the movies," the boy nodded. "The flying saucers."

"All those movies are made-up stories, Timmy. Like Jack and the Beanstalk, or Oz. Perhaps some creatures from space have come to see us sometime, but there is no good evidence that this is so. I feel sure there would be evidence if it had happened. There would have to be. If there were many such visits, ever, then at least one would have dropped the Martian equivalent of a McDonald's Big Mac box, or a used Sirian flash cube, and it would have been found and shown to be from somewhere other than the Earth. None ever has. So there are only three possible answers to Dr. Fermi's question. One, there is no other life. Two, there is, but they want to leave us alone. They don't want to contact us, perhaps because we frighten them with our violence, or for some reason we can't even guess at. And the third reason"—Elda made a quick gesture, but Malibert shook his head—"is that perhaps as soon as any people get smart enough to do all those things that get them into space—when they have all the technology we do—they also have such terrible bombs and weapons that they can't control them any more. So a war breaks out. And they kill themselves off before they are fully grown up."

"Like now," Timothy said, nodding seriously to show he understood. He had finished his soup, but instead of taking the plate away Elda hugged him in her arms and tried not to weep.

The world was totally dark now. There was no day or night, and would not be again for no one could say how long. The rains and snows had stopped. Without sunlight to suck water up out of the oceans there was no moisture left in the atmosphere to fall. Floods had been replaced by freezing droughts. Two meters down the soil of Iceland was steel hard, and the navvies could no longer dig. There was no hope of laying additional pipes. When more heat was needed all that could be done was to close off buildings and turn off their heating pipes. Elda's patients now were less likely to be frostbite and more to be the listlessness of radiation sickness as volunteers raced in and out of the Reykjavik ruins to find medicine and food. No one was spared that job. When Elda came back on a snowmobile from a foraging trip to the Loftleider Hotel she brought back a present for the boy. Candy bars and postcards from the gift shop; the candy bars had to be shared, but the postcards were all for him. "Do you know what these are?" she asked. The cards showed huge, squat, ugly men and women in the costumes of a thousand years ago. "They're trolls. We have myths in Iceland that the trolls lived here. They're still here, Timmy, or so they say; the mountains are trolls that just got too old and tired to move any more."

"They're made-up stories, right?" the boy asked seriously, and did not grin until she assured him they were. Then he made a joke. "I guess the trolls won," he said.

"Ach, Timmy!" Elda was shocked. But at least the boy was capable of joking, she told herself, and even graveyard humor was better than none. Life had become a little easier for her with the new patients—easier because for the radiation-sick there was very little that could be done—and she bestirred herself to think of ways to entertain the boy.

And found a wonderful one.

Since fuel was precious there were no excursions to see the sights of Iceland-under-the-ice. There was no way to see them anyway in the eternal dark. But when a hospital chopper was called up to travel empty to Stokksnes on the eastern shore to bring back a child with a broken back, she begged space for Malibert and Timmy. Elda's own ride was automatic, as duty nurse for the wounded child. "An avalanche crushed his house," she explained. "It is right under the mountains, Stokksnes, and landing there will be a little tricky, I think. But we can come in from the sea and make it safe. At least in the landing lights of the helicopter something can be seen."

They were luckier than that. There was more light. Nothing came through the clouds, where the billions of particles that had once been Elda's husband added to the trillions of trillions that had been Detroit and Marseilles and Shanghai to shut out the sky. But in the clouds and under them were snakes and sheets of dim color, sprays of dull red, fans of pale green. The aurora borealis did not give much light. But there was no other light at all except for the faint glow from the pilot's instrument panel. As their eyes widened they could see the dark shapes of the Vatnajökull slipping by below them. "*Big* trolls," cried the boy happily, and Elda smiled too as she hugged him.

The pilot did as Elda had predicted, down the slopes of the eastern range, out over the sea, and cautiously back in to the little fishing village. As they landed, red-tipped flashlights guiding them, the copter's landing lights picked out a white lump, vaguely saucer-shaped. "Radar dish," said Malibert to the boy, pointing.

Timmy pressed his nose to the freezing window. "Is it one of them, Daddy Harry? The things that could talk to the stars?"

The pilot answered: "Ach, no, Timmy—military, it is." And Malibert said:

"They wouldn't put one of those here, Timothy. It's too far north. You wanted a place for a big radio telescope that could search the whole sky, not just the little piece of it you can see from Iceland."

And while they helped slide the stretcher with the broken child into the helicopter, gently, kindly as they could be, Malibert was thinking about those places, Arecibo and Woomara and Socorro and all the others. Every one of them was now dead and certainly broken with a weight of ice and shredded by the mean winds. Crushed, rusted, washed away, all those eyes on space were blinded now; and the thought saddened Harry Malibert, but not for long. More gladdening than anything sad was the fact that, for the first time, Timothy had called him "Daddy."

In one ending to the story, when at last the sun came back it was too late. Iceland had been the last place where human beings survived, and Iceland had finally starved. There was nothing alive anywhere on Earth that spoke, or invented machines, or read books. Fermi's terrible third answer was the right one after all.

But there exists another ending. In this one the sun came back in time. Perhaps it was just barely in time, but the food had not yet run out when daylight brought the first touches of green in some parts of the world, and plants began to grow again from frozen or hoarded seed. In this ending Timothy lived to grow up. When he was old enough, and after Malibert and Elda had got around to marrying, he married one of their daughters. And of their descendants—two generations or a dozen generations later—one was alive on that day when Fermi's paradox became a quaintly amusing old worry, as irrelevant and comical as a fifteenth-century mariner's fear of falling off the edge of the flat Earth. On that day the skies spoke, and those who lived in them came to call.

Perhaps that is the true ending of the story, and in it the human race chose not to squabble and struggle with itself, and so extinguish itself finally into the dark. In this ending human beings survived, and saved all the science and beauty of life, and greeted their star-born visitors with joy . . .

But that is in fact what did happen!

At least, one would like to think so.

A DESPERATE CALCULUS

Gregory Benford

*Of course, to destroy the world, you don't need to push the
Button. As the bitter and despairing chiller that follows
demonstrates, going about business as usual, regardless of
the long-term consequences, is more than sufficient to bring
about the last days . . .*

*Gregory Benford is one of the modern giants of the field.
His 1980 novel* Timescape *won the Nebula Award, the John
W. Campbell Memorial Award, the British Science Fiction
Association Award, and the Australian Ditmar Award, and is
widely considered to be one of the classic novels of the last
two decades. His other novels include* The Stars in Shroud, In
the Ocean of Night, Against Infinity, Artifact, *and* Across the
Sea of Suns, Great Sky River, Tides of Light, Furious Gulf,
and Sailing Bright Eternity. *His short work has been collected in* Matter's End. *His most recent books are a new
addition to Isaac Asimov's Foundation series,* Foundation's
Fear, *and two new solo novels,* Cosm *and* Deep Time.
*Benford is a professor of physics at the University of
California, Irvine, and is one of the regular science colum-
nists for* The Magazine of Fantasy and Science Fiction. *As
Sterling Blake, under which name "A Desperate Calculus"
was originally published, he has written the novel* Chiller.

Amy inched shut the frail wooden door of her hotel room
and switched on the light. Cockroaches—or at least she
hoped they were mere cockroaches—scuttled for dark
corners. They were so big she could hear them bumping into
the tin plating along one wall.

She shucked off her dusty field jacket, threw it at the lone
pine chair and sprawled on the bed. Under the dangling, naked
light bulb she slit open her husband's letter eagerly, using a

dirty fingernail. Frying fat flavors seeped through the planking but she forgot the smells and noises of the African village. Her eyes raced along the lurching penmanship.

God, I do really need you. What's more, I know it's my 'juice' speaking—only been two weeks, but just at what point do I have to be reasonable? Hey, two scientists who work next to disasterville can afford a little loopy irrationality, right? Thinking about your alabaster breasts a lot. Our eagerly awaited rendezvous will be deep in the sultry jungle, in my tent. I recall your beautiful eyes that evening at Boccifani's and am counting the days . . .

This "superflu" thing is knocking our crew people down pretty fierce now. With our schedule already packed solid, now comes two-week Earth Summit V in São Paulo. Speeches, press, more talk, more dumb delay. Hoist a few with buddies, sure, but pointless, I think. Maybe I can scare up some more funding. Takes plenty juice!—just to keep this operation going! Wish me luck and I'll not even glance at the Latin beauties, promise. Really.

She rolled over onto her side to ease the ache in her back, keeping the letter in the yellow glow that seemed to be dimming. The crackly pages were wrinkled as if they had gotten wet in transit.

A distant generator coughed, stuttered, stopped. The light went out. She lay in the sultry dark, thinking about him and decoding all that the letter said and implied. In the distance a dog yapped and she smelled the sour lick of charcoal on the air. It did not cover the vile sickly-sweet odor of bodies left out in the street. Already they were swelling. Autumn was fairly warm in this brush-country slice of Tanzania and the village lay quiet with the still of the fallen. In a few minutes the generator huffed sluggishly back into its coughing rhythm and the bulb glowed. Watery light seeped into the room. Cockroaches scuttled again.

She finished the letter, which went on in rather impressively salacious detail about portions of her anatomy and did the job she knew Todd had intended. If any Tanzanian snoops got into her mail, they probably would not have the courage to admit it. And it did make her moist, yes.

• • •

The day's heavy heat now ebbed. A whispering breeze dispersed the wet, infesting warmth.

Todd got the new site coordinates from their uplink, through their microwave dish. He squatted beside the compact, black matte-finish module and its metallic ear, cupped to hear a satellite far out in chilly vacuum. That such a remote, desiccated, and silvery craft in the empty sky could be looked in electromagnetic embrace with this place of leafy heaviness, transfixed by sweet rot and the stink of distant fires, was to Todd a mute miracle.

Manuel yelled at him in Spanish from below. "Miz Cabrina says to come! Right away!"

"I'm nearly through."

"Right away! She says it is the cops!"

The kid had seen too much American TV. Cop spun like a bright coin in the syrup of thickly accented Spanish. Cops. Authorities. The weight of what he had to do. A fretwork of irksome memories. He stared off into infinity, missing Amy.

He was high up on the slope of thick forest. Toward him flew a rainbird. It came in languid slow motion, flapping in the mild breeze off the far Atlantic, a murmuring wind that lifted the warm weight from the stinging day. The bird's translucent shape flickered against big-bellied clouds and Todd thought of the bird as a gliding bag of genes, biological memories ancient and wrinkled and yet still coming forth. Distant time, floating toward him now across the layered air.

He waved to Manuel. "Tell her to stall them."

He finished getting the data and messages, letting the cool and precise part of him do the job. Every time some rural bigshot showed up his stomach lurched and he forced down jumpy confusions. He struggled to insulate the calm, unsettled center of himself so that he could work. He had thought this whole thing would get easier, but it never did.

The solar panels atop their van caught more power if he parked it in the day's full glare, but then he couldn't get into it without letting the interior cool off. He had driven up here to get a clear view of the rest of the team. He left the van and headed toward where the salvaging team was working.

Coming back down through kilometers of jungle took him through terrain that reflected his inner turmoil. Rotting logs shone with a vile, vivid emerald. Swirls of iridescent lichen engulfed thick-barked trees. He left the cross-country van on the clay road and continued, boots sinking into the thick mat.

Nothing held sway here for long. Hand-sized spiders scuttled like black motes across the intricate green radiance. Exotic vitality, myriad threats. A conservation biologist, he had learned to spot the jungle's traps and viper seductions. He sidestepped a blood vine's barbs, wisely gave a column of lime ants their way. Rustlings escorted him through dappled shadows which held a million minute violences. Carrion moths fluttered by on charcoal wings in search of the fallen. Tall grass blades cut the shifting sunlight. Birds cooed and warbled and stabbed insects from the air. Casually brutal beauty.

He vectored in on the salvaging site. As he worked downslope the insecticidal fog bombs popped off in the high canopy. Species pattered down through the branches, thumped on logs, a dying rain. The gray haze descended, touched the jungle floor, settled into nooks. Then a vagrant breeze blew it away. His team moved across the hundred-meter perimeter, sweeping uphill.

Smash and grab, Todd thought, watching the workers in floppy jeans and blue work shirts get down on hands and knees. They inched forward, digging out soil samples, picking up fallen insects, fronds, stems, small mammals. Everything, anything. Some snipped samples from the larger plants. Others shinnied up the slick-barked trees and rummaged for the resident ants and spiders and myriad creatures who had not fallen out when the fog hit them. A special team took leaves and branches—too much trouble to haul away whole trees. And even if they'd wanted to, the politicos would scream; timbering rights here had already been auctioned off.

Todd angled along behind the sweeping line of workers, all from Argentina. He caught a few grubs and leaves that had escaped and dropped them into a woman's bag. She smiled and nodded respectfully. Most of them were embarrassingly thankful to have a job. The key idea in the Bio-Salvage Program was to use local labor. That created a native constituency wherever they went. It also kept costs manageable. The urban North was funding this last-ditch effort. Only the depressed wages of the rural South made it affordable.

And here came the freezers. A thinner line of men carrying

foam dry ice boxes, like heavy-duty picnic coolers. Into these went each filled sack. Stapled to the neck of each bag was a yellow bar code strip giving location, date, terrain description. He had run them off in the van this morning. Three more batches were waiting in his pack for the day's work further up the valley.

His pack straps cut into his roll of shoulder muscle, reminding him of how much more remained to do. To save. He could see in the valley below the press of population on the lush land. A crude work camp sprawled like a tan fungus. Among the jungle's riot of emerald invention a dirt road wound like a dirty snake.

He left the team and headed toward the trouble, angling by faded stucco buildings. Puddles from a rain shower mirrored an iron cross over the entrance gate of a Catholic mission. The Pope's presence. Be fruitful, ye innocent, and multiply. Spread like locusts across God's green works.

Ramshackle sheds lay toward the work camp, soiling the air with greasy wood smoke. In the jungle beyond, chain saws snarled in their labors. Beside the clay ruts of the road lay crushed aluminum beer cans and a lurid tabloid about movie stars.

He reached the knot of men as Cabrina started shouting.

"Yes we do! Signed by your own lieutenant governor *especial!*"

She waved papers at three uniformed types, who wore swarthy scowls and revolvers in hip holsters.

"No, no." An officer jerked at the crowd. "These, they say it interferes with their toil."

Here at the edge of the work camp they had already attracted at least fifty. Worn men slouched against a stained yellow wall, scrawny and rawboned and faces slack with fatigue. They were sour twists of men, *maraneros* from the jungle, a machete their single tool, their worn skins sporting once-jaunty tattoos of wide-winged eagles and rampant bulls and grinning skulls.

"The hell it does." Cabrina crossed her arms over her red jumper and her lips whitened.

"The chemicals, they make coughing and—"

"We went through all that with the foreman. And I have documents—"

"These say nothing about—"

Todd turned out the details and watched lines deepen in the officer's face. Trouble coming, and fast. He was supposed to let Cabrina, as a native, run the interference. Trouble was, these were macho backcountry types. He nodded respectfully to the head officer and said, "Our schedule bothering them?"

The officer looked relieved to deal with a man. "They do not like the fumes or having to stay away from the area."

"Let's see if we can do something about that. Suppose they work upwind?"

So then it got into a back-and-forth negotiation. He hated cutting in on Cabrina but the officer had been near the breaking point. Todd gradually eased Cabrina back in and the officer saw how things were going to go. He accepted that with some facesaving talk and pretty soon it was settled.

Todd walked Cabrina a bit back toward the jungle. "Don't let them rile you. Just stick to the documents."

"But they are so stupid!" Flashing anger, a wrenched mouth.

"Tell me something new."

Their ice van growled into view. It already had the sample sacks from the fogging above. Time to move a kilometer on and repeat the process. All so they could get into this valley and take their samples before these butchers with their bovine complacency could chop it down for cropland or grazing or just to make charcoal. But Todd did not let any of this into his face. Instead he told Cabrina to show the van where to go. Then he went over and spoke to several of the men in his halting Spanish. Smoothing the way. He made sure to stand close to them and speak in the private and respectful way that worked around here.

Amy followed the rest of her team into the ward. It was the same as yesterday and the day before. All beds filled, patients on the floors, haggard faces, nurses looking as bad as the patients. The infection rate here was at least eighty percent of the population. These were just the cases which had made it to the hospital and then had the clout to get in.

Freddie went through the list prepared by the hospital director. They were there to survey and take blood samples but the director seemed to think his visitors bore some cure. Or at least advice.

"Fever, frequent coughing, swellings in the groin," Freddie

read, his long black hair getting in the way. He was French and found everything about this place a source of irritation. Amy did not blame him but it was not smart to show it. "Seven percent of cases display septic shock, indicating that the blood stream is directly infected."

"I hope these results will be of help to your researchers," the director said. He was a short man with a look that alternated between pleading and outright panic. Amy did her best to not look at him. His eyes were always asking, asking.

Freddie waved his clipboard. "All is consistent with spread directly among humans by inhalation of infected respiratory droplets?"

The director nodded rapidly. "But we cannot isolate the chain. It seems—"

"Yes, yes, it is so everywhere. The incubation period of the infection is at least two weeks, though it can be up to a month. By that time the original source is impossible to stipulate." Freddie rattled this off because he had said the same thing a dozen times already in Tanzania.

Amy said mildly, "I note that you have not attempted to isolate the septic cases."

The director jerked as if reprimanded and went into an explanation, which did not matter to anyone but would make him feel better, she was sure. She asked for and received limbic fluids, mucus, and blood samples from the deceased patients. The director wanted to talk to someone of higher authority and their international team filled that need. Not that it did any good. They had no vaccine, no real advice except to keep the patients cool and not to use sedation which would suppress their lung function. They told him this and then told his staff and then told him again because he just kept looking at them with those eyes. Then they went away.

In the next town Amy got to a telephone and could hook up her modem. She got an uplink with only a half hour wait. They drove back into the capital city over dusty roads while she read the printouts.

Summary View.

This present plague is certainly a derived form of influenza. It is well known that the "flu" virus undergoes "antigenic" drifts—point mutations in the virus's outer protein coat which can enhance the ability of the virus to attack the human immune system. New pandemic viruses emerge at unpredictable intervals on the order of decades, though the rate of shifts may be increasing. The present pathogenic outbreak, with its unusual two- to three-week incubation period, allows rapid spreading before populations can begin to take precautions—isolation, face masks, etc. Fatality rate is 3% in cases which do not recover within five days. Origin: The apparent derivation of this plague from southern Asia has been obscured by its rapid transmission to both Africa and South America. However, this Asian origin, recently unmasked by detailed hospital studies and demographics, verifies the suspicions of the United Nations Emergency Committee. Asia is the primary source of "flu" outbreaks because of the high incidence there of "integrated farming," which mingles fowl, pigs and fish close together. In Southeast Asia this has been an economic blessing, but a reverse-spin disaster for the North. Viruses from different species mix, recombining and undergoing gene reassortment at a rapid rate. Humans need time to synthesize specific antibodies as a defense. Genetic aspects: Preliminary results suggest that this is a recombinant virus. Influenza has seven segments of RNA, and several seem to have been modified. Some correlations suggest close connection to the swine flu from pigs. This is a shift, not a simple drift. Some recombination has occurred from another reservoir population—but which? Apparently, some rural environment in southern China.

She looked up as they jounced past scrubby farmland. No natural forest or grassland remained; humans had turned all arable land to crops. Insatiable appetite, eating nature itself.

Nobody visible. The superflu knocked everybody flat for at least three days, marvelously infective, and few felt like getting back to the fields right away. That would take another slice out of the food supply here. Behind the tide of illness would come some malnutrition. The U.N. would have to be ready for that, too.

Not my job, though, she thought, and mused longingly of Todd.

• • •

São Paulo. Earth Summit V, returning to South America for the first time since Summit I in the good old days of 1992. He was to give a talk about the program and then, by God, he'd be long gone.

On the drive in he had seen kindergarten-age children dig through cow dung, looking for corn kernels the cows hadn't digested. The usual colorful chaos laced with gray despair. Gangs of urchin thieves who didn't know their own last names. Gutters as sewers. Families living in cardboard boxes. Babies found discarded in trash heaps.

He had imagined that his grubby jeans and T-shirt made him look unremarkable, but desperation hones perceptions. The beggars were on him every chance. By now he had learned the trick which fended off the swarms of little urchins wanting Chiclets, the shadowy men with suitcases of silver jewelry, the women at traffic lights hawking bunches of roses. Natives didn't get their windshields washed unless they wanted it, nor did they say "no" a hundred times to accomplish the result. They just held up one finger and waggled it sideways, slowly. The pests magically dispersed. He had no idea what it meant, but it was so easy even a gringo could do it.

His "interest zone" at Earth Summit V was in a hodgepodge of sweltering tents erected in an outdoor park. The grass had been beaten into gray, flat blades. Already there was a dispute between the North delegates, who wanted a uniform pledge of seventy-five percent reduction in use of pesticides. Activists from the poor South worried about hunger more than purity, so the proposal died. This didn't stop anyone from dutifully signing the Earth Pledge which covered one whole wall in thick gray cardboard. After all, it wasn't legally binding.

Todd talked with a lot of the usual Northern crowd from the Nature Conservancy and World Wildlife Fund, who were major sponsors of BioSalvage. They were twittering about a Southern demand that everybody sign a "recognition of the historical, biological and cultural debt" the North owed the South. They roped him into it, because the background argument (in Spanish, so of course most of the condescending Northerners couldn't read it) named BioSalvage as "arrogantly entering our countries and pushing fashionable environmentalism over the needs of the people."

Todd heard this in a soft drink bar, swatting away flies. Before he could respond, a spindly man in a sack shirt elbowed his way into the Northern group. "I know who you are, Mr. Russell. We do not let your 'debt swap' thievery go by."

BioSalvage had some funding from agreements which traded money owed to foreign banks for salvaging rights and local labor. He smiled at the stranger. "All negotiated, friend."

"The debt was contracted illegally!" The man slapped the yellow plastic table, spilling Coke.

"By your governments."

"By your criminals!—who then stole great sums."

Todd spread his hands, still smiling though it was getting harder. "Hey, I'm no banker."

"You are part of a plot to keep us down," the man shot back.

"By saving some species?"

"You are killing them!"

"Yeah, maybe a few days before your countrymen get around to it."

Two other men and a woman joined the irate man. Todd was with several Northerners and a woman from Costa Rica who worked for the Environmental Defense Fund. He tried to keep his tone civil and easy but people started breaking in and pretty soon the Southerners were into Harangue Mode and it went to hell. The Northerners rolled their eyes and the Southerners accused them in quick, staccato jabs of being arrogant, impatient, irritated when somebody couldn't speak English, ready to walk out at the first sign of a long speech when there was so much to say after all.

Todd eased away from the table. The Northerners used words like "proactive" and "empowerment" and kept saying that before they were willing to discuss giving more grants they wanted accountability. They worried about corruption and got thin-lipped when told that they should give without being oppressors of the spirit by trying to manage the money. "*Imperialista!*" a Brazilian woman hissed, and Todd left.

He took a long walk down littered streets rank with garbage. Megacities. Humanity growing by a hundred million fresh souls per year, with disease and disorder in ample attendance. Twenty-nine megacities now with more than ten million population. Twenty-five in the "developing" world—only nobody was developing anymore. Tokyo topped the list, as always, at thirty-six million. São Paulo was coming up fast on the outside with thirty-four million. Lagos, Nigeria, which nobody ever thought about, festered with seventeen million despite the multitudes lost to AIDS.

He kicked a can and shrugged off beggars. A man with sores drooling down his face approached but Todd did not dare give him a bill. Uncomfortably he wagged his finger. Indifference was far safer.

Magacities spawned the return of microbes that had toppled empires down through history. Cholera, the old foe. New antibiotic-resistant strains. Cysticercosis, a tapeworm that invades the brain, caught from eating vegetables grown in the city's effluent. Half the world's urban population had at least one skin rash per year.

And big cities demand standardized, easily transported foods. Farmers respond with monocrops, which are more vulnerable to pests and disease and drought. Cities preyed on the cropland and forests which sustain them. Plywood apartment walls in Nagasaki chewed up Borneo's woodlands.

When he reached his hotel room—bare concrete, tin sink in the room, john down the hall—he found a light blinking on the satellite comm. He located the São Paulo nexus and got a fastprint letter on his private number. It was from Amy and he read it eagerly, the gray walls around him forgotten.

I'm pretty sure friend Freddie is now catching holy hell for not being on top of this superflu faster. There's a pattern, he says. Check out the media feeding frenzy, if you have the time. Use my access codes onto SciNet, too. I'm more worried about Zambia, our next destination. Taking no recognition of U.N. warnings, both sides violating the ceasefire. We'll have armed escorts. Not much use against a virus! All our programs are going slowly, with locals dropping like flies.

The sweetness of her seemed to swarm up into his nostrils then, blotting out the disinfectant smell from the cracked linoleum. He could see her electric black hair tumbling like rolling smoke about her shoulders, spilling onto her full breasts in yellow candle light. After a tough day he would lift her onto him, setting her astride his muscular arch. The hair wreathed them both, making a humid space that was theirs only, musk-rich and silent. She could bounce and stroke and coax from him the tensions of time, and later they would have dark rum laced with lemon. Her eyes could widen with comic rapt amazement, go slit-thin with anger, become suddenly womanly as they reflected the serenity of the languid candle flame.

Remember to dodge the electronic media blood hounds. Sniffers and lickers, I call 'em. Freddie handles them for us, but I'm paranoid—seeing insults spelled out in my alphabet soup. Remember that I love you. Remember to see Kuipers if you get sick! See you in two weeks—so very long!

His gray computer screen held a WorldNet news item, letters shimmering. Todd's program had fished it out of the torrent of news, and it confirmed the worst of his fears. He used her code-keys to gain entry and global search/scan found all the hot buzz:

SUPERFLU EPIDEMIC WIDENS. SECRETARY-GENERAL CALLS FOR AIR TRAVEL BAN. DISEASE CONTROL CENTER TRACING VECTOR CARRIERS.

(AP) A world-sweeping contagion has now leaped from Asia to Africa and on to South America. Simultaneous outbreaks in Cairo, Johannesburg, Mexico City and Buenos Aires confirmed fears that the infection is spreading most rapidly through air travelers. Whole cities have been struck silent and

prostrated as a majority of inhabitants succumb within a few days.

Secretary-General Imukurumba called for a total ban on international passenger air travel until the virus is better understood. Airlines have logged a sharp rise in ticket sales in affected regions, apparently from those fleeing.

The Center for Disease Control is reportedly attempting to correlate outbreaks with specific travelers, in an effort to pinpoint the source. Officials declined to confirm this extraordinary move, however.

He suspected that somebody at the CDC was behind this leak, but it might mean something more. More ominously, what point was there in tracing individuals? CDC was moving fast. This thing was a wildfire. And Amy was right in the middle of it.

He sat a long time at a fly-specked Formica table, staring at the remains of his lunch, a chipped blue plate holding rice and beans and a gnawed crescent of green tortilla. Todd felt the old swirl of emotions, unleashed as though they had lain in waiting all this time. Incoherent, disconnected images propelled him down musty corridors of self. Words formed on his lips but evaporated before spoken.

She hated autopsies. Freddie had told her to check this one, and the smell was enough to make her pass out. Slow fans churned at one end of the tiny morgue. Only the examining table was well lit. Its gutters ran with viscous, reeking fluids.

The slim black woman on the table was expertly "unzipped"—carved down from neck to pelvis, organs neatly extracted and lying across her chest and legs. Glistening tubes and lumpy vitals, so clean and smooth they seemed to be manufactured.

"A most interesting characteristic of these cases," the coroner went on in a serene voice that floated in the chilly room. He picked up an elongated gray sac. "The fallopians. Swollen, discolored. The ova sac is distended, you will be seeing here. And red."

Amy said, "Her records show very high temperatures. Could this be—"

"Being the cause of death, this temperature, yes. The contagion invaded the lower abdomen, however, causing further discomfort."

"So this is another variation on the, uh, superflu?"

"I think yes." The coroner elegantly opened the abdomen further and showed off kidneys and liver. "Here too, some swelling. But not as bad as in the reproductive organs."

Amy wanted desperately to get out of this place. Its cloying smells layered the air. Two local doctors stood beside her, watching her face more than the body. They were well-dressed men in their fifties and obviously had never seen a woman in a position of significance in their profession. She asked, "What percentage of your terminal cases display this?"

"About three quarters," the coroner said.

"In men and women alike?" Amy asked.

"Yes, though for the women these effects are more prominent."

"Well, thank you for your help." She nodded to them and

left. The two doctors followed her. When she reached the street her driver was standing beside the car with two soldiers. Three more soldiers got out of a big jeep and one of the doctors said, "You are please to come."

There wasn't much to do about it. Nobody was interested in listening to her assertion that she was protected by the Zambia-U.N. terms. They escorted her to a low, squat building on the outskirts of town. As they marched her inside she remarked that the place looked like a bunker. The officer with her replied mildly that it was.

General Movotubo wore crisp fatigues and introduced himself formally. He invited her to sit in a well-decorated office without windows. Coffee? Good. Biscuit? Very good. "And so you will be telling now what? That this disease is the product of my enemies."

"I am here as a United Nations—"

"Yes, yes, but the truth, it must come out. The Landuokoma, they have brought this disease here, is this not so?"

"We don't know how it got here." She tried to understand the expressions which flitted across the heavy-set man's face, which was shiny with nervous sweat.

"Then you cannot say that the Landuokoma did not bring it, this is right?"

Amy stood up. General Movotubo was shorter than her and she recognized now his expression: a look of caged fear. "Listen, staying holed up in here isn't going to protect you against superflu. Not if your personnel go in and out, anyway."

"Then I will go to the countryside! The people will understand. They will see that the Landuokoma caused me to do so."

She started for the door. "Believe me, neither I nor the U.N. cares what you say to your newspapers. Just let me go."

There was a crowd outside the bunker. They did not retreat when she emerged and she had to push and shove her way to her car. The driver sat inside, petrified. But nobody tried to stop them. The faces beyond the window glass were filled with stark dread, not anger.

She linked onto WorldNet back at the hotel. The serene liquid crystal screen blotted out the awareness of the bleak streets beyond the grand marble columns of the foyer.

PULLDOWN SIDEBAR: News Analysis MIXED REACTION TO PLAGUE OUTBREAK

Environmental Hard Liners Say "Inevitable"(AP) . . . "What I'm saying," Earth First! spokesman Josh Leonard said, "is that we're wasting our resources trying to hold back the tide. It's pointless. Here in the North we have great medical expertise. Plenty of research has gone into fathoming the human immune system, to fixing our cardiovascular plumbing, and the like. But to expend it trying to fix every disease that pops up in the South is anti-Darwinian, and futile. Nature corrects its own mistakes." . . . Many in the industrialized North privately admit being increasingly appalled with the South's runaway numbers. Their views are extreme. They point to how megacities sprawl, teeming with seedy, impoverished masses. Torrents of illegal immigration pour over borders. Responding to deprivation, Southern politico/religious movements froth and foment, few of them appetizing as seen from a Northern distance. "The more the North thinks of humanity as a malignancy," said psychophilosopher Norman Wills, "the more we will unconsciously long for disasters."

Amy was not really surprised. The Nets seethed with similar talk. Todd had been predicting this for years. That made her think of him, and she shut down her laptop.

He stopped at the BioSalvage Southern Repository to pick up the next set of instructions, maps, political spin. It was a huge complex—big, gray, concrete bunker-style for the actual freezing compartments, tin sheds for the sample processing. All the buzz and clatter of the rest of Caracas faded as he walked down alleys between the Repository buildings. Ranks of big liquid nitrogen dewars. Piping, automatic labeling machines, harried workers chattering in highly accented Spanish he could barely make out.

In the foyer a whole wall was devoted to the history of it. At the top was the abstract of Scott's first paper, proposing what he called the Library of Life. The Northern Repository was in fact called that, but here they were more stiff and official.

A broad program of freezing species in threatened eco-spheres could preserve biodiversity for eventual use by future generations. Sampling without studying can lower costs dramatically. Local labor can do most of the gathering. Plausible costs of collection and cryogenically

suspending the tropical rain forest species, at a sampling fraction of 10−6, are about two billion dollars for a full century. Much more information than species DNA will be saved, allowing future biotechnology to derive high information content and perhaps even resurrect then-extinct species. A parallel program of limited in situ *preservation is essential to allow later expression of frozen genomes in members of the same genus. This broad proposal should be debated throughout the entire scientific community.*

Todd had to wait for his appointment. He fidgeted in the foyer. A woman coming out of the executive area wobbled a bit, then collapsed, her clipboard clattering on marble. Nobody went to help. The secretaries and guards drew back, turned, were gone. Todd helped the woman struggle into a chair. She was already running a fever and could hardly speak. He knew there wasn't anything to do beyond getting her a glass of water. When he came back with one, a medical team was there. They simply loaded her onto a stretcher and took her out to an unmarked van. Probably they were just going to take her home. The hospitals were already jammed, he had heard.

He took his mind off matters by reading the rest of the Honor Wall, as it was labeled. Papers advocating the BioSalvage idea. A Nobel for Scott. Begrudging support from most conservation biologists.

Our situation resembles a browser in the ancient library at Alexandria, who suddenly notes that the trove he had begun inspecting has caught fire. Already a wing has burned, and the mobs outside seem certain to block any fire-fighting crews. What to do? There is no time to patrol the aisles, discerningly plucking forth a treatise of Aristotle, or deciding whether to leave behind Alexander the Great's laundry list. Instead, a better strategy is to run through the remaining library, tossing texts into a basket at random, sampling each section to give broad coverage. Perhaps it would be wise to take smaller texts, in order to carry more, and then flee into an unknown future.

"Dr. Russell? I am Leon Segueno."
The man in a severe black suit was not his usual monitor. "Where's Confuelos?"

"Ill, I believe. I'll give you the latest instructions."

Back into the executive area, another new wrinkle. Segueno went through the fresh maps with dispatch. Map coordinates, rendezvous points with the choppers, local authorities who would need soothing. A fresh package of local currency to grease palms, where necessary. Standard stuff.

"I take it you will be monitoring all three of your groups continuously?"

An odd question. Segueno didn't seem familiar with procedures. Probably a political hack.

"I get around as much as I can. Working the back roads, it isn't easy."

"You get to many towns."

"Gotta buy a few beers for the local brass hats."

"Have you difficulty with the superflu?"

"Some of the crew dropped out. We hired more."

"And you?"

"I keep away from anybody who's sniffling or coughing."

"But some say it is spread by ordinary breath."

He frowned. "Hadn't heard that."

"A United Nations team reported so."

"Might explain how it spreads so fast."

"*Sí, sí.* Your wife, I gather she is working for the U.N.?"

"On this same problem, right. I hadn't heard that angle, though."

"You must be very proud of her."

"Uh, yes." Where was this going?

"To be separated, it is not good. Will you see her soon?"

No reason to hide anything, even from an officious bureaucrat. "This week. She's joining me in the field."

Segueno chuckled. "Not the kind of reunion I would have picked. Well, good luck to you."

He tried to read the man's expression and got nothing but a polished blandness behind the eyes. Maybe the guy was angling for some kind of payoff? Nothing would surprise him anymore, even in the Repository.

He stopped off in the main bay. High sheet-metal ceiling, gantries, steel ramps. Stacks of blue plastic coolers, filled with the labeled sacks that teams like his own sent in. Sorting lines prepared them further. Each cooler was logged and integrated into a geographical inventory, so that future researchers could

study correlations with other regions. Then the coolers went
into big aluminum canisters. The gantries lowered these into
permanent place. Tubes hooked up, monitors added, and then
the liquid nitrogen pumped in with a hiss. A filmy fog, and
another slice of vanishing life was on its way to the next age.

Todd wondered just when biology would advance to the
point where these samples could be unfolded, their genes read.
And then? Nobody could dictate to the future. They might
resurrect extinct species, make leopards again pace the jungle
paths. Or maybe they would revive beetles—God must have
loved them, He made so many kinds, as Haldane himself had
remarked. Maybe there was something wonderful in those
shiny carapaces, and the future would need it.

Todd shrugged. It was reassuring to come here and feel a part
of it all.

Going out through the foyer, he stopped and read the rest of
the gilt lettering on polished black marble.

*We must be prudent. Leading figures in biodiversity argue
that a large scale species dieback seems inevitable,
leading to a blighted world which will eventually learn the
price of such folly. The political impact of such a disaster
will be immense. Politics comes and goes, but extinction is
forever. We may be judged harshly by our grandchildren,
our era labeled the Great Dying or the Age of Appetite.
A future generation could well reach out for means
to recover their lost biological heritage. If scientific
progress has followed the paths many envision today, they
will have the means to perform seeming miracles. They
will have developed ethical and social mechanisms we
cannot guess, but we can prepare now the broad outlines
of a recovery strategy, simply by banking biological
information. These are the crucial years for us to act, as
the Library of Life burns furiously around us, throughout
the world.*

He left. When he got into his rental Ford in the parking lot,
he saw Segueno looking down at him through a high window.

He had not expected to get a telephone call. On a one-day stop
in Goias, Brazil, to pick up more coolers and a fresh crew,

there was little time to hang around the hotel. But somehow she traced him and got through on the sole telephone in the manager's office. He recognized Amy's voice immediately despite the bad connection.

"Todd? I was worried."

"Nothing's gone wrong with your plans, has it?"

"No, no, I'll be there in two days. But I just heard from Freddie that a lot of people who were delegates at the Earth Summit have come down with superflu. Are you all right?"

"Sure, fine. How's it there?"

"I've got a million tales to tell. The civil war's still going on and we're pulling out. I wrote you a letter, I'll send it satellite squirt to your modem address."

"Great. God, I've missed you."

Her warm chuckle came through the purr of static. "I'll expect you to prove it."

"I'll be all set up in a fresh camp, just out from Maraba. A driver will pick you up."

"Terrif. Isn't it terrible, about the Earth Summit?"

"Nobody's immune."

"I guess not. We're seeing ninety percent affliction in some villages here."

"What about this ban on passenger travel? Will that—"

"It isn't sticking. Anyway, we have U.N. passes. Don't worry, lover, I'll get there if I have to walk."

He got her letter over modem within a few minutes.

We're pinning down the epidemiology. Higher fevers in women, but about 97% recover. Freddie's getting the lab results from the samples we sent in. He's convinced there'll be a vaccine, pronto.

But it's hard to concentrate, babe. This place is getting worse by the hour. We got a briefing on safety in Zambia, all very official, but most of the useful stuff we picked up from drivers, cops, locals on street corners. You have to watch details, like your license plates. I got some neutral plates from some distant country. People sell them in garages. Don't dare use the old dodge of putting a PRESS label on your car. Journalists draw fire here, and a TV label is worse. Locals see TV as more powerful than

the lowly word-artists of newspapers. TV's the big pro-
paganda club and everybody's got some reason to be mad
at it.

We got a four-wheel job that'll go off-road. Had to be
careful not to get one that looked like a military jeep. They
draw fire. We settled on a white Bighorn, figuring that
snipers might think we were U.N. peacekeeping forces.
On the other hand, there's undoubtedly some faction that
hates the U.N., too. Plenty of people here blame us—
Westerners—for the superflu. We get hostile stares, a few
thrown rocks. Freddie took a tomato in the chest today.
Rotten, of course. Otherwise, somebody'd have eaten it.

We go out in convoys, seeking superflu vectors. Single
cars are lots more vulnerable. And if we break down, like
yesterday, you've got help.

I picked up some tips in case we come under fire. (Now
don't be a nervous husband! You know I like field
work . . .) Bad idea to ride in the back seat of a two-
door—hard to get out fast. Sit in the front seat and keep
the door slightly open so you can dive out. Windows open,
too, so you can hear what's coming down.

Even in town we're careful with the lights. Minimal
flashlight use. Shrouds over camera lights as much as you
can. A camera crew interviewing us from CNN draped
dark cloth over their heads so nobody could see the dim
blue glow of the viewfinder leaking from around their
eyes.

Not what you wanted your wife to be doing, right? But
it's exciting! Sorry if this is unfeminine. You'll soon have
a chance to check out whether all this macho stuff has
changed my, uh, talents. Just a week! I'll try to be all
frilly-frilly. Lover, store up that juice of yours."

He stared at the glimmering phosphors of his laptop.
Superflu at the Earth Summit. Vaccine upcoming. Vectors
colliding, and always outside the teeming city with its hoarse
voices, squalling babies and swelling mothers, the rot of mad
growth. Could a species which produced so many mouths be
anything more than a blight? Their endless masses cast doubt
upon the importance of any individual, diminished the mind's
inner sense.

He read the letter again as if he were under water, bubbles springing from his lips and floating up into a filmy world he hoped someday to see. He and Amy struggled, knee-deep in the mud of lunatic mobs. How long, before they were dragged down? But at least for a few moments longer they had the shadowy recesses of each other.

He waited impatiently for her beside his tent. He had come back early from the crew sites and a visit to the local brass hats. It had gone pretty well but he could not repress his desire for her, his impatience. He calmed himself by sitting in his canvas-backed chair, boots propped up on a stump left by the land clearing. He had some background files from Amy and he idly paged through them on his laptop. A review paper in *Nature* tried to put the superflu in historical perspective.

There were in fact three bubonic plagues, each so named because the disease began with buboes—swollen lymph glands in the groin, armpit, neck. Its pneumonic form spread quickly, on breaths swarming with micro-organisms, every cough throwing micro-organisms to the wind. A bacterial disease, the bacillus *Pasteurella pestis* was carried by fleas on *Rattus rattus*.

In assessing the potentials of Superflu, consider the first bubonic pandemic. Termed the Plague of Justinian (540–590), who was the Caesar of the era, it began the decline of the Roman Empire, strengthened Christianity with its claims of an afterlife, and discredited Roman medicine, whose nostrums proved useless—thus strangling a baby science. By the second day of an everlasting fever, the victims saw phantoms which called, beckoning toward the grave. The plague ended only when it killed so many, up to half the population of some cities, that it ran out of carriers. It killed a hundred million, a third of the region's population, and four times the Black Death toll of 1346–1361.

Our Superflu closely resembles the Spanish Influenza, which actually originated in Kansas. It was history's worst outbreak, as rated by deaths per day—thirty million in a single fall season of 1918. The virus mutated quickly. Accidental Russian lab release of a frozen sample in 1977 caused a minor outbreak . . .

He lay on his cot, waiting for the sound of his jeep, bearing Amy. Through the heavy air came the oddly weak slap of a distant shot. Then three more, quick.

He stumbled outside the tent. Bird rustlings, something scampering in the bush. He was pretty sure the shots had come from up the hill, where the dirt road meandered down. It was impossible to see anything in the twilight trees.

He had envisioned this many times before but that did not help with the biting visceral alarm, the blur of wild thoughts. He thought he had no illusions about what might happen. He walked quickly inside and slapped his laptop shut. Two moths battered at the lone lantern in his tent, throwing a shrapnel of shadows on the walls, magnified anxiety.

Automatically he picked up the micro-disks which carried his decoding routines and vital records. He kept none of it on hard disk so he did not need to erase the laptop. His backpack always carried a day's food and water and he swung it onto his back as he left the tent and trotted into the jungle.

Evening falls heavily beneath the canopy. He went through a mat of vines, slapping aside the stinging flies which rose angrily.

Boots thumping behind him? No, up on the dirt road. A man's shout.

He bent over and worked his way down a steep slope. He wished he had remembered to bring his helmet. He crouched further to keep below the ferns but some caught him in the face. In the fading shafts of green radiance he went quietly, stooped forward. Cathedral pillars of old trees were furred wilth orange moss. The day's heat still thickened the air. He figured that if she got away from them she would go downhill. From the road that led quickly into a narrowing canyon. He angled to the left and ran along an open patch of rock and into the lip of the canyon about halfway down. Impossible to see anything in there but green masses.

There was enough light for them to search for her. She would keep moving and hope they didn't track her by the sound. Noise travels uphill better in a canyon. He plunged into lacerating fronds and worked his way toward where he knew a stream trickled down.

Somebody maybe twenty meters ahead and down slope. Todd angled up to get a look. His breath caught when he saw her, just a glimpse of her hair in a fading gleam of dusk. Branches snapped under his boots as he went after her. She heard as he had hoped and slipped behind a tree. He whispered, "Amy! Todd!" and there she was suddenly, gripping her pop-out pistol.

"Oh God!" she said and kissed him suddenly.

"Are you hurt?" he whispered.

"No." Her gaze ricocheted around the masses of green upslope from them. "I shot the driver of my jeep. In the shoulder, to make him stop. I had to, that Segueno—"

"Him. I wondered what the hell he was—Wait, what'd you shoot at after that?"

"The jeep behind us."

"They stopped?"

"Just around the curve, but they were running toward me."

"Where was Segueno?"

"In my jeep."

"He didn't shoot at you?"

"No, I don't think—"

"He probably didn't want to."

"Who is he? He said he was with World Emergency Services—"

"He's probably got a dozen IDs. Come on."

They forked off from the stream. It was clearer there and the obvious way to go so he figured to stay away from it and move laterally away from the camp. The best they could do would be to reach the highway about five kilometers away and hitch a ride before anybody covered that or stopped traffic. She had no more idea than he did how many people they had but the followup jeep implied they could get more pretty quickly. It probably had good comm gear in it. In the dark they would take several hours to reach the highway. Plenty of time to cover the escapes but they had to try it.

The thin light was almost gone now. Amy was gasping—probably from the shock more than anything else, he thought. She did look as though she had not been sleeping well. The leaden night was coming on fast when they stopped.

"What does he—"

She fished a crumpled page from her pocket. "I grabbed it to get his attention while I got this pistol out." She laughed suddenly, coughed. "He looked scared. I was really proud of myself. I didn't think I could ever use that little thing but when—"

Todd nodded, looking at the fax of his letter, words underlined:

God, I do really need you. What's more, I know it's my
"juice" speaking—only been two weeks, but just at what
point do I have to be reasonable? Hey, two scientists who
work next to disasterville can afford a little loopy irrationality, right? Thinking about your alabaster breasts a lot.
Our eagerly awaited rendezvous will be deep in the sultry
jungle, in my tent. I recall your beautiful eyes that evening
at Boccifani's and am counting the days . . .

"He thought he was being real smooth." She laughed again,
higher this time. Brittle. "Maybe he thought I'd break down or
something if he just showed me he was onto us." Todd saw that
she was excited still but that would fade fast.

"How many men you think he could get right away?"

She frowned. "I don't know. Who is he, why—"

He knew that she would start to worry soon and it would be
better to have her thinking about something else. "He's
probably some UN security or something, sniffed us out. He
may not know much."

"Special Operations, he told me." She was sobering, eyes
bleak.

"He said he was BioSalvage when I saw him in Caracas."

"He's been after us for over a week, then."

He gritted his teeth, eyeing the inky jungle. Twilight bird
calls came down from the canopy, soft and questioning.
Nothing more. Where were they? "I guess we were too
obvious."

"Rearranging Fibonacci into Boccifani? I thought it was
pretty clever."

Todd had felt that way, too, he realized ruefully. A simple
code: give an anagram of a mathematical series—Fibonacci's
was easy to remember in the field, each new term just the sum
of the two preceding integers—and then arranging the real
message in those words of the letter. A real code-breaker
probably thought of schemes like that automatically. Served
him right for being an arrogant smartass. He said, "I tried to
make the messages pretty vague."

Her smile was thin, tired. "I'll say. 'God I do need more juice
at next rendezvous.' I had to scramble to be sure virus-3 was
waiting at the Earth Summit."

"Sorry. I thought the short incubation strain might be more useful there."

She had stopped panting and now slid her arms around him. "I got that. 'This "superflu" thing knocking people with two-week delay. Juice!' I used that prime sequence—you got my letters?"

"Sure." That wasn't important now. Her heart was tripping, high and rapid against his chest.

"I . . . had some virus-4 with me."

"And now they have it. No matter."

Hesitantly she said, "We've . . . gotten farther than we thought we would, right?"

"It's a done deal. They can't stop it now."

"We're through then?" Eyes large.

"They haven't got us yet."

"Do you suppose they know about the others?"

"I hadn't thought of that." They probably tracked the contagion, correlated with travelers, popped up a list of suspects. He and several others had legitimate missions, traveled widely, and could receive frozen samples of the virus without arousing suspicion. Amy was a good nexus for messages, coded and tucked into her reports. All pretty simple, once somebody guessed that to spread varieties of the virus so fast demanded a systematic, international team. "They've probably got Esther and Clyde, then."

"Damn!" She hugged him fiercely.

Last glimmers of day gave a diffuse glow among the damp tangle of vines and fronds. A rustling alerted him. He caught a quick flitting shadow in time to turn.

A large man carrying a stubby rifle rushed at him. He pushed Amy away and the man came on, bringing the rifle down like a club. Todd ducked and drove a fist into the man's neck. They collided. Momentum slammed him into thick ferns. Rolling, elbows jabbing.

Together they slammed into a tree. Todd yanked on the man's hair, got a grip. He smacked the head against a prow of limestone that jutted up from the leafy forest floor. The man groaned and went limp.

Todd got up and looked for Amy and someone knocked him over from behind. The wind went out of him and when he rolled over there were two men, one holding Amy. The other was Mr. Segueno.

"It is pointless to continue," Segueno called.

"I thought some locals were raiding us." Might as well give it one more try.

No smile. "Of course you did."

The man Todd had knocked out was going to stay that way, apparently. Segueno and the other carried automatic pistols, both pointed politely at his feet. "What the hell is—"

"I assume you are not armed?"

"Look, Segueno—"

They took his pack and found the .38 buried beneath the packaged meals. Amy looked dazed, eyes large. They led them back along the slope. It was hard work and they were drenched in sweat when they reached his tent. There were half a dozen men wearing the subdued tan U.N. uniforms. One brought in a chair for Segueno.

Todd sat in his canvas chair and Amy on the bunk. She stretched out and stared numbly at the moths who still flailed against the unattainable lamp.

"What's this crap?" Todd asked, but he could not put any force into his voice. He wanted to make this easy on Amy. That was all he cared about now.

Segueno unfolded a tattered letter. "She did not destroy this—a mistake."

His letter to Amy. "It's personal. You have no right—"

"You are far beyond issues of rights, as I think you know."

"It was Freddie, wasn't it?" Amy said suddenly, voice sharp. "He was too friendly."

In the fluttering yellow light Segueno's smile gleamed. "I would never have caught such an adroit ruse. The name of a restaurant, a mathematical series. But then, I am not a code-breaker. And your second paragraph begins the sequence again—very economical."

Todd said nothing. One guard—he already thought of the uniformed types that way—blocked the tent exit, impassive, holding his 9mm automatic at the ready. Over the men outside talking tensely he heard soft bird calls. He had always liked the birds best of all things in the jungle. Tonight their songs were long and plaintive.

Segueno next produced copies of Amy's letters. "I must say we have not unpuzzled these. She is not using the same series."

Amy stared at the moths now.

"So much about cars, movement—perhaps she was communicating plans? But her use of 'juice' again suggests that she is bringing you some." Segueno pursed his lips, plainly enjoying this.

"You've stooped to intercepting private messages on satellite phone?"

"We have sweeping authority."

"And who's this 'we' anyway?"

"United Nations Special Operations. We picked up the trail of your group a month ago, as the superflu began to spread. Now, what is this 'juice'?"

Todd shook his head silently, trying to hear the birds high in the dark canopy. Segueno slapped him expertly. Todd took it and didn't even look up.

"I am an epidemiologist," Segueno said smoothly "Or rather, I was. And you are an asymptomatic carrier."

"Come on! How come my crew doesn't get it?" Might as well make him work for everything. Give Amy time to absorb the shock. She was still lying loosely, watching the moths seethe at the lamp.

"Sometimes they do. But you do not directly work with the local laborers, except by choice. Merely breathing in the vapor you emit can infect. And I suspect your immediate associates are inoculated—as, obviously, are you."

Todd hoped that Cabrina had gotten away. He wished he had worked out some alarm signal with her. He was an amateur at this.

"I want the whole story," Segueno said.

"I won't tell you the molecular description, if that's what you mean," Amy said flatly.

Segueno chuckled. "The University of California's Center for Molecular Genetics cracked that problem a week ago. That was when we knew someone had designed this plague."

Todd and Amy glanced at each other. Segueno smiled with relish. "You must have inoculated yourselves and all the rest in your conspiracy. Yet with some molecular twist, for you are all asymptomatic carriers."

"True." Amy's eyes were wary. "And I breathed in your face on my way in here."

Segueno laughed sourly. "I was inoculated three days ago. We already have a vaccine. Did you seriously think the best minds in medicine would take long to uncover this madness, and cure it?"

Todd said calmly, "Surprised it took this long."

"We have also tracked your contagion, spotted the carriers. You left a characteristic pattern. Quite intelligent, using those who had a legitimate mission and traveled widely. I gather you personally infected hundreds at Earth Summit V, Doctor Russell."

Todd shrugged. "I get around."

"To kill your colleagues."

"Call it a calculus of desperation," Todd said sharply. "Scientists are very mobile people. They spread a virus real well."

"A calculus? How can you be so—" Segueno caught himself, then went on, voice trembling slightly. "As an epidemiologist, I find puzzling two aspects. These strains vary in infectivity. Still, all seem like poor viral design, if one wants to plan a pandemic. First, they kill only a few percent of the cases. Even those are mostly the elderly, from the fever." He frowned scornfully. "Poor workmanship."

"Yeah, I guess we're just too dumb," Todd said.

"You and your gang—we estimate you number some hundred or more, correct?—are crazy, not stupid. So why, then, the concentration of the disorders in the abdominal organs? Influenza is most effective in the lungs."

Amy said crisply, "The virus had proteins which function as an ion channel. We modified those with amantadine to block the transport of fusion glycoproteins to the cell surface—but only in the lungs." She sounded as though she were reciting from something she had long ago planned to say. It was as stilted as the opening remarks in a seminar. "The modification enhances its effect in another specific site."

Segueno nodded. "We know the site—quite easy to trace, really. Abdominal."

"Game's over," Todd said soberly. The CDC must know by now. He felt a weight lifted from him. Their job was done. No need to conceal anything.

"This 'juice,' it is the virus, yes?"

Amy hesitated. Her skin was stretched over her high cheekbones and glassy beneath the yellow light. Todd went over and sat beside her on the cot and patted her hand reassuringly. "Nothing he can do anyway, hon."

Amy nodded cautiously. "Yes, the virus—but a different strain."

Todd said wryly, "To put a li'l spin on the game."

Segueno's face pinched. "You swine."

"Feel like slapping me again?" Todd sat with coiled energy He wished Segueno would come at him. He was pumped up from the fight earlier. His blood was singing the age-old adrenaline song. The guard was too far away. He watched Todd carefully.

Segueno visibly got control of himself. "Worse than that, I would like. But I am a man with principles."

"So am I."

"You? You are a pair of murderers."

Amy said stiffly, "We are soldiers."

"You are no troops. You are—crazed."

Her face hardened with the courage he so loved in her—the dedication they shared, that defined them. She said as if by rote, "We're fighting for something and we'll pay the price, too."

Segueno eyed Amy with distaste. "What I cannot quite fathom is why you bothered. The virus runs up temperature, but it does not damage the cubical cells or other constituents."

"The ovarian follicles," Amy said. "The virus stimulates production of luteinizing hormone."

Segueno frowned. "But that lasts only a few days."

"That's all it takes. That triggers interaction with the follicle-stimulating hormone." Amy spoke evenly, as though she had prepared herself for this moment, down through the years of work.

"So you force an ovarian follicle to rupture. Quite ordinary. That merely hastens the menstrual cycle."

"Not an ovarian follicle. All of them."

"All . . . ?" His brow wrinkled, puzzled—and then shock froze his face. "You trigger all the follicles? So that all the woman's eggs are released at once?"

Amy nodded. "Your people must know that by now, too."

Segueno nodded automatically, whispering. "I received a bulletin on the way here. Something about an unusual property . . ."

His voice trickled away. The moths threw frantic shadows over tight faces that gleamed with sweat.

"Then . . . they will recover. But be infertile."

Todd breathed out, tensions he did not know that he carried now released. "There. It's done."

"So you did not intend to kill many."

Amy said with cool deliberation, "That is an unavoidable side effect. The fever kills weak people, mostly elderly. We couldn't find any way to edit it out."

"My God . . . There will be no children."

Todd shook his head. "About fifteen percent of the time it doesn't work through all the ovarian follicles. The next generation will drop in population almost an order of magnitude."

Segueno's mouth compressed, lips white. "You are the greatest criminals of all time."

"Probably," Todd said. He felt suddenly tired now that the job was done. And he didn't much care what anybody thought.

"You will be executed."

"Probably," Amy said.

"How . . . how could you . . . ?"

"Our love got us through it," Todd said fiercely. "We could not have children ourselves—a tilted uterus. We simply extended the method."

Amy said in her flat, abstract tone, "We tried attaching an acrosome to sperm, but males can always make new ones. Females are the key. They've got a few hundred ova. Get those, you've solved the problem. Saved the world."

"To rescue the environment," Todd knew he had to say this right. "To stop the madness of more and more people."

Segueno looked at them with revulsion. "You know we will stop it. Distribute the vaccine."

Amy smiled, a slow sliding of lips beneath flinty eyes. "Sure. And you're wondering why we're so calm."

"That is obvious. You are insane. From the highest cultures, the most advanced—such savagery."

"Where else? We respect the environment. We don't breed like animals."

"You, you are . . ." Again Segueno's voice trickled away.

Todd saw the narrowed eyes, the straining jaw muscles, the sheen of sweat in this tight-lipped U.N. bureaucrat and wondered just how a man of such limited horizons could think his disapproval would matter to them. To people who had decided to give themselves to save the world. What a tiny, ordinary mind.

Amy hugged her husband. "At least now we'll be together."

Segueno said bitterly, "We shall try you under local statutes. Make an example. And the rest of your gang, too—we shall track them all down."

The two on the cot sat undisturbed, hugging each other tightly. Todd kissed Amy. They had lived through these moments in imagination many times.

Loudly Segueno said, "You shall live just long enough to see the vaccine stop your plan."

Amy kissed Todd, long and lingering, and then looked up. "Oh, really? And you believe the North will pay for it? When they can just drag their feet, and let it spread unchecked in the tropics?"

Todd smiled grimly. "After they've inoculated themselves, they'll be putting their energy into a 'womb race'—finding fertile women, a 'national natural resource.' Far too busy. And the superflu will do its job."

Segueno's face congested, reddened. Todd watched shock and fear and then rage flit across the man's face. The logic, the inevitable cool logic to it, had finally hit him.

Somehow this last twist had snagged somewhere in Segueno, pushed him over the line. Todd saw something compressed and dark in the face, too late. *My mouth*, he thought. *I've killed us both.*

Segueno snatched the pistol from the guard and Todd saw that they would not get to witness the last, pleasant irony, the dance of nations, acted out after all.

It was the last thing he thought, and yet it was only a mild regret.

EVOLUTION

Nancy Kress

We may have already made the fatal mistakes that will lead to our doom, as inevitable but unexpected consequences of decisions made long past—decisions so commonplace and everyday that we didn't even stop to think about them, like swallowing the pill your doctor prescribes for you when you're sick—relentlessly back us into corners nobody had ever foreseen. As portrayed in the unsettling story that follows, which takes us to an all-too-likely future (one that is, in fact, just about here) for a grim lesson in how evolution really works, however much we'd like to think that modern medical science has put us safely beyond its reach . . .

Nancy Kress began selling her elegant and incisive stories in the mid-'70s, and has since become a frequent contributor to Asimov's Science Fiction, The Magazine of Fantasy and Science Fiction, Omni, *and elsewhere. Her books include the novels* The Prince of Morning Bells, The Golden Grove, The White Pipes, An Alien Light, Brain Rose, *the novel version of her Hugo- and Nebula-winning story,* "Beggars in Spain," *and a sequel,* Beggars and Choosers, *and* Oaths & Miracles. *Her short work has been collected in* Trinity and Other Stories *and* The Aliens of Earth. *Her most recent novels are* Maximum Light *and* Stinger. *She has also won Nebula Awards for her stories* "Out of All Them Bright Stars" *and* "The Flowers of Aulit Prison." *Born in Buffalo, New York, she now lives in Silver Springs, Maryland, with her husband, SF writer Charles Sheffield.*

"**S**omebody shot and killed Dr. Bennett behind the Food Mart on April Street!" Ceci Moore says breathlessly as I take the washing off the line.

I stand with a pair of Jack's boxer shorts in my hand and

stare at her. I don't like Ceci. Her smirking pushiness, her need
to shove her scrawny body into the middle of every situation,
even ones she'd be better off leaving alone. She's been that way
since high school. But we're neighbors; we're stuck with each
other. Dr. Bennett delivered both Sean and Jackie. Slowly I fold
the boxer shorts and lay them in my clothes-basket.

"Well, Betty, aren't you even going to *say* anything?"

"Have the police arrested anybody?"

"Janie Brunelli says there's no suspects." Tom Brunelli is
one of Emerton's police officers, all five of them. He has
trouble keeping his mouth shut. "Honestly, Betty, you look like
there's a murder in this town every day!"

"Was it in the parking lot?" I'm in that parking lot behind the
Food Mart every week. It's unpaved, just hard-packed rocky
dirt sloping down to a low concrete wall by the river. I take
Jackie's sheets off the line. Belle, Ariel, and Princess Jasmine
all smile through fields of flowers.

"Yes, in the parking lot," Ceci says. "Near the dumpsters.
There must have been a silencer on the rifle, nobody heard
anything. Tom found two .22 250 semiautomatic cartridges."
Ceci knows about guns. Her house is full of them. "Betty, why
don't you put all this wash in your dryer and save yourself the
trouble of hanging it all out?"

"I like the way it smells line-dried. And I can hear Jackie
through the window."

Instantly Ceci's face changes. "Jackie's home from school?
Why?"

"She has a cold."

"Are you sure it's just a cold?"

"I'm sure." I take the clothespins off Sean's T-shirt. The
front says SEE DICK DRINK, SEE DICK DRIVE, SEE DICK DIE. "Ceci,
Jackie is not on any antibiotics."

"Good thing," Ceci says, and for a moment she studies her
fingernails, very casual. "They say Dr. Bennett prescribed
endozine again last week. For the youngest Nordstrum boy.
Without sending him to the hospital."

I don't answer. The back of Sean's t-shirt says DON'T BE A
DICK. Irritated by my silence, Ceci says, "I don't see how you
can let your son wear that obscene clothing!"

"It's his choice. Besides, Ceci, it's a health message. About not drinking and driving. Aren't you the one that thinks strong health messages are a good thing?"

Our eyes lock. The silence lengthens. Finally Ceci says, "Well, haven't *we* gotten serious all of a sudden."

I say, "Murder is serious."

"Yes. I'm sure the cops will catch whoever did it. Probably one of those scum that hang around the Rainbow Bar."

"Dr. Bennett wasn't the type to hang around with scum."

"Oh, I don't mean he *knew* them. Some lowlife probably killed him for his wallet." She looks straight into my eyes. "I can't think of any other motive. Can you?"

I look east, toward the river. On the other side, just visible over the tops of houses on its little hill, rise the three stories of Emerton Soldiers and Sailors Memorial Hospital. The bridge over the river was blown up three weeks ago. No injuries, no suspects. Now anybody who wants to go to the hospital has to drive ten miles up West River Road and cross at the Interstate. Jack told me that the Department of Transportation says two years to get a new bridge built.

I say, "Dr. Bennett was a good doctor. And a good man."

"Well, did anybody say he wasn't? Really, Betty, you should use your dryer and save yourself all that bending and stooping. Bad for the back. We're not getting any younger. Ta ta." She waves her right hand, just a waggle of fingers, and walks off. Her nails, I notice, are painted the delicate fragile pinky-white of freshly unscabbed skin.

"You have no proof," Jack says "Just some wild suspicions."

He has his stubborn face on. He sits with his Michelob at the kitchen table, dog-tired from his factory shift plus three hours overtime, and he doesn't want to hear this. I don't blame him. I don't want to be saying it. In the living room Jackie plays Nintendo frantically, trying to cram in as many electronic explosions as she can before her father claims the TV for *Monday Night Football*. Sean has already gone out with his friends, before his stepfather got home.

I sit down across from Jack, a fresh mug of coffee cradled between my palms. For warmth. "I know I don't have any proof, Jack. I'm not some detective."

"So let the cops handle it. It's their business, not ours. You stay out of it."

"I am out of it. You know that." Jack nods. We don't mix with cops, don't serve on any town committees, don't even listen to the news much. We don't get involved with what doesn't concern us. Jack never did. I add, "I'm just telling you what I think. I can do that, can't I?" and hear my voice stuck someplace between pleading and anger.

Jack hears it, too. He scowls, stands with his beer, puts his hand gently on my shoulder. "Sure, Bets. You can say whatever you want to me. But nobody else, you hear? I don't want no trouble, especially to you and the kids. This ain't our problem. Just be grateful *we're* all healthy, knock on wood."

He smiles and goes into the living room. Jackie switches off the Nintendo without being yelled at; she's good that way. I look out the kitchen window, but it's too dark to see anything but my own reflection, and anyway the window faces north, not east.

I haven't crossed the river since Jackie was born at Emerton Memorial, seven years ago. And then I was in the hospital less than twenty-four hours before I made Jack take me home. Not because of the infections, of course—that hadn't all started yet. But it has now, and what if next time instead of the youngest Nordstrum boy, it's Jackie who needs endozine? Or Sean?

Once you've been to Emerton Memorial, nobody but your family will go near you. And sometimes not even them. When Mrs. Weimer came home from surgery, her daughter-in-law put her in that back upstairs room and left her food on disposable trays in the doorway and put in a chemical toilet. Didn't even help the old lady crawl out of bed to use it. For a whole month it went on like that—surgical masks, gloves, paper gowns—until Rosie Weimer was positive Mrs. Weimer hadn't picked up any mutated drug-resistant bacteria in Emerton Memorial. And Hal Weimer didn't say a word against his wife.

"People are scared, but they'll do the right thing," Jack said, the only other time I tried to talk to him about it. Jack isn't much for talking. And so I don't. I owe him that.

But in the city—in all the cities—they're not just scared. They're terrified. Even without listening to the news I hear about the riots and the special government police and half the population sick with the new germs that only endozine cures—sometimes. I don't see how they're going to have much energy for one murdered small-town doctor. And I don't share Jack's conviction that people in Emerton will automatically do the right thing. I remember all too well that sometimes they don't. How come Jack doesn't remember, too?

But he's right about one thing: I don't owe this town anything.

I stack the supper dishes in the sink and get Jackie started on her homework.

The next day, I drive down to the Food Mart parking lot.

There isn't much to see. It rained last night. Next to the dumpster lie a wadded-up surgical glove and a piece of yellow tape like the police use around a crime scene. Also some of those little black cardboard boxes from the stuff that gets used up by the new holographic TV cameras. That's it.

"You heard what happened to Dr. Bennett?" I say to Sean at dinner. Jack's working again. Jackie sits playing with the Barbie doll she doesn't know I know she has on her lap.

Sean looks at me sideways, under the heavy fringe of his dark bangs, and I can't read his expression. "He was killed for giving out too many antibiotics."

Jackie looks up. "Who killed the doctor?"

"The bastards that think they run this town," Sean says. He flicks the hair out of his eyes. His face is ashy gray. "Fucking vigilantes'll get us all."

"That's enough, Sean," I say.

Jackie's lip trembles. "Who'll get us all? Mommy . . ."

"Nobody's getting anybody," I say. "Sean, stop it. You're scaring her."

"Well, she should be scared," Sean says, but he shuts up and stares bleakly at his plate. Sixteen now. I've had him for sixteen years. Watching him, his thick dark hair and sulky mouth, I think that it's a sin to have a favorite child. And that I can't help it, and that I would, God forgive me, sacrifice both Jackie and Jack for this boy.

"I want you to clean the garage tonight, Sean. You promised Jack three days ago now."

"Tomorrow. Tonight I have to go out."

Jackie says, "Why should I be scared?"

"Tonight," I say.

Sean looks at me with teenage desperation. His eyes are very blue. "Not tonight, I have to go out."

Jackie says, "Why should I—"

I say, "You're staying home and cleaning the garage."

"No." He glares at me, and then breaks. He has his father's looks, but he's not really like his father. There are even tears in the corners of his eyes. "I'll do it tomorrow, Mom, I promise. Right after school. But tonight I have to go out."

"Where?"

"Just out."

Jackie says, "Why should I be scared? Scared of what? Mommy!"

Sean turns to her. "You shouldn't be scared, Jack-o-lantern. Everything's going to be all right. One way or another."

I listen to the tone of his voice and suddenly fear shoots through me, piercing as childbirth. I say, "Jackie, you can play Nintendo now. I'll clear the table."

Her face brightens. She skips into the living room and I look at my son. "What does that mean? 'One way or another'? Sean, what's going on?"

"Nothing," he says, and then despite his ashy color he looks me straight in the eyes, and smiles tenderly, and for the first time—the very first time—I see his resemblance to his father. He can lie to me with tenderness.

Two days later, just after I return from the Food Mart, they contact me.

The murder was on the news for two nights, and then disappeared. Over the parking lot is scattered more TV-camera litter. There's also a wine bottle buried halfway into the hard ground, with a bouquet of yellow roses in it. Nearby is an empty basket, the kind that comes filled with expensive dried flowers at Blossoms by Bonnie, weighted down with stones. Staring at it, I remember that Bonnie Widelstein went out of business a few months ago. A drug-resistant abscess, and after she got out of Emerton Memorial, nobody on this side of the river would buy flowers from her.

At home, Sylvia James is sitting in my driveway in her black Algol. As soon as I see her, I put it together.

"Sylvia," I say tonelessly.

She climbs out of the sportscar and smiles a social smile. "Elizabeth! How good to see you!" I don't answer. She hasn't seen me in seventeen years. She's carrying a cheese kuchen, like some sort of key into my house. She's still blonde, still slim, still well dressed. Her lipstick is bright red, which is what her face should be.

I let her in anyway, my heart making slow hard thuds in my chest. *Sean. Sean.*

Once inside, her hard smile fades and she has the grace to look embarrassed. "Elizabeth—"

"Betty," I say. "I go by Betty now."

"Betty. First off, I want to apologize for not being . . . for not standing by you in that mess. I know it was so long ago, but even so, I—I wasn't a very good friend." She hesitates. "I was frightened by it all."

I want to say, *You* were frightened? But I don't.

I never think of the whole dumb story any more. Not even when I look at Sean. Especially not when I look at Sean.

Seventeen years ago, when Sylvia and I were seniors in high school, we were best friends. Neither of us had a sister, so we made each other into that, even though her family wasn't crazy about their precious daughter hanging around with someone like me. The Goddards live on the other side of the river. Sylvia ignored them, and I ignored the drunken warnings of my aunt, the closest thing I had to a family. The differences didn't matter. We were Sylvia-and-Elizabeth, the two prettiest and boldest girls in the senior class who had an academic future.

And then, suddenly, I didn't. At Elizabeth's house I met Randolf Satler, young resident in her father's unit at the hospital. And I got pregnant, and Randy dumped me, and I refused a paternity test because if he didn't want me and the baby I had too much pride to force myself on any man. That's what I told everyone, including myself. I was eighteen years old. I didn't know what a common story mine was, or what a dreary one. I thought I was the only one in the whole wide world who had ever felt this bad.

So after Sean was born at Emerton Memorial and Randy got engaged the day I moved my baby "home" to my dying aunt's, I bought a Smith & Wesson revolver in the city and shot out the windows of Randy's supposedly empty house across the river. I hit the gardener, who was helping himself to the Satler liquor cabinet in the living room. The judge gave me seven-and-a-half to ten, and I served five, and that only because my lawyer pleaded post-partum depression. The gardener recovered and retired to Miami, and Dr. Satler went on to become Chief of Medicine at Emerton Memorial and a lot of other important things in the city, and Sylvia never visited me once in Bedford Hills Correctional Facility. Nobody did, except Jack. Who, when Sylvia-and-Elizabeth were strutting their stuff at Emerton High, had already dropped out and was bagging groceries at the Food Mart. After I got out of Bedford, the only reason the foster care people would give me Sean back was because Jack married me.

We live in Emerton, but not of it.

Sylvia puts her kuchen on the kitchen table and sits down without being asked. I can see she'd done with apologizing. She's still smart enough to know there are things you can't apologize for.

"Eliz . . . Betty, I'm not here about the past. I'm here about Dr. Bennett's murder."

"That doesn't have anything to do with me."

"It has to do with all of us. Dan Moore lives next door to you."

I don't say anything.

"He and Ceci and Jim Dyer and Tom Brunelli are the ringleaders in a secret organization to close Emerton Memorial Hospital. They think the hospital is a breeding ground for the infections resistant to every antibiotic except endozine. Well, they're right about that—all hospitals are. But Dan and his group are determined to punish any doctor who prescribes endozine, so that no organisms develop a resistance to it, too, and it's kept effective in case one of *them* needs it."

"Sylvia—" the name tastes funny in my mouth, after all this time "—I'm telling you this doesn't have anything to do with me."

"And I'm telling you it does. We need you, Eliz . . . Betty. You live next door to Dan and Ceci. You can tell us when they leave the house, who comes to it, anything suspicious you see. We're not a vigilante group, Betty, like they are. We aren't doing anything illegal. We don't kill people, and we don't blow up bridges, and we don't threaten people like the Nordstrums who get endozine for their sick kids but are basically uneducated blue collar—"

She stops. Jack and I are basically uneducated blue collar. I say coldly, "I can't help you, Sylvia."

"I'm sorry, Betty. That wasn't what I meant. Look, this is more important than anything that happened a decade and a half ago! Don't you *understand?*" She leans toward me across the table. "The whole country's caught in this thing. It's already a public health crisis as big as the Spanish influenza epidemic of 1918, and it's only just started! Drug-resistant bacteria can produce a new generation every twenty minutes, they can swap resistant genes not only within a species but across *different* species. The bacteria are *winning*. And people like the Moores are taking advantage of that to contribute further to the breakdown of even basic social decency."

In high school Sylvia had been on the debating team. But so, in that other life, had I. "If the Moores' group is trying to keep endozine from being used, then aren't they also fighting against the development of more drug-resistant bacteria? And if that's so, aren't they the ones, not you, who are ultimately aiding the country's public health?"

"Through dynamiting. And intimidation. And murder. Betty, I know you don't approve of those things. I wouldn't be here telling you about our countergroup if I thought you did. Before I came here, we looked very carefully at you. At the kind of person you are. Are now. You and your husband are law-abiding people, you vote, you make a contribution to the Orphans of AIDS Fund, you—"

"How did you know about that? That's supposed to be a secret contribution!"

"—you signed the petition to protect the homeless from harassment. Your husband served on the jury that convicted Paul Keene of fraud, even though his real-estate scheme was so good for the economy of Emerton. You—"

"Stop it," I say. "You don't have any right to investigate me like I was some criminal!"

Only, of course, I was. Once. Not now. Sylvia's right about that—Jack and I believe in law and order, but for different reasons. Jack because that's what his father believed in, and his grandfather. Me, because I learned in Bedford that enforced rules are the only thing that even halfway restrains the kind of predators Sylvia James never dreamed of. The kind I want kept away from my children.

Sylvia says, "We have a lot of people on our side, Betty. People who don't want to see this town slide into the same kind of violence there is in Albany and Syracuse and, worst case, New York."

A month ago, New York Hospital in Queens was blown up. The whole thing, with a series of coordinated timed bombs. Seventeen hundred people dead in less than a minute.

"It's a varied group," she continues. "Some town leaders, some housewives, some teachers, nearly all the medical personnel at the hospital. All people who care what happens to Emerton."

"Then you've got the wrong person here," I say, and it comes out harsher than I want to reveal. "I don't care about Emerton."

"You have reasons," Sylvia says evenly. "And I'm part of your reasons, I know. But I think you'll help us, Elizabeth. I know you must be concerned about your son—we've all observed what a good mother you are."

So she brought up Sean's name first. I say, "You're wrong again, Sylvia. I don't need you to protect Sean, and if you've let him get involved in helping you, you'll wish you'd never been born. I've worked damn hard to make sure that what happened seventeen years ago never touches him. He doesn't need to get mixed up in any way with your 'medical personnel at the hospital.' And Sean sure the hell doesn't owe this town anything, there wasn't even anybody who would take him in after my aunt died, he had to go to—"

The look on her face stops me. Pure surprise. And then something else.

"Oh my God," she says. "Is it possible you don't know? Hasn't Sean told you?"

"Told me what?" I stand up, and I'm seventeen years old again, and just that scared. Sylvia-and-Elizabeth.

"Your son isn't helping our side. He's working for Dan Moore and Mike Dryer. They use juveniles because if they're caught, they won't be tried as severely as adults. We think Sean was one of the kids they used to blow up the bridge over the river."

I look first at the high school. Sean isn't there; he hadn't even shown up for homeroom. No one's home at his friend Tom's house, or at Keith's. He isn't at the Billiard Ball or the Emerton Diner or the American Bowl. After that, I run out of places to search.

This doesn't happen in places like Emerton. We have fights at basketball games and grand theft auto and smashed store windows on Halloween and sometimes a drunken tragic car crash on prom night. But not secret terrorists, not counter terrorist vigilante groups. Not in Emerton.

Not with my son.

I drive to the factory and make them page Jack.

He comes off the line, face creased with sweat and dirt. The air is filled with clanging machinery and grinding drills. I pull him outside the door, where there are benches and picnic tables for workers on break. "Betty! What is it?"

"Sean," I gasp. "He's in danger."

Something shifts behind Jack's eyes. "What kind of danger?"

"Sylvia Goddard came to see me today. Sylvia James. She says Sean is involved with the group that blew up the bridge, the ones who are trying to get Emerton Memorial closed, and . . . and killed Dr. Bennett."

Jack peels off his bench gloves, taking his time. Finally he looks up at me. "How come that bitch Sylvia Goddard comes to you with this? After all this time?"

"Jack! Is that all you can think of? Sean is in trouble!"

He says gently, "Well, Bets, it was bound to happen sooner or later, wasn't it? He's always been a tough kid to raise. Rebellious. Can't tell him anything."

I stare at Jack.

"Some people just have to learn the hard way."

"Jack . . . this is serious! Sean might be involved in terrorism! He could end up in jail!"

"Couldn't ever tell him anything," Jack says, and I hear the hidden satisfaction in his voice, that he doesn't even know is there. Not his son. Dr. Randy Satler's son. Turning out bad.

"Look," Jack says, "when the shift ends I'll go look for him, Bets. Bring him home. You go and wait there for us." His face is gentle, soothing. He really will find Sean, if it's possible. But only because he loves me.

My sudden surge of hatred is so strong I can't even speak.

"Go on home, Bets. It'll be all right. Sean just needs to have the nonsense kicked out of him."

I turn and walk away. At the turning in the parking lot, I see Jack walking jauntily back inside, pulling on his gloves.

I drive home, because I can't think what else to do. I sit on the couch and reach back in my mind for that other place, the place I haven't gone to since I got out of Bedford. The gray granite place that turns you to granite, too, so you can sit and wait for hours, for weeks, for years, without feeling very much. I go into that place, and I become the Elizabeth I was then, when Sean was in foster care someplace and I didn't know who had him or what they might be doing to him or how I would get him back. I go into the gray granite place to become stone.

And it doesn't work.

It's been too long. I've had Sean too long. Jack has made me feel too safe. I can't find the stony place.

Jackie is spending the night at a friend's. I sit in the dark, no lights on, car in the garage. Sean doesn't come home, and neither does Jack. At two in the morning, a lot of people in dark clothing cross the back lawn and quietly enter Dan and Ceci's house next door, carrying bulky packages wrapped in black cloth.

Jack staggers in at six-thirty in the morning. Alone. His face droops with exhaustion.

"I couldn't find him, Betty. I looked everywhere."

"Thank you," I say, and he nods. Accepting my thanks. This was something he did for me, not for Sean. Not for himself, as Sean's stepfather. I push down my sudden anger and say, "You better get some sleep."

"Right." He goes down the narrow hallway into our bedroom. In three minutes he's snoring.

I let the car coast in neutral down the driveway. Our bedroom faces the street. The curtains don't stir.

The West River Road is deserted, except for a few eighteen-wheelers. I cross the river at the Interstate and start back along the east side. Three miles along, in the middle of farmland, the smell of burned flesh rolls in the window.

Cows, close to the pasture fence. I stop the car and get out. Fifteen or sixteen Holsteins. By straining over the fence, I can see the bullet holes in their heads. Somebody herded them together, shot them one by one, and started a half-hearted fire among the bodies with neatly cut firewood. The fire had gone out; it didn't look as if it was supposed to burn long. Just long enough to attract attention that hadn't come yet.

I'd never heard that cows could get human diseases. Why had they been shot?

I get back in my car and drive the rest of the way to Emerton Memorial.

This side of town is deathly quiet. Grass grows unmowed in yard after yard. One large, expensive house has old newspapers piled on the porch steps, ten or twelve of them. There are no kids waiting for school buses, no cars pulling out of driveways on the way to work. The hospital parking lot has huge empty stretches between cars. At the last minute I drive on through the lot, parking instead across the street in somebody's empty driveway, under a clump of trees.

Nobody sits at the information desk. The gift shop is locked. Nobody speaks to me as I study the directory on the lobby wall, even though two figures in gowns and masks hurry past. CHIEF OF MEDICINE, DR. RANDOLF SATLER. Third floor, east wing. The elevator is deserted.

It stops at the second floor. When the doors open a man stands there, a middle-aged farmer in overalls and work boots, his eyes red and swollen like he's been crying. There are tinted windows across from the elevators and I can see the back of him reflected in the glass. Coming and going. From somewhere I hear a voice calling, "Nurse, oh nurse, oh God . . ." A gurney sits in hallway, the body on it covered by a sheet up to the neck. The man in overalls looks at me and raises both hands to ward off the elevator, like it's some kind of demon. He steps backward. The doors close.

I grip the railing on the elevator wall.

The third floor looks empty. Bright arrows lead along the hallways: yellow for PATHOLOGY and LAB SERVICES, green for RESPIRATORY THERAPY, red for SUPPORT SERVICES. I follow the yellow arrow.

It dead-ends at an empty alcove with chairs, magazines thrown on the floor. And three locked doors off a short corridor that's little more than an alcove.

I pick the farthest door and pound on it. No words, just regular blows of my fist. After a minute, I start on the second one. A voice calls, "Who's there?"

I recognize the voice, even through the locked door. Even after seventeen years. I shout, "Police! Open the door!"

And he does. The second it cracks, I shove it hard and push my way into the lab.

"*Elizabeth*?"

He's older, heavier, but still the same. Dark hair, blue eyes . . . I look at that face every day at dinner. I've looked at it at soccer matches, in school plays, in his playpen. Dr. Satler looks more shaken to see me than I would have thought, his face white, sweat on his forehead.

"Hello, Randy."

"Elizabeth. You can't come in here. You have to leave—"

"Because of the staph? Do you think I care about that? After all, I'm in the hospital, right, Randy? This is where the endozine is. This place is safe. Unless it gets blown up while I'm standing here."

He stares at my left hand, still gripping the doorknob behind me. Then at the gun in my right hand. A seventeen-year-old Smith & Wesson, and for five of those years the gun wasn't cleaned or oiled, hidden under my aunt's garage. But it still fires.

"I'm not going to shoot you, Randy. I don't care if you're alive or dead. But you're going to help me. I can't find my son—" *your son* "—and Sylvia Goddard told me he's mixed up with that group that blew up the bridge. He'd hiding with them someplace, probably scared out of his skull. You know everybody in town, everybody with power, you're going to get on that phone there and find out where Sean is."

"I would do that anyway," Randy says, and now he looks the way I remember him: impatient and arrogant. But not completely. There's still sweat on his pale face. "Put that stupid thing away, Elizabeth."

"No."

"Oh, for . . ." He turns his back on me and punches at the phone.

"Cam? Randy Satler here. Could you . . . no, it's not about that . . . No. Not yet."

Cameron Witt. The mayor. His son is chief of Emerton's five cops.

"I need a favor. There's a kid missing. . . . I know that, Cam. You don't have to lecture *me* on how bad delay could . . . But you might know about this kid. Sean Baker."

"Pulaski. Sean Pulaski." He doesn't even know that.

"Sean Pulaski. Yeah, that one . . . okay. Get back to me . . . I told you. *Not yet.*" He hands up. "Cam will hunt around and call back. Now will you put that stupid gun away, Elizabeth?"

"You still don't say thank you for anything." The words just come out. Fuck, fuck, fuck.

"To Cam, or to you for not shooting me?" He says it evenly, and the evenness is the only way I finally see how furious he is. People don't order around Dr. Randy Satler at gunpoint. A part of my mind wonders why he doesn't call security.

I said, "All right, I'm here. Give me a dose of endozine, just in case."

He goes on staring at me with that same level, furious gaze. "Too late, Elizabeth."

"What do you mean, too late? Haven't you got endozine?"

"Of course we do." Suddenly he staggers slightly, puts out one hand behind him, and holds onto a table covered with glassware and papers.

"Randy. You're sick."

"I am. And not with anything endozine is going to cure. Ah, Elizabeth, why didn't you just phone me? I'd have looked for Sean for you."

"Oh, right. Like you've been so interested and helpful in raising him."

"You never asked me."

I see that he means it. He really believes his total lack of contact with his son is my fault. I see that Randy gives only what he's asked to. He waits, lordly, for people to plead for his help, beg for it, and then he gives it. If it suits him.

I say, "I'll bet anything your kids with your wife are turning out really scary."

The blood rushes to his face, and I know I guessed right. His blue eyes darken and he looks like Jack looks just before Jack explodes. But Randy isn't Jack. An explosion would be too clean for him. He says instead, "You were stupid to come here. Haven't you been listening to the news?"

I haven't.

"The CDC publicly announced just last night what medical personnel have seen for weeks. A virulent strain of staphylococcus aureus has incorporated endozine-resistant plasmids from enterococcus." He pauses to catch his breath. "And pneumococcus may have done the same thing."

"What does that mean?"

"It means, you stupid woman, that now there are highly contagious infections that we have no drugs to cure. No antibiotics at all, not even endozine. This staph is resistant to them all. And it can live everywhere."

I lower the gun. The empty parking lot. No security to summon. The man who wouldn't get on the elevator. And Randy's face. "And you've got it."

"We've all got it. Everyone . . . in the hospital. And for forcing your way in here, you probably do, too."

"You're going to die," I say, and it's half a hope.

And he *smiles*.

He stands there in his white lab coat, sweating like a horse; barely able to stand up straight, almost shot by a woman he'd once abandoned pregnant, and he smiles. His blue eyes gleam. He looks like a picture I once saw in a book, back when I read a lot. It takes me a minute to remember that it was my high school World History book. A picture of some general.

"Everybody's going to die eventually," Randy says. "But not me right now. At least . . . I hope not." Casually he crosses the floor toward me, and I step backward. He smiles again.

"I'm not going to deliberately infect you, Elizabeth. I'm a *doctor*. I just want the gun."

"No."

"Have it your way. Look, how much do you know about the bubonic plague of the fourteenth century?"

"Nothing," I say, although I do. Why had I always acted stupider around Randy than I actually am?

"Then it won't mean anything to you to say that this mutated staph has at least that much potential—" again he paused and gulped air "—for rapid and fatal transmission. It flourishes everywhere. Even on doorknobs."

"So why the fuck are you *smiling?*" Alexander. That was the picture of the general. Alexander the Great.

"Because I . . . because the CDC distributed . . . I was on the national team to discover . . ." His face changes again. Goes even whiter. And he pitches over onto the floor.

I grab him, roll him face up, and feel his forehead. He's

burning up. I bolt for the door. "Nurse! Doctor! There's a sick doctor here!"

Nobody comes.

I run down the corridors. Respiratory Therapy is empty. So is Support Services. I jab at the elevator button, but before it comes I run back to Randy.

And stand above him, lying there crumpled on the floor, laboring to breathe.

I'd dreamed about a moment like this for years. Dreamed it waking and asleep, in Emerton and in Bedford Hills and in Jack's arms. Dreamed it in a thousand ridiculous melodramatic versions. And here it is, Randy helpless and pleading, and me strong, standing over him, free to walk away and let him die. Free.

I wring out a towel in cold water and put it on his forehead. Then I find ice in the refrigerator in a corner of the lab and substitute that. He watches me, his breathing wheezy as old machinery.

"Elizabeth. Bring me . . . syringe in a box on . . . that table."

I do it. "Who should I get for you, Randy? Where?"

"Nobody. I'm not . . . as bad . . . as I sound. Yet. Just the initial . . . dyspnea." He picks up the syringe.

"Is there medicine for you in there? I thought you said endozine wouldn't work on this new infection." His color is a little better now.

"Not medicine. And not for me. For you."

He looks at me steadily. And I see that Randy would never plead, never admit to helplessness. Never ever think of himself as helpless.

He lowers the hand holding the syringe back to the floor. "Listen, Elizabeth. You have . . . almost certainly have . . ."

Somewhere, distantly, a siren starts to wail. Randy ignores it. All of a sudden his voice becomes much firmer, even though he's sweating again and his eyes burn bright with fever. Or something.

"This staph is resistant to everything we can throw it. We cultured it and tried. Cephalosporins and aminoglycosides and vancomycin, even endozine . . . I'll go into gram-positive septic shock. . . ." His eyes glaze, but after a moment he seems to find his thought again. "We exhausted all points of counterattack. Cell wall, bacterial ribosome, folic acid pathway. Microbes just evolve countermeasures. Like beta-lactamase."

I don't understand this language. Even talking to himself, he's making me feel stupid again. I ask something I do understand.

"Why are people killing cows? Are the cows sick, too?"

He focuses again. "Cows? No, they're not sick. Farmers use massive doses of antibiotics to increase meat and milk production. Agricultural use of endozine has increased the rate of resistance development by over a thousand percent since—Elizabeth, this is irrelevant! Can't you pay attention to what I'm saying for three minutes?"

I stand up and look down at him, lying shivering on the floor. He doesn't even seem to notice, just keeps on lecturing.

"But antibiotics weren't invented by humans. They were invented by the microbes themselves to use . . . against each other and . . . they had two billion years of evolution at it before we even showed up. . . . We should have—where are you going?"

"Home. Have a nice life, Randy."

He says quietly, "I probably will. But if . . . you leave now, you're probably dead. And your husband and kids, too."

"Why? Damn it, stop lecturing and tell me why!"

"Because you're infected, and there's no antibiotic for it, but there *is* another bacteria that will attack the drug-resistant staph."

I look at the syringe in his hand.

"It's a Trojan horse plasmid. That's a . . . never mind. It can get into the staph in your blood and deliver a lethal gene. One that will kill the staph. It's an incredible discovery. But the only way to deliver it so far is to deliver the whole bacteria."

My knees all of a sudden get shaky. Randy watches me from his position on the floor. He looks shakier himself. His breathing turns raspier again.

"No, you're not sick yet, Elizabeth. But you will be."

I snap, "From the staph germs or from the cure?"

"Both."

"You want to make me sicker. With two bacteria. And hope one will kill the other."

"Not hope. I *know*. I actually saw . . . it on the electromicrograph. . . ." His eyes roll, refocus. ". . . could package just the lethal plasmid on a transpon if we had time . . . no time. Has to be the whole bacteria." And then, stronger, "The CDC team is working on it. But *I* actually caught it on the electromicrograph!"

I say, before I know I'm going to, "Stop congratulating yourself and give me the syringe. Before you die."

I move across the floor toward him, put my arms around him to prop him in a sitting position against the table leg. His whole body feels on fire. But somehow he keeps his hands steady as he injects the syringe into the inside of my elbow. While it drains sickness into me I say, "You never actually wanted me, did you, Randy? Even before Sean?"

"No," he says. "Not really." He drops the syringe.

I bend my arm. "You're a rotten human being. All you care about is yourself and your work."

He smiles the same cold smile. "So? My work is what matters. In a larger sense than you could possibly imagine. You were always a weak sentimentalist, Elizabeth. Now, go home."

"Go *home?* But you said . . ."

"I said you'd infect everyone. And you will—with the bacteria that attacks staph. It should cause only a fairly mild illness. Jenner . . . smallpox . . ."

"But you said I have the mutated staph, too!"

"You almost certainly do. Yes . . . And so will everyone else, before long. Deaths . . . in New York State alone . . . passed one million this morning. Six and a half percent of the . . . population. . . . Did you really think you could hide on your side of . . . the . . . river . . . ?"

"Randy!"

"Go . . . home."

I strip off his lab coat and wad it up for a pillow, bring more ice from the refrigerator, try to get him to drink some water.

"Go . . . home. Kiss everybody." He smiles to himself, and starts to shake with fever. His eyes close.

I stand up again. Should I go? Stay? If I could find someone in the hospital to take care of him—

The phone rings. I seize it. "Hello? Hello?"

"Randy? Excuse me, can I talk to Dr. Satler? This is Cameron Witt."

I try to sound professional. "Dr. Satler can't come to the

phone right now. But if you're calling about Sean Pulaski, Dr.
Satler asked me to take the message."

"I don't . . . oh, all right. Just tell Randy the Pulaski boy is
with Richard and Sylvia James. He'll understand." The line
clicks.

I replace the receiver and stare at Randy, fighting for breath
on the floor, his face as gray as Sean's when Sean realized it
was murder he'd gotten involved with. No, not as gray.
Because Sean had been terrified, and Randy is only sick.

My work is what matters.

But how had Sean known to go to Sylvia? Even if he knew
from Ceci who was on the other side, how did he know which
people would hide him, would protect him when I could not,
Jack could not? Sylvia-and-Elizabeth. How much did Sean
actually know about the past I'd tried so hard to keep from
touching him?

I reach the elevator, my finger almost touching the button,
when the first explosion rocks the hospital.

It's in the west wing. Through the windows opposite the
elevator banks I see windows in the far end of the building
explode outward. Thick greasy black smoke billows out the
holes. Alarms begin to screech.

Don't touch the elevators. Instructions remembered from
high school, from grade-school fire drills. I race along the hall
to the fire stairs. What if they put a bomb in the stairwell? What
if *who* put a bomb in the stairwell? *A lot of people in dark
clothing cross the back lawn and quietly enter Dan and Ceci's
house next door, carrying bulky packages wrapped in black
cloth.*

A last glimpse through a window by the door to the firestairs.
People are running out of the building, not many, but the ones
I see are pushing gurneys. A nurse staggers outside, three small
children in her arms, on her hip, clinging to her back.

They aren't setting off any more bombs until people have a
chance to get out.

I let the fire door close. Alarms scream. I run back to
Pathology and shove open the heavy door.

Randy lies on the floor, sweating and shivering. His lips
move but if he's muttering aloud, I can't hear it over the alarm.
I tug on his arm. He doesn't resist and he doesn't help, just lies
like a heavy dead cow.

There are no gurneys in Pathology. I slap him across the face, yelling "Randy! Randy! Get up!" Even now, even here, a small part of my mind thrills at hitting him.

His eyes open. For a second, I think he knows me. It goes away, then returns. He tries to get up. The effort is enough to let me hoist him over my shoulder in a fireman's carry. I could never have carried Jack, but Randy is much slighter, and I'm very strong.

But I can't carry him down three flights of stairs. I get him to the top, prop him up on his ass, and shove. He slides down one flight, bumping and flailing, and glares at me for a minute. "For . . . God's sake . . . Janet!"

His wife's name. I don't think about this tiny glimpse of his marriage. I give him another shove, but he grabs the railing and refuses to fall. He hauls himself—I'll never know how—back to a sitting position, and I sit next to him. Together, my arm around his waist, tugging and pulling, we both descend the stairs the way two-year-olds do, on our asses. Every second I'm waiting for the stairwell to blow up. Sean's gray face at dinner: *Fucking vigilantes'll get us all.*

The stairs don't blow up. The firedoor at the bottom gives out on a sidewalk on the side of the hospital away from both street and parking lot. As soon as we're outside, Randy blacks out.

This time I do what I should have done upstairs and grab him under the armpits. I drag him over the grass as far as I can. Sweat and hair fall in my eyes, and my vision keeps blurring. Dimly I'm aware of someone running toward us.

"It's Dr. Satler! Oh my God!"

A man. A large man. He grabs Randy and hoists him over his shoulder, a fireman's carry a lot smoother than mine, barely glancing at me. I stay behind them and, at the first buildings, run in a wide loop away from the hospital.

My car is still in the deserted driveway across the street. Fire trucks add their sirens to the noise. When they've torn past, I back my car out of the driveway and push my foot to the floor, just as a second bomb blows in the east wing of the hospital, and then another, and the air is full of flying debris as thick and sharp as the noise that goes on and on and on.

• • •

Three miles along the East River Road, it suddenly catches up
with me. All of it. I pull the car off the road and I can't stop
shaking. Only a few trucks pass me, and nobody stops. It's
twenty minutes before I can start the engine again, and there
has never been a twenty minutes like them in my life, not even
in Bedford. At the end of them, I pray that there never will be
again.

I turn on the radio as soon as I've started the engine.

"—in another hospital bombing in New York City, St.
Clare's Hospital in the heart of Manhattan. Beleaguered police
officials say that a shortage of available officers make impossible the kind of protection called for by Mayor Thomas
Flanagan. No group has claimed credit for the bombing, which
caused fires that spread to nearby businesses and at least one
apartment house.

"Since the Centers for Disease Control's announcement last
night of a widespread staphylococcus resistant to endozine, and
its simultaneous release of an emergency counterbacteria in
twenty-five metropolitan areas around the country, the violence
has worsened in every city transmitting reliable reports to
Atlanta. A spokesperson for the national tam of pathologists
and scientists responsible for the drastic countermeasure released an additional set of guidelines for its use. The spokesperson declined to be identified, or to identify any of the
doctors on the team, citing fear of reprisals if—"

A burst of static. The voice disappears, replaced by a shrill
hum.

I turn the dial carefully, looking for another station with
news.

By the time I reach the west side of Emerton, the streets are
deserted. Everyone has retreated inside. It looks like the
neighborhoods around the hospital look. Had looked. My body
still doesn't feel sick.

Instead of going straight home, I drive the deserted streets to
the Food Mart.

The parking lot is as empty as everywhere else. But the
basket is still there, weighted with stones. Now the stones
hold down a pile of letters. The top one is addressed in blue
Magic Marker: TO DR. BENNETT. The half-buried wine bottle
holds a fresh bouquet, chrysanthemums from somebody's

garden. Nearby a foot-high American flag sticks in the ground, beside a white candle on a foam plate, a stone crucifix, and a Barbie doll dressed like an angel. Saran Wrap covers a leather-bound copy of *The Prophet*. There are also five anti-NRA stickers, a pile of seashells, and a battered peace sign on a gold chain like a necklace. The peace sign looks older than I am.

When I get home, Jack is still asleep.

I stand over him, as a few hours ago I stood over Randy Satler. I think about how Jack visited me in prison, week after week, making the long drive from Emerton even in the bad winter weather. About how he'd sit smiling at me through the thick glass in the visitors' room, his hands with their grease-stained fingers resting on his knees, smiling even when we couldn't think of anything to say to each other. About how he clutched my hand in the delivery room when Jackie was born, and the look on his face when he first held her. About the look on his face when I told him Sean was missing: the sly, secret, not-my-kid triumph. And I think about the two sets of germs in my body, readying for war.

I bend over and kiss Jack full on the lips.

He stirs a little, half wakes, reaches for me. I pull away and go into the bathroom, where I use his toothbrush. I don't rinse it. When I return, he's asleep again.

I drive to Jackie's school, to retrieve my daughter. Together, we will go to Sylvia Goddard's—Sylvia James's—and get Sean. I'll visit with Sylvia, and shake her hand, and kiss her on the cheek, and touch everything I can. When the kids are safe at home, I'll visit Ceci and tell her I've thought it over and I want to help fight the overuse of antibiotics that's killing us. I'll touch her, and anyone else there, and everyone that either Sylvia or Ceci introduces me to, until I get too sick to do that. If I get that sick. Randy said I wouldn't, not as sick as he is. Of course, Randy has lied to me before. But I have to believe him now, on this.

I don't really have any choise. Yet.

A month later, I am on my way to Albany to bring back another dose of the counterbacteria, which the news calls "a reengineered prokaryote." They're careful not to call it a germ.

I listen to the news every hour now, although Jack doesn't

like it. Or anything else I'm doing. I read, and I study, and now I know what prokaryotes are, and beta-lactamase, and plasmids. I know how bacteria fight to survive, evolving whatever they need to wipe out the competition and go on producing the next generation. That's all that matters to bacteria. Survival by their own kind.

And that's what Randy Satler meant, too, when he said, "My work is what matters." Triumph by his own kind. It's what Ceci believes, too. And Jack.

We bring in the reengineered prokaryotes in convoys of cars and trucks, because in some other places there's been trouble. People who don't understand, people who won't understand. People whose family got a lot sicker than mine. The violence isn't over, even though the CDC says the epidemic itself is starting to come under control.

I'm early. The convoy hasn't formed yet. We leave from a different place in town each time. This time we're meeting behind the American Bowl. Sean is already there, with Sylvia. I take a short detour and drive, for the last time, to the Food Mart.

The basket is gone, with all its letters to the dead man. So are the American flag and the peace sign. The crucifix is still there, but it's broken in half. The latest flowers in the wine bottle are half wilted. Rain has muddied the Barbie doll's dress, and her long blonde hair is a mess. Someone ripped up the anti-NRA stickers. The white candle on a foam plate and the pile of seashells are untouched.

We are not bacteria. More than survival matters to us, or should. The individual past, which we can't escape, no matter how hard we try. The individual present, with its unsafe choices. The individual future. And the collective one.

I search in my pockets. Nothing but keys, money clip, lipstick, tissues, a blue marble I must have stuck in my pocket when I cleaned behind the couch. Jackie likes marbles.

I put the marble beside the candle, check my gun, and drive to join the convoy for the city.

A MESSAGE TO THE KING OF BROBDINGNAG

Richard Cowper

Sometimes, even trying to solve the problems that beset us may be in itself enough to bring about a global Armageddon—after all, as we all know, the road to hell is often paved with the very best of intentions. As in the story that follows, where earnest attempts to unseat one of the oldest and most terrible of the Four Horsemen, the pale spectre of starvation, leads us down the path to a global catastrophe of a frighteningly possible kind, one that could happen tomorrow—or today.

English writer Richard Cowper—the pseudonym of John Middleton Murry Jr.—is perhaps best known in the United States for his lyrical post-holocaust novella "Piper at the Gates of Dawn," a Nebula and Hugo finalist that was later expanded into the novel The Road to Corlay, published in 1978. Two sequels, A Dream of Kinship and A Tapestry of Time, appeared throughout the early years of the '80s, and his Corlay trilogy is generally considered to be the capstone of Cowper's career; since the mid-'80s, he has published only the occasional short story, with nothing at all by him appearing in the decade of the '90s to date as far as we know, and it remains to be seen if he will return to science fiction writing in the new century to come. Cowper's other books include—in addition to four non-SF novels as Colin Murry and Colin Middleton Murry—the novels The Twilight of Briareus, Clone, Kuldesak, Domino, Breakthrough, Profundis, Worlds Apart, and Time out of Mind, and the collections The Custodians, Out there Where the Big Ships Go, The Web of the Magi, and The Tithonian Factor.

Last night I dreamed I was a child again, watching my father grafting yet another shoot onto the apple tree in our kitchen garden. He had his back to me, and though I called out to him, he would not turn round and acknowledge me. True, it was only a dream, but if the finger is to be pointed at anyone, should it not be pointed at my father? I wonder what he would say to that if he were alive. Would he pass the buck on to *his* father—and so down the line forever and ever? Sometimes I think that there *are* no identifiable beginnings, only ends. And that surely is what we have here—the last full stop, the ultimate quietus. Unless, of course, you still believe in miracles.

Dad's life ambition was to produce one single tree that carried as many different varieties of fruit as he could induce it to adopt. Two years before his death in 1981, he had four kinds of apple, three kinds of pear, and two different sorts of plum all producing fruit on the same tree. That summer a photographer from the local paper came round and took a picture of him beside his remarkable creation. They printed it over the caption: "Local Plant Wizard Displays the Fruits of His Skill." In the article that accompanied the picture, my father was quoted as saying: "If we work with her and not against her, she'll provide us all with another Garden of Eden." The "her" he referred to was, of course, "Mother Nature."

When my father had his heart attack I was twenty-five years old and eighteen months into my first paid research job with Biotek. As soon as I heard the news I drove down to Chelmsford from Lincolnshire and went straight to the hospital. My mother and sister were already there. Dad was lying back with his eyes closed, looking gray and shriveled among the pillows. He was wired up to a monitor that was winking away steadily in a corner. A gurney with two gas cylinders was standing beside the bed, and a face mask lay ready to hand. Mother had just begun telling me in a strained whisper how it happened, when Dad opened his eyes. "Hello, Dad," I said. "How are you feeling?"

"Is that you, Clive?" His voice was so weak I barely recognized it.

"That's right," I said. "Who did you think it was?"

"What are *you* doing here, Son?"

"I've come to see how you are."

"It's that bad, is it?"

"Oh, they'll have you out of here in next to no time," I said. "They need the beds."

He managed a faint smile. "How are things up in Grantham?"

"Busy as ever."

"No messages for the king, yet?"

"Not yet," I said. "Just give me a year or two."

At which point a nurse came in, followed by a couple of doctors, and we were ushered out of the room.

"What did he mean about a message for the king?" asked my sister as I was driving her home.

"It's a sort of private joke," I told her. "Something out of *Gulliver's Travels.*"

"Go on."

"I can't remember it offhand," I said. "I'll look it up when we get back."

While she was putting the kettle on, I went into Dad's cubbyhole of a study, hunted out his ancient copy of *Gulliver's Travels*, and, after some searching, found the passage I was looking for. I carried the book through into the kitchen. "Here we are, Lou," I said. "It's where the King of Brobdingnag is talking to Gulliver." And I read out: *He gave it for his opinion that whoever could make two ears of corn, or two blades of grass grow upon a spot of ground where only one grew before; would deserve better of Mankind, and do more essential service for his country, than the whole race of politicians put together.*

Lou was just pouring out the tea when the phone rang. It was Mother. Would we could back to hospital straightaway? Dad had just had another attack. As luck would have it, we got snarled up in the rush-hour traffic, and by the time we arrived, it was all over.

The funeral took place five days later. As we trailed along the puddled path behind the coffin, the sun came out. A few minutes later, a brilliant rainbow had unfurled itself above the distant Roding. I remember how I chose to see it as a sort of omen—a message of hope for the future—as though Dad had somehow contrived to send me a benign blessing from wherever he was now. The wish was both father and mother to the thought.

As soon as I could decently do so, I went back to work. Driving north through the flat, lush Cambridgeshire landscape, I found myself recalling a host of incidents from my childhood—long walks with my father through the summer fields and beside the slow, reedy East Anglian rivers; walks during which he had taught me the names of the birds and the flowers and the trees and had talked to me about his mysterious "Mother Nature." I remembered him poignantly as a man of great gentleness and compassion, and I was only slightly consoled by recalling how happy he had been when the news of my Open Scholarship had come through. That evening we had sat side by side, drinking to my future in glasses of his homemade wine and watching a documentary on the television about the ravages of the drought in Ethiopia. In my mind's eye I can still see those seemingly interminable lines of articulated skeletons wandering from nowhere to nowhere along a sort of crazy-paved highway of baked mud in a dried-up riverbed, while all around them wheeled the ominous shadows of the ever-present vultures. It was then that I noticed Dad was weeping. Now, recalling the shock I experienced, I think it was that grief of his as much as my own feelings of impotent horror at the pictures on the screen that made me decide how my own life would be spent.

After the film ended, he went out into his study, brought back his tattered old copy of *Gulliver's Travels*, and read me out the bit I'd read to Lou. We talked for hours, ranging back and forth across the world. In our imaginations the sterile desert bloomed; the granaries of Asia, Africa, and South America overflowed; and the specter of Famine was banished forever from the face of the earth. As we were tottering off to our beds in the small hours, Dad paused on the stairs, peered down at me owlishly over the banisters, and said: "One of these days, Clive, we'll write our own postscript to *Gulliver*. We'll call it 'A Message to the King of Brobdingnag.' All it'll say is: 'Your Majesty's sacred mission is finally accomplished. Over and out.'"

I giggled tipsily and saluted. "Message received and understood, Dad," I responded. "Over and out."

• • •

Almost twelve months to the day after Dad's death, I attended a three-day international conference at Cambridge that was being arranged under the aegis of UNIDO. For the afternoon of the second day the organizers had laid on an inspection trip to the A.R.C.'s plant-breeding institute. After lunch we piled into a fleet of coaches and were driven off. By chance I found myself sitting next to a young woman whose identity badge proclaimed her to be "Dr. N. E. Sheran." I introduced myself and asked her what her specialty was. She told me she was a microbiologist. "And where are you from?" I said.

"I'm from Sussex."

"With Professor Dawlish?"

She nodded.

"Hey! Are you researching nitrogen fixers?"

"We're researching lots of things."

"It's those nifs I'm really interested in," I told her. "What's the point of developing high-yield strains of cereals if none of the Third World countries can afford the fertilizers to reap the benefit?"

She smiled. "So maybe we should all be researching ways of producing cheaper fertilizers."

We spent that afternoon on a conducted tour of the trial plots and in listening to an account of the P.L.B.'s latest colchicine experiments. I was very impressed. By cutting the twelve years it takes to produce a genuinely new variety down to eight years, they seemed to have stolen half a march on the inexorable Malthusian progression, which decrees that the mouths to be fed will forever outstrip the production of the wherewithal to feed them on.

As we rode back to Cambridge, I expatiated on this theme to Dr. Sheran. "A world population headed for over 6 billion by the year 2000 means we've got to increase food production by at least 50 percent just to keep starvation down to its *present* level. What we need are shortcuts."

"Or efficient birth control," she suggested mildly.

"That's bound to come with the rise in the standard of living."

"But to achieve *that* you'll have to increase your food production by at least 100 percent. Do you really think it's possible?"

"To make two ears of corn grow where only one grew before?" I said. "Of course it's possible."

"In twenty years?"

"Improving the species is only one aspect of it," I said. "Improving your methods of agriculture—better irrigation, soil conservation, cheaper fertilizers—they're all vital. It has to be a broad-front operation. But it *can* be done. It must be."

"You know, you sound exactly like my father," she remarked with a smile.

"To me I sound just like *my* father," I told her.

That evening we both attended a film show sponsored by I.C.I., and after it we ended up in the hotel bar. By then I'd discovered that her first name was Natasha. Now, under further questioning, she told me that her mother was Russian and her father Eurasian. "An F_2 hybrid!" I exclaimed rapturously. "That's really exciting. Are you married?"

She shook her head.

"But you're going to be?"

"Am I?"

"You're not telling me there isn't a bloke swanning around in the background?" I protested. "I mean—well, you're really something special, Natasha. You're far and away the most fantastic microbiologist I've ever laid eyes on. And an F_2 hybrid into the bargain!"

I wasn't lying, either. She had the sort of looks of one or two of the girls I'd occasionally seen dangling from the arms of well-heeled Tory twits in the lounge bar of The Marquis of Grantham—sweet peaches growing in an orchard on the other side of a barbed-wire fence. I couldn't believe my luck.

Adroitly she changed the subject to what I was doing at Biotek. I told her how I was trying to isolate improved strains of the nitrogen-fixing bacteria *Rhizobia* and induce them to cooperate with cereals. I said I believed that the answer lay in getting *Rhizobium* genes into cereals so that the plants would be persuaded to form root nodules and hence create their own soluble nitrates. I added that I also had a hunch that somewhere in the world a strain of wild grain already existed that had succeeded in solving the problem for itself. If only we could track it down and then maybe exploit the P.B.I. colchicine techniques to improve its yield, we'd have the battle more than half-won.

We talked and talked, bouncing ideas back and forth, until eventually I became aware that the lights were being turned off in the lounge. I glanced at my watch, saw to my astonishment that it was long after midnight, and realized that I'd just passed the most exciting and enjoyable three hours of my life.

I spent the final morning of that conference in Natasha's company and succeeded in convincing her that her afternoon would be more profitably passed with me in a boat on the river than in attending an illustrated lecture on reafforestation programs in the Kashmir. As soon as we were afloat, I picked up where I'd left off the night before. I cross-questioned her about her line of research at Sussex and learned that for the past year she'd been working on the insertion of nif genes into chloroplast DNA. The aim of the exercise was to persuade the host plant to fix nitrogen directly in its leaves. I found the idea appealing as an *idea*, but it seemed a terribly long shot, and I told her so.

"No longer than yours," she retorted. "No one's anywhere near to interpreting the DNA code that allows *Rhizobium* to cooperate with its hosts."

"Well, if you ever happen to find it out, promise me you'll let me know," I said. "I really could do with some help."

"Do you mean that?"

Something in the tone of her voice brought me up short. I stared at her. "Yes, I do mean it," I said. "I really do. Why do you ask?"

"I just wondered."

I suppose I must have sensed that there was something else underlying her seemingly casual question, but I also knew that I lacked the subtlety to elicit it without appearing unbearably nosy. I tucked it away in the back of my mind, and that evening, when we were halfway through our second drink, I contrived to revert to it in a roundabout sort of way. Thus it was that I discovered she was even then in the painful process of extricating herself from a pretty intense relationship with one of her Sussex colleagues.

"Does that mean you're looking around for a change of scene?" I suggested ingenuously.

"It might have its attractions," she agreed. "Always providing I could find something in my own specialized field. Last month I got as far as writing off for application forms for a post with Unilever, but then I changed my mind."

At that point my own mind went into accelerated overdrive. I whipped out my diary and a pen and handed them across to her. "Jot down your address and phone number," I told her. "When I get back to Grantham I'll have a word with our Big White Chief. I'm pretty sure there may be something coming up at Biotek in the very near future."

"Really?" she said, scribbling down the information. "What sort of 'something'?"

"There've been rumors floating around the department for months," I told her. "The one thing I *am* sure is that they're stepping up our genetic research funding. That's bound to mean taking on some more bodies. Why shouldn't one of them be a gorgeous Ph.D. microbiologist specializing in DNA transfer? I bet we'd pay you more than you get at Sussex."

"No takes on that,"she said with a grin, and handed back my diary and pen.

Thinking about it over these past months, I believe I've succeeded in isolating five distinct episodes in my life that have led me directly to this particular point. Maybe "episodes" isn't quite the right word, but it will have to do. The first was, of course, Dad—his inspiration, his encouragement, and above all his belief in me. Without that, I might never have got started in science at all. The second was my discovery of Natie at that UNIDO conference in Cambridge in '82. The third, unquestionably, was my meeting with Dr. Sancharez at Ayacucho.

What got Natie and me out to South America in the summer of '88 was largely a series of flukes, starting with the takeover of Biotek by Monagri in '86. When that happened Natie and I were distinctly apprehensive about what it might entail, but in the space of eighteen months we'd both been upgraded, and my *Rhizobium* project had been singled out for special encouragement—thanks largely to the promising field trials with GX3.

Being a U.S.-based multinational, Monagri had all sorts of Third World links that were completely beyond the scope of Biotek's largely U.K./European operation. Furthermore, they believed strongly in what they liked to think of as "multinational cross-fertilization." When the GX3 reports filtered through to Los Angeles and were fed into the computer, what came out was, I presume, a recommendation that Dr. Clive Woodhouse be flown out to South America to scatter some of his intellectual pollen around sundry outposts of the far-flung Monagrian empire. Fortunately, Dr. Woodhouse was now in a position to stipulate that his colleague Dr. Sheran should accompany him, and on May 3, 1988, Natie and I found ourselves descending the gangway of a transcontinental jet at Sao Paulo on the first leg of a journey that was to take us to five countries in three and a half weeks. The supreme irony is that Ayacucho didn't even feature on our itinerary!

We were supposed to spend two days at Cajamarca in Peru, fly on to Quito in Ecuador for a further four days, and then return home by way of Bogotá. What happened was that somewhere about halfway between La Paz and Lima, the private company jet that was ferrying us around developed engine trouble and had to make an emergency landing at Ayacucho. I managed to put through a phone call to the Monagri people at Cajamarca, and explained what had happened. They said they'd get back to us as soon as possible. We checked into the airport hotel and then wandered out to take a look at the town. When we returned to the hotel a couple of hours later, we were met by a lean, leather-faced, gray-haired man who introduced himself in excellent American English as Dr. Jaime Sancharez and informed us regretfully that our plane would have to remain grounded for at least twenty-four hours. In the meantime, he trusted that we would do him the inestimable honor of being the guests of himself and his wife at the Botanical Institute, which was situated a mere thirty minutes' drive outside the town.

We never did discover precisely what Dr. Sancharez's link with Monagri amounted to—he referred vaguely to some departmental funding connection via the University of Lima—but he told us that over the past ten years he had sent more than fifty species of wild plants and seeds to the N.S.S. lab in Colorado, and that he spent at least four months of each year on field trips up in the mountains. His real enthusiasm was reserved for the potato, of which he contended he had personally identified no fewer than eighty-three different kinds, seven of them previously unknown varieties.

We passed that afternoon examining his collection, and then he took us on a personally conducted tour of the steeply terraced gardens of the institute, which were perched on the hillside high above the town. After that we risked heart failure by plunging into a deep pool that was fed by a mountain stream. Later we sat on the Sancharezes' terrace, sipping tall glasses of iced sangria while we watched the sun go down, and chatted about our experiences in Bolivia and Brazil. Then, over a truly excellent dinner, we told him something about our present line of research at Biotek and explained how it had led directly to our being there enjoying his hospitality. As we were on the point of retiring to bed, there came a phone call from our pilot at the airport to say that the plane had been repaired and that we were now free to continue our journey.

Early next morning Dr. Sancharez drove us back into Ayacucho. We exchanged addresses, promised to keep in touch, and half an hour later were airborne once more and on our way to Cajamarca.

When we got back to the U.K. at the beginning of June, I wrote to Dr. Sancharez and his wife thanking them for having been so kind to us, and, that done, prepared to let the whole episode slip from my mind. It was briefly recalled when the photographs we had taken on our trip were developed, and among them I found one of Natie swimming naked as a naiad in the mountain pool and another of Dr. and Señora Sancharez standing with their arms about each other, smiling at us on their terrace.

Five months later, out of the blue, I received an airmail letter from Peru. Inside I found a hastily scribbled note together with a small, sealed plastic packet containing half a dozen seeds. All the note said was: "I found these growing in a high valley off the Apurimac. They could be worth trying—J.S."

I examined the seeds under the microscope and discovered them to be some primitive variety of maize. They were far smaller than any I had ever seen, and I wondered what could possibly have led Dr. Sancharez to suppose they might interest me—nothing in his note gave me the slightest clue—but I handed them over to our chief horticulturist and asked her to do her best by them. Three weeks later, she told me that five out of the six had germinated.

It was some days before I got around to taking a look at them for myself, and what I saw did not cause me to change my opinion. By then I had written back to Dr. Sancharez thanking

him for his sample and asking him what it was that had led him
to suppose the seeds might be anything out of the ordinary. By
the time I received his reply I had already discovered the
answer for myself. *All five plants had begun to develop
unmistakable signs of N_2 tubercles on their roots!*

But it was when I received Dr. Sancharez's second letter that
I was really rocked back on my heels. Having described in
some detail the general area in which he had discovered the
plants, he concluded: "The altitude was a good five hundred
meters higher than any where I have ever found wild maize
before, which to me suggests an exceptionally short life cycle.
The soil was *very* poor—low-grade loess. My guess is that
these plants may have acquired not only a symbiotic N_2
Rhizobium, but also maybe a species of cooperative bacterium
that acts as a phosphate accumulator. Is this possible, do you
think?"

Sancharez was certainly right about the length of the life cycle.
The plants matured at three months. By February '89 we had
collected sufficient seed to risk our first limited trials. From
that second crop Natie succeeded in extracting a hitherto
unknown motile flagellate bacerium that appeared to flourish in
and around the N_2 nodules and seemed to possess precisely
those characteristics that Sancharez had suspected. We named
it *Phosphomonas sancharezii* in his honor and crossed our
fingers. For the first time since December, Natie and I began to
talk—though only between ourselves and very, very guard-
edly—of a real breakthrough.

For the next three years we worked flat out at transferring the
nif genes from the wild maize to our high-yielding strains. Our
first real success came with GX14. The colchicine-crossed
progeny had a four-month cycle, bred true to three generations,
and carried a yield of anything up to four times that of the wild
stock. Meanwhile, Natie and her colleague were forging ahead,
adapting and culturing *P. sancharezii*. In two years they had
succeeded in persuading it to work in harmony with both wheat
and rice. When the results of those first Grantham cereal field
trials came in, they showed increased yeilds of from 30 to 50
percent right across the board, and no adverse side effects!
Natie and I were on top of the world: 1992 was our golden year,
and I see it now as the fourth of my five particular episodes.

It was also the year when she and I finally regularized our relationship by getting married. We'd put off doing it before, partly from inertia and partly because of the tax situation. Now she suddenly decided that she'd like to start a family. I pointed out that if things went according to plan, we'd soon find ourselves rushing around the world supervising our tropical field trials. But she had quite made up her mind that Science could spare her to Nature for a year or two, and once I'd realized just how strongly she felt about it, I discovered that I rather fancied the idea of becoming a father. Anyway, it didn't happen straightaway.

By this time Monagri was totally convinced that in *P. sancharezii* we were onto an out-and-out all-time winner. They dropped the security shutters while they set about feverishly devising the best means of exploiting our discovery to maximum financial advantage. Yet even with that holdup, I estimated that it would take us at least ten more years before we could expect to see any significant advance in our campaign against the ancient enemy world hunger. Fortunately, we were still free to press ahead with GX14.

The results of the first tropical field trials were frankly disappointing—yields were on average less than half those we had been obtaining in the U.K.—but even so, GX14 proved itself conclusively capable of flourishing in soils that were notably deficient in both nitrates and phosphates. I estimated that it could eventually increase the Third World's agrarian potential by anything up to 10 percent. And there was still our vastly improved strain of *P. sancharezii* to come!

In April '93 Natie finally achieved her ambition of getting herself pregnant. We set off on our annual holiday in the third week of June, driving down to a villa we'd rented on the Côte d'Azur. On our way we called in to see Mother at Chelmsford, broke the good news about the baby, and then set off to catch the night ferry from Dover. As we approached the northern end of the Dartford tunnel, we were waved down at a police checkpoint and asked to show our identity cards and work permits. I noticed that all the patrolmen were carrying guns. They opened the trunk of the car and poked around among our suitcases. I asked one of them what they were looking for, but all he said was, "We'll tell you if we find it." Then they slammed the trunk shut and waved us on.

As we drove up the ramp on the far side of the tunnel, we saw more armed police, a fire engine, and the burned-out shells of two container trucks that had been dragged aside into a lay-by. On the concrete wall beside them was a crudely daubed sign of a sickle and clenched fist of the Right to Work Movement. I switched on the car radio, hoping to pick up a local newscast, but all I could find was the usual Muzak pap. The highjacking of a couple of foreign juggernauts probably didn't rate even a solitary news flash anymore.

But that incident, slight as it was, started Natie and me talking in a way we hadn't really talked to each other for years. I think it dawned on both of us at the same time how *insulated* our lives had become. All our closest friends were in the same highly specialized field as ourselves; we were earning far more money than we knew what to do with; neither of us had any strong political allegiance (we voted S.D.P.); and yet, without either of us ever actually saying it, there was no doubt that we both believed we were somehow intrinsically superior to practically everyone else in the world. After all, we *knew* what we were doing and we knew *why* we were doing it. It's easy to say we were both smug and self-righteous and perfectly happy to be so. But I don't honestly think that we were altogether to blame. Look on us, if you like, as the refined product of our social conditioning, highly specialized cells, pampered, flattered, and richly rewarded for our successes. We could hardly have been expected to probe all the ethical subtleties of our situation when we knew that what we were engaged upon was the practical realization of one of mankind's few truly altruistic dreams.

But during that holiday we discussed it more than once. And it was always Natie who brought the subject up. Maybe it was something to do with her being pregnant. I remember us lying side by side after we'd made love one afternoon, and suddenly she came out with: "Do you sometimes think we're playing at being God?"

"What on earth are you talking about?" I said.

"I'm not sure myself," she admitted. "It's just a feeling."

"You don't *believe* in God, do you, Natie?"

She didn't answer straightaway, so I repeated my question.

"I don't know if I do or not," she said at last. "But now and again I think I'd like to. I'd like to feel safe."

"You mean you *don't* feel safe?"

"I can't explain it exactly," she said, "but just occasionally I get a sort of uncomfortable feeling that the bottom could drop right out of the world and I could fall through. And I know that if that happens, I'll just go on falling and falling forever."

I felt her give a sudden shiver. "Did you remember to take your vitamins this morning?" I asked.

"You don't know *what* I've been talking about, do you?" she said. "Go on. Admit it."

I started to protest, then caught sight of her sideways on. My imagination switched into an altogether different and more exciting gear. I don't remember her ever reverting to the subject of God.

In September I was informed in strict confidence that all the necessary arrangements had been made for three simultaneous tropical field trials of *P. sancharezii*. One was to take place in Brazil, another in Zimbabwe, and the third in Northern Queensland. Given the choice of which I'd attend in person, I opted for Queensland simply because I knew Sam Wallace and I'd never been to Australia before. Since the baby was due at the end of January, Natie elected to stay at home.

I flew into Darwin on December 3rd and within an hour was airborne again, heading east over the Arnhem Land Reserve to Nhulunbuy on the coast of the Gulf of Carpentaria. At Nhulunbuy a company helicopter was waiting to ferry me down to the experimental Queensland Station near Arrowsmith.

We reached our destination shortly before six o'clock in the evening and circled briefly over the rice paddies before setting down on the outfield of the station's cricket ground. I was greeted by Sam Wallace, who was O.i.C. of the Queensland Station, and an Indian colleague of his whom he introduced as "Ami." Sam took me over to the bungalow that was to be my home for the next week, and then the three of us went across to the main lab, where I was shown the current field plan and the rice paddy charts.

Two small feeder streams ran down into the valley from the densely wooded hills behind. At the top of the valley an earth dam had been constructed to provide a fallback reservoir in the unlikely event of a prolonged drought. The single outlet from this artificial lake supplied the irrigation network through a main artery and an ingeniously engineered system of capillary channels that were in turn controlled by a series of manually operated sluice gates.

Sam pointed out two plots on the chart, one at the bottom of the paddy ladder and one about halfway up. "Those are your best bets," he said. "The upper one's Balinese J. hybrid, and the lower one's a variety of Sumatra long-grain. They're both well established, and they're both good *Azospirillum* cooperators, so nitrogen starvation won't be a problem."

"Whatever you say, Sam," I said. "You're the man in charge."

"That's settled, then," he said. "C7 and D5. Now let's go and open up some beers."

Early the next morning, without any undue ceremony, I loaded up a pressure spray with a 500-to-1 dilute culture of *Phosphomonas sancharezii* and handed it over to one of Sam's assistants. Then I pulled on a pair of borrowed waders and followed Sam and Ami up the track to plot C7.

The plants were well in flower, and the N_2-fixing alga *Anabaena* was clearly visible as a green scum on the surface of the water. I nodded to Sam and gave a thumbs-up sign to the boy who was working the spray. He waded out into the center of the plot, switched on the motor of the sprayer, and began laying down a fine mist of *P. sancharezii* across the surface of the paddy. It took him about ten minutes. Then we made our way down to the lower plot and repeated the operation. There was just sufficient culture solution for a comprehensive treatment of both paddies. After it was done we strolled back down the hill in the warm sunshine for a well-earned breakfast.

Over our meal I talked to Sam and Ami about the other element of the test program and told them what it was we were aiming for. They both looked a bit skeptical when I said I was anticipating anything up to a 50 percent increase in gross crop yield. "It sounds like black magic to me," said Sam. "Hell, we were over the moon when we got 8 percent with our first Sumatra cross. *And* we were supplementing with phosphate."

"Yes, I know," I said, and held up my crossed fingers, "but if we're right—and I think we *are* right, Sam—this one looks like the breakthrough we've all been praying for since the days of the Reverend Thomas Malthus."

After breakfast I sent off a prearranged coded message via the radio-phone to our office in Brisbane, letting Monagri know that everything had gone according to plan. I followed this up with a cable to Natie telling her I'd arrived safely and that things were looking good. Then, still feeling the effects of jetlag, I strolled off up the valley to relax beside the lake at the back of the dam.

A couple of hours later, as I was making my way down again, I saw Ami running up the track toward me. The sun was pretty fierce by then, and I remember wondering what on earth he could be in such a tearing hurry about in that heat. "Come," he gasped. "Come quick, Clive! We are in bad trouble!"

"Trouble?" I said. "What sort of trouble?"

"The alga. The alga on the paddy."

"What about it?"

"It has gone crazy."

I stared at him. I just couldn't focus mentally on what he was saying. "Gone crazy?" I repeated vaguely. "What's that supposed to mean?"

"You'll soon see," he panted. "Sam thinks your culture's triggered off a reproductive explosion in the *Anabaena*. We've shut off the sluices to try and contain it."

Almost without my realizing it, I found I was sprinting back down the path. When I reached a point that allowed me a view across the paddy fields, I stopped dead in my tracks. The two plots that we'd treated with *P. sancharezii* were now completely covered over with a vivid, lettuce-green carpet of algae bloom. Half a dozen men with face masks and backpack sprays were wading to and fro through the scum, laying down a smoky mist that I guessed must be a biocide. "Christ Almighty," I whispered. "Who'd have believed it?"

I found Sam in the lab, bent over a microscope. He looked up as I entered, and beckoned me forward to see for myself. I watched with a sort of horrified fascination as the *Anabaena* cells guzzled the nutrients that the foraging *P. sancharezii* bacteria provided, then grew fat and divided and multiplied with an almost unbelievable rapidity. The microscopic predatory organisms that should have prevented this from occurring were seemingly rendered powerless by the algae's newfound capacity to monopolize the entire supply of phosphorus. I felt a chilly sweat break out all across my back. "Jesus Christ,

Sam," I muttered. "Do you realize what might have happened if . . . ?"

"Don't I just," he said grimly. "I've radioed to Nhulunbuy for fifty drums of biocide and a spray chopper. As it is, there's still no guarantee we've got it cordoned off. It was at least two hours after the treatment before we closed off the main sluice. But I've had a five-man crew out working downstream for the past hour or so. Let's go and see how they're making out."

The sun beat down on us like a hammer as we set off along the riverside track below the compound. By now there was only a thread of water trickling in the bottom of the channel, and the mud was drying out and starting to steam. Some of the grass along the bank that had caught the biocide spray drift was already beginning to wilt. "How long can you keep the channel dry?" I asked.

"For about twelve hours, give or take a couple. After that the lake'll spill over the sluice gate. Still, maybe that's twelve hours more than we deserve. We can count ourselves lucky the monsoon's late. There hasn't been any rain to speak of up in the hills for over a week."

We discovered plenty of traces of the rogue *Anabaena,* but it was obvious that the biocide had already done its work. I found that the clenched fist in my stomach was beginning to relax. Then I suddenly remembered the other two tropical trials and let out a strangled yelp. Sam asked what was up. When I told him, he gave a sort of grunt and said: "Oh, I forgot to tell you. I already radioed Brisbane and L.A. on your behalf. You weren't around to ask, and it seemed prudent."

"Sam—" I began, and then couldn't seem to find the words I wanted.

He winked at me. "That's O.K., chum," he said. "I guess you'd have done the same for me in similar circumstances."

At about three in the afternoon, two helicopters appeared, one equipped for aerial spraying and the other loaded with extra drums of poison. Within minutes of its arrival, the sprayer was in the air again, clattering back and forth over the rice paddies and along the now dry irrigation channel below the station. By the time the sun was low over the western hills, there couldn't have been an inch of the ground that hadn't been treated at least three times over. We had seen the work of a dozen years virtually destroyed in a single afternoon.

That evening I asked Sam how long he thought it would be before he could have the station operating again. "I'm not even thinking about it," he said. "Ask me the same question in a week's time and maybe I'll have an answer. Right now all I'm concerned with is 100 percent sterilization. But I'll tell you something, Clive, when I get around to writing up my report on this little malfunction, I'll make damned sure one copy gets to Canberra and another to the United Nations."

"But what about your contract? Doesn't Monagri stipulate—"

"I don't give a whore's fuck about my contract! If we don't blow the lid right off this one, they'll only go and try it again somewhere else. Where d'you think we'd be now if I hadn't just happened to take a stroll up to the paddies when I did?"

"I know. I know," I said. "When I saw what had happened, my heart damn near stopped. I had a sort of nightmare vision of the whole valley vanishing under a spew of green slime. I don't think I've ever been more scared in my life. You deserve a gold medal."

"Maybe I do at that," he said thoughtfully. "If I *have* done it."

"Christ!" I exclaimed. "If you haven't, what else *can* we do?"

"We can spray, and spray, and then we can spray some more," he said. "Even if it means killing off every single living green thing from here down to the gulf. What we've cooked up here is an insatiable algalbacterial cancer. Unless we manage to cut it out completely and utterly right here and now, we might as well get down on our knees and say amen."

"But surely we *have* cut it out."

"I hope so," he said. "I really do. But I'll be a whole lot easier in my mind if by this time tomorrow we haven't found a solitary trace of rogue alga within five miles of this place. Now I'm off to bed, and my advice to you is to do the same. We've got a pretty nail-biting twenty-four hours ahead of us."

I did as he suggested, but it was a long time before I got to sleep. I lay and stared up at the ceiling, going over and over in my mind the twists and turns of the trail that had brought me to this point. And then I found myself thinking about Natie and the baby, and for the first time since I was a small child, I found myself praying.

• • •

I was awakened by the cough and clatter of a helicopter starting up. I leaped out of bed, dragged on some clothes, and ran outside just in time to see one of the machines lift and head off down the valley toward the coast. Ami was making his way back toward the compound. I shouted to him. He waved his arm and turned in my direction. "Ah, good morning, Clive."

"Let's hope you're right," I said. "I didn't sleep too well last night."

"Nor me," he agreed.

"Was that Sam I saw going off?"

"Yes, he has gone to reconnoiter downstream. The lake started to spill over at about four this morning. That was later than we had expected."

"And how are the paddies?"

"They seem to be clear, thank God. But we shall go over them once more just to be doubly sure. Would you like some coffee?"

"Wouldn't I just," I said.

We sat on the veranda of the cookhouse, sipping scalding black coffee and talking over the events of the previous day. Long, slim fingers of silvery light thrust themselves abruptly through a band of clouds low down on the eastern horizon, showing where the sun was about to rise. "I expect you are very disappointed by what has happened," he said. "All those years of hard work gone up the spout."

"D'you know, I hadn't even begun to think of that side of it," I said. "But I daresay it'll hit me soon enough. At this moment every hope I have is riding on Sam and those drums of biotoxin."

"Yes, indeed," he murmured. "Has it not struck you as strange, Clive, that you experienced no such side effects in your trials at home?"

"That's what tropical trials are all about," I said. "And I don't mind telling you I still wouldn't believe it if I hadn't seen it with my own eyes. It really was such a beautiful piece of applied biotechnology, Ami—a truly sweet equation. It should have been worth a couple of dozen Nobel prizes any day. Jesus, I'll bet our overlords are feeling pretty sick right now."

"You are forgetting that Monagri is into phosphates, too," he observed with a wry smile.

After we'd drunk our coffee we went up to take another look
at the paddies. They were truly a dismal sight. The water had
all been diverted into the main channel, and the drying plots lay
shrouded under a sort of graveyard quilting of yellowy gray
cobweb. The effect was curiously *alien*—sinister. I surveyed it
for a few minutes, then walked the hundred or so yards across
to the arterial channel and peered down into the stream. Almost
at once I saw a splodge of blue-green algal bloom about the
size of a dinner plate sailing down the center of the channel.
Another followed it, and then a third. I shouted to Ami. He
hurried over, saw what had alarmed me, and smiled reassuringly. "Oh, that is perfectly innocent, Clive. It is coming down
from the reservoir. When we shut off the main sluice, the water
level rose. Now it is spilling over. That is just surface alga. It
has been coming down like that since early this morning."

I gazed down at a fresh lump that was trundling cheerfully
along. "Have you been up there to check?" I asked.

"No," he admitted. "But what is the point? The alga could
never move upstream against the current. So how could the
lake be infected?"

"I don't know," I said. "Maybe I've just got a heavy attack
of the jitters. But I'm going up to take a look. Just for my own
piece of mind, you understand. Will you come with me?"

He shook his head. "I have promised Sam I will organize the
respraying of the paddies. I will see you at breakfast."

I set off up the track beside the stream. In one place a thick
clot of algal bloom had piled up against some invisible
obstruction. When I saw that it was pieces of this mass that the
current was prizing loose and launching down the channel, I
breathed more easily. Ami was right. Our problem, if it still
existed, lay down at the far end of the valley where Sam was
investigating. But having come this far I did not turn back.

The tallest of the trees that covered the hills were already
catching the early sunlight as I started to plot my way up the
face slope of the dam. A single invisible bird was making a
strange, sad, two-noted call—*lo-ee, lo-ee, lo-ee*—on and on in
the depths of the forest, but that apart, there was only the noise
of the stream to break the silence.

And then I saw the lake!

The sensation I experienced at that moment was purely
physical. I felt exactly as if my stomach had been ripped open

and all my intestines were spilling out around my ankles. I remember that I lifted my hands and began pushing childishly at the air in front of my face as though by so doing I could make the vision go away, not *he*. Above all, I wanted to wake myself up out of my nightmare.

Where, the day before, there had been a few small islands of water hyacinth floating serenely on a cloud-dappled, sky-blue mirror, now, except for one small patch of clear water close to the mouth of the sluice, the surface was completely covered in a dense, mantling bloom of *Anabaena*. All across its seething skin little bubbles of gas were constantly forming and breaking. They seemed to wink at me like a billion tiny, bright, incurious eyes.

I stood as though I had been nailed to the ground, staring out across that evil broth with a feeling of such horror in my heart that I can't even begin to express it. And then I threw back my head and gave a sort of wild-animal howl of terror and anguish. Startled a pair of ducks rose clattering from the slime, circled once above the nearby trees, and then flew off toward the south.

As I watched them grow small and vanish in the distance, I suddenly realized what must have happened, what was going to happen again, and what would surely go on happening unless some miracle could be found to prevent it. Just one small shred of rogue alga clinging to the foot of one of those birds would have been enough. Doubling itself every fifteen minutes in the warm waters of the lake, knowing nothing but its own insatiable appetite to feed and to grow, in twenty-four hours or maybe even less it would have engulfed the whole surface.

Then I saw that in places it had already begun to expand outward across the margin of reed and grass that separated the lake from the nearby trees. The sight unlocked my rigor. I turned my back on the sickening scene and fled away down the path toward the distant station. And all the way down my mind was filled with an appalling vision of those two birds planing down through the calm air somewhere far away, and rinsing off their trailing ribbons of slime into some quiet marsh or stream whose waters were just beginning to feel the first mothering warmth of the morning sun.

• • •

The events of the next twenty-four hours are still a sort of hazy chaos in my memory. I remember the expression on Ami's face as I blurted out what I had discovered. I remember helping to load up a truck with half a dozen drums of biocide and ordering two of the men to drive up to the top of the lake and pour the stuff straight into the feeder streams, then to start hand-spraying wherever they found signs of the alga spreading under the trees. I remember a white-faced Sam returning an hour later with a grim news that they'd found unmistakable evidence of *Anabaena* on a quite different stream over three miles away. And I remember most vividly how he swore and banged his fists against his forehead when I told him what I suspected about the birds.

He gave immediate orders for the helicopter's tanks to be refilled and told the pilot to douse any patch of open water he could find between us and the gulf, because "if ever it finds its way down to the sea, we haven't got a hope in hell of holding it!" Then he took me with him into the radio room, and we spent the next four hours pleading desperately for help from the government, from the army, from Monagri, from *anyone* we thought we might persuade to take us seriously.

That evening Sam summoned a council of war in the main lab. By then four more helicopters had flown in, together with a fuel-supply tanker and just about enough biocide to transform the whole valley into a sterile desert. A man of the surrounding district was projected onto a screen. Sam divided it up into half a dozen operation areas and detailed off the pilots. These men, all of whom worked for state agricultural combines, couldn't seem to grasp just how desperate the situation was. One of them asked Sam what he was so scared of. "Hell, we're talking about that stuff that grows on the top of duck ponds, aren't we?"

Sam agreed that we were, more or less.

"And that's *dangerous?*"

Sam nodded. "I could be wrong," he said. "I hope to God I *am* wrong. But what I think we've got here is something that could make all the atom bombs in the world look about as dangerous as a cold in the head. Unless we wipe this stuff out absolutely, totally and completely, here and now, within the next couple of days, then in a month's time I'll lay you odds there won't be anything left that you'd recognize as Queensland—no forests, no rivers, no fields, no sea, no animals, nothing. Just a blanket of blue-green scum over everything. And after us it'll be the turn of the rest of the world."

"Jesus," breathed his questioner, visibly shaken. "How the hell did this thing start?"

Sam glanced across at me. "I guess you'd have to say it's a direct result of doing the wrong deed for the right reasons," he said. "The point is, are we going to be able to stop it?"

All next day from sunup to sundown, the helicopters droned up and down and back and forth across the valley, laying down a dense mist of biocide. No longer was it a question of selecting targets. This was an obliteration attack designed to wipe out every last trace of *Anabaena* across an area of some four miles by five of hinterland. While it was in progress, Sam contacted Canberra, reported on what was happening, and demanded to speak directly with the prime minister. Somehow he managed it, though I never discovered exactly how. Nor do I know for certain what he said—Sam's own account of their conversation was not particularly coherent—but I do know that he did his utmost to persuade Prime Minister Brownlee that, should all else fail, he must order an immediate and total evacuation of the whole Arnhem peninsula and then drop a thermonuclear bomb on it. The plea was turned down flat. At the time I thought Sam was just trying to give the ultimate emphasis to his point. Which simply goes to show that even I still could not bring myself to face up to the true nature of the situation.

I don't think I slept at all that night. At first light I joined Sam and Ami in the radio room and listened to the helicopter pilots calling in their dawn reports. As they patrolled farther and farther out and the ring of red crosses finally petered out on Sam's map, Ami and I looked at one another with an unspoken question in our eyes. Neither of us cared to tempt fate by saying that it looked as if the operation had succeeded. Sam further extended the perimeter of the search by three miles, and still there was nothing. When the final report came in "all clear," Ami said: "Someone is going to have to say it. We've won, haven't we, Sam?"

Sam gazed down abstractedly at the map on the table and began hatching in a grid of scarlet lines across the blue triangle that represented the lake. "Maybe we have," he said. "But with cancer it's always the secondaries you can never be quite sure of. If Clive hadn't spotted those bloody ducks yesterday, I think I'd have to agree with you. As it is. . . ." And he left the sentence unfinished.

The helicopters, their mission completed, returned to the station. Over breakfast the pilots confirmed their reports. *Anabaena*—and just about everything else, too—had been wiped out. Sam told them they had done a first-rate job, and then followed this up with the news that they were going to have to go out and spray it all over again. They took it better than I had expected, but then I didn't know what they were being paid.

In the afternoon I flew with Sam down to the coast. We found the shore littered with dead fish and seabirds, innocent victims of the tons of poison we'd poured into the water. But there was no sign of live *Anabaena* anywhere. We flew south as far as Bickerton, then swung inland. It was all clear. "Go on, you've got to admit it now, Sam," I said. "You've won."

He turned toward me and was, I know, on the point of agreeing with me, when the radio crackled. "Sam? Sam? Ami here."

"Go ahead, Ami."

"We've just had a report in from Nhulunbuy, Sam. They say there's *Anabaena* in Arnhem Bay!"

"*Arnhem Bay!* Sweet Mother of Christ! Are they *sure?*"

"The pilot of the mail plane from Darwin reported it. He went down and took a close look. He says it's covering both rivers and spreading along about five miles of the south shore."

If ever I've seen death in a man's face, I saw it in Sam's at that moment. He closed his eyes for a few seconds, then drew in a deep breath and said: "We'll be with you inside fifteen minutes, Ami. Get Mike to put out that total-panic call to Darwin. And get hold of Bill Rawlings. Hold him till I get there. See you, boy."

"Where's Arnhem Bay, Sam?" I said.

"Over on the far side of the peninsula. All of forty bloody miles from here!"

We looked at one another, and then, lost for words, we looked away.

• • •

All that happened four months ago. Perhaps if we had been *believed*, then it might still have been prevented. But by the time the Australian government was at last convinced that we had not all gone stark raving mad, it was much too late. Carried by the southern equatorial current, the alga was already well on its way to the Indian Ocean. When I flew back to England three days before Christmas, I could see the green stain spread right out across the Timor Sea. The bitterest irony of all is that when Sam and I flew down to Canberra and made our last desperate and ineffectual appeal for a hydrogen bomb to be dropped on Arnhem Land, there were no fewer than four nuclear subs on exercise in the Coral Sea, each one capable of sterilizing the whole of Queensland twenty times over. As Sam said to me that night while we were doing our best to drink ourselves into oblivion in the airport bar: "There's one gulf in the human imagination that's deeper than the Mariana Trench. Although men are prepared to insult Nature, to abuse her, even to rape her, they just can't *conceive* the possibility that she isn't immortal. But why in God's name should you and I have been the ones chosen to prove them wrong?"

I don't know if he was expecting me to supply an answer. I don't even know if there *is* an answer. All I know for sure is what I've written down here.

Since then, every one of his predictions has come true. For the past six weeks the atmospheric sulfur count has been climbing steadily, and the last satellite scan I saw a week ago showed infestation well out into the Pacific and as far south as Madagascar. We have passed a sentence of death on the biosphere, and there is no court of appeal. It is only a question of time—or God. Fifty years from now, all trace of *Anabaena* and *Phosphomonas sancharezii* will have vanished as though they had never been: in destroying the world, it will destroy itself, too. Ultimately, inevitably, the planet Earth will become indistinguishable from any other sterile satellite trailing its lifeless way through the empty corridors of space until the end of time.

As for *"that most Pernicious Race of little odious Vermin that Nature ever Suffered to crawl upon the face of the Earth"*—which was how the King of Brobdingnag finally summed us up—my own rough estimate is that we have about a year left. So it will be somewhere around Cissie's first and last birthday that I'll be in a position to send Dad's message back: "Your Majesty's sacred mission is finally accomplished. Over and out."

". . . THE WORLD, AS WE KNOW'T"

Howard Waldrop

But even the most dry, academic, and innocuous of scientific theorizing, seemingly devoid of any practical implications, can be enough to unlock the gates that lead to Armageddon. In the wry, elegant, and meticulously researched story that follows, we take a close look at one of the most widely accepted scientific theories of the eighteenth century—and the unfortunate consequences that might have followed for the entire world if it had turned out to be accurate after all!

Howard Waldrop is widely considered to be one of the best short-story writers in the business, and his famous story, "The Ugly Chickens," won both the Nebula and the World Fantasy Awards in 1981. His work has been gathered in the collections Howard Who?, All About Strange Monsters of the Recent Past: Neat Stories by Howard Waldrop, *and* Night of the Cooters: More Neat Stories by Howard Waldrop, *with more collections in the works. Waldrop is also the author of the novel* The Texas-Israeli War: 1999, *in collaboration with Jake Saunders, and of two solo novels,* Them Bones *and* A Dozen Tough Jobs. *He is at work on a new novel, tentatively entitled* The Moon World. *His most recent book is a new collection,* Going Home Again. *A longtime Texan, Waldrop now lives in the tiny town of Arlington, Washington, outside Seattle, as close to a trout stream as he can possibly get without actually living in it.*

The *neptunists and* vulcanists were going at it hammer and tongs.

The fight had begun just after Curwell's demonstration on counteracting the effects of garlic on the compass. His meth-

ods, which would open the seas to safe passage of condiments
and spices, had been wildly applauded by his peers in the
Lunatick Society.

He had graciously accepted their accolades, and was making
a few extemporary remarks. He seemed the essence of charm
and grace as he answered questions from the audience, until he
made the unfortunate mistake of mentioning the age of the
earth.

Canes had begun rapping on the floor, there were whistles,
words of dispute, and then the yelling had begun.

The president of the Society gaveled for quiet. Fists were
brandished in faces. "Gentlemen! Order, please. Order."

This only infuriated them the more.

"I maintain," someone shouted from the back of the hall,
"that the earth is no less than . . ."

They yelled him down.

To make matters worse, the argument began to eddy and
splinter around the main one. The gradualist uniformitarians,
who thought the land masses had been uncovered from a once
all-pervading ocean, were yelling at the catastrophic vulcanists
who were gathered in one corner of the hall.

". . . The earth has been made over," yelled one of the latter
in the face of one of the former, "by terrible volcanic upheavals
something approaching twenty-seven consecutive times!"

"Faddle."

"Hear, hear!"

Across the aisle, a catastrophic neptunist climbed atop his
chair and shouted at both groups. "You people can't use your
own eyes to see that the rocks of the Northwest Territory were
carried there by the action of a series of deluges, more than
seven, but no more than ten in number, as has . . ."

Instantly, members of *all* the other factions turned on him.

The president kept gaveling for order.

Sir Robert Athole, mounting the platform, shook hands with
Curwell, who was smiling and watching the uproar he had
caused.

"They really are in some mood tonight," said Lawrence
Curwell, who was a young man with a broad handsome face.

"It's really too bad you gave them no points to dispute in
your presentation, which was quite remarkable," said Sir
Robert.

They were bumped from behind by a black man who was taking models and equipment to the raised stage, where the gavel kept pounding and having absolutely no effect on the turmoil.

"Sorry, sir, so sorry," said the black.

Curwell took no notice.

"Thank you for the compliment," said Curwell. "I've already turned the results over to your Maritime Commission. I hope no more tragedies of the kind which took the *Bon Apetit* and the *Lucie Marie* to their watery graves will occur again because of my researches."

There were dull thuds from the back of the room. The two men turned to watch cane-brandishing men be pulled apart by their friends to the uttering of great vile oaths and epithets.

"Shall you be visiting the States long?" asked Sir Robert to Curwell. "If it's at all possible, I should like you to come visit and see the progress of my researches. They might interest you."

"I'd love to. I hear you're doing splendid things. I look forward to your presentation tonight."

Sir Robert Athole began to bow, but paused to turn and watch as one of the more elderly philosophs bounded across the aisle and began to vigorously choke a younger man. They were absorbed in the crowd.

Then "oohs" and "ahhs" raced from the front of the room toward the back. It became very quiet and somber, and some bowed their heads.

For up on the dais, the president of the Society had signaled for the sergeant-at-arms to bring in a small square box and place it in the center of the president's desk.

"Franklin's spectacles," whispered someone. The whisper susurrated through the room. Persons righted their overturned chairs, straightened their wigs, took their seats.

"Order," said the president. The two raps of his small gavel now sounded like the slamming of the great gates of a fort in the still hall.

"The next item on the agenda," he said, "will be a presentation by Sir Robert Athole on the absolute nature of phlogiston."

•   •   •

The room itself was old, huge, and dark. It was lit by chandeliers and by candle sconces along the walls. The odor of wig powder, soot and sweat filled the hall. Through several doors leading in, household servants could be seen coming and going, preparing the traditional meal which would end the monthly meeting of the Lunatick Society.

Velvet and brocade rustled as the men moved about in their upholstered chairs. A snort, sniff and occasional sneeze broke the quiet as one or another of them took snuff. A cane rolled from a lap and clattered loudly to the floor.

The black man indicated to Sir Robert that the models were ready. He came a little closer. "Go easy on the cylinder," he said. "I think it might have cracked a little on the way over in the wagon."

"Very good, Hamp," said Sir Robert, and nodded to the president. There was polite applause for him as he stepped to the rostrum, on which sat a whale-oil lamp smoking quietly.

He looked out at the mass of faces and wigs flickering slowly in the dim light, and saw them as bubbles in the darkening pudding that was the world. No matter. He smiled and began.

He started with the history of combustion and with mention of the works of Becher and Stahl.

"Phlogiston is thought to permeate all things in finely inseparable parts. It is characterized by setting up a violent motion within substances in the presence of heat. This motion results in flame, and as long as the air is not kept from it, the motion will continue until only earthy ash remains."

He then described *terra pinguis* and the fatty earths, and the search for the phlogistic principle itself. His audience continued to listen intently, even a little restlessly. So far he had told them nothing new.

"Recently Cavendish thought he had found the most highly phlogiston-charged substance in his inflammable gas, which is lighter than common air, and is used to lift aerostatic vehicles to heretofore unheard-of heights. Inflammable gas burns violently in air, sometimes to the point of detonation. But, as others, including Dr. Priestley, have shown, a mixture of inflammable gas and eminently respirable air explodes, but leaves as residue a wet liquid, indistinguishable from common water.

"And water, as you know, is the enemy of phlogiston. It seems to me therefore, that a mixture of phlogiston and any other substance *could not* give a residue of its exact opposite. Cavendish, however . . ."

"Question!"

Sir Robert looked up.

"Yes?"

"According to the leading French theorists, eminently respirable air is . . ."

"The French," said someone else, "are a bunch of rabble who cannot even carry out a revolution in the accepted manner, as did we."

There was a matter of agreement.

"You were going to say," said Sir Robert to his questioner, "that the French New Chemistry, which denies the phlogistic principle, attributes other causes to combustion and calcination. Most of these concern the properties of the eminently respirable air, or oxygine, as it is named. Instead of phlogiston being given off by substances in combustion, the New Chemistry says substances combine with this oxygine in the presence of heat. And you are asking what I think of this theory?"

"Yes."

"Not much," said Sir Robert. "I *have* read the French Chemistry. If you must deal with the devil, first you must know him." There was hearty applause from the back. "I have decided to ignore most of these theories, insofar as is possible. For I believe it is now within the power of science to isolate phlogiston itself."

"No! No! Impossible! Wrong!" they shouted.

Oaths crossed the air again as others took his side.

Sir Robert raised his hand for quiet.

"I have come here tonight to outline my plans and to show you models of the operations by which I intend to carry out . . ."

"Phlogiston . . . ," said a voice, ". . . is present to some extent in all matter, and indivisible. Might as well try and weigh or separate sunlight itself!"

"Hear! Hear!"

Sir Robert looked them down. A tremor passed through his

hand then, something he had noticed as happening more often since he began experimenting with his mercuric pneumatic troughs. He raised it as the tremor passed. "Some say phlogiston drifts down from the shooting stars through the aether. Others say it *comes* from the very sun. Perhaps if I succeed in isolating the phlogistic principle, we shall find, indeed, the true nature of even that great sun overhead."

That was too much for even the devout phlogistians in the audience. They came to their feet, arguing against him.

"Nevertheless," said Sir Robert, rolling up his manuscript. "Nevertheless, I have had special equipment ordered, and will carry through . . ." The president stood up and pounded with his gavel. ". . . I will prevail in my work, and expect within a fortnight to have all ready. Such of you as may want shall be invited to witness. . . " The roar rose above his words for a space and he paused. ". . . to witness this great thing, and those of you who don't can go to the very devil himself!"

He stomped from the dais. Hamp drove home in the wagon down the snow-covered ruts which passed for a road. The ground was lit by the cold still glow of the full moon, on whose closest Monday night the Lunatick Society sat, and for whose shining light it was named.

At noon two days later, Lawrence Curwell arrived. Sir Robert and Lady Margurite Athole met him on the wide carriage porch in the light of a bright cold sun.

Curwell bowed to Lady Margurite. "Your servant, madam."

"Sorry Hamp isn't here, too," said Sir Robert. "He's out in the laboratory, unpacking the new globe which arrived this forenoon from Philadelphia."

"I'm sure my note arrived rather late the night of the meeting," said Curwell. "I was surrounded by disputants during your speech. It's only luck we kept Hazzard from plunging his penknife into Revecher. What a contentious lot!"

Lawrence Curwell, like Sir Robert, was from Britain. Unlike the elder scientist, he could return, being in America to check on his brother's tobacco holdings. This was possible only because the new Constitution had been adopted, and relations between the two countries were normalizing again after the shaky years of the Confederation.

Sir Robert, who had once been a notorious supporter of the

Colonies in their rebellion, had been hounded to the States, much like his contemporary—Priestley who now lived in Pennsylvania.

Curwell, who was young and still loyal to Britain, and Sir Robert, in his fifties, experienced, but now apolitical, met only on the common ground of a devotion to knowledge and the empire of science. They shared another opinion that the American philosophs were hotheaded, opinionated, prejudiced, and had no science to match the new country's ideals. With a few exceptions: the late, lamented Franklin, Priestley, who really didn't count, Bartram of Carolina.

"I trust they'll sing another tune if you succeed," said Curwell.

"They'll have to," said Lady Margurite.

"Do we have time to see how Hamp's getting on before lunch?" asked Sir Robert.

Lady Margurite gave a knowing smile. "Surely," she said.

"Will you come with us?" asked Curwell, who was very taken with her beauty.

"Not presently. I have to see to the servants," she said, and turned to go into the house, which was an imposing, square, white three-story structure with a green roof.

"This way," said Sir Robert.

They followed a flagstone path around the house. A vista opened up to the flat rolling hills toward the west. Here was a barn, there poultry houses, stables and servant quarters larger than the cottage Curwell lived in. Past those was a wide field and beyond that a low squat edifice of fieldstones with many smokestacks and chimneys protruding from it. As Curwell neared it, he saw a huge pile of sand under the fire bell tower which stood near the doorway. One of the many large windows showed blackened signs of scorching.

"An accident late last year," said Sir Robert.

There were still a few patches of snow here and there in the shadows of the building and trees across the field. The wind was from the north but spring was in the air.

"This is quite a marvelous globe flask," said Sir Robert as they entered the building through a low rickety door. Several white servants and the black man were busy with crates and boxes. "It has a diameter of three feet, its sides are two and one-half inches in thickness, stoppable ports and conduits for sparking. I had it made especially for the grand experiment."

"Hamp," said Sir Robert. The black man looked up from his work, rubbed his hands on a chamois, came over. "Hamp. Lawrence Curwell. Lawrence, Hampton Hamilton."

"Pleased, indeed," said Hampton, and offered his hand.

It was the first time Lawrence Curwell had been offered the hand of a black man. He shook it nonetheless. He had assumed at the meeting that the man had been Sir Robert's slave.

"Hamp runs the laboratory for me, and is in charge of all the equipment and requisitioning. How's the globe, Hamp?"

"Excellent, indeed," said Hamp. Turning to the great transparent globe before them supported on sawhorses, he said, "The ports fit so tightly that I doubt we shall need wax and quicklime to seal the joints tight."

"Good, good," said Sir Robert. "Let me see the bill of lading, will you? Excuse me, Lawrence . . ."

While they put their heads together, Lawrence Curwell looked around the laboratory. He was struck by the spaciousness and cleanliness of the place and its supplies. Where most chemists got on with two or three small furnaces, Sir Robert had no less than seven—three of them large reverberatory cones, two forced-draft furnaces, two smaller ones spread down the length of the room, each with its own stack or chimney.

At one end stood large jugs—gallons of water, vitriol, spirit of wine, acid, distilled waters. In other places were ceramic buckets marked sulfur, antimony, lead, earth of rhubarb, Mohr's salt.

Shelf after shelf stretched across the walls with tins, vials and flasks—the most completely stocked workroom Curwell had ever seen—syrup of violets, oil of Dippel, ley of oxblood, Icy Butter, Starkeys Soap, salt of Gall, Glauber's salt, liquor of flints, Minderer's spirit. Numberless others.

At the far end of the laboratory were pumps and basins for washing. Near each end were large workbenches covered with experiments in progress.

In the center of the room were pneumatic troughs for the recovery of gases. Two were filled with water, the third with four inches of mercury. Seven glass bottles, some filled with a reddish air, stood upside down in each.

Curwell walked to the workbench where retorts and a Woulfe bottle caught his eye. In a few seconds he recognized it as the cohobation of some solid. At another spot he found lixiviation in process—how long it had been going on he did not know. He had seen some last for half a year, with virtually no result.

He followed to another spot where some matter was being edulcorated from acid by a water bath.

There seemed no order to the experiments, nowhere they should be leading. There was no thread holding them together, except perhaps that of refinement. Maybe Sir Robert was getting the best possible metals and calxes together before using them in his actual work.

"Lawrence," said Sir Robert. "Here, come over here." He was now standing near one of his pneumatic troughs, while behind him Hamp and the others busied themselves once more with the boxes.

"Here." He pointed at one of the inverted bottles. "I've been doing things with a gas collected over sulfur and nitre. Would you like to see?"

He began by showing Curwell some of the properties of the gas, talking occasionally of how it would be a part of the great experiment. They began moving from table to trough to bench as one or another thing they should try came to them. At one point they took off their frock coats, and sometime later their wigs. Curwell suggested other properties, other processes. They took bottles from workbench to crucible to mortar and pestle. The workmen came and left, came again. They ignored the two men huddling over the trough.

At some time Hamp lit candles in the room, finished the unpacking. Then he left. The candles burned down.

At 11 P.M. the two scientists stumbled back to the house, talking, gesturing, happy as mice and famished as wolves. Everyone was asleep.

It was the second week of Curwell's stay. Something was bothering Sir Robert, and both Margurite and Hampton could tell. Sir Robert seemed distracted in the middle of conversations or experiments. He drew plans on sheets of foolscap with a thick graphite pencil, then discarded them in lumps around the house or the laboratory.

Most of them dealt with clockwork devices, cogs, fuses. None seemed to satisfy him.

Curwell had begun to see that all the experiments and processes in the laboratory were coming together in a great design. It was ambitious, complicated, and to Curwell's mind it would probably not work. Most of it centered on fixing the phlogiston, much as fixed air is obtained from common air. He thought there were too many variables, and it depended on timing of at least four major processes. But Sir Robert's enthusiasm stirred him, and he and Hamp set about putting together minor portions of the apparatus and materials. Sir Robert talked less and less, worked more and more, and became still more dissatisfied.

One morning as he and Curwell walked toward the laboratory, they were interrupted by a halloo. Turning, they saw Athole's gamekeeper riding slowly toward them down the road. On the wagon-rut before him walked a trussed man dressed in deerskin trousers and jacket who seemed much the worse for wear.

"Caught a live one, Your Lordship," said the gamekeeper, who was Irish. "He made the best shot I've ever seen. Right into one of your heath hens," he continued, and produced the feathered evidence from his saddlepack. "Am I to take him to the constable, or shall I pummel him unmercifully?"

"As if you haven't already!" grumbled the man in leather.

"Quiet, you!" said the gamekeeper, and yanked on the rope.

Sir Robert was staring as if transfixed. "What rifle did he use?"

"Here," said the gamekeeper, and handed down a Kentucky rifle.

"I didn't do anything," said the man.

"Quite right," said the gamekeeper, and dealt him a smart blow behind the ear with his own rifle butt.

"No need for that, McCartney," said Sir Robert.

"Ow Ow Ow!" said the man, who had fallen to the ground.

"How far was the hen?" asked Sir Robert.

"Between eighty and a hundred paces, my lord," said McCartney.

"It was a hundred or I'm damned," said the man on the road.

"And could you make a shot at a quarter mile?"

"How big a target, and with what gun?" asked the man.

Sir Robert thought a moment. "A target two feet across, and with whatever weapon you need."

"It'd take a Philadelphia rifle of .60 caliber," said the man, "and I could do it."

"Done!" said Sir Robert. "Be here at dawn on the twenty-first of the month. You shall have the Philadelphia rifle, and yours to keep, and a gold crown for making the shot."

"What's the catch?" asked the man.

"None whatever. You've solved a problem of great weight for me."

"I'm not going to have to kill a man, am I?"

"No, no! What's your name, man?"

"Bumppo," he said.

"Well, Bumppo, make this shot, you have all I named before and free hunting on my land besides, in perpetuity. What say?"

"But, sir—" said McCartney.

"Untie the man, McCartney," said Sir Robert, "so he can shake hands on the deal." Then he danced a little jig on the edge of the road.

The ropes came off. Humbly, Bumppo shook Sir Robert's hand.

They set up the apparatus for the Great Experiment in a field near the woods two miles from the house. It was a quarter mile from an old Indian mound which Sir Robert thought would serve as an excellent vantage point for the spectators.

The experiment had many stops, all leading to the great glass globe which was at the center of the setup. It was surrounded by charcoal buckets, basins and jars. Over all they had erected canvas to protect it from the elements.

The invitations had been posted for the morning of the twenty-first, weather permitting.

On the afternoon of the nineteenth, they were linking the last of the equipment in place. There came to them a far-off noise, like low thunder or fireworks on the Fourth of July.

Sir Robert came out from under a basin he was installing. "What's that?"

Hampton turned to the south, from where the noise rose.

He smiled. "Pigeons," he said.

The rumble heightened like a great wind from a storm.

"Here they come," said Hamp.

To the south was a ragged blot on the horizon which wound in on itself, then spread.

"Pigeons?" asked Curwell, his face covered with soot from a charcoal bucket. "That noise?"

He stood beside the black man, who pointed.

"Passenger pigeons," he said. "Coming north again to nest. This time every year."

The line covered a quarter of the southern horizon. The sound was like a droning flutter, and the shape moved toward them with the inexorability of the rising tide. It seemed a solid mass which only resolved itself as they drew near the zenith.

They were brown and blue specks which flashed pink. They were packed more densely than Curwell had ever seen birds, ten or twenty sleek shapes to the cubic yard. They flew in a column thirty feet thick and two miles wide and—Curwell tried to count. "What's their rate of flight?"

"A mile to the minute," said Hamp, who watched a hawk diving at one of the edges of the flock. Where the predator flew the pigeons eddied and swirled, but still the column came on.

Curwell looked at his watch. The sun was blotted out as the pigeons passed over, and the fluttering roar was omnipresent.

"Under the awning!" said Hamp, and pulled Curwell back. White flashes like snow, and occasional feathers began to drift down. Passenger pigeon excrement dotted the ground in spots, then more, and fell like a gentle white rain.

Through the flutter of wings, shots could be heard from the neighboring estates. Curwell saw great clumps of pigeons drop a mile away on a surrounding farm.

Then one fell a few feet outside the canvas, struggled and lay still. It must have been hit some distance away and flown this far.

Curwell ran out, picked it up and brought it inside the tent.

It was the most beautiful bird he had ever seen, even in death. Its back was blue, its neck and stomach bronze, its chest pink and dull red, with an iridescent sheen to all the feathers. Its beak was dark, and its legs, feet and eyes were a brilliant orange-red. He placed it on the bench and examined it minutely.

Still the fluttering roared overhead, and the ground was as white as in a snow flurry. The sky outside was an interrupted play of darkness and light where the cloud of birds went in transit across the sun.

Curwell went back to work in the artificial gloom, occasionally looking out to make sure the flock was still traveling Gunshots came more frequently from the nearby roads and fields.

Sometime later, the sound subsided. Curwell came out of the tent in time to see the last of the flock rocket overhead. The late evening sun began to shine again.

He looked at his watch. Two hours and forty minutes had elapsed. The column had been one hundred and sixty miles long. At ten birds to the yard, ten yards thick, 1,700 yards to the mile, two miles wide . . .

Sir Robert looked at Curwell. "About sixteen million birds, I'd say."

"I've seen more," said Hamp "When I was a boy I saw a flock that took from noon to dusk to pass. It got dark at midday, and we never saw the sun go down. We had only morning that day." He pounded a copper pipe in place with a maul. He stopped to look at the encrusted ground for a moment.

Then they all went back to work.

All was in readiness.

The spectators, scientific men for the most part, had begun arriving in the early hours of the morn. Dawn was approaching. Then men on the Indian mound waited while Curwell, Hampton and Sir Robert Athole walked up the intervening field from the apparatus, which looked to be a jumble of metal and glass to the unaided eye at this distance.

Bumppo stood well back from the others. McCartney kept an eye on him. The leather-clad man was testing the feel of his new Philadelphia rifle, swinging it up and down from his shoulder.

Sir Robert came to the top of the mound and stood beside Lady Margurite.

"Gentlemen," he said. "Lady. Others."

"You are here to witness what I hope is a grand event in scientific progress. On yonder field," he pointed, "are working apparatus for the generation of gases and airs—of dephlogisticated, or eminently respirable, air; of flammable gas, of sulfur air, of phosphorus. They are all working and generating as we stand here, and shall be in fruition soon.

"They enter into conduits taken to the glass globe which you see at the center. They will enter the glass when Mr. Bumppo . . ." Here Bumppo held up his hand shyly, and a ragged cheer went up from the spectators, ". . . fires at his target disk. These phlogiston-rich gases and liquids will rush together. They should produce the essence of fire, of combustion, of calcination viz. phlogiston itself. A clockwork will then be put in motion, and fifteen seconds later, the mixture will be sparked by means of a circuit from a Leyden jar. This should fix the phlogiston itself, much as common air becomes fixed air in the presence of the electric principle, and allow us the examination for the first time, of one of the principles, of one of the elements itself.

"That is my Great Experiment."

Some applauded.

"Question?"

"Yes?"

"You're mixing inflammable air, dephlogisticated air and phosphorus in the presence of common air, and sparking it?"

"That is my plan."

"Then what you'll get," said the voice, after a moment's reckoning, "is a gentle explosion, a small quantity of fixed air, and a small field fire to fight."

Some laughed.

"I doubt that," said Sir Robert Athole. "I have taken the precaution of removing us to this distance in case of some apparatus failure, and the leakage of noxious fumes."

The sun topped the small ridge to the east, and the field and mound were bathed in a frosty light.

"Win or lose," said Sir Robert, "I feel on the edge of great things."

"And I," said Curwell.

"I, too," said Lady Margurite, and took her husband's hand.

"Mr. Bumppo," said Sir Robert. "You see your target?"

"That I do," said Bumppo.

"Then earn your crown, man!"

The leather-clad man stepped to the front of the mound. Smoothly he raised the weapon as if it were part of him, pulled back the dog-ear hammer, aimed and fired.

The smoke from the muzzle wafted away.

Even without his spyglass, Sir Robert saw the great globe turn milky white. But it was not the milk-white of residue gases. It roiled and swirled slowly. An "ooh" went up from the small crowd. Winks of light seemed to play across the equipment from the globe. All the apparatus was bathed in a white light.

Sir Robert felt the muscles of his stomach twitch.

For the requisite few more seconds, nothing happened.

Then it did.

Shaken and dazed, Sir Robert pulled himself from the ground in the blinding light. He was near the bottom of the mound. Some of the others were getting up as well as they could. One man lay with a branch through his chest. A few lay unmarked but unmoving. Hampton, near him, held his arm crookedly the wrong way.

There was a roaring in their ears, and it did not subside. Sir Robert stumbled back to the top of the mound, shielding his eyes.

To the west was a great roiling white cloud, too bright to be looked at directly. Bright blooms and bursts of light flew out from it like those from a pan of burning phosphorus. Sir Robert could tell that it was moving slowly away from him to the westward.

He turned. The cloud stretched to north and south, horizon to horizon, moving laterally to its progress westward. Ribbons of red flame shot through the bright white wall.

The smell of burnt wood permeated all the air. As the cloud moved away, it continued to grow in height.

The wind rose from the east, first gently, then in gusts, then faster and faster. The earth to the west was charred to the surface. Matchstick trees poked up. As Sir Robert watched, a puff of wind blew them to ash before his eyes.

The numbed scientists were milling around behind the mound. The wind rose to gale force.

"It's moving west with the rotation of the earth," said Hampton Hamilton. He knew, as did any schoolboy, that the air moves with the surface under it falling behind, from whence rise winds.

Sir Robert turned to see Curwell helping Lady Margurite up. They both seemed safe, though Lady Margurite's skirts flapped immodestly in the racking wind. Sir Robert noticed his wig was gone as he saw Hamp's wig blow off and be lost in the western distance toward the bright cloud. They climbed down the Indian mound against the force of the wind.

"How long will it burn?" asked Curwell.

"I have no idea," said Sir Robert. "It was not supposed to burn at all. It was supposed to fix in the globe. I just don't understand."

"It may burn until it reaches the Western Ocean," said Hampton, and he had voiced all their fears.

"Surely, surely not," said Athole, yelling to be heard above the wind.

"But you must have succeeded," said someone else. "You *must* have released all the phlogiston in the mixed matter. There's no telling what will happen with it. It could burn that far!"

"Then the water will put it out. The water!" said Sir Robert. He felt a spasm go through him and he lost consciousness.

He awakened with smoke and the smell of soot in his nostrils. The light outside was murky. A wind whistled around the rafters outside the house, but it was no longer the gale it had been. A brown darkness of smoke lapped against the windows.

He sat up on the couch where they had lain him.

Lady Margurite was crying on the sofa opposite.

"Everything to the west is gone, Robert," she said quietly when she saw him rouse.

"*Everything?*"

"As far as a horse and man can ride, before it becomes too hot to continue. And that was hours ago, when the scout from the township came back from his reconnoiter."

"The barometer," said Lawrence Curwell, tapping the great Dresden instrument atop the mantlepiece. "The barometer has dropped a full six inches since this morning, and is still falling."

"Oh, great Jehovah!" said Sir Robert. "What have I done?"

"Nothing any of us wouldn't have done," said Hampton Hamilton tiredly from another chair. "It only seems you succeeded much better than you had planned."

"Why didn't you stop me?"

"I don't know" said Hampton. "I doubt you would have stopped me."

"What time is it?"

"A little after five."

"We'll know in fourteen hours, then," said Curwell. He continued to stare at the barometer, as if to drag secrets from it.

They tried to eat after darkness fell, but no one was hungry. Tins of molasses had begun to pop their lids in the pantry. Sir Robert imagined it was harder to breathe, but knew better.

They sat in the parlor until no one could stand the waiting and the heat any longer.

"Damn it!" Sir Robert jumped to his feet. "If it's going to happen, I want to look it in the face. We'll go to the ocean."

They looked at him a moment, then climbed from their chairs. It was better than waiting here, where each ticking of the clock sounded loud as a carpenter's hammer to them.

The wagon bounced on the rutted road. The horse labored.

Sir Robert drove in front with Hampton; Curwell and Lady Margurite were in back with a picnic basket and blankets.

It was nearing midnight. The air was filled with the odors of burning—of a thousand things, burnt wood, grass, feathers, calcined metals, gunpowder smells. The wind brought warmth. Through rifts in the smoky sky they saw the stars—larger and colder than they had ever looked before, and they hardly twinkled.

The temperature was still rising, and the barometer had bottomed out an hour ago. It was now decidedly harder to breathe.

They topped the hill overlooking the port town of New Sharpton. Candles burned in the houses, torches moved in the streets as knots of people formed together and dispersed. An occasional rider left on the road down the coast.

"Over here will be fine," said Sir Robert, guiding the horse to a spot beneath a group of trees atop the hill.

They spread the blankets on the seaward side of the hill and lay back, watching the still Atlantic.

•   •   •

Sir Robert drifted in and out of sleep as from fatigue. The air was hot and close, as if he were shut up in a chimney in the middle of summer.

Curwell had gone down the hill toward the bay. It had taken him a long time to go the few hundred yards. He had stopped frequently and rested.

The horse, which had been unhitched from the wagon, was in distress, as if it had been galloped miles, instead of being walked the few from the estate to the sea.

"The water temperature is rising, and the streams coming to it are out of their banks from melted snow," said Curwell, when he had labored up the hill and lay down. "There are shoals of dead fish away from the stream outlet. There are so many we could smell from here were it not for this infernal smoke."

"It just can't be true," said Sir Robert. "It just cannot. Water *will not* burn!"

"Maybe," said Hampton, where he lay on the ground above them, holding his splinted and broken arm. "Maybe the New Chemistry has some truths. Perhaps water is *not* an element. Perhaps it, too, contains phlogiston, or inflammable gas, which . . ." For the first time in his life, Hampton was having trouble following a line of thought. He shook his head to clear it. ". . . Inflammable gas. Perhaps a constituent like the oxygine principle. Perhaps it was separated by the heat from the land. Perhaps the fire is fueled from it. Maybe it will have to pass over the Earth innumerable times before it is all combusted with phlogiston . . ."

Sir Robert lay back on the blanket. He held Lady Margurite's hand.

"All gone," he said at last.

"The buffalo. The Indians," said Margurite.

"The Chinese. The bold Russians. The Turks," said Hampton.

"The French. *Britain!*" said Curwell.

"Now us," said Hampton Hamilton, and pointed.

The east was beginning to lighten, though it was still an hour before dawn. The wind blew toward the sea, but it was still a gentle wind, a thin wind. It had very little force.

From north to south the bright white boiling line appeared, like the sun breaking through under a late afternoon storm. But much brighter.

"Shall we be burned?" asked Lady Margurite. Her arm sprouted gooseflesh. "The thought of burning is the worst."

"I think not," said Curwell. "Like the martyrs, I think the air will be too saturated with phlogiston for us to breathe before the fire reaches us." He paused as a great tongue of flame licked out of the roil toward them.

The hill and the village were bathed in the glaring artificial dawn. Screams came from the town from those who were still able to scream.

The thin wind rose more.

They watched the burning line quietly, each locked in their thoughts. The edge of the great combusting cloud was still more than two hundred miles away.

"Phlogiston!" said Sir Robert Athole and turned and passed away.

"I want to stand up," said Hamp. They heard him stir and fall behind them.

"The French _were_ right, partly . . ." said Curwell.

"Robert . . . ?" asked Lady Margurite.

Curwell looked at the enormous burning wall.

"It's the end of . . ."

The sentence was the only thing left unfinished.

THE PEACEMAKER

Gardner Dozois

And, of course, after all but the most potent of those Armageddons that we can bring down on ourselves, whether it is war or plague or environmental disaster, there will be survivors, survivors who will have to pick up the pieces and try to start again—survivors, as the Nebula-winning story that follows suggests, who will also have to deal with their own guilt for having survived . . .

Gardner Dozois has won two Nebula Awards for his own short fiction, as well as ten Hugo Awards as the year's Best Editor. He is the editor of Asimov's Science Fiction *magazine, and also the editor of the annual anthology series* The Year's Best Science Fiction, *now up to its Fifteenth Annual Collection. He is the author or editor of over seventy books, including a long string of Ace anthologies co-edited with Jack Dann. His own short fiction was most recently collected in* Geodesic Dreams: The Best Short Fiction of Gardner Dozois.

Roy had dreamed of the sea, as he often did. When he woke up that morning, the wind was sighing through the trees outside with a sound like the restless murmuring of surf, and for a moment he thought that he was home, back in the tidy brick house by the beach, with everything that had happened undone, and hope opened hotly inside him, like a wound.

"Mom?" he said. He sat up, straightening his legs, expecting his feet to touch the warm mass that was his dog, Toby. Toby always slept curled at the foot of his bed, but already everything was breaking up and changing, slipping away, and he blinked through sleep-gummed eyes at the thin blue light coming in through the attic window, felt the hardness of the old Army cot under him, and realized that he wasn't home, that there was no home anymore, that for him there could never be a home again.

He pushed the blankets aside and stood up. It was bitterly cold in the big attic room—winter was dying hard, the most terrible winter he could remember—and the rough wood planking burned his feet like ice, but he couldn't stay in bed anymore, not now.

None of the other kids were awake yet; he threaded his way through the other cots—accidently bumping against one of them so that its occupant tossed and moaned and began to snore in a higher register—and groped through cavernous shadows to the single high window. He was just tall enough to reach it, if he stood on tiptoe. He forced the window open, the old wood of its frame groaning in protest, plaster dust puffing, and shivered as the cold dawn wind poured inward, hitting him in the face, tugging with ghostly fingers at his hair, sweeping past him to rush through the rest of the stuffy attic like a restless child set free to play.

The wind smelled of pine resin and wet earth, not of salt flats and tides; and the bird-sound that rode in on that wind was the burbling of wrens and the squawking of bluejays, not the raucous shrieking of seagulls . . . but even so, as he braced his elbows against the window frame and strained up to look out, his mind still full of the broken fragments of dreams, he half-expected to see the ocean below, stretched out to the horizon, sending patient wavelets to lap against the side of the house. Instead he saw the nearby trees holding silhouetted arms up against the graying sky, the barn and the farmyard, all still lost in shadow, the surrounding fields, the weathered macadam line of the road, the forested hills rolling away into the distance. Silver mist lay in pockets of low ground, retreated in wraithlike streamers up along the ridges.

Not yet. The sea had not chased him here—yet.

Somewhere out there to the east, still invisible, were the mountains, and just beyond those mountains was the sea that he had dreamed of, lapping quietly at the dusty Pennsylvania hill towns, coal towns, that were now, suddenly, seaports. There the Atlantic waited, held at bay, momentarily at least, by the humpbacked wall of the Appalachians, still perhaps forty miles from here, although closer now by leagues of swallowed land and drowned cities than it had been only three years before.

He had been down by the seawall that long-ago morning, playing some forgotten game, watching the waves move in slow oily swells, like some heavy, dull metal in liquid form, watching the tide come in . . . and come in . . . and come *in*. . . . He had been excited at first, as the sea crept in, way above the high-tide line, higher than he had ever seen it before, and then, as the sea swallowed the beach entirely and began to lap patiently against the base of the seawall, he had become uneasy, and *then*, as the sea continued to rise up toward the top of the seawall itself, he had begun to be afraid. . . . The sea had just kept coming in, rising slowly and inexorably, swallowing the land at a slow walking pace, never stopping, always coming *in*, always rising higher. . . . By the time the sea had swallowed the top of the seawall and begun to creep up the short grassy slope toward his house, sending glassy fingers probing almost to his feet, he had started to scream, and as the first thin sheet of water rippled up to soak his sneakers, he had whirled and run frantically up the slope, screaming hysterically for his parents, and the sea had followed patiently at his heels. . . .

A "marine transgression," the scientists called it. Ordinary people called it, inevitably, the Flood. Whatever you called it, it had washed away the old world forever. Scientists had been talking about the possibility of such a thing for years—some of them even pointing out that it was already as warm as it had been at the peak of the last interglacial, and getting warmer—but few had suspected just how *fast* the Antarctic ice could melt. Many times during those chaotic weeks, one scientific King Canute or another had predicted that the worst was over, that the tide would rise this high and no higher . . . but each time the sea had come inexorably on, pushing miles and miles further inland with each successive high-tide, rising almost 300 feet in the course of one disastrous summer, drowning lowlands around the globe until there *were* no lowlands anymore. In the United States alone, the sea had swallowed most of the East Coast of the Appalachians, the West Coast west of the Sierras and the Cascades, much of Alaska and Hawaii, Florida, the Gulf Coast, East Texas, taken a big wide scoop out of the lowlands of the Mississippi Valley, thin fingers of water penetrating north to Iowa and Illinois, and caused the St. Lawrence and the Great Lakes to overflow and drown their shorelines. The Green Mountains, the White Mountains, the Adirondacks, the Poconos and the Catskills, the Ozarks, the Pacific Coast Ranges—all had been transformed to archipelagos, surrounded by the invading sea.

The funny thing was . . . that as the sea pursued them relentlessly inland, pushing them from one temporary refuge to another, he had been unable to shake the feeling that *he* had caused the Flood: that he had done something that day while playing atop the seawall, inadvertently stumbled on some magic ritual, some chance combination of gesture and word that had untied the bonds of the sea and sent it sliding up over the land . . . that it was chasing *him*, personally. . . .

A dog was barking out there now, somewhere out across the fields toward town, but it was not *his* dog. His dog was dead, long since dead, and its whitening skull was rolling along the ocean floor with the tides that washed over what had once been Brigantine, New Jersey, three hundred feet down.

Suddenly he was covered with gooseflesh, and he shivered, rubbing his hands over his bare arms. He returned to his cot and dressed hurriedly—no point in trying to go back to bed, Sara would be up to kick them all out of the sack in a minute or two anyway. The day had begun; he would think no further ahead than that. He had learned in the refugee camps to take life one second at a time.

As he moved around the room, he thought that he could feel hostile eyes watching him from some of the other bunks. It was much colder in here now that he had opened the window, and he had inevitably made a certain amount of noise getting dressed, but although they all valued every second of sleep they could scrounge, none of the other kids would dare to complain. The thought was bittersweet, bringing both pleasure and pain, and he smiled at it, a thin, brittle smile that was almost a grimace. No, they would watch sullenly from their bunks, and pretend to be asleep, and curse him under their breath, but they would say nothing to anyone about it. Certainly they would say nothing to *him*.

He went down through the still-silent house like a ghost, and out across the farmyard, through fugitive streamers of mist that wrapped clammy white arms around him and beaded his face with dew. His uncle Abner was there at the slit-trench before him. Abner grunted a greeting, and they stood pissing side by side for a moment in companionable silence, their urine steaming in the gray morning air.

Abner stepped backward and began to button his pants. "You start playin' with yourself yet, boy?" he said, not looking at Roy.

Roy felt his face flush. "No," he said, trying not to stammer, "no sir."

"You growin' hair already," Abner said. He swung himself slowly around to face Roy, as if his body was some ponderous machine that could only be moved and aimed by the use of pulleys and levers. The hard morning light made his face look harsh as stone, but also sallow and old. Tired, Roy thought. Unutterably weary, as though it took almost more effort than he could sustain just to stand there. Worn out, like the overtaxed fields around them. Only the eyes were alive in the eroded face; they were hard and merciless as flint, and they looked at you as if they were looking right through you to some distant thing that nobody else could see. "I've tried to explain to you about remaining pure," Abner said, speaking slowly. "About how important it is for you to keep yourself pure, not to let yourself be sullied in any way. I've tried to explain that, I hope you could understand—"

"Yes, sir," Roy said.

Abner made a groping hesitant motion with his hand, fingers spread wide, as though he were trying to sculpt meaning from the air itself. "I mean—it's important that you understand, Roy. Everything has to be *right*. I mean, everything's got to be just . . . *right* . . . or nothing else will mean anything. You got to be right in your *soul*, boy. You got to let the Peace of God into your soul. It all depends on *you* now—you got to let that Peace inside yourself, no one can do it for you. And it's so important . . ."

"Yes, sir," Roy said quietly, "I understand."

"I wish . . . ," Abner said, and fell silent. They stood there for a minute, not speaking, not looking at each other. There was wood-smoke in the air now, and they heard a door slam somewhere on the far side of the house. They had instinctively been looking out across the open land to the east, and now, as they watched, the sun rose above the mountains, splitting the plum-and-ash sky open horizontally with a long wedge of red, distinguishing the rolling horizon from the lowering clouds. A lance of bright white sunlight hit their eyes, thrusting straight in at them from the edge of the world.

"You're going to make us proud, boy, I know it," Abner said, but Roy ignored him, watching in fascination as the molten disk of the sun floated free of the horizon-line, squinting against the dazzle until his eyes watered and his sight blurred. Abner put his hand on the boy's shoulder. The hand felt heavy and hot, proprietary, and Roy shook it loose in annoyance, still not looking away from the horizon. Abner sighed, started to say something, thought better of it, and instead said, "Come on in the house, boy, and let's get some breakfast inside you."

Breakfast—when they finally did get to sit down to it, after the usual rambling grace and invocation by Abner—proved to be unusually lavish. For the brethren, there were hickory-nut biscuits, and honey, and cups of chicory, and even the other refugee kids—who on occasion during the long bitter winter had been fed as close to nothing at all as law and appearances would allow—got a few slices of fried fatback along with their habitual cornmeal mush. Along with his biscuits and honey, Roy got wild turkey eggs, Indian potatoes, and a real pork chop. There was a good deal of tension around the big table that morning: Henry and Luke were stern-faced and tense, Raymond was moody and preoccupied, Albert actually looked frightened; the refugee kids were round-eyed and silent, doing their best to make themselves invisible; the jolly Mrs. Crammer was as jolly as ever, shoveling her food in with gusto, but the grumpy Mrs. Zeigler, who was feared and disliked by all the kids, had obviously been crying, and ate little or nothing; Abner's face was set like rock, his eyes were hard and bright, and he looked from one to another of the brethren, as if daring them to question his leadership and spiritual guidance. Roy ate with good appetite, unperturbed by the emotional convection currents that were swirling around him, calmly but deliberately concentrating on mopping up every morsel of food on his plate—in the last couple of months he had put back some of the weight he had lost, although by the old standards, the ones his Mom would have applied four years ago, he was still painfully thin. At the end of the meal, Mrs. Reardon came in from the kitchen and, beaming with the well-justified pride of someone who is about to do the impossible, presented Roy with a small, rectangular object wrapped in shiny brown paper. He was startled for a second, but yes, by God, it *was*: a Hershey bar, the first one he'd seen in years. A black market item, of course, difficult to get hold of in the impoverished East these days, and probably expensive as hell. Even some of the brethren were looking at him enviously now, and the refugee kids were frankly gaping. As he picked up the Hershey bar and slowly and caressingly peeled the wrapper back, exposing the pale chocolate beneath, one of the other kids actually began to drool.

After breakfast, the other refugee kids—"wetbacks," the townspeople sometimes called them, with elaborate irony— were divided into two groups. One group would help the brethren work Abner's farm that day, while the larger group would be loaded onto an ox-drawn dray (actually an old flatbed truck, with the cab knocked off) and sent out around the countryside to do what pretty much amounted to slave labor: road work, heavy farm work, helping with the quarrying or the timbering, rebuilding houses and barns and bridges damaged or destroyed in the chaotic days after the Flood. The federal government—or what was left of the federal government, trying desperately, and not always successfully, to keep a battered and Balkanizing country from flying completely apart, struggling to put the Humpty Dumpty that was America back together again—the federal government paid Abner (and others like him) a yearly allowance in federal scrip or promise-of-merchandise notes for giving room and board to refugees from the drowned lands . . . but times being as tough as they were, no one was going to complain if Abner also helped ease the burden of their upkeep by hiring them out locally to work for whomever could come up with the scrip, or sufficient barter goods, or an attractive work-swap offer; what was left of the state and town governments also used them on occasion (and the others like them, adult or child), gratis, for work-projects "for the common good, during this time of emergency . . ."

Sometimes, hanging around the farm with little or nothing to do, Roy almost missed going out on the work-crews, but only almost: he remembered too well the backbreaking labor performed on scanty rations . . . the sickness, the accidents, the staggering fatigue . . . the blazing sun and the swarms of mosquitoes in summer, the bitter cold in winter, the snow, the icy wind . . . He watched the dray go by, seeing the envious and resentful faces of kids he had once worked beside—Stevie, Enrique, Sal—turn toward him as it passed, and, reflexively, he opened and closed his hands. Even two months of idleness and relative luxury had not softened the thick and roughened layers of callus that were the legacy of several seasons spent on the crews. . . . No, boredom was infinitely preferable.

By mid-morning, a small crowd of people had gathered in the road outside the farmhouse. It was hotter now; you could smell the promise of summer in the air, in the wind, and the sun that beat down out of a cloudless blue sky had a real sting to it. It must have been uncomfortable out there in the open, under that sun, but the crowd made no attempt to approach—they just stood there on the far side of the road and watched the house, shuffling their feet, occasionally muttering to each other in voices that, across the road, were audible only as a low wordless grumbling.

Roy watched them for a while from the porch door; they were townspeople, most of them vaguely familiar to Roy, although none of them belonged to Abner's sect, and he knew none of them by name. The refugee kids saw little of the townspeople, being kept carefully segregated for the most part. The few times that Roy had gotten into town he had been treated with icy hostility—and God help the wetback kid who was caught by the town kids on a deserted stretch of road! For that matter, even the brethren tended to keep to themselves, and were snubbed by certain segments of town society, although the sect had increased its numbers dramatically in recent years, nearly tripling in strength during the past winter alone; there were new chapters now in several of the surrounding communities.

A gaunt-faced woman in the crowd outside spotted Roy, and shook a thin fist at him. "Heretic!" she shouted. "Blasphemer!" The rest of the crowd began to buzz ominously, like a huge angry bee. She spat at Roy, her face contorting and her shoulders heaving with the ferocity of her effort, although she must have known that the spittle had no chance of reaching him. "Blasphemer!" she shouted again. The veins stood out like cords in her scrawny neck.

Roy stepped back into the house, but continued to watch from behind the curtained front windows. There was shouting inside the house as well as outside—the brethren had been

cloistered in the kitchen for most of the morning, arguing, and
the sound and ferocity of their argument carried clearly through
the thin plaster walls of the crumbling old house. At last the
sliding door to the kitchen slammed open, and Mrs. Zeigler
strode out into the parlor, accompanied by her two children and
her scrawny, pasty-faced husband, and followed by two other
families of brethren—about nine people altogether. Most of
them were carrying suitcases, and a few had backpacks and
bindles. Abner stood in the kitchen doorway and watched them
go, his anger evident only in the whiteness of his knuckles as
he grasped the doorframe. "*Go*, then," Abner said scornfully.
"We spit you up out of our mouths! Don't ever think to come
back!" He swayed in the doorway, his voice tremulous with
hate. "We're better off without you, you hear? You *hear* me?
We don't *need* the weak-willed and the short-sighted."

Mrs. Zeigler said nothing, and her steps didn't slow or falter,
but her homely hatchet-face was streaked with tears. To Roy's
astonishment—for she had a reputation as a harridan—she
stopped near the porch door and threw her arms around him.
"Come with us," she said, hugging him with smothering
tightness, "Roy, *please* come with us! You can, you know—
we'll find a place for you, everything will work out fine." Roy
said nothing, resisting the impulse to squirm—he was uncomfortable in her embrace; in spite of himself, it touched some
sleeping corner of his soul he had thought was safely bricked-
over years before, and for a moment he felt trapped and
panicky, unable to breathe, as though he were in sudden danger
of wakening from a comfortable dream into a far more terrible and less desirable reality. "Come *with* us," Mrs. Zeigler
said again, more urgently, but Roy shook his head gently and
pulled away from her. "You're a goddamned fool then!" she
blazed, suddenly angry, her voice ringing harsh and loud, but
Roy only shrugged, and gave her his wistful, ghostly smile.
"Damn it—" she started to say, but her eyes filled with tears
again, and she whirled and hurried out of the house, followed
by the other members of her party. The children—wetbacks
were kept pretty much segregated from the children of the
brethren as well, and he had seen some of these kids only at
meals—looked at Roy with wide, frightened eyes as they
passed.

Abner was staring at Roy now, from across the room; it was

a hard and challenging stare, but there was also a trace of desperation in it, and in that moment Abner seemed uncertain and oddly vulnerable. Roy stared back at him serenely, unblinkingly meeting his eyes, and after a while some of the tension went out of Abner, and he turned and stumbled out of the room, listing to one side like a church steeple in the wind.

Outside, the crowd began to buzz again as Mrs. Zeigler's party filed out of the house and across the road. There was much discussion and arm-waving and head-shaking when the two groups met, someone occasionally gesturing back toward the farmhouse. The buzzing grew louder, then gradually died away. At last, Mrs. Zeigler and her group set off down the road for town, accompanied by some of the locals. They trudged away dispiritedly down the center of the dusty road, lugging their shabby suitcases, only a few of them looking back.

Roy watched them until they were out of sight, his face still and calm, and continued to stare down the road after them long after they were gone.

About noon, a carload of reporters arrived outside, driving up in one of the bulky new methane-burners that were still rarely seen east of Omaha. They circulated through the crowd of townspeople, pausing briefly to take photographs and ask questions, working their way toward the house, and Roy watched them as if they were unicorns, strange remnants from some vanished cycle of creation. Most of the reporters were probably from State College or the new state capital at Altoona—places where a few small newspapers were again being produced—but one of them was wearing an armband that identified him as a bureau man for one of the big Denver papers, and that was probably where the money for the car had come from. It was strange to be reminded that there were still areas of the country that were . . . not unchanged, no place in the world could claim that . . . and not rich, not by the old standards of affluence anyway . . . but, at any rate, better off than *here*. The whole western part of the country—from roughly the 95th meridian on west to approximately the 122nd—had been untouched by the flooding, and although the west had also suffered severely from the collapse of the national economy and the consequent social upheavals, at least much of their industrial base had remained intact. Denver—

one of the few large American cities built on ground high
enough to have been safe from the rising waters—was the new
federal capital, and, if poorer and meaner, it was also bigger
and busier than ever.

Abner went out to herd the reporters inside and away from
the unbelievers, and after a moment or two Roy could hear
Abner's voice going out there, booming like a church organ. By
the time the reporters came in, Roy was sitting at the dining
room table, flanked by Raymond and Aaron, waiting for them.

They took photographs of him sitting there, while he stared
calmly back at them, and they took photographs of him while
he politely refused to answer questions, and then Aaron handed
him the pre-prepared papers, and he signed them, and repeated
the legal formulas that Aaron had taught him, and they took
photographs of that, too. And then—able to get nothing more
out of him, and made slightly uneasy by his blank composure
and the remoteness of his eyes—they left.

Within a few more minutes, as though everything were over,
as though the departure of the reporters had drained all possible
significance from anything else that might still happen, most of
the crowd outside had drifted away also, only one or two
people remaining behind to stand quietly waiting, like vultures,
in the once-again empty road.

Lunch was a quiet meal. Roy ate heartily, taking seconds of
everything, and Mrs. Crammer was as jovial as ever, but
everyone else was subdued, and even Abner seemed shaken by
the schism that had just sundered his church. After the meal,
Abner stood by and began to pray aloud. The brethren sat
resignedly at the table, heads partially bowed, some listening,
some not. Abner was holding his arms up toward the big
blackened rafters of the ceiling, sweat runneling his face, when
Peter came hurriedly in from outside and stood hesitating in the
doorway, trying to catch Abner's eye. When it became obvious
that Abner was going to keep right on ignoring him, Peter
shrugged, and said in a loud flat voice, "Abner, the sheriff is
here."

Abner stopped praying. He grunted, a hoarse, exhausted
sound, the kind of sound a baited bear might make when,
already pushed beyond the limits of endurance, someone jabs it
yet again with a spear. He slowly lowered his arms and was still
for a long moment, and then he shuddered, seeming to shake

himself back to life. He glanced speculatively—and, it almost seemed, beseechingly—at Roy, and then straightened his shoulders and strode from the room.

They received the sheriff in the parlor, Raymond and Aaron and Mrs. Crammer sitting in the battered old armchairs, Roy sitting unobtrusively to one side of the stool from a piano that no longer worked, Abner standing a little to the fore with his arms locked behind him and his boots planted solidly on the oak planking, as if he were on the bridge of a schooner that was heading into a gale. County Sheriff Sam Braddock glanced at the others—his gaze lingering on Roy for a moment—and then ignored them, addressing himself to Abner as if they were alone in the room. "Mornin', Abner," he said.

"Mornin', Sam," Abner said quietly. "You here for some reason other than just t'say hello, I suppose."

Braddock grunted. He was a short, stocky, grizzled man with iron-gray hair and a tired face. His uniform was shiny and old and patched in a dozen places, but clean, and the huge old revolver strapped to his hip looked worn but serviceable. He fidgeted with his shapeless old hat, turning it around and around in his fingers—he was obviously embarrassed, but he was determined as well, and at last he said, "The thing of it is, Abner, I'm here to talk you out of this damned tomfoolery."

"Are you, now?" Abner said.

"We'll do whatever we damn well want to do—" Raymond burst out, shrilly, but Abner waved him to silence. Braddock glanced lazily at Raymond, then looked back at Abner, his tired old face settling into harder lines. "I'm not going to allow it," he said, most harshly. "We don't want this kind of thing going on in this country."

Abner said nothing.

"There's not a thing you can do about it, sheriff," Aaron said, speaking a bit heatedly, but keeping his melodious voice well under control. "It's all perfectly legal, all the way down the line."

"Well, now," Braddock said, "I don't know about that . . ."

"Well, I *do* know, sheriff," Aaron said calmly. "As a legally sanctioned and recognized church, we are protected by law all the way down the line. There is ample precedent, most of it recent, most of it upheld by appellate decisions within the last year: Carlton *versus* the State of Vermont, Trenholm *versus* the

State of West Virginia, the Church of Souls *versus* the State of New York. There was that case up in Tylersville, just last year. Why, the Freedom of Worship Act *alone* . . ."

Braddock sighed, tacitly admitting that he knew Aaron was right—perhaps he had hoped to bluff them into obeying. "The 'Flood Congress' of '93," Braddock said, with bitter contempt. "They were so goddamned panic-stricken and full of sick chatter about Armageddon that you could've rammed *any* nonsense down their throats. That's a bad law, a pisspoor law . . ."

"Be that as it may, sheriff, you have no authority whatsoever—"

Abner suddenly began to speak, talking with a slow heavy deliberateness, musingly, almost reminiscently, ignoring the conversation he was interrupting—and indeed, perhaps he had not even been listening to it. "My grandfather lived right here on this farm, and *his* father before him—you know that, Sam? *They* lived by the old ways, and they survived and prospered. Greatgranddad, there wasn't hardly anything he needed from the outside world, anything he needed to *buy,* except maybe nails and suchlike, and he could've made them himself, too, if he'd needed to. Everything they needed, everything they ate, or wore, or used, they got from the woods, or from out of the soil of this farm, right here. *We* don't know how to do that anymore. We forgot the old ways, we turned our faces away, which is why the Flood came on us as a Judgment, a Judgment and a scourge, a scouring, a winnowing. The Old Days have come back again, and we've forgotten so goddamned *much,* we're almost helpless now that there's no goddamned K-mart down the goddamned street. We've got to go back to the old ways, or we'll pass from the earth, and be seen no more in it . . ." He was sweating now, staring earnestly at Braddock, as if to compel him by force of will alone to share the vision. "But it's so *hard,* Sam. . . . We have to *work* at relearning the old ways, we have to reinvent them as we go, step by step . . ."

"Some things we were better off without," Braddock said grimly.

"Up at Tylersville, they *doubled* their yield last harvest. Think what that could mean to a country as hungry as this one has been—"

Braddock shook his iron-gray head and held up one hand, as

if he were directing traffic. "I'm telling you, Abner, the town won't stand for this—I'm bound to warn you that some of the boys just might decide to go outside the law to deal with this thing." He paused. "And, unofficially of course, I just might be inclined to give them a hand. . . ."

Mrs. Crammer laughed. She had been sitting quietly and taking all of this in, smiling good-naturedly from time to time, and her laugh was a shocking thing in that stuffy little room, harsh as a crow's caw. "You'll do *nothing,* Sam Braddock," she said jovially. "And neither will anybody else. More than half the county's with us already, nearly all the country folk, and a good part of the town, too." She smiled pleasantly at him, but her eyes were small and hard. "Just you remember, we *know* where *you* live, Sam Braddock. And we know where your sister lives, too, and your sister's child, over to Framington . . ."

"Are you threatening an officer of the law?" Braddock said, but he said it in a weak voice, and his face, when he turned it away to stare at the floor, looked sick and old. Mrs. Crammer laughed again, and then there was silence.

Braddock kept his face turned down for another long moment, and then he put his hat back on, squashing it down firmly on his head, and when he looked up he pointedly ignored the brethren and addressed his next remark to Roy. "You don't have to stay with these people, son," he said. "*That's* the law, too." He kept his eyes fixed steadily on Roy. "You just say the word, son, and I'll take you straight out of here, right now." His jaw was set, and he touched the butt of his revolver, as if for encouragement. "They can't stop us. How about it?"

"No, thank you," Roy said quietly. "I'll stay."

That night, while Abner wrung his hands and prayed aloud, Roy sat half-dozing before the parlor fire, unconcerned, watching the firelight throw Abner's gesticulating shadow across the white-washed walls. There was something in the wine they kept giving him, Roy knew, maybe somebody's saved-up Quäāludes, but he didn't need it. Abner kept exorting him to let the Peace of God into his heart, but he didn't need that either. He didn't need anything. He felt calm and self-possessed and remote, disassociated from everything that went on around him, as if he were looking down on the world through the wrong end of a telescope, feeling only a mild scientific interest as he watched the tiny mannequins swirl and pirouette. . . .

Like watching television with the sound off. If this were the Peace of God, it had settled down on him months ago, during the dead of that terrible winter, while he had struggled twelve hours a day to load foundation-stone in the face of icestorms and the razoring wind, while they had all, wetbacks and brethren alike, come close to starving. About the same time that word of the goings-on at Tylersville had started to seep down from the brethren's parent church upstate, about the same time that Abner, who until then had totally ignored their kinship, had begun to talk to him in the evenings about the old ways. . . .

Although perhaps the great dead cold had started to settle in even earlier, that first day of the new world, while they were driving off across foundering Brigantine, the water already up over the hubcaps of the Toyota, and he had heard Toby barking frantically somewhere behind them. . . . His dad had died that day, died of a heart-attack as he fought to get them onto an overloaded boat that would take them across to the "safety" of the New Jersey mainland. His mother had died months later in one of the sprawling refugee camps, called "Floodtowns," that had sprung up on high ground everywhere along the new coastlines. She had just given up—sat down in the mud, rested her head on her knees, closed her eyes, and died. Just like that. Roy had seen the phenomenon countless times in the Floodtowns, places so festeringly horrible that even life on Abner's farm, with its Dickensian bleakness, forced labor, and short rations, had seemed—and was—a distinct change for the better. It was odd, and wrong, and sometimes it bothered him a little, but he hardly ever thought of his mother and father anymore—it was as if his mind shut itself off every time he came to those memories; he had never even cried for them, but all he had to do was close his eyes and he could see Toby, or his cat, Basil, running toward him and meowing with his tail held up over his back like a flag, and grief would come up like black bile at the back of his throat. . . .

It was still dark when they left the farmhouse. Roy and Abner and Aaron walked together, Abner carrying a large tattered carpetbag. Hank and Raymond ranged ahead with shotguns, in case there was trouble, but the last of the afternoon's gawkers had been driven off hours before by the cold and the road was empty, a dim charcoal line through the slowly lightening darkness. No one spoke, and there was no sound other than the sound of boots crunching on gravel. It was chilly again that morning, and Roy's bare feet burned against the macadam, but he trudged along stoically, ignoring the bite of cinders and pebbles. Their breath steamed faintly against the paling stars. The fields stretched dark and formless around them to either side of the road, and once they heard the rustling of some unseen animal fleeing away from them through the stubble. Mist flowed slowly down the road to meet them, sending out gleaming silver fingers to curl around their legs.

The sky was graying to the east, where the sea slept behind the mountains. Roy could imagine the sea rising higher and higher until it found its patient way around the roots of the hills and came spilling into the tableland beyond, flowing steadily forward like the mist, spreading out into a placid sheet of water that slowly swallowed the town, the farmhouse, the fields, until only the highest branches of the trees remained, held up like the beckoning arms of the drowned, and then they too would slide slowly, peacefully, beneath the water. . . .

A bird was crying out now, somewhere in the darkness, and they were walking through the fields, away from the road, cold mud squelching underfoot, the dry stubble crackling around them. Soon it would be time to sow the spring wheat, and after that, the corn. . . .

They stopped. Wind sighed through the dawn, muttering in the throat of the world. Still no one had spoken. Then hands were helping him remove the old bathrobe he'd been wearing. . . . Before leaving the house, he had been bathed, and annointed with a thick fragrant oil, and with a tiny silver scissors Mrs. Reardon had clipped a lock of his hair for each of the brethren.

Suddenly he was naked, and he was being urged forward again, his feet stumbling and slow.

They had made a wide ring of automobile flares here, the flares spitting and sizzling luridly in the wan dawn light, and in the center of the ring, they had dug a hollow in the ground.

He lay down in the hollow, feeling his naked back and buttocks settle into the cold mud, feeling it mat the hair on the back of his head. The mud made little sucking noises as he moved his arms and legs, settling in, and then he stretched out and lay still. The dawn breeze was cold, and he shivered in the mud, feeling it take hold of him like a giant's hand, tightening around him, pulling him down with a grip old and cold and strong. . . .

They gathered around him, seeming, from his low perspective, to tower miles into the sky. Their faces were harsh and angular, gouged with lines and shadows that made them look like something from a stark old woodcut. Abner bent down to rummage in the carpetbag, his harsh woodcut face close to Roy's for a moment, and when he straightened up again he had the big fine-honed hunting knife in his hand.

Abner began to speak now, groaning out the words in a loud, harsh voice, but Roy was no longer listening. He watched calmly as Abner lifted the knife high into the air, and then he turned his head to look last, as if he could somehow see across all the intervening miles of rock and farmland and forest to where the sea waited behind the mountains. . . .

Is this enough? he thought disjointedly, ignoring the towering scarecrow figures that were swaying in closer over him, straining his eyes to look last, to where the Presence lived . . . speaking now only to that Presence, to the sea, to that vast remorseless deity, bargaining with it cannily, hopefully, shrewdly, like a country housewife at market, proffering it the fine rich red gift of his death. Is this enough? Will this do?

Will you stop now?

THE
SCREWFLY SOLUTION

Raccoona Sheldon

And then, sometimes, if you want to destroy the world, it's good to have a little help. And what's really unnerving, as the classic shocker that follows shows us in unrelenting detail, is how little help the human race really needs in order to destroy itself. Just a tweak. Just the smallest bit of encouragement. Just something to urge us a bit farther down the road we're already on . . .

As most of you probably know, multiple Hugo and Nebula winning author James Tiptree Jr. was actually the pseudonym of the late Dr. Alice Sheldon, a semiretired experimental psychologist and former member of the American Intelligence community who also wrote occasionally under the name of Raccoona Sheldon. Dr. Sheldon's tragic death in 1987 put an end to "both" careers, but not before she had won two Nebula and Hugo Awards as Tiptree, won another Nebula Award as Raccoona Sheldon, and established herself, under whatever name, as one of the very best science fiction writers of our times. As Tiptree, Dr. Sheldon published two novels, Up the Walls of the World *and* Brightness Falls from the Air, *and nine short-story collections:* Ten Thousand Light Years from Home, Warm Worlds and Otherwise, Starsongs of an Old Primate, Out of the Everywhere, Tales of the Quintana Roo, Byte Beautiful, The Starry Rift, *the posthumously published* Crown of Stars, *and the posthumous retrospective collection,* Her Smoke Rose up Forever.

The *young man* sitting at 2° N, 75° W sent a casually venomous glance up at the nonfunctional shoofly *ventilador* and went on reading his letter. He was sweating heavily,

stripped to his shorts in the hot box of what passed for a
hotel room in Cuyapán.

> *How do other wives do it? I stay busy-busy with the Ann
> Arbor grant review programs and the seminar, saying
> brightly, "Oh yes, Alan is in Columbia setting up a
> biological pest control program, isn't it wonderful?" But
> inside I imagine you surrounded by nineteen-year-old
> raven-haired cooing beauties, every one panting with
> social dedication and filthy rich. And forty inches of
> bosom bursting out of her delicate lingerie. I even figured
> it in centimeters, that's 101.6 centimeters of busting. Oh,
> darling, darling, do what you want only come home safe.*

Alan grinned fondly, briefly imagining the only body he longed
for. His girl, his magic Anne. Then he got up to open the window another cautious notch. A long pale mournful face looked
in—a goat. The room opened on the goatpen, the stench was
vile. Air, anyway. He picked up the letter.

> *Everything is just about as you left it, except that the
> Peedsville horror seems to be getting worse. They're
> calling it the Sons of Adam cult now. Why can't they do
> something, even if it is a religion? The Red Cross has set
> up a refugee camp in Ashton, Georgia. Imagine, refugees
> in the U.S.A. I heard two little girls were carried out all
> slashed up. Oh, Alan.*
>
> *Which reminds me, Barney came over with a wad of
> clippings he wants me to send you. I'm putting them in a
> separate envelope; I know what happens to very fat letters
> in foreign POs. He says, in case you don't get them, what
> do the following have in common? Peedsville, São Paulo,
> Phoenix, San Diego, Shanghai, New Delhi, Tripoli, Bris-
> bane, Johannesburg and Lubbock, Texas. He says the hint
> is, remember where the Intertropical Convergence Zone is
> now. That makes no sense to me, maybe it will to your
> superior ecological brain. All I could see about the
> clippings was that they were fairly horrible accounts of
> murders or massacres of women. The worst was the New
> Delhi one, about "rafts of female corpses" in the river.
> The funniest (!) was the Texas Army officer who shot his*

*wife, three daughters and his aunt, because God told him
to clean the place up.*

*Barney's such an old dear, he's coming over Sunday to
help me take off the downspout and see what's blocking it.
He's dancing on air right now, since you left his spruce
budworm-moth antipheromone program finally paid off.
You know he tested over 2,000 compounds? Well, it seems
that good old 2,097 really works. When I asked him what
it does he just giggled, you know how shy he is with
women. Anyway, it seems that a one-shot spray program
will save the forests without harming a single other thing.
Birds and people can eat it all day, he says.*

*Well sweetheart, that's all the news except Amy goes
back to Chicago to school Sunday. The place will be a
tomb, I'll miss her frightfully in spite of her being at the
stage where I'm her worst enemy. The sullen sexy sub-
teens, Angie says. Amy sends love to her Daddy. I send you
my whole heart, all that words can't say.*

Your Anne

Alan put the letter safely in his notefile and glanced over the
rest of the thin packet of mail, refusing to let himself dream of
home and Anne. Barney's "fat envelope" wasn't there. He
threw himself on the rumpled bed, yanking off the lightcord a
minute before the town generator went off for the night. In the
darkness the list of places Barney had mentioned spread themselves around a misty globe that turned, troublingly, briefly in
his mind. Something . . .

But then the memory of the hideously parasitized children he
had worked with at the clinic that day took possession of his
thoughts. He set himself to considering the data he must
collect. *Look for the vulnerable link in the behavioral chain—*
inside his skull. Where was it, where? In the morning he would
start work on bigger canefly cages. . . .

At that moment, five thousand miles north, Anne was writing:

*Oh, darling, darling, your first three letters are here, they
all came together. I knew you were writing. Forget what
I said about swarthy heiresses, that was all a joke. My
darling I know, I know . . . us. Those dreadful canefly*

*larvae, those poor little kids. If you weren't my husband
I'd think you were a saint or something. (I do anyway.)*

*I have your letters pinned up all over the house, makes
it a lot less lonely. No real news here except things feel
kind of quiet and spooky. Barney and I got the downspout
out, it was full of a big rotted hoard of squirrel nuts. They
must have been dropping them down the top. I'll put a
wire over it. (Don't worry, I'll use a ladder this time.)*

*Barney's in an odd, grim mood. He's taking this Sons of
Adam thing very seriously, it seems he's going to be on the
investigation committee if that ever gets off the ground.
The weird part is that nobody seems to be doing anything,
as if it's just too big. Selina Peters has been printing some
acid comments, like When one man kills his wife you call
it murder, but when enough do it we call it a lifestyle. I
think it's spreading, but nobody knows because the media
have been asked to downplay it. Barney says it's being
viewed as a form of contagious hysteria. He insisted I
send you this ghastly interview. It's not going to be
published, of course. The quietness is worse, though, it's
like something terrible was going on just out of sight. After
reading Barney's thing I called up Pauline in San Diego
to make sure she was all right. She sounded funny, as if
she wasn't saying everything . . . my own sister. Just
after she said things were great she suddenly asked if she
could come and stay here a while next month. I said come
right away, but she wants to sell her house first. I wish
she'd hurry.*

*Oh, the diesel car is okay now, it just needed its filter
changed. I had to go out to Springfield to get one but
Eddie installed it for only $2.50. He's going to bankrupt
his garage.*

*In case you didn't guess, those places of Barney's are
all about latitude 30° N or S—the horse latitudes. When
I said not exactly, he said remember the equatorial
convergence zone shifts in winter, and to add to Libya,
Osaka, and a place I forget—wait, Alice Springs, Austra-
lia. What has this to do with anything, I asked. He said,
"Nothing—I hope." I leave it to you, great brains like
Barney can be weird.*

My dearest, here's all of me to all of you. Your letters

*make life possible. But don't feel you have to, I can tell
how tired you must be. Just know we're together, always
everywhere.*

Your Anne

*PS I had to open this to put Barney's thing in, it wasn't the
secret police. Here it is. All love again. A.*

In the goat-infested room where Alan read this, rain was
drumming on the roof. He put the letter to his nose to catch the
faint perfume once more, and folded it away. Then he pulled
out the yellow flimsy Barney had sent and began to read,
frowning.

PEEDSVILLE CULT/SONS OF ADAM SPECIAL. Statement by driver
Sgt. Willard Mews, Globe Fork, Ark. We hit the roadblock
about 80 miles west of Jacksonville. Major John Heinz of
Ashton was expecting us, he gave us an escort of two riot
vehicles headed by Capt. T Parr. Major Heinz appeared
shocked to see that the NIH medical team included two
women doctors. He warned us in the strongest terms of the
danger. So Dr. Patsy Putnam (Urbana, Ill.), the psychologist, decided to stay behind at the Army cordon. But Dr.
Elaine Fay (Clinton, N.J.) insisted on going with us,
saying she was the epi-something (epidemiologist).

We drove behind one of the riot cars at 30 mph for
about an hour without seeing anything unusual. There
were two big signs saying "SONS OF ADAM—LIBERATED
ZONE." We passed some small pecan packing plants and a
citrus processing plant. The men there looked at us but did
not do anything unusual, I didn't see any children or
women of course. Just outside Peedsville we stopped at a
big barrier made of oil drums in front of a large citrus
warehouse. This area is old, sort of a shantytown and
trailer park. The new part of town with the shopping
center and developments is about a mile further on. A
warehouse worker with a shotgun came out and told us to
wait for the Mayor. I don't think he saw Dr. Elaine Fay
then, she was sitting sort of bent down in back.

Mayor Blount drove up in a police cruiser and our
chief, Dr. Premack, explained our mission from the

Surgeon General. Dr. Premack was very careful not to make any remarks insulting to the Mayor's religion. Mayor Blount agreed to let the party go on into Peedsville to take samples of the soil and water and so on and talk to the doctor who lives there. The Mayor was about 6'2", weight maybe 230 or 240, tanned, with grayish hair. He was smiling and chuckling in a friendly manner.

Then he looked inside the car and saw Dr. Elaine Fay and he blew up. He started yelling we had to all get the hell back. But Dr. Premack talked to him and cooled him down and finally the Mayor said Dr. Fay should go into the warehouse office and stay there with the door closed. I had to stay there too and see she didn't come out, and one of the Mayor's men would drive the party.

So the medical people and the Mayor and one of the riot vehicles went on into Peedsville and I took Dr. Fay back into the warehouse office and sat down. It was real hot and stuffy. Dr. Fay opened a window, but when I heard her trying to talk to an old man outside I told her she couldn't do that and closed the window. The old man went away. Then she wanted to talk to me but I told her I did not feel like conversing. I felt it was real wrong, her being there.

So then she started looking through the office files and reading papers there. I told her that was a bad idea, she shouldn't do that. She said the government expected her to investigate. She showed me a booklet or magazine they had there, it was called *Man Listens to God* by Reverend McIllhenny. They had a carton full in the office. I started reading it and Dr. Fay said she wanted to wash her hands. So I took her back along a kind of enclosed hallway beside the conveyor to where the toilet was. There were no doors or windows so I went back. After a while she called out that there was a cot back there, she was going to lie down. I figured that was all right because of the no windows, also I was glad to be rid of her company.

When I got to reading the book it was very intriguing. It was very deep thinking about how man is now on trial with God and if we fulfill our duty God will bless us with a real new life on Earth. The signs and portents show it. It wasn't like, you know, Sunday school stuff. It was deep.

After a while I heard some music and saw the soldiers

from the other riot car were across the street by the gas tanks, sitting in the shade of some trees and kidding with the workers from the plant. One of them was playing a guitar, not electric, just plain. It looked so peaceful.

Then Mayor Blount drove up alone in the cruiser and came in. When he saw I was reading the book he smiled at me sort of fatherly, but he looked tense. He asked me where Dr. Fay was and I told him she was lying down in back. He said that was okay. Then he kind of sighed and went back down the hall, closing the door behind him. I sat and listened to the guitar man, trying to hear what he was singing. I felt really hungry, my lunch was in Dr. Premack's car.

After a while the door opened and Mayor Blount came back in. He looked terrible, his clothes were messed up and he had bloody scrape marks on his face. He didn't say anything, he just looked at me hard and fierce, like he might have been disoriented. I saw his zipper was open and there was blood on his clothing and also on his (private parts).

I didn't feel frightened. I felt something important had happened. I tried to get him to sit down. But he motioned me to follow him back down the hall, to where Dr. Fay was. "You must see," he said. He went into the toilet and I went into a kind of little room there, where the cot was. The light was fairly good, reflected off the tin roof from where the walls stopped. I saw Dr. Fay lying on the cot in a peaceful appearance. She was lying straight, her clothing was to some extent different but her legs were together. I was glad to see that. Her blouse was pulled up and I saw there was a cut or incision on her abdomen. The blood was coming out there, or it had been coming out there, like a mouth. It wasn't moving at this time. Also her throat was cut open.

I returned to the office. Mayor Blount was sitting down, looking very tired. He had cleaned himself off. He said, "I did it for you. Do you understand?"

He seemed like my father, I can't say it better than that. I realized he was under a terrible strain, he had taken a lot on himself for me. He went on to explain how Dr. Fay was very dangerous. She was what they called a cripto-female (crypto?), the most dangerous kind. He had exposed her and purified the situation. He was very straightforward, I didn't feel confused at all. I knew he had done what was right.

We discussed the book, how man must purify himself and show God a clean world. He said some people raise the question of how can man reproduce without women but such people miss the point. The point is that as long as man depends on the old filthy animal way God won't help him. When man gets rid of his animal part, which is woman, this is the signal God is waiting. Then God will reveal the new true clean way, maybe angels will come bringing new souls, or maybe we will live forever, but it is not our place to speculate, only to obey. He said some men here had seen an Angel of the Lord. This was very deep, it seemed like it echoed inside me, I felt it was an inspiration.

Then the medical party drove up and I told Dr. Premack that Dr. Fay had been taken care of and sent away, and I got in the car to drive them out of the Liberated Zone. However four of the six soldiers from the roadblock refused to leave. Capt. Parr tried to argue them out of it but finally agreed they could stay to guard the oil-drum barrier.

I would have liked to stay too, the place was so peaceful, but they needed me to drive the car. If I had known there would be all this hassle I never would have done them the favor. I am not crazy and I have not done anything wrong and my lawyer will get me out. That is all I have to say.

In Cuyapán the hot afternoon rain had temporarily ceased. As Alan's fingers let go of Sgt. Willard Mews's wretched document he caught sight of pencil-scrawled words in the margin. Barney's spider hand. He squinted.

Man's religion and metaphysics are the voices of his glands. Schönweiser, 1878.

Who the devil Schönweiser was Alan didn't know, but he knew what Barney was conveying. This murderous crackpot religion of McWhosis was a symptom, not a cause. Barney believed something was physically affecting the Peedsville men, generating psychosis, and a local religious demagogue had sprung up to "explain" it.

Well, maybe. But cause or effect, Alan thought only of one thing: eight hundred miles from Peedsville to Ann Arzor. Anne should be safe. She *had* to be.

He threw himself on the lumpy cot, his mind going back exultantly to his work. At the cost of a million bites and cane-cuts he was pretty sure he'd found the weak link in the canefly cycle. The male mass-mating behavior, the comparative scarcity of ovulant females. It would be the screwfly solution all over again with the sexes reversed. Concentrate the pheromone, release sterilized females. Luckily the breeding populations were comparatively isolated. In a couple of seasons they ought to have it. Have to let them go on spraying poison meanwhile, of course; damn pity, it was slaughtering everything and getting in the water, and the caneflies had evolved to immunity anyway. But in a couple of seasons, maybe three, they could drop the canefly populations below reproductive viability. No more tormented human bodies with those stinking larvae in the nasal passages and brain. . . . He drifted off for a nap, grinning.

Up north, Anne was biting her lip in shame and pain.

Sweetheart, I shouldn't admit it but your wife is scared a bit jittery. Just female nerves or something, nothing to worry about. Everything is normal up here. It's so eerily normal, nothing in the papers, nothing anywhere except what I hear through Barney and Lillian. But Pauline's phone won't answer out in San Diego; the fifth day some strange man yelled at me and banged the phone down. Maybe she's sold her house—but why wouldn't she call?

Lillian's on some kind of Save-the-Women committee, like we were an endangered species, ha-ha—you know Lillian. It seems the Red Cross has started setting up camps. But she says, after the first rush, only a trickle are coming out of what they call "the affected areas." Not many children, either, even little boys. And they have some airphotos around Lubbock showing what look like mass graves. Oh, Alan . . . so far it seems to be mostly spreading west, but something's happening in St. Louis, they're cut off. So many places seem to have just vanished from the news. I had a nightmare that there isn't a woman left alive down there. And nobody's doing anything. They talked about spraying with tranquillizers for a while and then that died out. What could it do? Somebody at the U.N. has proposed a convention on—you won't believe this—femicide. It sounds like a deodorant spray.

Excuse me, honey, I seem to be a little hysterical. George Searles came back from Georgia talking about God's Will—Searles the life-long atheist. Alan, something crazy is happening.

But there aren't any facts. Nothing. The Surgeon General issued a report on the bodies of the Rahway Rip-Breast Team—I guess I didn't tell you about that. Anyway, they could find no pathology. Milton Baines wrote a letter saying in the present state of the art we can't distinguish the brain of a saint from a psychopathic killer, so how could they expect to find what they don't know how to look for?

Well, enough of these jitters. It'll be all over by the time you get back, just history. Everything's fine here, I feel the car's muffler again. And Amy's coming home for the vacation, that'll get my mind off faraway problems.

Oh, something amusing to end with—Angie told me what Barney's enzyme does to the spruce budworm. It seems it blocks the male from turning around after he connects with the female, so he mates with her head instead. Like clockwork with a cog missing. There're going to be some pretty puzzled female spruceworms. Now why couldn't Barney tell me that? He really is such a sweet shy old dear. He's given me some stuff to put in, as usual. I didn't read it.

Now don't worry, my darling, everything's fine.

I love you, I love you so.

Always, all ways your Anne

Two weeks later in Cuyapán when Barney's enclosures slid out of the envelope, Alan didn't read them either. He stuffed them into the pocket of his bush jacket with a shaking hand and started bundling his notes together on the rickety table, with a scrawled note to Sister Dominique on top. The hell with the canefly, the hell with everything except that tremor in his Anne's firm handwriting. The hell with being five thousand miles away from his woman, his child, while some deadly madness raged. He crammed his meager belongings into his duffel. If he hurried he could catch the bus through to Bogotá and maybe make the Miami flight.

He made it, but in Miami he found the planes north jammed. He failed a quick standby; six hours to wait. Time to call Anne. When the call got through some difficulty he was unprepared for the rush of joy and relief that burst along the wires.

"Thank God—I can't believe it—Oh, Alan, my darling, are you really—I can't believe—"

He found he was repeating too, and all mixed up with the canefly data. They were both laughing hysterically when he finally hung up.

Six hours. He settled in a frayed plastic chair opposite Aerolineas Argentinas, his mind half back at the clinic, half on the throngs moving by him. Something was oddly different here, he perceived presently. Where was the decorative fauna he usually enjoyed in Miami, the parade of young girls in crotchtight pastel jeans? The flounces, boots, wild hats and hairdos, and startling expanses of newly-tanned skin, the brilliant fabrics barely confining the bob of breasts and buttocks? Not here—but wait; looking closely, he glimpsed two young faces hidden under unbecoming parkas, their bodies draped in bulky, non-descript skirts. In fact, all down the long vista he could see the same thing: hooded ponchos, heaped-on clothes, and baggy pants, dull colors. A new style? No, he thought not. It seemed to him their movements suggested furtiveness, timidity. And they moved in groups. He watched a lone girl struggle to catch up with others ahead of her, apparently strangers. They accepted her wordlessly.

They're frightened, he thought. Afraid of attracting notice. Even that gray-haired matron in a pantsuit, resolutely leading a flock of kids. was glancing around nervously.

And at the Argentine desk opposite he saw another odd thing: two lines had a big sign over them, *Mujeres*. Women. They were crowded with the shapeless forms and very quiet.

The men seemed to be behaving normally; hurrying, loung-ing, griping, and joking in the lines as they kicked their luggage along. But Alan felt an undercurrent of tension, like an irritant in the air. Outside the line of storefronts behind him a few isolated men seemed to be handing out tracts. An airport attendant spoke to the nearest man; he merely shrugged and moved a few doors down.

To distract himself Alan picked up a *Miami Herald* from the next seat. It was surprisingly thin. The international news occupied him for a while; he had seen none for weeks. It too had a strange, empty quality, even the bad news seemed to have dried up. The African war which had been going on seemed to be over, or went unreported. A trade summit meeting was haggling over grain and steel prices. He found himself at the obituary pages, columns of close-set type dominated by the photo of a defunct ex-senator. Then his eye fell on two announcements at the bottom of the page. One was too flowery for quick comprehension, but the other stated in bold plain type:

THE FORSETTE FUNERAL HOME REGRET-
FULLY ANNOUNCES
IT WILL NO LONGER ACCEPT FEMALE
CADAVERS

Slowly he folded the paper, staring at it numbly. On the back was an item headed *Navigational Hazard Warning*, in the shipping news. Without really taking it in, he read:

AP/NASSAU: The excursion liner *Carib Swallow* reached port under tow today after striking an obstruction in the Gulf Stream, off Cape Hatteras. The obstruction was identified as part of a commercial trawler's seine floated by female corpses. This confirms reports from Florida and the Gulf of the use of such seines, some of them over a mile in length. Similar reports coming from the Pacific coast and as far away as Japan indicate a growing hazard to coastwise shipping.

Alan flung the thing into the trash receptacle and sat rubbing his forehead and eyes. Thank God he had followed his impulse to come home. He felt totally disoriented, as though he had landed by error on another planet. Four and a half hours more to wait. . . . At length he recalled the stuff from Barney he had thrust in his pocket, and pulled it out and smoothed it.

The top item was from the *Ann Arbor News*. Dr. Lillian Dash, together with several hundred other members of her organization, had been arrested for demonstrating without a permit in front of the White House. They had started a fire in a garbage can, which was considered particularly heinous. A number of women's groups had participated, the total struck Alan as more like thousands than hundreds. Extraordinary security precautions were being taken despite the fact that the President was out of town at the time.

The next item had to be Barney's acerbic humor.

UP/VATICAN CITY, 19 JUNE. Pope John IV today intimated that he does not plan to comment officially on the so-called Pauline Purification cults advocating the elimination of women as a means of justifying man to God. A spokesman emphasized that the Church takes no position on these cults but repudiates any doctrine involving a "challenge" to or from God to reveal His further plans for man.

Cardinal Fazzoli, spokesman for the European Pauline movement, reaffirmed his view that the Scriptures define woman as merely a temporary companion and instrument of Man. Women, he states, are nowhere defined as human, but merely as a transitional expedient or state. "The time of transition to full humanity is at hand," he concluded.

The next item was a thin-paper Xerox from a recent issue of *Science*:

SUMMARY REPORT OF THE AD HOC
EMERGENCY COMMITTEE ON FEMICIDE

The recent world-wide though localized outbreaks of femicide appear to represent a recurrence of similar outbreaks by groups or sects which are not uncommon in world history in times of psychic stress. In this case the root cause is undoubtedly the speed of social and technological change augmented by population pressure, and the spread and scope are aggravated by instantaneous world communications, thus exposing more susceptible persons.

It is not viewed as a medical or epidemiological problem; no physical pathology has been found. Rather it is more akin to the various manias which swept Europe in the seventeenth century, e.g., the Dancing Manias; and like them, should run its course and disappear. The chiliastic cults which have sprung up around the affected areas appear to be unrelated, having in common only the idea that a new means of human reproduction will be revealed as a result of the "purifying" elimination of women.

We recommended that (1) inflammatory and sensational reporting be suspended; (2) refugee centers be set up and maintained for women escapees from the focal areas; (3) containment of affected areas by military cordon be continued and enforced; and (4) after a cooling-down period and the subsidence of the mania, qualified mental health teams and appropriate professional personnel go in to undertake rehabilitation.

SUMMARY OF THE MINORITY
REPORT OF THE AD HOC COMMITTEE

The nine members signing this report agree that there is no evidence for epidemiological contagion of femicide in the strict sense. *However*, the geographical relation of the focal areas of outbreak strongly suggests that they cannot be dismissed as purely psychosocial phenomena. The initial outbreaks have occurred around the globe near the 30th parallel, the area of principal atmospheric downflow of upper winds coming from the Intertropical Convergence Zone. An agent or condition in the upper equatorial atmosphere would thus be expected to reach ground level along the 30th parallel, with certain seasonal variations. One principal variation is that the downflow moves north over the East Asian continent during the late winter months, and those areas south of it (Arabia, Western India, parts of North Africa) have in fact been free of outbreaks until recently, when the downflow zone moved south. A similar downflow occurs in he Southern Hemisphere, and outbreaks have been reported along the 30th parallel running through Pretoria, and Alice Springs, Australia. (Information from Argentina is currently unavailable.)

This geographical correlation cannot be dismissed, and it is therefore urged that an intensified search for a physical cause be instituted. It is also urgently recommended that the rate of spread from known focal points be correlated with wind conditions. A watch for similar outbreaks along the secondary down-welling zones at 60° north and south should be kept.

(signed for the minority)
Barnhard Braithwaite

Alan grinned reminiscently at his old friend's name, which seemed to restore normalcy and stability to the world. It looked as if Barney was onto something, too, despite the prevalence of horses' asses. He frowned, puzzling it out.

Then his face slowly changed as he thought how it would be, going home to Anne. In a few short hours his arms would be around her, the tall, secretly beautiful body that had come to obsess him. Theirs had been a late-blooming love. They'd married, he supposed now, out of friendship, even out of friends' pressure. Everyone said they were made for each other, he big and chunky and blond, she willowy brunette; both shy, highly controlled, cerebral types. For the first few years the friendship had held, but sex hadn't been all that much. Conventional necessity. Politely reassuring each other, privately— he could say it now—disappointing.

But then, when Amy was a toddler, something had happened. A miraculous inner portal of sensuality had slowly opened to them, a liberation into their own secret unsuspected heaven of fully physical bliss . . . Jesus, but it had been a wrench when the Columbia thing had come up. Only their absolute sureness of each other had made him take it. And now, to be about to have her again, trebly desirable from the spice of separation— feeling-seeing-hearing-smelling-grasping. He shifted in his seat to conceal his body's excitement, half mesmerized by fantasy.

And Amy would be there, too; he grinned at the memory of that prepubescent little body plastered against him. She was going to be a handful, all right. His manhood understood Amy a lot better than her mother did; no cerebral phase for Amy. . . . But Anne, his exquisite shy one, with whom he'd found the way into the almost unendurable transports of the flesh. . . . First the conventional greeting, he thought; the news, the unspoken, savored, mounting excitement behind their eyes; the light touches; then the seeking of their own room, the falling clothes, the caresses, gentle at first—the flesh, the *nakedness*—the delicate teasing, the grasp, the first thrust—

A terrible alarm bell went off in his head. Exploded from his dream, he started around, then finally down at his hands. *What was he doing with his open clasp-knife in his fist?*

Stunned, he felt for the last shreds of his fantasy and realized that the tactile images had not been of caresses, but of a frail neck strangling in his fist, the thrust had been the plunge of a blade seeking vitals. In his arms, legs, phantasms of striking and trampling, bones cracking. And Amy—

Oh God, Oh God—

Not sex, bloodlust.

That was what he had been dreaming. The sex was there, but it was driving some engine of death.

Numbly he put the knife away, thinking over and over, it's got me. It's got me. Whatever it is, it's got me. *I can't go home.*

After an unknown time he got up and made his way to the United counter to turn in his ticket. The line was long. As he waited, his mind cleared a little. What could he do, here in Miami? Wouldn't it be better to get back to Ann Arbor and turn himself in to Barney? Barney could help him, if anyone could. Yes, that was best. But first he had to warn Anne.

The connection took even longer this time. When Anne finally answered he found himself blurting unintelligibly, it took a while to make her understand he wasn't talking about a plane delay.

"I tell you, I've caught it. Listen, Anne, for God's sake. If I should come to the house don't let me come near you. I mean it. I'm going to the lab, but I might lose control and try to get to you. Is Barney there?"

"Yes, but darling—"

"Listen. Maybe he can fix me, maybe this'll wear off. But I'm not safe, Anne. Anne, I'd kill you, can you understand? Get a—get a weapon. I'll try not to come to the house. But if I do, don't let me get near you. Or Amy. It's a sickness, it's real. Treat me—treat me like a fucking wild animal. Anne, say you understand, say you'll do it."

They were both crying when he hung up.

He went shaking back to sit and wait. After a time his head seemed to clear a little more. *Doctor, try to think.* The first thing he thought of was to take the loathsome knife and throw it down a trash slot. As he did so he realized there was one more piece of Barney's material in his pocket. He uncrumpled it; it seemed to be a clipping from *Nature*.

At the top was Barney's scrawl: *Only guy making sense. U.K. infected now, Oslo, Copenhagen out of communication. Damfools still won't listen. Stay put.*

COMMUNICATION FROM
PROFESSOR IAN MACINTYRE, GLASGOW UNIV.

A potential difficulty for our species has always been implicit in the close linkage between the behavioural expression of aggression/prediction and sexual reproduction in the male. This close linkage involves (a) many neuromuscular pathways which are utilized both in predatory and sexual pursuit: grasping, mounting, etc., and (b) similar states of adrenergic arousal which are activated in both. The same linkage is seen in the males of many other species; in some, the expression of aggression and copulation alternate or even coexist, an all-too-familiar example being the common house cat. Males of many species bite, claw, bruise, tread, or otherwise assault receptive females during the act of intercourse; indeed, in some species the male attack is necessary for female ovulation to occur.

In many if not all species it is the aggressive behaviour which appears first, and then changes to copulatory behaviour when the appropriate signal is presented (e.g., the three-tined stickleback and the European robin). Lacking the inhibiting signal, the male's fighting response continues and the female is attacked or driven off.

It seems therefore appropriate to speculate that the present crisis might be caused by some substance, perhaps at the viral or enzymatic level, which effects a failure of the switching or triggering function in the higher primates. (Note: Zoo gorillas and chimpanzees have recently been observed to attack or destroy their mates; rhesus not.)

Such a dysfunction could be expressed by the failure of mating behaviour to modify or supervene over the aggressive/predatory response; i.e., sexual stimulation would produce attack only, the stimulation discharging itself through the destruction of the stimulating object.

In this connection it might be noted that exactly this condition is a commonplace of male functional pathology in those cases where murder occurs as a response to, and apparent completion of, sexual desire.

It should be emphasized that the aggression/copulation linkage discussed here is specific to the male; the female response (e.g., lordotic reflex) being of a different nature.

Alan sat holding the crumpled sheet a long time; the dry, stilted Scottish phrases seemed to help clear his head, despite the sense of brooding tension all around him. Well, if pollution or whatever had produced some substance, it could presumably be countered, filtered, neutralized. Very, very carefully, he let himself consider his life with Anne, his sexuality. Yes; much of their loveplay could be viewed as genitalized, sexually-gentled savagery. Play-predation. . . . He turned his mind quickly away. Some writer's phrase occurred to him: "The panic element in all sex." Who? Fritz Leiber? The violation of social distance, maybe; another threatening element. Whatever, it's our weak link, he thought. Our vulnerability . . . The dreadful feeling of *rightness* he had experienced when he found himself knife in hand, fantasizing violence, came back to him. As though it was the right, the only way. Was that what Barney's budworms felt when they mated with their females wrong-end-to?

At long length, he became aware of body need and sought a toilet. The place was empty, except for what he took to be a heap of clothes blocking the door of the far stall. Then he saw the red-brown pool in which it lay, and the bluish mounds of bare, thin buttocks. He backed out, not breathing, and fled into the nearest crowd, knowing he was not the first to have done so.

Of course. Any sexual drive. Boys, men, too.

At the next washroom he watched to see men enter and leave normally before he ventured in.

Afterward he returned to sit, waiting, repeating over to

himself; *Go to the lab. Don't go home. Go straight to the lab.*
Three more hours; he sat numbly at 26° N, 81° W, breathing,
breathing. . . .

Dear diary. Big scene tonite, Daddy came home!!! Only
he acted so funny, he had the taxi wait and just held onto
the doorway, he wouldn't touch me or let us come near
him. (I mean funny weird, not funny ha-ha). He said, I
have something to tell you, this is getting worse not better.
I'm going to sleep in the lab but I want you to get out,
Anne, Anne, I can't trust myself any more. First thing in
the morning you both get on the plane for Martha's and
stay there. So I thought he had to be joking, I mean with
the dance next week and Aunt Martha lives in Whitehorse
where there's nothing nothing nothing. So I was yelling
and Mother was yelling and Daddy was groaning. Go
now! And then he started crying. Crying!! So I realized,
wow, this is serious, and I started to go over to him but
Mother yanked me back and then I saw she had this big
KNIFE!! And she shoved me in back of her and started
crying too Oh Alan, Oh Alan, like she was insane. So I
said, Daddy, I'll never leave you, it felt like the perfect
thing to say. And it was thrilling, he looked at me real sad
and deep like I was a grown-up while Mother was treating
me like I was a mere infant as usual. But Mother ruined it,
raving Alan the child is mad, darling go. So he ran out the
door yelling Be gone, Take the car, Get out before I come
back.

Oh I forgot to say I was wearing what but my gooby
green with my curltites still on, wouldn't you know of all
the shitty luck, how could I have known such a beautiful
scene was ahead we never know life's cruel whimsy. And
mother is dragging out suitcases yelling Pack your things
hurry! So she's going I guess but I am not repeat not going
to spend the fall sitting in Aunt Martha's grain silo and
lose the dance and all my summer credits. And Daddy was
trying to communicate with us, right? I think their
relationship is obsolete. So when she goes upstairs I am
splitting, I am going to go over to the lab and see Daddy.

Oh PS Diane tore my yellow jeans she promised me I
could use her pink ones Ha-ha that'll be the day.

•   •   •

I ripped that page out of Amy's diary when I heard the squad car coming. I never opened her diary but when I found she'd gone I looked. . . . Oh, my darling girl. She went to him, my little girl, my poor little fool child. Maybe if I'd taken time to explain, maybe—

Excuse me, Barney. The stuff is wearing off, the shots they gave me. I didn't feel anything. I mean, I knew somebody's daughter went to see her father and he killed her. And cut his throat. But it didn't mean anything.

Alan's note, they gave me that but then they took it away. Why did they have to do that? His last handwriting, the last words he wrote before his hand picked up the, before he—

I remember it. "*Sudden and light as that, the bonds gave/And we learned of finalities besides the grave.* The bonds of our humanity have broken, we are finished. I love—"

I'm all right, Barney, really. Who wrote that, Robert Frost? *The bonds gave.* . . . Oh, he said tell Barney: *The terrible rightness.* What does that mean?

You can't answer that, Barney dear. I'm just writing this to stay sane, I'll put it in your hidey-hole. Thank you, thank you, Barney dear. Even as blurry as I was, I knew it was you. All the time you were cutting off my hair and rubbing dirt on my face, I knew it was right because it was you. Barney, I never thought of you as those horrible words you said. You were always Dear Barney.

By the time the stuff wore off I had done everything you said, the gas, the groceries. Now I'm here in your cabin. With those clothes you made me put on I guess I do look like a boy, the gas man called me "Mister."

I still can't really realize, I have to stop myself from rushing back. But you saved my life, I know that. The first trip in I got a paper, I saw where they bombed the Apostle Islands refuge. And it had about those three women stealing the Air Force plane and bombing Dallas, too. Of course, they shot them down, over the Gulf. Isn't it strange how we do nothing? Just get killed by ones and twos. Or more, now they've started on the refugees. . . . Like hypnotized rabbits. We're a toothless race.

Do you know I never said, "we" meaning women before? "We" was always me and Alan, and Amy of course. Being killed selectively encourages group identification. . . . You see how sane-headed I am.

But I still can't really realize.

My first trip in was for salt and kerosine. I went to that little Red Deer store and got my stuff from the old man in the back, as you told me—you see, I remembered! He called me "Boy," but I think maybe he suspects. He knows I'm staying at your cabin.

Anyway, some men and boys came in the front. They were all so *normal*, laughing and kidding. I just couldn't believe, Barney. In fact I started to go out past them when I heard one of them say, "Heinz saw an angel." An *angel*. So I stopped and listened. They said it was big and sparkly. Coming to see if man is carrying out God's Will, one of them said. And he said, Moosonee is now a liberated zone, and all up by Hudson Bay. I turned and got out the back, fast. The old man had heard them too. He said to me quietly, "I'll miss the kids."

Hudson Bay, Barney, that means it's coming from the north too, doesn't it? That must be about 60°.

But I have to go back once again, to get some fishhooks. I can't live on bread. Last week I found a deer some poacher had killed, just the head and legs. I made a stew. It was a doe. Her eyes; I wonder if mine look like that now.

I went to get the fishhooks today. It was bad, I can't ever go back. There were some men in front again, but they were different. Mean and tense. No boys. And there was a new sign out in front. I couldn't see it; maybe it says Liberated Zone too.

The old man gave me the hooks quick and whispered to me, "Boy, them woods'll be full of hunters next week." I almost ran out.

About a mile down the road a blue pickup started to chase me. I guess he wasn't from around there. I ran the VW into a logging draw and he roared on by. After a long while I drove out and came on back, but I left the car about a mile from here and hiked in. It's surprising how hard it is to pile enough brush to hide a yellow VW.

Barney, I can't stay here. I'm eating perch raw so nobody will see my smoke, but those hunters will be coming through. I'm going to move my sleeping bag out to the swamp by that big rock. I don't think many people go there.

•   •   •

Since the last lines I moved out. It feels safer. Oh, Barney, how did this *happen*?

Fast, that's how. Six months ago I was Dr. Anne Alstein. Now I'm a widow and bereaved mother, dirty and hungry, squatting in a swamp in mortal fear. Funny if I'm the last woman left alive on Earth. I guess the last one around here, anyway. May be some holed out in the Himalayas, or sneaking through the wreck of New York City. How can we last?

We can't.

And I can't survive the winter here, Barney. It gets to 40° below. I'd have to have a fire, they'd see the smoke. Even if I worked my way south, the woods end in a couple hundred miles. I'd be potted like a duck. No. No use. Maybe somebody is trying something somewhere, but it won't reach here in time . . . and what do I have to live for?

No. I'll just make a good end, say up on that rock where I can see the stars. After I go back and leave this for you. I'll wait to see the beautiful color in the trees one last time.

Goodbye, dearest dearest Barney.

I know what I'll scratch for an epitaph.

HERE LIES THE SECOND MEANEST
PRIMATE ON EARTH.

I guess nobody will ever read this, unless I get the nerve to take it back to Barney's. Probably I won't. Leave it in a Baggie, I have one here; maybe Barney will come and look. I'm up on the big rock now. The moon is going to rise soon, I'll do it then. Mosquitoes, be patient. You'll have all you want.

The thing I have to write down is that I saw an angel too. This morning. It was big and sparkly, like the man said; like a Christmas tree without the tree. But I knew it was real because the frogs stopped croaking and two bluejays gave alarm calls. That's important; it was *really there*.

I watched it, sitting under my rock. It didn't move much. It sort of bent over and picked up something, leaves or twigs, I couldn't see. Then it did something with them around its middle, like putting them into an invisible sample pocket.

Let me repeat—it was *there*. Barney, if you're reading this,

THERE ARE THINGS HERE. And I think they've done whatever it is to us. Made us kill ourselves off.

Why? Well, it's a nice place, if it wasn't for people. How do you get rid of people? Bombs, death-rays—all very primitive. Leave a big mess. Destroy everything, craters, radioactivity, ruin the place.

This way there's no muss, no fuss. Just like what we did for the screwfly. Pinpoint the weak link, wait a bit while we do it for them. Only a few bones around; make good fertilizer.

Barney dear, goodbye. I saw it. It was there.

But it wasn't an angel.

I think I saw a real-estate agent.

A PAIL OF AIR

Fritz Leiber

But the universe doesn't need us to destroy the world!
(It doesn't even need hostile, meddling aliens.)

Until now, we've been examining scenarios where humanity is responsible for its own destruction, either inadvertently or through a deliberate act of war or global terrorism—but even if humanity were behaving itself in a totally blameless way, even if we'd achieved the war-free, pollution-free, hatred-free one-world Utopia of the most optimistic science fiction, even if we were as blissfully innocent of sin and responsibility as the dinosaurs, the world could still be destroyed in an eyeblink by the blank, blind, grinding, mindless, uncaring, remorseless forces of Nature—as vividly demonstrated by the five stories that follow, which offer us a smorgasbord of cosmic catastrophes, any one of which could obliterate the human race (and perhaps all life on Earth) at any time, in a heartbeat, perhaps before you can turn the next page . . .

First up is Fritz Leiber, one of the giants of the field, to demonstrate that air is a commonplace commodity that everyone takes for granted and nobody thinks twice about—until you don't have *any.*

With a fifty-year career that stretched from the "Golden Age" Astounding of the '40s to the beginning of the '90s, the late Fritz Leiber was an indispensable figure in the development of modern science fiction, fantasy, and horror. It is impossible to imagine what those genres would be like today without him, except to say that they would be the poorer for it. Probably no other figure of his generation (with the possible exception of L. Sprague de Camp) wrote in as many different genres as Leiber, or was as important as he was to the development of each. Leiber can be considered to be one of the fathers of modern "heroic fantasy," and his long sequence of stories about Fafhrd and the Gray Mouser remains one of the most complex and intelligent bodies of work in the entire subgenre of "Sword & Sorcery" (which term Leiber himself is usually credited with coining). He may also be one of the best—if not the best—writers of the super- natural horror tale since Lovecraft and Poe, and was writing updated "modern" or "urban" horror stories like "Smoke Ghost" and the classic Conjure Wife *long before the work of Stephen King engendered the big horror boom of the middle '70s and brought that form to wide popular attention.*

Leiber was also a towering Ancestral Figure in science fiction as well, having been one of the major writers of both Campbell's "Golden Age" Astounding *of the '40s—with works like* Gather, Darkness—*and H. L. Gold's* Galaxy *in the '50s—with works like the classic "Coming Attraction" and the superb novel* The Big Time, *which still holds up as one of the best SF novels ever written—and then going on to contribute a steady stream of superior fiction to the maga- zines and anthologies of the '60s, the '70s, and '80s, as well as powerful novels such as* The Wanderer *and* Our Lady of Darkness. The Big Time *won a well-deserved Hugo in 1959, and Leiber also won a slew of other awards: all told, six Hugos and four Nebulas, plus three World Fantasy Awards— one of them the prestigious Life Achievement Award—and a Grandmaster of Fantasy Award.*

Fritz Leiber's other books include The Green Millennium, A Spectre Is Haunting Texas, The Big Engine, *and* The Silver Eggheads, *the collections* The Best of Fritz Leiber, The Book of Fritz Leiber, The Change War, Night's Dark Agents, Heroes and Horrors, The Mind Spider, *and* The Ghost Light, *and the seven volumes of Fafhrd–Gray Mouser stories, now being reissued in massive omnibus trade-paperback editions; the most recent such volume is* Return to Lankhmar.

Pa had sent me out to get an extra pail of air. I'd just about scooped it full and most of the warmth had leaked from my fingers when I saw the thing.

You know, at first I thought it was a young lady. Yes, a beautiful young lady's face all glowing in the dark and looking at me from the fifth floor of the opposite apartment, which hereabouts is the floor just above the white blanket of frozen air four storeys thick. I'd never seen a live young lady before, except in the old magazines—Sis is just a kid and Ma is pretty sick and miserable—and it gave me such a start that I dropped the pail. Who wouldn't, knowing everyone on Earth was dead except Pa and Ma and Sis and you?

Even at that, I don't suppose I should have been surprised. We all see things now and then. Ma sees some pretty bad ones, to judge from the way she bugs her eyes at nothing and just screams and screams and huddles back against the blankets hanging around the Nest. Pa says it is natural we should react like that sometimes.

When I'd recovered the pail and could look again at the opposite apartment, I got an idea of what Ma might be feeling at those times, for I saw it wasn't a young lady at all but simply a light—a tiny light that moved stealthily from window to window, just as if one of the cruel little stars had come down out of the airless sky to investigate why the Earth had gone away from the Sun, and maybe to hunt down something to torment or terrify, now that the Earth didn't have the Sun's protection.

I tell you, the thought of it gave me the creeps. I just stood there shaking, and almost froze my feet and did frost my helmet so solid on the inside that I couldn't have seen the light even if it had come out of one of the windows to get me. Then I had the wit to go back inside.

Pretty soon I was feeling my familiar way through the thirty or so blankets and rugs and rubbery sheets Pa has got hung and braced around to slow down the escape of air from the Nest, and I wasn't quite so scared. I began to hear the tick-ticking of the clouds in the Nest and knew I was getting back into air, because there's no sound outside in the vacuum, of course. But my mind was still crawly and uneasy as I pushed through the last blankets—Pa's got them faced with aluminum foil to hold in the heat—and came into the Nest.

Let me tell you about the Nest. It's low and snug, just room for the four of us and our things. The floor is covered with thick woolly rugs. Three of the sides are blankets, and the blankets roofing it touch Pa's head. He tells me it's inside a much bigger room, but I've never seen the real walls or ceiling.

Against one of the blanket-walls is a big set of shelves, with tools and books and other stuff, and on top of it a whole row of clocks. Pa's very fussy about keeping them wound. He says we must never forget time, and without a sun or moon, that would be easy to do.

The fourth wall has blankets all over except around the fireplace, in which there is a fire that must never go out. It keeps us from freezing and does a lot more besides. One of us must always watch it. Some of the clocks are alarm and we can use them to remind us. In the early days there was only Ma to take turns with Pa—I think of that when she gets difficult—but now there's me to help, and Sis too.

It's Pa who is the chief guardian of the fire, though. I always think of him that way: a tall man sitting cross-legged, frowning anxiously at the fire, his lined face golden in its light, and every so often carefully placing on it a piece of coal from the big heap beside it. Pa tells me there used to be guardians of the fire sometimes in the very old days—vestals, he calls them—although there was unfrozen air all around then and a sun too and you didn't really need a fire.

He was sitting just that way now, though he got up quick to take the pail from me and bawl me out for loitering—he'd spotted my frozen helmet right off. That roused Ma and she joined in picking on me. She's always trying to get the load off her feelings, Pa explains. He shut her up pretty fast. Sis let off a couple of silly squeals too.

Pa handled the pail of air in a twist of cloth. Now that it was inside the Nest, you could really feel its coldness. It just seemed to suck the heat out of everything. Even the flames cringed away from it as Pa put it down close by the fire.

Yet it's that glimmery blue-white stuff in the pail that keeps us alive. It slowly melts and vanishes and refreshes the Nest and feeds the fire. The blankets keep it from escaping too fast. Pa'd like to seal the whole place, but he can't—building's too earthquake-twisted, and besides he has to leave the chimney open for smoke. But the chimney has special things Pa calls baffles up inside it, to keep the air from getting out too quick that way. Sometimes Pa, making a joke, says it baffles him they keep on working, or work at all.

Pa says air is tiny molecules that fly away like a flash if there isn't something to stop them. We have to watch sharp not to let the air run low. Pa always keeps a big reserve supply of it in buckets behind the first blankets, along with extra coal and cans of food and bottles of vitamins and other things, such as pails of snow to melt for water. We have to go way down to the bottom floor for that stuff, which is a mean trip, and get it through a door to outside.

You see, when the Earth got cold, all the water in the air froze first and made a blanket ten feet thick or so everywhere, and then down on top of that dropped the crystals of frozen air, making another mostly white blanket sixty or seventy feet thick maybe.

Of course, all the parts of the air didn't freeze and snow down at the same time.

First to drop out was the carbon dioxide—when you're shoveling for water, you have to make sure you don't go too high and get any of that stuff mixed in, for it would put you to sleep, maybe for good, and make the fire go out. Next there's the nitrogen, which doesn't count one way or the other, though it's the biggest part of the blanket. On top of that and easy to get at, which is lucky for us, there's the oxygen that keeps us alive. It's pale blue, which helps you tell it from the nitrogen. It has to be colder for oxygen to freeze solid than nitrogen. That's why the oxygen snowed down last.

Pa says we live better than kings ever did, breathing pure oxygen, but we're used to it and don't notice.

Finally, at the very top, there's a slick of liquid helium, which is funny stuff.

All of these gases are in neat separate layers. Like a pussy caffay, Pa laughingly says, whatever that is.

I was busting to tell them all about what I'd seen, and so as soon as I'd ducked out of my helmet and while I was still climbing out of my suit, I cut loose. Right away Ma got nervous and began making eyes at the entry-slit in the blankets and wringing her hands together—the hand where she'd lost three fingers from frostbite inside the good one, as usual. I could tell that Pa was annoyed at me scaring her and wanted to explain it all away quickly, yet I knew he knew I wasn't fooling.

"And you watched this light for some time, son?" he asked when I finished.

I hadn't said anything about first thinking it was a young lady's face. Somehow that part embarrassed me.

"Long enough for it to pass five windows and go to the next floor."

"And it didn't look like stray electricity or crawling liquid or starlight focused by a growing crystal, or anything like that?"

He wasn't just making up those ideas. Odd things happen in a world that's about as cold as can be, and just when you think matter would be frozen dead, it takes on a strange new life. A slimy stuff comes crawling toward the Nest, just like an animal snuffing for heat—that's the liquid helium. And once, when I was little, a bolt of lightning—not even Pa could figure where it came from—hit the nearby steeple and crawled up and down it for weeks, until the glow finally died.

"Not like anything I ever saw," I told him.

He stood for a moment frowning. Then, "I'll go out with you, and you show it to me," he said.

Ma raised a howl at the idea of being left alone, and Sis joined in, too, but Pa quieted them. We started climbing into our outside clothes—mine had been warming by the fire. Pa made them. They have triple-pane plastic headpieces that were once big double-duty transparent food cans, but they keep heat and air in and can replace the air for a little while, long enough for our trips for water and coal and food and so on.

Ma started moaning again, "I've always known there was something outside there, waiting to get us. I've felt it for years—something that's part of the cold and hates all warmth and wants to destroy the Nest. It's been watching us all this time, and now it's coming after us. It'll get you and then come for me. Don't go, Harry!"

Pa had everything on but his helmet. He knelt by the fireplace and reached in and shook the long metal rod that goes up the chimney and knocks off the ice that keeps trying to clog it. Once a week he goes up on the roof to check if it's working all right. That's our worst trip and Pa won't let me make it alone.

"Sis," Pa said quietly, "come watch the fire. Keep an eye on the air, too. If it gets low or doesn't seem to be boiling fast enough, fetch another bucket from behind the blanket. But mind your hands. Use the cloth to pick up the bucket."

Sis quit helping Ma be frightened and came over and did as she was told. Ma quieted down pretty suddenly, though her eyes were still kind of wild as she watched Pa fix on his helmet tight and pick up a pail and the two of us go out.

Pa led the way and I took hold of his belt. It's a funny thing, I'm not afraid to go by myself, but when Pa's along I always want to hold on to him. Habit, I guess, and then there's no denying that this time I was a bit scared.

You see, it's this way. We know that everything is dead out there. Pa heard the last radio voices fade away years ago, and had seen some of the last folks die who weren't as lucky or well-protected as us. So we knew that if there was something groping around out there, it couldn't be anything human or friendly.

Besides that, there's a feeling that comes with it always being night, *cold* night. Pa says there used to be some of that feeling even in the old days, but then every morning the Sun would come and chase it away. I have to take his word for that, not ever remembering the Sun as being anything more than a big star. You see, I hadn't been born when the dark star snatched us away from the Sun, and by now it's dragged us out beyond the orbit of the planet Pluto, Pa says, and taking us farther out all the time.

We can see the dark star as it crosses the sky because it blots out stars, and especially when it's outlined by the Milky Way. It's pretty big, for we're closer to it than the planet Mercury was to the Sun, Pa says, but we don't care to look at it much and Pa won't set his clocks by it.

I found myself wondering whether there mightn't be something on the dark star that wanted us, and if that was why it had captured the Earth. Just then we came to the end of the corridor and I followed Pa out on the balcony.

I don't know what the city looked like in the old days, but now it's beautiful. The starlight lets you see it pretty well — there's quite a bit of light in those steady points speckling the blackness above. (Pa says the stars used to twinkle once, but that was because there was air.) We are on a hill and the shimmery plain drops away from us and then flattens out, cut up into neat squares by the troughs that used to be streets. I sometimes make my masked potatoes look like it, before I pour on the gravy.

Some taller buildings push up out of the feathery plain,

topped by rounded caps of air crystals, like the fur hood Ma
wears, only whiter. On those buildings you can see the darker
squares of windows, underlined by white dashes of air crystals.
Some of them are on a slant, for many of the buildings are
pretty badly twisted by the quakes and all the rest that
happened when the dark star captured the Earth.

Here and there a few icicles hang, water icicles from the first
days of the cold, other icicles of frozen air that melted on the
roofs and dropped and froze again. Sometimes one of those
icicles will catch the light of a star and send it to you so brightly
you think the star has swooped into the city. That was one of
the things Pa had been thinking of when I told him about the
light, but I had thought of it myself first and known it wasn't so.

He touched his helmet to mine so we could talk easier and he
asked me to point out the windows to him. But there wasn't any
light moving around inside them now, or anywhere else. To my
surprise, Pa didn't bawl me out and tell me I'd been seeing
things. He looked all around quite a while after filling his pail,
and just as we were going inside he whipped around without
warning, as if to take some peeping thing off guard.

I could feel it, too. The old peace was gone. There was
something lurking out there, watching, waiting, getting ready.

Inside, he said to me, touching helmets, "If you see something like that again, son, don't tell the others. Your Ma's sort
of nervous these days and we owe her all the feeling of safety
we can give her. Once—it was when your sister was born—I
was ready to give up and die, but your Mother kept me trying.
Another time she kept the fire going a whole week all by
herself when I was sick. Nursed me and took care of two of
you, too.

"You know that game we sometimes play, sitting in a square
in the Nest, tossing a ball around? Courage is like a ball, son.
A person can hold it only so long, and then he's got to toss it
to someone else. When it's tossed your way, you've got to
catch it and hold it tight—and hope there'll be someone else to
toss it to when you get tired of being brave."

His talking to me that way made me feel grown-up and good.
But it didn't wipe away the thing outside from the back of my
mind—or the fact that Pa took it seriously.

•   •   •

It's hard to hide your feelings about such a thing. When we got back in the Nest and took off our outside clothes, Pa laughed about it all and told them it was nothing and kidded me for having such an imagination, but his words fell flat. He didn't convince Ma and Sis any more than he did me. It looked for a minute like we were all fumbling the courage-ball. Something had to be done, and almost before I knew what I was going to say, I heard myself asking Pa to tell us about the old days, and how it all happened.

He sometimes doesn't mind telling that story, and Sis and I sure like to listen to it, and he got my idea. So we were all settled around the fire in a wink, and Ma pushed up some cans to thaw for supper, and Pa began. Before he did, though, I noticed him casually get a hammer from the shelf and lay it down beside him.

It was the same old story as always—I think I could recite the main thread of it in my sleep—though Pa always puts in a new detail or two and keeps improving it in spots.

He told us how the Earth had been swinging around the Sun ever so steady and warm, and the people on it fixing to make money and wars and have a good time and get power and treat each other right or wrong, when without warning there comes charging out of space this dead star, this burned out sun, and upsets everything.

You know, I find it hard to believe in the way those people felt, any more than I can believe in the swarming number of them. Imagine people getting ready for the horrible sort of war they were cooking up. Wanting it even, or at least wishing it were over so as to end their nervousness. As if all folks didn't have to hang together and pool every bit of warmth just to keep alive. And how can they have hoped to end danger, any more than we can hope to end the cold?

Sometimes I think Pa exaggerates and makes things out too black. He's cross with us once in a while and was probably cross with all those folks. Still, some of the things I read in the old magazines sound pretty wild. He may be right.

The dark star, as Pa went on telling it, rushed in pretty fast and there wasn't much time to get ready. At the beginning they tried to keep it a secret from most people, but then the truth came out, what with the earthquakes and floods—imagine, oceans of *unfrozen* water!—and people seeing stars blotted out by something on a clear night. First off they thought it would hit the Sun, and then they thought it would hit the Earth. There was even the start of a rush to get to a place called China, because people thought the star would hit on the other side. Not that that would have helped them, they were just crazy with fear. But then they found it wasn't going to hit either side, but was going to come very close to the Earth.

Most of the other planets were on the other side of the Sun and didn't get involved. The Sun and the newcomer fought over the Earth for a little while—pulling it this way and that, in a twisty curve, like two dogs growling over a bone, Pa described it this time—and then the newcomer won and carried us off. The Sun got a consolation prize, though. At the last minute he managed to hold on to the Moon.

That was the time of the monster earthquakes and floods, twenty times worse than anything before. It was also the time of the Big Swoop, as Pa calls it, when the Earth speeded up, going into a close orbit around the dark star.

I've asked Pa, wasn't the Earth yanked then, just as he has done to me sometimes, grabbing me by the collar to do it, when I've been sitting too far from the fire. But Pa says no, gravity doesn't work that way. It was like a yank, but nobody felt it. I guess it was like being yanked in a dream.

You see, the dark star was going through space faster than the Sun, and in the opposite direction, and it had to speed up the world a lot in order to take it away.

The Big Swoop didn't last long. It was over as soon as the Earth was settled down in its new orbit around the dark star. But the earthquakes and floods were terrible while it lasted, twenty times worse than anything before. Pa says that all sorts of cliffs and buildings toppled, oceans slopped over, swamps and sandy deserts gave great sliding surges that buried nearby lands. Earth's blanket of air, still up in the sky then, was stretched out and got so thin in spots that people keeled over and fainted—though of course, at the same time, they were getting knocked down by the earthquakes that went with the Big Swoop and maybe their bones broke or skulls cracked.

We've often asked Pa how people acted during that time, whether they were scared or brave or crazy or stunned, or all four, but he's sort of leery of the subject, and he was again tonight. He says he was mostly too busy to notice.

You see, Pa and some scientist friends of his had figured out part of what was going to happen—they'd known we'd get captured and our air would freeze—and they'd been working like mad to fix up a place with airtight walls and doors, and insulation against the cold, and big supplies of food and fuel and water and bottled air. But the place got smashed in the last earthquakes and all Pa's friends were killed then and in the Big Swoop. So he had to start over and throw the Nest together quick without any advantages, just using any stuff he could lay his hands on.

I guess he's telling pretty much the truth when he says he didn't have any time to keep an eye on how other folks behaved, either then or in the Big Freeze that followed—followed very quick, you know, both because the dark star was pulling us away very fast and because Earth's rotation had been slowed by the tug-of-war and the tides, so that the nights were longer.

Still, I've got an idea of some of the things that happened from the frozen folk I've seen, a few of them in other rooms in our building, others clustered around the furnaces in the basements where we go for coal.

In one of the rooms, an old man sits stiff in a chair, with an arm and a leg in splints. In another, a man and woman are huddled together in a bed with heaps of covers over them. You can just see their heads peeking out, close together. And in another a beautiful young lady is sitting with a pile of wraps huddled around her, looking hopefully toward the door, as if waiting for someone who never came back with warmth and food. They're all still and stiff as statues, of course, but just like life.

Pa showed them to me once in quick winks of his flashlight, when he still had a fair supply of batteries and could afford to waste a little light. They scared me pretty bad and made my heart pound, especially the young lady.

Now, with Pa telling his story for the umpteenth time to take our minds off another scare, I got to thinking of the frozen folk again. All of a sudden I got an idea that scared me worse than anything yet. You see, I'd just remembered the face I'd thought

I'd seen in the window. I'd forgotten about that on account of trying to hide it from the others.

What, I asked myself, if the frozen folk were coming to life? What if they were like the liquid helium that got a new lease on life and started crawling toward the heat just when you thought its molecules ought to freeze solid forever? Or like the electricity that moves endlessly when it's just about as cold as that? What if the ever-growing cold, with the temperature creeping down the last few degrees to the last zero, had mysteriously wakened the frozen folk to life—not warm-blooded life, but something icy and horrible?

That was a worse idea than the one about something coming down from the dark star to get us.

Or maybe, I thought, both ideas might be true. Something coming down from the dark star and making the frozen folk move, using them to do its work. That would fit with both things I'd seen—the beautiful young lady and the moving, starlike light.

The frozen folk with minds from the dark star behind their unwinking eyes, creeping, crawling, snuffing their way, following the heat to the Nest, maybe wanting the heat, but more likely hating it and wanting to chill it forever, snuff out our fire.

I tell you, that thought gave me a very bad turn and I wanted very badly to tell the others my fears, but I remembered what Pa had said and clenched my teeth and didn't speak.

We were all sitting very still. Even the fire was burning silently. There was just the sound of Pa's voice and the clocks.

And then, from beyond the blankets, I thought I heard a tiny noise. My skin tightened all over me.

Pa was telling about the early years in the Nest and had come to the place where he philosophizes.

"So I asked myself then," he said, "what's the use of dragging it out for a few years? Why prolong a doomed existence of hard work and cold and loneliness? The human race is done. The Earth is done. Why not give up, I asked myself—and all of a sudden I got the answer."

Again I heard the noise, louder this time, a kind of uncertain, shuffling tread, coming closer. I couldn't breathe.

"Life's always been a business of working hard and fighting the cold," Pa was saying. "The earth's always been a lonely place, millions of miles from the next planet. And no matter how long the human race might have lived, the end would have come some night. Those things don't matter. What matters is that life is good. It has a lovely texture, like some thick fur or the petals of flowers—you've never seen those, but you know our ice-flowers—or like the texture of flames, never twice the same. It makes everything else worth while. And that's as true for the last man as the first."

And still the steps kept shuffling closer. It seemed to me that the inmost blanket trembled and bulged a little. Just as if they were burned into my imagination, I kept seeing those peering, frozen eyes.

"So right then and there," Pa went on, and now I could tell that he heard the steps, too, and was talking loud so we maybe wouldn't hear them, "right then and there I told myself that I was going on as if we had all eternity ahead of us. I'd have children and teach them all I could. I'd get them to read books. I'd plan for the future, try to enlarge and seal the Nest. I'd do what I could to keep everything beautiful and growing. I'd keep alive my feeling of wonder even at the cold and the dark and the distant stars."

But then the blanket actually did move and lift. And there was a bright light somewhere behind it. Pa's voice stopped and his eyes turned to the widening slit and his hand went out until it touched and gripped the handle of the hammer beside him.

In through the blanket stepped the beautiful young lady. She stood there looking at us the strangest way, and she carried something bright and unwinking in her hand. And two other faces peered over her shoulders—men's faces, white and staring.

Well, my heart couldn't have been stopped for more than four or five beats before I realized she was wearing a suit and helmet like Pa's homemade ones, only fancier, and that the men were, too—and that the frozen folk certainly wouldn't be wearing those. Also, I noticed that the bright thing in her hand was just a kind of flashlight.

Sinking down very softly, Ma fainted.

The silence kept on while I swallowed hard a couple of times, and after that there was all sorts of jabbering and commotion.

They were simply people, you see. We hadn't been the only

ones to survive; we'd just thought so, for natural enough
reasons. These three people had survived, and quite a few
others with them. And when we found out *how* they'd survived,
Pa let out the biggest whoop of joy.

They were from Los Alamos and they were getting their heat
and power from atomic energy. Just using the uranium and
plutonium intended for bombs, they had enough to go on for
thousands of years. They had a regular little airtight city, with
airlocks and all. They even generated electric light and grew
plants and animals by it. (At this Pa let out a second whoop,
waking Ma from her faint.)

But if we were flabbergasted at them, they were double-
flabbergasted at us.

One of the men kept saying, "But it's impossible, I tell you.
You can't maintain an air supply without hermetic sealing. It's
simply impossible."

That was after he had got his helmet off and was using our
air. Meanwhile, the young lady kept looking around at us as if
we were saints, and telling us we'd done something amazing,
and suddenly she broke down and cried.

They'd been scouting around for survivors, but they never
expected to find any in a place like this. They had rocket ships
at Los Alamos and plenty of chemical fuel. As for liquid
oxygen, all you had to do was go out and shovel the air blanket
at the top level. So after they'd got things going smoothly at
Los Alamos, which had taken years, they'd decided to make
some trips to likely places where there might be other survivors. No good trying long-distance radio signals, of course,
since there was no atmosphere, no ionosphere, to carry them
around the curve of the Earth. That was why all the radio
signals had died out.

Well, they'd found other colonies at Argonne and Brook-
haven and way around the world at Harwell and Tanna Tuva.
And now they'd been giving our city a look, not really
expecting to find anything. But they had an instrument that
noticed the faintest heat waves and it had told them there was
something warm down here, so they'd landed to investigate. Of
course we hadn't heard them land, since there was no air to
carry the sound, and they'd had to investigate around quite a
while before finding us. Their instruments had given them a

wrong steer and they'd wasted some time in the building across the street.

By now, all five adults were talking like sixty. Pa was demonstrating to the men how he worked the fire and got rid of the ice in the chimney and all that. Ma had perked up wonderfully and was showing the young lady her cooking and sewing stuff, and even asking about how the women dressed at Los Alamos. The strangers marveled at everything and praised it to the skies. I could tell from the way they wrinkled their noses that they found the Nest a bit smelly, but they never mentioned that at all and just asked bushels of questions.

In fact, there was so much talking and excitement that Pa forgot about things, and it wasn't until they were all getting groggy that he looked and found the air had all boiled away in the pail. He got another bucket of air quick from behind the blankets. Of course that started them all laughing and jabbering again. The newcomers even got a little drunk. They weren't used to so much oxygen.

Funny thing, though—I didn't do much talking at all and Sis hung on to Ma all the time and hid her face when anybody looked at her. I felt pretty uncomfortable and disturbed myself, even about the young lady. Glimpsing her outside there, I'd had all sorts of mushy thoughts, but now I was just embarrassed and scared of her, even though she tried to be nice as anything to me.

I sort of wished they'd all quit crowding the Nest and let us be alone and get our feelings straightened out.

And when the newcomers began to talk about our all going to Los Alamos, as if that were taken for granted, I could see that something of the same feeling struck Pa and Ma, too. Pa got very silent all of a sudden and Ma kept telling the young lady, "But I wouldn't know how to act there and I haven't any clothes."

The strangers were puzzled like anything at first, but then they got the idea. As Pa kept saying, "It just doesn't seem right to let this fire go out."

Well, the strangers are gone, but they're coming back. It hasn't been decided yet just what will happen. Maybe the Nest will be kept up as what one of the strangers called a "survival school."

Or maybe we will join the pioneers who are going to try to establish a new colony at the uranium mines at Great Slave Lake or in the Congo.

Of course, now that the strangers are gone, I've been thinking a lot about Los Alamos and those other tremendous colonies. I have a hankering to see them for myself.

You ask me, Pa wants to see them, too. He's been getting pretty thoughtful, watching Ma and Sis perk up.

"It's different, now that we know others are alive," he explains to me. "Your mother doesn't feel so hopeless any more. Neither do I, for that matter, not having to carry the whole responsibility for keeping the human race going, so to speak. It scares a person."

I looked around at the blanket walls and the fire and the pails of air boiling away and Ma and Sis sleeping in the warmth and the flickering light.

"It's not going to be easy to leave the Nest," I said, wanting to cry, kind of. "It's so small and there's just the four of us. I get scared at the idea of big places and a lot of strangers."

He nodded and put another piece of coal on the fire. Then he looked at the little pile and grinned suddenly and put a couple of handfuls on, just as if it was one of our birthdays or Christmas.

"You'll quickly get over that feeling, son," he said. "The trouble with the world was that it kept getting smaller and smaller, till it ended with just the Nest. Now it'll be good to start building up to a real huge world again, the way it was in the beginning.

I guess he's right. You think the beautiful young lady will wait for me till I grow up? I asked her that and she smiled to thank me and then she told me she's got a daughter almost my age and that there are lots of children at the atomic places. Imagine that.

THE GREAT NEBRASKA SEA

Allan Danzig

The steadiness and permanence of the ground beneath our feet is another of those things we take for granted. And even if the idea that the ground could suddenly move and buck and break beneath us does cross our minds, most Americans dismiss the possibility, smugly content to think of earthquakes as something that only happens in California.

Not true. Not only can earthquakes happen anywhere, far outside those areas where they are considered to be most probable, but geologic forces can make the Earth move on a scale and with a horrific intensity not seen in historical times, perhaps not seen since humanity came down from the trees. A visit to the tortured rock wastelands of the American Southwest, though, is enough to demonstrate that earth-movements of unimaginable magnitude have happened in the past, and could just as easily happen again.

As elegantly demonstrated in the classic story that follows, one of only a handful written by Allan Danzig during a too-brief career, but one that is sufficient all by itself to gain him a distinguished place in genre history—a story not dated in any significant way in spite of being over thirty years old, and one that reminds us we'd better not be too complaisant about things remaining "the way they've always been," even things as seemingly unchanging as the mountains and the prairies and the sea.

Everyone—all the geologists, at any rate—had known about the Kiowa Fault for years. That was before there was anything very interesting to know about it. The first survey of Colorado traced its course north and south in the narrow valley of Kiowa Creek about twenty miles east of Denver; it extended south to the Arkansas River. And that was about all even the professionals were interested in knowing. There was never so much as a landslide to bring the Fault to the attention of the general public.

It was still a matter of academic interest when in the late '40s geologists speculated on the relationship between the Kiowa Fault and the Conchas Fault farther south, in New Mexico, and which followed the Pecos as far south as Texas.

Nor was there much in the papers a few years later when it was suggested that the Niobrara Fault (just inside and roughly parallel to the eastern border of Wyoming) was a northerly extension of the Kiowa. By the mid-sixties it was definitely established that the three Faults were in fact a single line of fissure in the essential rock, stretching almost from the Canadian border well south of the New Mexico–Texas line.

It is not really surprising that it took so long to figure out the connection. The population of the states affected was in places as low as five people per square mile! The land was so dry it seemed impossible that it could ever be used except for sheep farming.

It strikes us today as ironic that from the late '50s there was grave concern about the level of the water table throughout the entire area.

The even more ironic solution to the problem began in the summer of 1973. It had been a particularly hot and dry August, and the Forestry Service was keeping an anxious eye out for the fires it knew it could expect. Dense smoke was reported rising above a virtually uninhabited area along Black Squirrel Creek, and a plane was sent out for a report.

The report was—no fire at all. The rising cloud was not smoke, but dust. Thousands of cubic feet of dry earth rising lazily on the summer air. Rock slides, they guessed; certainly no fire. The Forestry Service had other worries at the moment, and filed the report.

But after a week had gone by, the town of Edison, a good twenty miles away from the slides, was still complaining of the dust. Springs were going dry, too, apparently from underground disturbances. Not even in the Rockies could anyone remember a series of rock slides as bad as this.

Newspapers in the mountain states gave it a few inches on

the front page; anything is news in late August. And the geologists became interested. Seismologists were reporting unusual activity in the area, tremors too severe to be rock slides. Volcanic activity? Specifically, a dust volcano? Unusual, they knew, but right on the Kiowa Fault—could be.

Labor Day crowds read the scientific conjectures with late summer lassitude. Sunday supplements ran four-color artists' conceptions of the possible volcano. "Only Active Volcano in U. S.?" demanded the headlines, and some papers even left off the question mark.

It may seem odd that the simplest explanation was practically not mentioned. Only Joseph Schwartzberg, head geographer of the Department of the Interior, wondered if the disturbance might not be a settling of the Kiowa Fault. His suggestion was mentioned on page nine or ten of the Monday newspapers (page 27 of the *New York Times*). The idea was not nearly so exciting as a volcano, even a lava-less one, and you couldn't draw a very dramatic picture of it.

To excuse the other geologists, it must be said that the Kiowa Fault had never acted up before. It never sidestepped, never jiggled, never, never produced the regular shows of its little sister out in California, which almost daily bounced San Francisco or Los Angeles, or some place in between. The dust volcano was on the face of it a more plausible theory.

Still, it was only a theory. It had to be proved. As the tremors grew bigger, along with the affected area, as several towns including Edison were shaken to pieces by incredible earthquakes, whole bus- and plane-loads of geologists set out for Colorado, without even waiting for their university and government departments to approve budgets.

They found, of course, that Schwartzberg had been perfectly correct.

They found themselves on the scene of what was fast becoming the most violent and widespread earthquake North America—probably the world—has ever seen in historic times. To describe it in the simplest terms, land east of the Fault was settling, and at a precipitous rate.

Rock scraped rock with a whining roar. Shuddery as a squeaky piece of chalk raked across a blackboard, the noise was deafening. The surfaces of the land east and west of the Fault seemed no longer to have any relation to each other. To the west, tortured rock reared into cliffs. East, where sharp reports and muffled wheezes told of continued buckling and dropping, the earth trembled downward. Atop the new cliffs, which seemed to grow by sudden inches from heaving rubble, dry earth fissured and trembled, sliding acres at a time to fall, smoking, into the bucking, heaving bottom of the depression.

There the devastation was even more thorough, if less spectacular. Dry earth churned like mud, and rock shards weighing tons bumped and rolled about like pebbles as they shivered and cracked into pebbles themselves. "It looks like sand dancing in a child's sieve," said the normally impassive Schwartzberg in a nationwide broadcast from the scene of disaster. "No one here has ever seen anything like it." And the landslip was growing, north and south along the Fault.

"Get out while you can," Schwartzberg urged the population of the affected area. "When it's over you can come back and pick up the pieces." But the band of scientists who had rallied to his leadership privately wondered if there would be any pieces.

The Arkansas River, at Avondale and North Avondale, was sluggishly backing north into the deepening trough. At the rate things were going, there might be a new lake the entire length of El Paso and Pueblo counties. And, warned Schwartzberg, this might only be the beginning.

By 16 September the landslip had crept down the Huerfano River past Cedarwood. Avondale, North Avondale and Boone had totally disappeared. Land west of the Fault was holding firm, though Denver had recorded several small tremors; everywhere east of the Fault, to almost twenty miles away, the now-familiar lurch and steady fall had already sent several thousand Coloradans scurrying for safety.

All mountain climbing was prohibited on the eastern slope because of the danger of rock slides from minor quakes. The geologists went home to wait.

There wasn't much to wait for. The news got worse and worse. The Platte River, now, was creating a vast mud puddle where the town of Orchard had been. Just below Masters, Colorado, the river leaped seventy-foot cliffs to add to the heaving chaos below. And the cliffs were higher every day as the land beneath them groaned downward in mile-square gulps.

As the Fault moved north and south, new areas quivered into unwelcome life. Fields and whole mountainsides moved with deceptive sloth down, down. They danced "like sand in a sieve"; dry, they boiled into rubble. Telephone lines, railroad tracks, roads snapped and simply disappeared. Virtually all east-west land communication was suspended, and the President declared a national emergency.

By 23 September the Fault was active well into Wyoming on the north, and rapidly approaching the border of New Mexico to the south. Trinchera and Branson were totally evacuated, but even so the over-all death toll had risen above one thousand.

Away to the east the situation was quiet but even more ominous. Tremendous fissures opened up perpendicular to the Fault, and a general subsidence of the land was noticeable well into Kansas and Nebraska. The western borders of these states, and soon of the Dakotas and Oklahoma as well, were slowly sinking.

On the actual scene of the disaster (or the *scenes;* it is impossible to speak of anything this size in the singular) there was a horrifying confusion. Prairie and hill cracked open under intolerable strains as the land shuddered downward in gasps and leaps. Springs burst to the surface in hot geysers and explosions of steam.

The downtown section of North Platte, Nebraska, dropped eight feet, just like that, on the afternoon of 4 October. "We must remain calm," declared the Governor of Nebraska. "We must sit this thing out. Be assured that everything possible is being done." But what could be done, with his state dropping straight down at a mean rate of a foot a day?

The Fault nicked off the southeast corner of Montana. It worked its way north along the Little Missouri. South, it ripped past Roswell, New Mexico, and tore down the Pecos toward Texas. All the upper reaches of the Missouri were standing puddles by now, and the Red River west of Paris, Texas, had begun to run backward.

Soon the Missouri began slowly slipping away westward over the slowly churning land. Abandoning its bed, the river spread uncertainly across farmland and prairie, becoming a sea of mud beneath the sharp new cliffs which rose in rending line, ever taller as the land continued to sink, almost from Canada to the Mexican border. There were virtually no floods, in the usual sense. The water moved too slowly, spread itself with no real direction or force. But the vast sheets of sluggish water and jellylike mud formed deathtraps for the countless refugees now streaming east.

Perhaps the North Platte disaster had been more than anyone could take. One hundred ninety-three people had died in that one cave-in. Certainly by 7 October it had to be officially admitted that there was an exodus of epic proportion. Nearly two million people were on the move, and the U.S. was faced with a gigantic wave of refugees. Rails, roads and airlanes were jammed with terrified hordes who had left everything behind to crowd eastward.

All through October hollow-eyed motorists flocked into Tulsa, Topeka, Omaha, Sioux Falls and Fargo. St. Louis was made distributing center for emergency squads which flew everywhere with milk for babies and dog food for evacuated pets. Gasoline trucks boomed west to meet the demand for gas, but once inside the "zone of terror," as the newspapers now called it, they found their route blocked by eastbound cars on the wrong side of the road. Shops left by their fleeing owners were looted by refugees from further west; an American Airlines plane was wrecked by a mob of would-be passengers in Bismarck, North Dakota. Federal and state troops were called out, but moving two million people was not to be done in an orderly way.

And still the landslip grew larger. The new cliffs gleamed in the autumn sunshine, growing higher as the land beneath them continued its inexorable descent.

On 21 October, at Lubbock, Texas, there was a noise variously described as a hollow roar, a shriek and a deep musical vibration like a church bell. It was simply the tortured rock of the substrata giving way. The second phase of the national disaster was beginning.

The noise traveled due east at better than eighty-five miles per hour. In its wake the earth to the north "just seemed to collapse on itself like a punctured balloon," read one newspaper report. "Like a cake that's failed," said a Texarkana housewife who fortunately lived a block *south* of Thayer Street, where the fissure raced through. There was a sigh and a great cloud of dust, and Oklahoma subsided at the astounding rate of about six feet per hour.

At Biloxi, on the Gulf, there had been uneasy shufflings under foot all day. "Not tremors, exactly," said the captain of a fishing boat which was somehow to ride out the coming flood, "but like as if the land wanted to be somewhere else."

Everyone in doomed Biloxi would have done well to have been somewhere else that evening. At approximately 8:30 P.M. the town shuddered, seemed to rise a little like the edge of a hall carpet caught in a draft, and sank. So did the entire Mississippi and Alabama coast, at about the same moment. The tidal wave which was to gouge the center from the U.S. marched on the land.

From the north shore of Lake Pontchartrain to the Appalachicola River in Florida, the Gulf coast simply disappeared. Gulfport, Biloxi, Mobile, Pensacola, Panama City; two hundred miles of shoreline vanished, with over two and a half million people. An hour later a wall of water had swept over every town from Dothan, Alabama, to Bogalusa on the Louisiana-Mississippi border.

"We must keep panic from our minds," said the Governor of Alabama in a radio message delivered from a hastily arranged all-station hookup. "We of the gallant southland have faced and withstood invasion before." Then, as ominous creakings and groanings of the earth announced the approach of the tidal wave, he flew out of Montgomery half an hour before the town disappeared forever.

One head of the wave plunged north, eventually to spend itself in the hills south of Birmingham. The main sweep followed the lowest land. Reaching west, it swallowed Vicksburg and nicked the corner of Louisiana. The whole of East Carroll Parish was scoured from the map.

The Mississippi River now ended at about Eudora, Arkansas, and minute by minute the advancing flood bit away miles of riverbed, swelling north. Chicot, Jennie, Lake Village, Arkansas City, Snow Lake, Elaine, Helena and Memphis felt the tremors. The tormented city shuddered through the night. The earth continued its descent, eventually tipping 2½ degrees down to the west. The "Memphis Tilt" is today one of the unique and charming characteristics of the gracious Old Town, but during the night of panic Memphis residents were sure they were doomed.

South and west the waters carved deeply into Arkansas and Oklahoma. By morning it was plain that all of Arkansas was going under. Waves advanced on Little Rock at almost one hundred miles an hour, new crests forming, overtopping the wave's leading edge as towns, hills and the thirst of the soil temporarily broke the furious charge.

Washington announced the official hope that the Ozarks would stop the wild gallop of the unleashed Gulf, for in northwest Arkansas the land rose to over two thousand feet. But nothing could save Oklahoma. By noon the water reached clutching fingers around Mt. Scott and Elk Mountain, deluging Hobart and almost all of Greer County.

Despite hopeful announcements that the wave was slowing, had virtually stopped after inundating Oklahoma City, was being swallowed up in the desert near Amarillo, the wall of water continued its advance. For the land was still sinking, and the floods were constantly replenished from the Gulf. Schwartzberg and his geologists advised the utmost haste in evacuating the entire area between Colorado and Missouri, from Texas to North Dakota.

Lubbock, Texas, went under. On a curling reflex the tidal wave blotted out Sweetwater and Big Spring. The Texas panhandle disappeared in one great swirl.

Whirlpools opened. A great welter of smashed wood and human debris was sucked under, vomited up and pounded to pieces. Gulf water crashed on the cliffs of New Mexico and fell back on itself in foam. Would-be rescuers on the cliffs along what had been the west bank of the Pecos River afterward recalled the hiss and scream like tearing silk as the water broke furiously on the newly exposed rock. It was the most terrible sound they had ever heard.

"We couldn't hear any shouts, of course, not that far away and with all the noise," said Dan Weaver, Mayor of Carlsbad. "But we knew there were people down there. When the water hit the cliffs, it was like a collision between two solid bodies. We couldn't see for over an hour, because of the spray."

Salt spray. The ocean had come to New Mexico.

The cliffs proved to be the only effective barrier against the westward march of the water, which turned north, gouging out lumps of rock and tumbling down blocks of earth onto its own back. In places scoops of granite came out like ice cream. The present fishing town of Rockport, Colorado, is built on a harbor created in such a way.

The water had found its farthest westering. But still it poured north along the line of the original Fault. Irresistible fingers closed on Sterling, Colorado, on Sidney, Nebraska, on Hot Springs, South Dakota. The entire tier of states settled, from south to north, down to its eventual place of stability one thousand feet below the level of the new sea.

Memphis was by now a seaport. The Ozarks, islands in a mad sea, formed precarious havens for half drowned humanity. Waves bit off a corner of Missouri, flung themselves on Wichita. Topeka, Lawrence and Belleville were the last Kansas towns to disappear. The Governor of Kansas went down with his State.

Daniel Bernd of Lincoln, Nebraska, was washed up half-drowned in a cove of the Wyoming cliffs, having been sucked from one end of vanished Nebraska to the other. Similar hairbreadth escapes were recounted on radio and television.

Virtually the only people saved out of the entire population of Pierre, South Dakota, were the six members of the Creeth family. Plucky Timothy Creeth carried and dragged his aged parents to the loft of their barn on the outskirts of town. His brother Geoffrey brought along the younger children and what provisions they could find—"Mostly a ham and about half a ton of vanilla cookies," he explained to his eventual rescuers. The barn, luckily collapsing in the vibration as the waves bore down on them, became an ark in which they rode out the disaster.

"We must of played cards for four days straight," recalled genial Mrs. Creeth when she afterwards appeared on a popular television spectacular. Her rural good humor undamaged by an ordeal few women can ever have been called on to face, she added, "We sure wondered why flushes never came out right. Jimanettly, we'd left the king of hearts behind, in the rush!"

But such lightheartedness and such happy endings were by no means typical. The world could only watch aghast as the water raced north under the shadow of the cliffs which occasionally crumbled, roaring, into the roaring waves. Day by

day the relentless rush swallowed what had been dusty farmland, cities and towns.

Some people were saved by the helicopters which flew
mercy missions just ahead of the advancing waters. Some
found safety in the peaks of western Nebraska and the Dakotas.
But when the waters came to rest along what is roughly the
present shoreline of our inland sea, it was estimated that over
fourteen million people had lost their lives.

No one could even estimate the damage to property; almost
the entirety of eight states, and portions of twelve others, had
simply vanished from the heart of the North American continent forever.

It was in such a cataclysmic birth that the now-peaceful
Nebraska Sea came to America.

Today, nearly one hundred years after the unprecedented—
and happily unrepeated—disaster, it is hard to remember the
terror and despair of those weeks in October and November,
1973. It is inconceivable to think of the United States without
its beautiful and economically essential curve of interior ocean.
Two-thirds as long as the Mediterranean, it graduates from the
warm waters of the Gulf of Mexico through the equally blue
waves of the Mississippi Bight, becoming cooler and greener
north and west of the pleasant fishing isles of the Ozark
Archipelago, finally shading into the gray-green chop of the
Gulf of Dakota.

What would the United States have become without the
5,600-mile coastline of our inland sea? It is only within the last
twenty years that any but the topmost layer of water has cleared
sufficiently to permit a really extensive fishing industry. Mud
still held in suspension by the restless waves will not precipi-
tate fully even in our lifetimes. Even so, the commercial
fisheries of Missouri and Wyoming contribute no small part to
the nation's economy.

Who can imagine what the Middle West must have been like
before the amelioration of climate brought about by the
proximity of a warm sea? The now-temperate state of Minnesota (to say nothing of the submerged Dakotas) must have been
Siberian. From contemporary accounts Missouri, our second
California, was unbelievably muggy, almost uninhabitable
during the summer months. Our climate today, from Ohio and

North Carolina to the rich fields of New Mexico and the orchards of Montana, is directly ameliorated by the marine heart of the continent.

Who today could imagine the United States without the majestic sea cliffs in stately parade from New Mexico to Montana? The beaches of Wyoming, the American Riviera, where fruit trees grow almost to the water's edge? Or incredible Colorado, where the morning skier is the afternoon bather, thanks to the monorail connecting the highest peaks with the glistening white beaches?

Of course there have been losses to balance slightly these strong gains. The Mississippi was, before 1973, one of the great rivers of the world. Taken together with its main tributary, the Missouri, it vied favorably with such giant systems as the Amazon and the Ganges. Now, ending as it does at Memphis and drawing its water chiefly from the Appalachian Mountains, it is only a slight remnant of what it was. And though the Nebraska Sea today carries many times the tonnage of shipping in its ceaseless traffic, we have lost the old romance of river shipping. We may only guess what it was like when we look upon the Ohio and the truncated Mississippi.

And transcontinental shipping is somewhat more difficult, with trucks and the freight-railroads obliged to take the sea ferries across the Nebraska Sea. We shall never know what the United States was like with its numerous coast-to-coast highways busy with trucks and private cars. Still, the ferry ride is certainly a welcome break after days of driving, and for those who wish a glimpse of what it must have been like, there is always the Cross-Canada Throughway and the magnificent U.S. Highway 73 looping north through Minnesota and passing through the giant port of Alexis, North Dakota, shipping center for the wheat of Manitoba and crossroad of a nation.

The political situation has long been a thorny problem. Only tattered remnants of the eight submerged states remained after the flood, but none of them wanted to surrender its autonomy. The tiny fringe of Kansas seemed, for a time, ready to merge with contiguous Missouri, but following the lead of the Arkansas Forever faction, the remaining population decided to retain political integrity. This has resulted in the continuing anomaly of the seven "fringe states" represented in Congress by the usual two senators each, though the largest of them is barely the size of Connecticut and all are economically indistinguishable from their neighboring states.

Fortunately it was decided some years ago that Oklahoma, the only one of the eight to have completely disappeared, could not in any sense be considered to have a continuing political existence. So, though there are still families who proudly call themselves Oklahomans, and the Oklahoma Oil Company continues to pump oil from its submerged real estate, the state has in fact disappeared from the American political scene.

But this is by now no more than a petty annoyance, to raise a smile when the talk gets around to the question of States' rights. Not even the tremendous price the country paid for its new sea—fourteen million dead, untold property destroyed— really offsets the asset we enjoy today. The heart of the continent, now open to the shipping of the world, was once dry and landlocked, cut off from the bustle of trade and the ferment of world culture.

It would indeed seem odd to an American of the '50s or '60s of the last century to imagine sailors from the merchant fleets of every nation walking the streets of Denver, fresh ashore at Newport, only fifteen miles away. Or to imagine Lincoln, Fargo, Kansas City and Dallas as world ports and great manufacturing centers. Utterly beyond their ken would be Roswell, New Mexico; Benton, Wyoming; Westport, Missouri; and the other new ports of over a million inhabitants each which have developed on the new harbors of the inland sea.

Unimaginable too would have been the general growth of population in the states surrounding the new sea. As the water tables rose and manufacturing and trade moved in to take advantage of the just-created axis of world communication, a population explosion was touched off of which we are only now seeing the diminution. This new westering is to be ranked with the first surge of pioneers which created the American west. But what a difference! Vacation paradises bloom, a new fishing industry thrives; her water road is America's main artery of trade, and fleets of all the world sail . . . where once the prairie schooner made its laborious and dusty way west!

INCONSTANT MOON

Larry Niven

The life-giving sun is another of those things, like the air and the ground beneath our feet, that we take for granted, whose constancy we count on without really thinking much about it. But as the compelling and Hugo-winning story that follows suggests, our sun can become a very fractious star indeed under the right circumstances, a death-giver rather than a life-giver, sweeping the hapless Earth with hard radiation that could mean the end of the world—unless you're clever enough to figure out a way to survive it . . .

Larry Niven made his first sale to Worlds of If *magazine in 1964, and soon established himself as one of the best new writers of "hard" science fiction since Robert Heinlein. By the end of the '70s, Niven had won several Hugo and Nebula awards, published* Ringworld, *one of the most acclaimed technological novels of its decade, and had written several best-selling novels in collaboration with Jerry Pournelle, including* The Mote in God's Eye. *Niven's books include the novels* Protector, World of Ptavvs, A Gift from Earth, Ringworld Engineers, Smoke Ring, *and* Destiny's Road, *and the collections* Tales of Known Space, Inconstant Moon, Neutron Star, N-Space, *and* Playground of the Mind. *His most recent book is a new novel,* Rainbow Mars.

I

I was watching the news when the change came, like a flicker of motion at the corner of my eye. I turned toward the balcony window. Whatever it was, I was too late to catch it.

The moon was very bright tonight.

I saw that, and smiled, and turned back. Johnny Carson was just starting his monologue.

When the first commercials came on I got up to reheat some coffee. Commercials came in strings of three and four, going on midnight. I'd have time.

The moonlight caught me coming back. If it had been bright before, it was brighter now. Hypnotic. I opened the sliding glass door and stepped out onto the balcony.

The balcony wasn't much more than a railed ledge, with standing room for a man and a woman and a portable barbecue set. These past months the view had been lovely, especially around sunset. The Power and Light Company had been putting up a glass-slab-style office building. So far it was only a steel framework of open girders. Shadow-blackened against a red sunset sky, it tended to look stark and surrealistic and hellishly impressive.

Tonight . . .

I had never seen the moon so bright, not even in the desert. *Bright enough to read by,* I thought, and immediately, *but that's an illusion.* The moon was never bigger (I had read somewhere) than a quarter held nine feet away. It couldn't possibly be bright enough to read by.

It was only three-quarters full!

But, glowing high over the San Diego Freeway to the west, the moon seemed to dim even the streaming automobile headlights. I blinked against its light, and thought of men walking on the moon, leaving corrugated footprints. Once, for the sake of an article I was writing, I had been allowed to pick up a bone-dry moon rock and hold it in my hand . . .

I heard the show starting again, and I stepped inside. But, glancing once behind me, I caught the moon growing even brighter—as if it had come from behind a wisp of scudding cloud.

Now its light was brain-searing, lunatic.

The phone rang five times before she answered.

"Hi," I said. "Listen—"

"Hi," Leslie said sleepily, complainingly. Damn. I'd hoped she was watching television, like me.

I said, "Don't scream and shout, because I had a reason for calling. You're in bed, right? Get up and— Can you get up?"

"What time is it?"

"Quarter of twelve."

"Oh, Lord."

"Go out on your balcony and look around."

"Okay."

The phone clunked. I waited. Leslie's balcony faced north and west, like mine, but it was ten stories higher, with a correspondingly better view.

Through my own window, the moon burned like a textured spotlight.

"Stan? You there?"

"Yah. What do you think of it?"

"It's gorgeous. I've never seen anything like it. What could make the moon light up like that?"

"I don't know, but isn't it gorgeous?"

"You're supposed to be the native." Leslie had only moved out here a year ago.

"Listen, I've *never* seen it like this. But there's an old legend," I said. "Once every hundred years the Los Angeles smog rolls away for a single night, leaving the air as clear as interstellar space. That way the gods can see if Los Angeles is still there. If it is, they roll the smog back so they won't have to look at it."

"I used to know all that stuff. Well, listen, I'm glad you woke me up to see it, but I've got to get to work tomorrow."

"Poor baby."

"That's life. 'Night."

"'Night."

Afterward I sat in the dark, trying to think of someone else to call. Call a girl at midnight, invite her to step outside, and look at the moonlight . . . and she may think it's romantic or she may be furious, but she won't assume you called six others.

So I thought of some names. But the girls who belonged to them had all dropped away over the past year or so, after I started spending all my time with Leslie. One could hardly blame them. And now Joan was in Texas and Hildy was getting married, and if I called Louise I'd probably get Gordie too. The English girl? But I couldn't remember her number. Or her last name.

Besides, everyone I knew punched a time clock of one kind

or another. Me, I worked for a living, but as a freelance writer I picked my hours. Anyone I woke up tonight, I'd be ruining her morning. Ah, well . . .

The Johnny Carson show was a swirl of gray and a roar of static when I got back to the living room. I turned the set off and went back out on the balcony.

The moon was brighter than the flow of headlights on the freeway, brighter than Westwood Village off to the right. The Santa Monica Mountains had a magical pearly glow. There were no stars near the moon. Stars could not survive that glare.

I wrote science and how-to articles for a living. I ought to be able to figure out what was making the moon do that. Could the moon be suddenly larger? Inflating like a balloon? No.

Closer, maybe. The moon falling?

Tides! Waves fifty feet high . . . and earthquakes! San Andreas Fault splitting apart like the Grand Canyon! Jump in my car, head for the hills . . . no, too late already . . .

Nonsense. The moon was brighter, not bigger. I could see that. And what could possibly drop the moon on our heads like that?

I blinked, and the moon left an afterimage on my retinae. It was *that* bright.

A million people must be watching the moon right now, and wondering, like me. An article on the subject would sell big . . . if I wrote it before anyone else did . . .

There must be some simple, obvious explanation.

Well, how could the moon grow brighter? Moonlight was reflected sunlight. Could the sun have gotten brighter? It must have happened after sunset, then, or it would have been noticed . . .

I didn't like that idea.

Besides, half the Earth was in direct sunlight. A thousand correspondents for *Life* and *Time* and *Newsweek* and Associated Press would all be calling in from Europe, Asia, Africa . . . unless they were all hiding in cellars. Or dead. Or voiceless, because the sun was blanketing everything with static, radio and phone systems and televisions . . . Television. Oh my God.

I was just barely beginning to be afraid.

All right, start over. The moon had become very much brighter. Moonlight, well, moonlight was reflected sunlight;

any idiot knew that. Then . . . something had happened to the
sun.

II

"Hello?"

"Hi. Me," I said, and then my throat froze solid. Panic! What
was I going to *tell* her?

"I've been watching the moon," she said dreamily. "It's
wonderful. I even tried to use my telescope, but I couldn't see
a thing; it was too bright. It lights up the whole city. The hills
are all silver."

That's right, she kept a telescope on her balcony. I'd forgotten.

"I haven't tried to go back to sleep," she said. "Too much
light."

I got my throat working again. "Listen, Leslie love, I started
thinking about how I woke you up and how you probably
couldn't get back to sleep, what with all this light. So let's go
out for a midnight snack."

"Are you out of your mind?"

"No, I'm serious. I mean it. Tonight isn't a night for sleeping.
We may never have a night like this again. To hell with your
diet. Let's celebrate. Hot fudge sundaes, Irish coffee—"

"That's different. I'll get dressed."

"I'll be right over."

Leslie lived on the fourteenth floor of Building C of the
Barrington Plaza. I rapped for admission, and waited.

And waiting, I wondered without any sense of urgency: Why
Leslie?

There must be other ways to spend my last night on Earth
than with one particular girl. I could have picked a different
particular girl, or even several not too particular girls, except
that that didn't really apply to me, did it? Or I could have called
my brother, or either set of parents . . .

Well, but brother Mike would have wanted a good reason for
being hauled out of bed at midnight. "But, Mike, the moon is
so beautiful . . ." Hardly. Any of my parents would have

reacted similarly. Well, I had a good reason, but would they believe me?

And if they did, what then? I would have arranged a kind of wake. Let 'em sleep through it. What I wanted was someone who would join my . . . farewell party without asking the wrong questions.

What I wanted was Leslie. I knocked again.

She opened the door just a crack for me. She was in her underwear. A stiff, misshapen girdle in one hand brushed my back as she came into my arms. "I was about to put this on."

"I came just in time, then." I took the girdle away from her and dropped it. I stooped to get my arms under her ribs, straightened up with effort, and walked us to the bedroom with her feet dangling against my ankles.

Her skin was cold. She must have been outside.

"So!" she demanded. "You think you can compete with a hot fudge sundae, do you?"

"Certainly. My pride demands it." We were both somewhat out of breath. Once in our lives I had tried to lift her cradled in my arms, in conventional movie style. I'd damn near broken my back. Leslie was a big girl, my height, and almost too heavy around the hips.

I dropped us on the bed, side by side. I reached around her from both sides to scratch her back, knowing it would leave her helpless to resist me, *ah* ha hahahaha. She made sounds of pleasure to tell me where to scratch. She pulled my shirt up around my shoulders and began scratching my back.

We pulled pieces of clothing from ourselves and each other, at random, dropping them over the edges of the bed. Leslie's skin was warm now, almost hot . . .

All right, now *that's* why I couldn't have picked another girl. I'd have had to teach her how to scratch. And there just wasn't time.

Some nights I had a nervous tendency to hurry our lovemaking. Tonight we were performing a ritual, a rite of passage. I tried to slow it down, to make it last. I tried to make Leslie like it more. It paid off incredibly. I forgot the moon and the future when Leslie put her heels against the backs of my knees and we moved into the ancient rhythm.

But the image that came to me at the climax was vivid and

frightening. We were in a ring of blue-hot fire that closed like a noose. If I moaned in terror and ecstasy, then she must have thought it was ecstasy alone.

We lay side by side, drowsy, torpid, clinging together. I was minded to go back to sleep then, renege on my promise, sleep and let Leslie sleep . . . but instead I whispered into her ear: "Hot fudge sundae." She smiled and stirred and presently rolled off the bed.

I wouldn't let her wear the girdle. "It's past midnight. Nobody's going to pick you up, because I'd thrash the blackguard, right? So why not be comfortable?" She laughed and gave in. We hugged each other once, hard, in the elevator. It felt much better without the girdle.

III

The gray-haired counter waitress was cheerful and excited. Her eyes glowed. She spoke as if confiding a secret. "Have you noticed the moonlight?"

Ship's was fairly crowded, this time of night and this close to UCLA. Half the customers were university students. Tonight they talked in hushed voices, turning to look out through the glass walls of the twenty-four-hour restaurant. The moon was low in the west, low enough to compete with the street globes.

"We noticed," I said. "We're celebrating. Get us two hot fudge sundaes, will you?" When she turned her back I slid a ten-dollar bill under the paper place mat. Not that she'd ever spend it, but at least she'd have the pleasure of finding it. I'd never spend it either.

I felt loose, casual. A lot of problems seemed suddenly to have solved themselves.

Who would have believed that peace could come to Vietnam and Cambodia in a single night?

This thing had started around eleven-thirty, here in California. That would have put the noon sun just over the Arabian Sea, with all but a few fringes of Asia, Europe, Africa, and Australia in direct sunlight.

Already Germany was reunited, the Wall melted or smashed by shock waves. Israelis and Arabs had laid down their arms. Apartheid was dead in Africa.

And I was free. For me there were no more consequences.
Tonight I could satisfy all my dark urges, rob, kill, cheat on my
income tax, throw bricks at plate-glass windows, burn my
credit cards. I could forget the article on explosive metal
forming, due Thursday. Tonight I could substitute cinnamon
candy for Leslie's Pills. Tonight—

"Think I'll have a cigarette."

Leslie looked a me oddly. "I thought you'd given that up."

"You remember. I told myself if I got any overpowering
urges, I'd have a cigarette. I did that because I couldn't stand
the thought of never smoking again."

She laughed. "But it's been months!"

"But they keep putting cigarette ads in my magazines!"

"It's a plot. All right, go have a cigarette."

I put coins in the machine, hesitated over the choice, finally
picked a mild filter. It wasn't that I wanted a cigarette. But
certain events call for champagne, and others for cigarettes.
There is the traditional last cigarette before a firing squad . . .

I lit up. *Here's to lung cancer.*

It tasted just as good as I remembered; though there was a
faint stale undertaste, like a mouthful of old cigarette butts. The
third lungful hit me oddly. My eyes unfocused and everything
went very calm. My heart pulsed loudly in my throat.

"How does it taste?"

"Strange. I'm buzzed," I said.

Buzzed! I hadn't heard the word in fifteen years. In high
school we'd smoked to get that buzz, that quasi-drunkenness
produced by capillaries constricting in the brain. The buzz had
stopped coming after the first few times, but we'd kept
smoking, most of us . . .

I put it out. The waitress was picking up our sundaes.

Hot and cold, sweet and bitter; there is no taste quite like that
of a hot fudge sundae. To die without tasting it again would
have been a crying shame. But with Leslie it was a *thing,* a
symbol of all rich living. Watching her eat was more fun than
eating myself.

Besides . . . I'd killed the cigarette to taste the ice cream.
Now, instead of savoring the ice cream, I was anticipating Irish
coffee.

Too little time.

Leslie's dish was empty. She stage-whispered, "Aahh!" and patted herself over the navel.

A customer at one of the small tables began to go mad.

I'd noticed him coming in. A lean scholarly type wearing sideburns and steel-rimmed glasses, he had been continually twisting around to look out at the moon. Like others at other tables, he seemed high on a rare and lovely natural phenomenon.

Then he got it. I saw his face changing, showing suspicion, then disbelief, then horror, horror and helplessness.

"Let's go," I told Leslie. I dropped quarters on the counter and stood up."

"Don't you want to finish yours?"

"Nope. We've got things to do. How about some Irish coffee?"

"And a Pink Lady for me? Oh, look!" She turned full around.

The scholar was climbing up on a table. He balanced, spread wide his arms and bellowed, "Look out your windows!"

"You get down from there!" a waitress demanded, jerking emphatically at his pants leg.

"The world is coming to an end! Far away on the other side of the sea, death and hellfire—"

But we were out the door, laughing as we ran. Leslie panted. "We may have—escaped a religious—riot in there!"

I thought of the ten I'd left under my plate. Now it would please nobody. Inside, a prophet was shouting his message of doom to all who would hear. The gray-haired woman with the glowing eyes would find the money and think: They knew it too.

Buildings blocked the moon from the Red Barn's parking lot. The street lights and the indirect moonglare were pretty much the same color. The night only seemed a bit brighter than usual.

I didn't understand why Leslie stopped suddenly in the driveway. But I followed her gaze, straight up to where a star burned very brightly just south of the zenith.

"Pretty," I said.

She gave me a very odd look.

There were no windows in the Red Barn. Dim artificial lighting, far dimmer than the queer cold light outside, showed

on dark wood and quietly cheerful customers. Nobody seemed
aware that tonight was different from other nights.

The sparse Tuesday night crowd was gathered mostly around
the piano bar. A customer had the mike. He was singing some
half-familiar song in a wavering weak voice, while the black
pianist grinned and played a schmaltzy background.

I ordered two Irish coffees and a Pink Lady. At Leslie's
questioning look I only smiled mysteriously.

How ordinary the Red Barn felt. How relaxed; how happy.
We held hands across the table, and I smiled and was afraid to
speak. If I broke the spell, if I said the wrong thing . . .

The drinks arrived. I raised an Irish coffee glass by the stem.
Sugar, Irish whiskey, and strong black coffee, with thick
whipped cream floating on top. It coursed through me like a
magical potion of strength, dark and hot and powerful.

The waitress waved back my money. "See that man in the
turtleneck, there at the end of the piano bar? He's buying,"
she said with relish. "He came in two hours ago and handed the
bartender a hundred-dollar bill."

So that was where all the happiness was coming from. Free
drinks! I looked over, wondering what the guy was celebrating.

A thick-necked, wide-shouldered man in a turtleneck and
sports coat, he sat hunched over into himself, with a wide bar
glass clutched tight in one hand. The pianist offered him the
mike, and he waved it by, the gesture giving me a good look at
his face. A square, strong face, now drunk and miserable and
scared. He was ready to cry from fear.

So I knew what he was celebrating.

Leslie made a face. "They didn't make the Pink Lady right."

There's one bar in the world that makes a Pink Lady the way
Leslie likes it, and it isn't in Los Angeles. I passed her the other
Irish coffee, grinning an I-told-you-so grin. Forcing it. The
other man's fear was contagious. She smiled back, lifted her
glass and said, "To the blue moonlight."

I lifted my glass to her, and drank. But it wasn't the toast I
would have chosen.

The man in the turtleneck slid down from his stool. He
moved carefully toward the door, his course slow and straight
as an ocean liner cruising into dock. He pulled the door wide,
and turned around, holding it open, so that the weird blue-white
light streamed past his broad black silhouette.

Bastard. He was waiting for someone to figure it out, to shout out the truth to the rest. *Fire and doom—*

"Shut the door!" someone bellowed.

"Time to go," I said softly

"What's the hurry?"

The hurry? He might *speak!* But I couldn't say that . . .

Leslie put her hand over mine. "I know. I *know.* But we can't run away from it, can we?"

A fist closed hard on my heart. She'd known, and I hadn't noticed?

The door closed, leaving the Red Barn in reddish dusk. The man who had been buying drinks was gone.

"Oh, God. When did you figure it out?"

"Before you came over," she said. "But when I tried to check it out, it didn't work."

"Check it out?"

"I went out on the balcony and turned the telescope on Jupiter. Mars is below the horizon these nights. If the sun's gone nova, all the planets ought to be lit up like the moon, right?"

"Right. Damn." I should have thought of that myself. But Leslie was the stargazer. I knew some astrophysics, but I couldn't have found Jupiter to save my life.

"But Jupiter wasn't any brighter than usual. So then I didn't know *what* to think."

"But then—" I felt hope dawning fiery hot. Then I remembered. "That star, just overhead. The one you stared at."

"Jupiter."

"All lit up like a fucking neon sign. Well, that tears it."

"Keep your voice down."

I *had* been keeping my voice down. But for a wild moment I wanted to stand up on a table and scream! *Fire and doom*—What right had they to be ignorant?

Leslie's hand closed tight on mine. The urge passed. It left me shuddering. "Let's get out of here. Let 'em think there's going to be a dawn."

"There is." Leslie laughed a bitter, barking laugh like nothing I'd ever heard from her. She walked out while I was reaching for my wallet—and remembering that there was no need.

Poor Leslie. Finding Jupiter its normal self must have looked like a reprieve—until the white spark flared to shining glory an hour and a half late. An hour and a half, for sunlight to reach Earth by the way of Jupiter.

When I reached the door Leslie was half-running down Westwood toward Santa Monica. I cursed and ran to catch up, wondering if she'd suddenly gone crazy.

Then I noticed the shadows ahead of us. All along the other side of Santa Monica Boulevard: moon shadows, in horizontal patterns of dark and blue-white bands.

I caught her at the corner.

The moon was setting.

A setting moon always looks tremendous. Tonight it glared at us through the gap of sky beneath the freeway, terribly bright, casting an incredible complexity of lines and shadows. Even the unlighted crescent glowed pearly bright with earth-shine.

Which told me all I wanted to know about what was happening on the lighted side of Earth.

And on the moon? The men of Apollo 19 must have died in the first few minutes of nova sunlight. Trapped out on a lunar plain, hiding perhaps behind a melting boulder . . . Or were they on the night side? I couldn't remember. Hell, they could outlive us all. I felt a stab of envy and hatred.

And pride. We'd put them there. We reached the moon before the nova came. A little longer, we'd have reached the stars.

The disc changed oddly as it set. A dome, a flying saucer, a lens, a line . . .

Gone.

Gone. Well, that was that. Now we could forget it; now we could walk around outside without being constantly reminded that something was *wrong*. Moonset had taken all the queer shadows out of the city.

But the clouds had an odd glow to them. As clouds glow after sunset, tonight the clouds shone livid white at their western edges. And they streamed too quickly across the sky. As if they tried to run . . .

When I turned to Leslie, there were big tears rolling down her cheeks.

"Oh, damn." I took her arm. "Now stop it. Stop it."

"I can't. You know I can't stop crying once I get started."

"This wasn't what I had in mind. I thought we'd do things we've been putting off, things we like. It's our last chance. Is this the way you want to die, crying on a street corner?"

"I don't want to die at all."

"Tough shit!"

"Thanks a lot." Her face was all red and twisted. Leslie was crying as a baby cries, without regard for dignity or appearance. I felt awful. I felt guilty, and I *knew* the nova wasn't my fault, and it made me angry.

"I don't want to die either!" I snarled at her. "You show me a way out and I'll take it. Where would we go? The South Pole? It'd just take longer. The moon must be molten all across its day side. Mars? When this is over Mars will be part of the sun, like the Earth. Alpha Centauri? The acceleration we'd need, we'd be spread across a wall like peanut butter and jelly—"

"Oh, shut up."

"Right."

"Hawaii. Stan, we could get to the airport in twenty minutes. We'd get two hours extra, going west! Two hours more before sunrise!"

She had something there. Two hours was worth any price! But I'd worked this out before, staring at the moon from my balcony. "No. We'd die sooner. Listen, love, we saw the moon go bright about midnight. That means California was at the back of the Earth when the sun went nova."

"Yes, that's right."

"Then we must be farthest from the shock wave."

She blinked. "I don't understand."

"Look at it this way. First the sun explodes. That heats the air and the oceans, all in a flash, all across the day side. The steam and superheated air expand *fast*. A flaming shock wave comes roaring over into the night side. It's closing on us right now. Like a noose. But it'll reach Hawaii first. Hawaii is two hours closer to the sunset line."

"Then we won't see the dawn. We won't live even that long."

"No."

"You explain things so well," she said bitterly. "A flaming shock wave. So graphic."

"Sorry. I've been thinking about it too much. Wondering what it will be like."

"Well, stop it." She came to me and put her face in my shoulder. She cried quietly. I held her with one arm and used the other to rub her neck, and I watched the streaming clouds, and I didn't think about what it would be like.

Didn't think about the ring of fire closing on us.

It was the wrong picture anyway.

I thought of how the oceans must have boiled on the day side, so that the shock wave had been mostly steam to start with. I thought of the millions of square miles of ocean it had to cross. It would be cooler and wetter when it reached us. And the Earth's rotation would spin it like the whirlpool in a bathtub.

Two counterrotating hurricanes of live steam, one north, one south. That was how it would come. We were lucky. California would be near the eye of the northern one.

A hurricane wind of live steam. It would pick a man up and cook him in the air, strip the steamed flesh from him and cast him aside. It was going to hurt like hell.

We would never see the sunrise. In a way that was a pity. It would be spectacular.

Thick parallel streamers of cloud were drifting across the stars, too fast, their bellies white by city light. Jupiter dimmed, then went out. Could it be starting already? Heat lightning jumped—

"Aurora," I said.

"What?"

"There's a shock wave from the sun, too. There should be an aurora like nothing anybody's ever seen before."

Leslie laughed suddenly, jarringly. "It seems so strange, standing on a street corner talking like this! Stan, are we dreaming it?"

"We could pretend—"

"No. Most of the human race must be dead already."

"Yah."

"And there's nowhere to go."

"Damn it, you figured that out long ago, all by yourself. Why bring it up now?"

"You could have let me sleep," she said bitterly. "I was dropping off to sleep when you whispered in my ear."

I didn't answer. It was true.

"'Hot fudge sundae,'" she quoted. Then, "It wasn't a bad idea, actually. Breaking my diet."

I started to giggle.

"Stop that."

"We could go back to your place now. Or my place. To sleep."

"I suppose. But we couldn't sleep, could we? No, don't say it. We take sleeping pills, and five hours from now we wake up screaming. I'd rather stay awake. At least we'll know what's happening."

But if we took all the pills . . . but I didn't say it. I said, "Then how about a picnic?"

"Where?"

"The beach, maybe. Who cares? We can decide later."

IV

All the markets were closed. But the liquor store next to the Red Barn was one I'd been using for years. They sold us foie gras, crackers, a couple of bottles of chilled champagne, six kinds of cheese and a hell of a lot of nuts—I took one of everything—more crackers, a bag of ice, frozen rumaki hors d'oeuvres, a fifth of an ancient brandy that cost twenty-five bucks, a matching fifth of Cherry Heering for Leslie, six-packs of beer and Bitter Orange . . .

By the time we had piled all that into a dinky store cart, it was raining. Big fat drops spattered in flurries across the acre of plate glass that fronted the store. Wind howled around the corners.

The salesman was in a fey mood, bursting with energy. He'd been watching the moon all night. "And now this!" he exclaimed as he packed our loot into bags. He was a small, muscular old man with thick arms and shoulders. "It *never* rains like this in California. It comes down straight and heavy, when it comes at all. Takes days to build up."

"I know." I wrote him a check, feeling guilty about it. He'd known me long enough to trust me. But the check was good. There were funds to cover it. Before opening hours the check would be ash, and all the banks in the world would be bubbling in the heat of the sun. But that was hardly my fault.

He piled our bags in the cart, set himself at the door. "Now when the rain lets up, we'll run these out. Ready?" I got ready to open the door. The rain came like someone had thrown a bucket of water at the window. In a moment it had stopped, though water still streamed down the glass. "Now!" cried the salesman, and I threw the door open and we were off. We reached the car laughing like maniacs. The wind howled around us, sweeping up spray and hurling it at us.

"We picked a good break. You know what this weather reminds me of? Kansas," said the salesman. "During a tornado."

Then suddenly the sky was full of gravel! We yelped and ducked, and the car rang to a million tiny concussions, and I got the car door unlocked and pulled Leslie and the salesman in after me. We rubbed our bruised heads and looked out at white gravel bouncing everywhere.

The salesman picked a small white pebble out of his collar. He put it in Leslie's hand, and she gave a startled squeak and handed it to me, and it was cold.

"Hail," said the salesman. "Now I really don't get it."

Neither did I. I could only think that it had something to do with the nova. But what? How?

"I've got to get back," said the salesman. The hail had expended itself in one brief flurry. He braced himself, then went out of the car like a marine taking a hill. We never saw him again.

The clouds were churning up there, forming and disappearing, sliding past each other faster than I'd ever seen clouds move; their bellies glowing by city light.

"It must be the nova," Leslie said shivering.

"But how? If the shock were here already, we'd be *dead*—or at least deaf. Hail?"

"Who cares? Stan, we don't have *time!*"

I shook myself. "All right. What would you like to do most, right now?"

"Watch a baseball game."

"It's two in the morning," I pointed out

"That lets out a lot of things, doesn't it?"

"Right. We've hopped our last bar. We've seen our last play, and our last clean movie. What's left?"

"Looking in jewelry store windows."

"Seriously? Your last night on Earth?"

She considered, then answered. "Yes."

By damn, she meant it. I couldn't think of anything duller. "Westwood or Beverly Hills?"

"Both."

"Now, *look*—"

"Beverly Hills, then."

We drove through another spatter of rain and hail—a capsule tempest. We parked half a block from the Tiffany salesroom.

The sidewalk was one continuous puddle. Secondhand rain dripped on us from various levels of the buildings overhead. Leslie said, "This is great. There must be half a dozen jewelry stores in walking distance."

"I was thinking of driving."

"No no no, you don't have the proper attitude. One must window-shop on foot. It's in the rules."

"But the rain!"

"You won't die of pneumonia. You won't have time," she said, too grimly.

Tiffany's had a small branch office in Beverly Hills, but they didn't put expensive things in the windows at night. There were a few fascinating toys, that was all.

We turned up Rodeo Drive—and struck it rich. Tibor showed an infinite selection of rings, ornate and modern, large and small, in all kinds of precious and semiprecious stones. Across the street, Van Cleef & Arpels showed brooches, men's wristwatches of elegant design, bracelets with tiny watches in them, and one window that was all diamonds.

"Oh, lovely," Leslie breathed, caught by the flashing diamonds. "What they must look like in daylight! . . . Wups—"

"No, that's a good thought. Imagine them at dawn, flaming with nova light, while the windows shatter to let the raw daylight in. Want one? The necklace?"

"Oh, *may* I? Hey, hey, I was kidding! Put that down, you idiot, there must be alarms in the glass."

"Look, nobody's going to be wearing any of that stuff

between now and morning. Why shouldn't we get some good out of it?"

"We'd be caught!"

"Well, you *said* you wanted to window-shop . . ."

"I don't want to spend my last hour in a cell. If you'd brought the car we'd have *some* chance—"

"Of getting away. Right. I *wanted* to bring the car—" But at that point we both cracked up entirely, and had to stagger away holding onto each other for balance.

There were a good half-dozen jewelry stores on Rodeo. But there was more. Toys, books, shirts and ties in odd and advanced styling. In Francis Orr, a huge plastic cube full of new pennies. A couple of damn strange clocks farther on. There was an extra kick in window shopping, knowing that we could break a window and take anything we wanted badly enough.

We walked hand in hand, swinging our arms. The sidewalks were ours alone; all others had fled the mad weather. The clouds still churned overhead.

"I wish I'd known it was coming," Leslie said suddenly. "I spent the whole day fixing a mistake in a program. Now we'll never run it."

"What would you have done with the time? A baseball game?"

"Maybe. No. The standings don't matter now." She frowned at dresses in a store window. "What would you have done?"

"Gone to the Blue Sphere for cocktails," I said promptly. "It's a topless place. I used to go there all the time. I hear they've gone full nude now."

"I've never been to one of those. How late are they open?"

"Forget it. It's almost two-thirty."

Leslie mused, looking at giant stuffed animals in a toy store window. "Isn't there someone you would have murdered, if you'd had the time?"

"Now, you *know* my agent lives in New York."

"Why him?"

"My child, why would any writer want to murder his agent? For the manuscripts he loses under other manuscripts. For his ill-gotten ten percent, and the remaining ninety percent that he sends me grudgingly and late. For—"

Suddenly the wind roared and rose up against us. Leslie

pointed, and we ran for a deep doorway that turned out to be Gucci's. We huddled against the glass.

The wind was suddenly choked with hail the size of marbles. Glass broke somewhere, and alarms lifted thin, frail voices into the wind. There was more than hail in the wind! There were rocks!

I caught the smell and taste of sea water.

We clung together in the expensively wasted space in front of Gucci's. I coined a short-lived phrase and screamed, "Nova weather! How the blazes did it—" But I couldn't hear myself, and Leslie didn't even know I was shouting.

Nova weather. How did it get here so fast? Coming over the pole, the nova shock wave would have to travel about four thousand miles—at least a five-hour trip.

No. The shock wave would travel in the stratosphere, where the speed of sound was higher, then propagate down. Three hours was plenty of time. Still, I thought, it should not have come as a rising wind. On the other side of the world, the exploding sun was tearing our atmosphere away and hurling it at the stars. The shock should have come as a single vast thunderclap.

For an instant the wind gentled, and I ran down the sidewalk pulling Leslie after me. We found another doorway as the wind picked up again. I thought I heard a siren coming to answer the alarm.

At the next break we splashed across Wilshire and reached the car. We sat there panting, waiting for the heater to warm up. My shoes felt squishy. The wet clothes stuck to my skin.

Leslie shouted, "How much longer?"

"I don't know! We ought to have *some* time."

"We'll have to spend our picnic indoors!"

"Your place or mine? Yours," I decided, and pulled away from the curb.

V

Wilshire Boulevard was flooded to the hubcaps in spots. The spurts of hail and sleet had become a steady, pounding rain. Fog lay flat and waist-deep ahead of us, broke swirling over our hood, churned in a wake behind us. Weird weather.

Nova weather. The shock wave of scalding superheated

steam hadn't happened. Instead, a mere hot wind roaring through the stratosphere, the turbulence eddying down to form strange storms at ground level.

We parked illegally on the upper parking level. My one glimpse of the lower level showed it to be flooded. I opened the trunk and lifted two heavy paper bags.

"We must have been crazy," Leslie said, shaking her head. "We'll never use all this."

"Let's take it up anyway."

She laughed at me. "But why?"

"Just a whim. Will you help me carry it?"

We took double armfuls up to the fourteenth floor. That still left a couple of bags in the trunk. "Never mind them," Leslie said. "We've got the rumaki and the bottles and the nuts. What more do we need?"

"The cheeses. The crackers. The foie gras."

"Forget 'em."

"No."

"You're out of your mind," she explained to me, slowly so that I would understand. "You could be steamed dead on the way down. We might not have more than a few minutes left, and you want food for a week! *Why?*"

"I'd rather not say."

"Go then!" She slammed the door with terrible force.

The elevator was an ordeal. I kept wondering if Leslie was right. The shrilling of the wind was muffled, here at the core of the building. Perhaps it was about to rip electrical cables somewhere, leave me stranded in a darkened box. But I made it down.

The upper level was knee-deep in water.

My second surprise was that it was lukewarm, like old bathwater, unpleasant to wade through. Steam curdled on the surface, then blew away on a wind howled through the concrete echo chamber like the screaming of the damned.

Going up was another ordeal. If what I was thinking was wish fulfillment, if a roaring wind of live steam caught me now . . . I'd feel like such an idiot . . . But the doors opened, and the lights hadn't even flickered.

Leslie wouldn't let me in.

"Go away!" She shouted through the locked door. "Go eat your cheese and crackers somewhere else!"

"You got another date?"

That was a mistake. I got no answer at all.

I could almost see her viewpoint. The extra trip for the extra bags was no big thing to fight about; but why did it have to be? How long was our love affair going to last, anyway? An hour, with luck. Why back down on a perfectly good argument, to preserve so ephemeral a thing?

"I wasn't going to bring this up," I shouted, hoping she could hear me through the door. The wind must be three times as loud on the other side. "We may need food for a week! And a place to hide!"

Silence. I began to wonder if I could kick the door down. Would I be better off waiting in the hall? Eventually she'd have to—

The door opened. Leslie was pale. "That was cruel," she said quietly.

"I can't promise anything. I wanted to wait, but you forced it. I've been wondering if the sun really has exploded."

"That's cruel. I was just getting used to the idea." She turned her face to the doorjamb. Tired, she was tired. I'd kept her up too late . . .

"Listen to me. It was all wrong," I said. "There should have been an aurora borealis to light up the night sky from pole to pole. A shock wave of particles exploding out of the sun, traveling at an inch short of the speed of light, would rip into the atmosphere like—why, we'd have seen blue fire over every building!

"Then, the storm came too slow," I screamed, to be heard above the thunder. "A nova would rip away the sky over half the planet. The shock wave would move around the night side with a sound to break all the glass in the world, all at once! And crack concrete and marble—and, Leslie love, it just hasn't happened. So I started wondering."

She said it in a mumble. "Then what is it?"

"A flare. The worst—"

She shouted it at me like an accusation. "A flare! A solar flare! You think the sun could light up like that—"

"Easy, now—"

"—could turn the moon and planets into so many torches, then fade out as if nothing had happened! Oh, you idiot—"

"May I come in?"

She looked surprised. She stepped aside, and I bent and picked up the bags and walked in.

The glass doors rattled as if giants were trying to beat their way in. Rain had squeezed through cracks to make dark puddles on the rug.

I set the bags on the kitchen counter. I found bread in the refrigerator, dropped two slices in the toaster. While they were toasting I opened the foie gras.

"My telescope's gone," she said. Sure enough, it was. The tripod was all by itself on the balcony, on its side.

I untwisted the wire on a champagne bottle. The toast popped up, and Leslie found a knife and spread both slices with foie gras. I held the bottle near her ear, figuring to trip conditioned reflexes.

She did smile fleetingly as the cork popped. She said, "We should set up our picnic grounds here. Behind the counter. Sooner or later the wind is going to break those doors and shower glass all over everything."

That was a good thought. I slid around the partition, swept all the pillows off the floor and the couch and came back with them. We set up a nest for ourselves.

It was kind of cosy. The kitchen counter was three and a half feet high, just over our heads, and the kitchen alcove itself was just wide enough to swing our elbows comfortably. Now the floor was all pillows. Leslie poured the champagne into brandy snifters, all the way to the lip.

I searched for a toast, but there were just too many possibilities, all depressing. We drank without toasting. And then carefully set the snifters down and slid forward into each other's arms. We could sit that way, face to face, leaning sideways against each other.

"We're going to die," she said.

"Maybe not."

"Get used to the idea. I have," she said. "Look at you, you're all nervous now. Afraid of dying. Hasn't it been a lovely night?"

"Unique. I wish I'd known in time to take you to dinner."

Thunder came in a string of six explosions. Like bombs in an air raid. "Me too," she said when we could hear again.

"I wish I'd known this afternoon."

"Pecan pralines!"

"Farmer's Market. Double-roasted peanuts. Who would *you* have murdered, if you'd had the time?

"There was a girl in my sorority   "

—and she was guilty of sibling rivalry, so Leslie claimed. I named an editor who kept changing his mind. Leslie named one of my old girl friends, I named her only old boy friend that I knew about, and it got to be kind of fun before we ran out. My brother Mike had forgotten my birthday once. The fiend.

The lights flickered, then came on again.

Too casually, Leslie asked, "Do you really think the sun might go back to normal?"

"It better *be* back to normal. Otherwise we're dead anyway. I wish we could see Jupiter."

"Dammit it, answer me! Do you think it was a flare?"

"Yes."

"Why?"

"Yellow dwarf stars don't go nova "

"What if ours did?"

"The astronomers know a lot about novas," I said. "More than you'd guess. They can see them coming months ahead. Sol is a gee-nought yellow dwarf. They don't go nova at all. They have to wander off the main sequence first, and that takes millions of years."

She pounded a fist softly on my back. We were cheek to cheek; I couldn't see her face. "I don't want to believe it. I don't dare. Stan, nothing like this has ever happened before. How can you know?"

"Something did."

"What? I don't believe it. We'd remember."

"Do you remember the first moon landing? Aldrin and Armstrong?"

"Of course. We watched it at Earl's Lunar Landing Party."

"They landed on the biggest, flattest place they could find on the moon. They sent back several hours of jumpy home movies, took a lot of very clear pictures, left corrugated footprints all over the place. And they came home with a bunch of rocks.

"Remember? People said it was a long way to go for rocks. But the first thing anyone noticed about those rocks was that they were half-melted.

"Sometime in the past—oh, say, the past hundred thousand

years, there's no way of marking it closer than that—the sun
flared up. It didn't stay hot enough long enough to leave any
marks on the Earth. But the moon doesn't have an atmosphere
to protect it. All the rocks melted on one side."

The air was warm and damp. I took off my coat, which was
heavy with rainwater. I fished the cigarettes and matches out, lit
a cigarette and exhaled past Leslie's ear.

"We'd remember. It *couldn't* have been this bad."

"I'm not so sure. Suppose it happened over the Pacific? It
wouldn't do *that* much damage. Or over the American continents. It would have sterilized some plants and animals and
burned down a lot of forests, and who'd know? The sun went
back to normal, that time. It might again. The sun is a four
percent variable star. Maybe it gets a touch more variable than
that, every so often."

Something shattered in the bedroom. A window? A wet wind
touched us, and the shriek of the storm was louder.

"Then we could live through this," Leslie said hesitantly.

"I believe you've put your finger on the crux of the matter.
Skål!" I found my champagne and drank deep. It was past three
in the morning, with a hurricane beating at our doors.

"Then shouldn't we be doing something about it?"

"We are."

"Something like trying to get up into the hills! Stan, there're
going to be floods!"

"You bet your ass there are, but they won't rise this high.
Fourteen stories. Listen, I've thought this through. We're in a
building that was designed to be earthquake-proof. You told me
so yourself. It'd take more than a hurricane to knock it over.

"As for heading for the hills, what hills? We won't get far
tonight, not with the streets flooded already. Suppose we could
get up into the Santa Monica Mountains; then what? Mud-
slides, that's what. That area won't stand up to what's coming.
The flare must have boiled away enough water to make another
ocean. It's going to rain for forty days and forty nights! Love,
this is the safest place we could have reached tonight."

"Suppose the polar caps melt?"

"Yeah . . . well, we're pretty high, even for that. Hey,
maybe that last flare was what started Noah's flood. Maybe it's
happening again. Sure as hell, there's not a place on Earth that
isn't the middle of a hurricane. Those two great counterrotating

hurricanes, by now they must have broken up into hundreds of little storms—"

The glass doors exploded inward. We ducked, and the wind howled about us and dropped rain and glass on us.

"At least we've got food!" I shouted. "If the floods maroon us here, we can last it out!"

"But if the power goes, we can't cook it! And the refrigerator—"

"We'll cook everything we can. Hardboil all the eggs—"

The wind rose about us. I stopped trying to talk.

Warm rain sprayed us horizontally and left us soaked. Try to cook in a hurricane? I'd been stupid; I'd waited too long. The wind would tip boiling water on us if we tried it. Or hot grease.

Leslie screamed, "We'll have to use the oven!"

Of course. The oven couldn't possibly fall on us.

We set it for 400° and put the eggs in, in a pot of water. We took all the meat out of the meat drawer and shoved it in on a broiling pan. Two artichokes in another pot. The other vegetables we could eat raw.

What else? I tried to think.

Water. If the electricity went, probably the water and telephone lines would too. I turned on the faucet over the sink and started filling things: pots with lids, Leslie's thirty-cup percolator that she used for parties, her wash bucket. She clearly thought I was crazy, but I didn't trust the rain as a water source; I couldn't control it.

The sound. Already we'd stopped trying to shout through it. Forty days and nights of this and we'd be stone-deaf. Cotton? Too late to reach the bathroom. Paper towels! I tore and wadded and made four plugs for our ears.

Sanitary facilities? Another reason for picking Leslie's place over mine. When the plumbing stopped, there was always the balcony.

And if the flood rose higher than the fourteenth floor, there was the roof. Twenty stories up. If it went higher than that, there would be damn few people when it was over.

And if it was a nova?

I held Leslie a bit more closely, and lit another cigarette one-handed. All the wasted planning, if it was a nova. But I'd have been doing it anyway. You don't stop planning just because there's no hope.

And when the hurricane turned to live steam, there was always the balcony. At a dead run, and over the railing, in preference to being boiled alive.

But now was not the time to mention it.

Anyway, she'd probably thought of it herself.

The lights went out about four. I turned off the oven, in case the power should come back. Give it an hour to cool down, then I'd put all the food in Baggies.

Leslie was asleep, sitting up in my arms. How could she sleep, not knowing? I piled pillows behind her and let her back easy.

For some time I lay on my back, smoking, watching the lightning make shadows on the ceiling. We had eaten all the foie gras and drunk one bottle of champagne. I thought of opening the brandy, but decided against it, with regret.

A long time passed. I'm not sure what I thought about. I didn't sleep, but certainly my mind was in idle. It only gradually came to me that the ceiling, between lightning flashes, had turned gray.

I rolled over, gingerly, soggily. Everything was wet.

My watch said it was nine-thirty.

I crawled around the partition into the living room. I'd been ignoring the storm sounds for so long that it took a faceful of warm whipping rain to remind me. There was a hurricane going on. But charcoal-gray light was filtering through the black clouds.

So. I was right to have saved the brandy. Flood, storms, intense radiation, fires lit by the flare—if the toll of destruction was as high as I expected, then money was about to become worthless. We would need trade goods.

I was hungry. I ate two eggs and some bacon—still warm—and started putting the rest of the food away. We had food for a week, maybe . . . but hardly a balanced diet. Maybe we could trade with other apartments. This was a big building. There must be empty apartments, too, that we could raid for canned soup and the like. And refugees from the lower floors to be taken care of, if the waters rose high enough . . .

Damn! I missed the nova. Life had been simplicity itself last night. Now . . . Did we have medicines? Were there doctors in the building? There would be dysentery and other plagues.

And hunger. There was a supermarket near here; could we find a scuba rig in the building?

But I'd get some sleep first. Later we could start exploring the building. The day had become a lighter charcoal gray. Things could be worse, far worse. I thought of the radiation that must have sleeted over the far side of the world, and wondered if our children would colonize Europe, or Asia, or Africa.

THE LAST SUNSET

Geoffrey A. Landis

And when the last days have come at last, when the end of the world really is at hand and the human race is about to vanish from the Earth, perhaps the last thing to matter is the style with which you face the End . . .

A physicist who works for NASA, and who has recently been working on the Martian Lander program, Geoffrey A. Landis is a frequent contributor to Analog *and* Asimov's Science Fiction, *and has also sold stories to markets such as* Interzone, Amazing *and* Pulphouse. *Landis is not a prolific writer, by the high-production standards of the genre, but he is popular. His story, "A Walk in the Sun," won him a Nebula and a Hugo Award in 1992; his story, "Ripples in the Dirac Sea," won him a Nebula Award in 1990; and his story, "Elemental," was on the final Hugo ballot a few years back. His first book was the collection,* Myths, Legends, and True History, *and he has recently sold his first novel. He lives in Brook Park, Ohio.*

Like an enemy fighter in an old movie about flying aces, the comet came out of the sun, invisible against the glare until it was far too late. There was nothing left to do, Christopher thought, but wait for the inevitable impact, and to calculate where it would hit.

Chris was the astronomy group's pet computer whiz. The comet had been discovered by the astronomers, but the calculation of orbit, and hence finding the time and location of the impact, was his responsibility. He'd been extraordinarily careful with the calculation, checking the critical lunar perturbation by three different methods before he was confident of the results. It was close, almost a miss. Had the Earth been ten minutes further along its orbit, it *would* have been a miss.

It was a hit.

"Shit," said Martin, one of the astronomers. They were gathered in the computer division's conference room, not that the results couldn't have been printed out in any one of their offices. "Forty miles? The impact is forty miles east of here? You're sure?"

Christopher nodded. "I'm sorry."

"Huh? Not your fault," the astronomer said. "What irony. We'll be at ground zero, then, or just about. The fireball will be a hundred miles across. We won't even see it."

"No consolation," said Tibor, the second astronomer on the team, "but, if it matters to you, yes, we'll see it. It will take about a minute for the fireball to expand."

"I'm sorry," said the first astronomer. "I really wanted to see my kids grow up. I did." He was crying now, awkwardly. "Not that it makes any difference what I wanted. I'm sorry. I'm going home now. I think I want to be with my family."

Tibor looked at his watch. "Go ahead and call the newspapers, if you want."

"Why bother?" Martin said, already halfway out the door. "I don't see much point in it."

Tibor tossed the page of printout on the floor. "Yeah. Guess I'm going to go home, too." He looked up at Christopher. "You know, you're lucky," he said, shaking his head. "You're not married. Never thought I'd envy somebody for that."

"Some luck," Christopher said softly, but by then the astronomers had both left, and he was alone in the bright silence of the conference room.

An hour and a half to the end of the world. There was no sense running, Christopher knew. When the end of the world falls like the sword of God out of the sky, there was no place far enough to run. He walked back to his office and stared at the books and papers piled helter-skelter across his desk. They didn't matter. Nothing mattered now; nothing at all.

He closed the door.

Kara was in her office two doors down, reading a journal. She was the newest hire in the University Research Institute's computer division—she'd been there only a year—but of all the group, he liked working with her best. Occasionally they went out for coffee together; once they'd gone to a movie.

She looked up when he passed her door. "Say, Chris, where is the astronomy group off to?" she asked. "I was just looking for Tibor, but he's not here, and his car's not in the lot."

"He went home early today," Chris said. "So did Martin."

"Oh," Kara said. "No big deal. Guess I'll have to catch him tomorrow." She went back to her reading.

Christopher worked well with her, but sometimes he thought he didn't really know her. Kara was four years younger than he was, and at times the difference seemed like an abyss. Sometimes it seemed to him that she was gently flirting with him, and then a moment later she would be nothing but business, friendly and casual in a completely professional way. She was smart and extremely competent; he never had to explain anything to her twice. He liked working with her.

She was a bit shy, he knew, although she hid it well. One time he'd seen Kara with her kid sister, and the difference had been striking. She'd been simultaneously more grown up, and also younger, laughing and kidding. That day, he thought, was probably when he'd fallen in love with her. He'd known better than to try to make a pass at somebody he worked with; far too often, that led to disaster.

But he'd thought about it many times over the last year. And now, he thought, he could do it now. Now that nothing mattered.

"Hey, Kara," he said, and waited for her to look up again. "Coffee?"

She looked at her watch. "Well—"

"Come on," he said. "You need the break. It's after four."

She looked at the stack of papers on her desk, a bit neater than the piles on his, but still formidable. "Thanks, but I can't. I've really got a lot of work."

"Oh, come on. If it was the end of the world, would any of this really matter?"

She smiled. "Well, okay. Give me five minutes."

It was more like twenty minutes before she came by his office. Chris spent the time writing names on a list of people he ought to call, then crossing them off again.

They went down Thayer Street, to a coffee shop popular with undergraduates, and grabbed a corner table. It had been raining all day, but the sky had finally cleared, and the late afternoon sun glinted in the puddles. Chris's stomach was wound tight.

He had to say something now, but he couldn't find words. He felt like he was in high school again, dry-mouthed at the thought of asking a girl to dance. And, indeed, what could he say? He realized that he didn't want to threaten their friendship with a pass, and suddenly knew that he wasn't going to ask her anything. It would be too crude. He wanted her to like him too much. He felt like a fool. It was the end of the world, and even so, he was tongue-tied. Nothing could change him.

Kara didn't seem to notice his silence. Perhaps she had things on her mind, too. He didn't even know if she had a boyfriend. She never mentioned one, but why should she? There was so much he didn't know about her; so much he would never get a chance to know.

Christopher turned away, pretending to watch the sunset reflected in the puddles, and worked hard to blink away his tears. Two minutes left. When he thought he could speak without his voice breaking, he said, "Say, grab your coffee, and let's go sit by the observatory to watch the sunset."

Kara shrugged. "Okay."

Walking down the street, on a sudden impulse he reached out and took her hand. She gave him a sidelong glance, but didn't pull her hand away. Her hand was cool, her fingers surprisingly small against his palm. It was enough, he decided, enough just to walk down the street with her and hold her hand on the last night of the world. It was not what he wanted; he wanted to hold her close to him, to spend his life with her, to share all her secrets and her joys. But holding hands was enough. It was a promise; a promise meant for a someday that, now, would never be. Holding her hand would have to be enough for a lifetime.

Opposite the sunset, a deep red glow was rising silently into the sky, backlighting the clouds low on the horizon. "Look," he said, and she turned around and stopped, her eyes brilliant in the glow.

"Why, it's beautiful," she said. "I've never seen a sunset do that before. What is it?"

The red stretched nearly from horizon to horizon now, and in the east it was turning an intense blue-violet, brighter than the sun. "It's the end of the world," he said, and then, at last, there was nothing left to say.

DOWN IN THE DARK

william Barton

But, as a contemporary sage once said, "It's not over until it's over."

Here we visit the frozen moons of Saturn, in the wake of a cosmic catastrophe that has destroyed all life on Earth, to a time when the human race has been backed into the tightest of tight corners and is on the verge of extinction, for a compelling and somberly lyrical study of how flickers of light can sometimes show up from the most unexpected of sources, even at the blackest of times, even when you're down in the dark, and it seems that all hope is gone.

William Barton was born in Boston in 1950 and currently resides in Durham, North Carolina. For most of his life, he has been an engineering technician, specializing in military and industrial technology. He was at one time employed by the Department of Defense, working on the nation's nuclear submarine fleet, and is currently a freelance writer and computer consultant. His stories have appeared in Aboriginal SF, Asimov's Science Fiction, Amazing, Interzone, Tomorrow, Full Spectrum, and other markets. His books include the novels Hunting on Kunderer, A Plague of All Cowards, Dark Sky Legion, When Heaven Fell, The Transmigration of Souls *(which was a finalist for the Philip K. Dick Award), and* Acts of Conscience, *and, in collaboration with Michael Capobianco,* Iris, Fellow Traveler, *and* Alpha Centauri. *His most recent novels are* White Light, *in collaboration with Michael Capobianco, and the new solo novel,* When We Were Real.

Yesterday, August 4, 2057, was my fifty-third birthday. I don't think anyone noticed. No one said anything. Maybe birthdays don't count anymore.

I sat in the half-track's cockpit, wearing my pressure suit, gloves off, helmet thrown back, steering by memory, as if caught in a dream. Four months. Four more months and I would've gone home, home to Lisa, whose letters said she was still waiting for me after all these years. But then the world came to an end, and all that ended along with it.

Sometimes, when I'm asleep, I still see the ending itself, see the newsreels transmitted after the fact from Moonbase. Just a nickel-iron asteroid twenty-three kilometers across, that's all. Knew about it for more than a year, they said, keeping it secret so there'd be no panic, making their plans in secret, carrying them off the same way.

Big rock like that, you'd think they'd've known about it for decades, but that long elliptical orbit, taking it out past Neptune . . . no number. No name on it but ours.

See those six bright flashes? Six thirty-year-old thermonuclear bombs going off, blowing the damned thing to bits. Now see the pretty pieces? Notice how they entrain and continue on their way? Twelve of them hit the Earth, one right after another, during the course of a long and interesting day.

I imagined people, imagined my old friends, seeing those secret nuclear flashes in the deep night sky, going, What the hell . . . ?

The biggest one hit the South Pole, coming in almost level, and damn if you couldn't see the West Antarctic ice sheet lift right off, breaking to a trillion glittery bits as it flew into orbit.

The last one came down dead square in the middle of North America, not far from Kansas City. Not far from my house. I kept imagining, hoping anyway, that Lisa was asleep just then. But she was probably out in the backyard with all our old friends, maybe watching with my binoculars as . . .

I had the cabin lights off, surrounded by the dull red glow of a few necessary dials, the bluer glow of a half dozen small plasma screens, so I could see outside, watch bits of landscape jump into the headlights' wash, low hummocks of waxy ice, pinkish snow the color of the stuff that sometimes grows down in the bowl of a dirty toilet.

Following old ruts outside, my own tracks, driven over and over again.

The saddleback came up, ground leveling out, forming a very shallow caldera. I pulled over to my familiar place, pink snow mashed flat, glazed yellow from environmental heating, parked where I'd parked a hundred times already, killed the headlights, dimmed the panel lights as much as they'd go without full powerdown, waited for my eyes to catch up.

The world came out of its own background gloom, like a ghost ship coasting from a fog, landscape tumbling down away from me, dull purplish hills and blue half-mountains, rolling away in the mist like the Adirondacks in springtime, rolling all the way to the shores of the Waxsea. More mist out there, then pale, glassy red nothing disappearing long before it got to where the horizon should've been.

From the heights of the Aethurst Range, pressure ridge complex puckering the midline of Terra Noursae, maybe seven klicks from where *Huygens* set down, just a few weeks before I was born, you get one of the best views in the solar system. Maybe why I stop for it every time.

Overhead, the sky was bright now, though it was near the middle of an eight-day night. Maybe my eyes are learning to adapt quicker, quicker with each passing day. Maybe I'm at home here now.

Sure as hell can't be home anywhere else.

Everyone says the sky is orange here, even more orange than the sky on Venus, but it isn't. Hell, I've been to Venus. I know what that sky looks like. Not at all the same.

Sometimes, I try to imagine what the sky must look like from my old backyard. Sometimes, I imagine it just the way it was when I last saw it, not so many years ago. Other times I get a quick image of all those meters of ejecta that must be . . . well. Those times I let it go.

From overhead, Earth's sky looks dull gray-brown, lit up here and there, day and night, by a tawny red-orange glow. Moonbase newsreels say there's no free oxygen down there anymore, so the glow must be lava. Something like that.

Far above, hundreds of meters up, a flat snowdrift sailed along, potato chip waxflakes tumbling end over end in slow motion, twinkling, shiny, bouncing off each other, drift keeping its shape the way a terrestrial cloud keeps its shape in the wind. I clutched the Stirlings and brought the rpms as far down as the safeties would let me. Cut the cabin blower and listened to what the hull mikes were hearing.

There.

First, the dry-as-dust creaking of the landscape, stretching gently to and fro under Saturn's tidal strain. Then the dull, faraway moan of the wind. Not like an Earthly wind, wind blowing around the eaves of your house, groaning like a ghost through the branches of dead trees. Deeper here, almost subsonic, a wind that'd never been alive.

Finally . . . like dry, dead leaves, fallen leaves blowing along the gutter on a cold, gray fall morning, the sound of snow, drifting through the sky.

Saturn was barely visible behind the haze, nearly full, like a huge, featureless yellow moon, striated and edgeless. When it's daytime up here, if you know how to look, you can see the rings from their backscatter, like diamonds in the sky, arcing round the sooty smudge of Saturn's nightside shadow. Not now. Just that yellow disk, sitting up there, looking like an eyeless face.

I was out on Phoebe just once, fixing broken hardware. One-fifty degrees inclination to the ecliptic. Christ. It was a hell of sight, even from thirteen million klicks out. Maybe, someday . . .

Running late, I powered up the halftrack's systems and got going. With the headlights on, Titan was just a murky moonscape under a vaguely orange indigo sky.

Down by the Waxsea, down where the atmospheric pressure can hit two thousand millibars, the sky is opaque, Sun, Saturn, stars, and pale, iridescent blue Rhea, all lost. It's not really orange, even here. Brown might be a better word.

I pulled out of a gray defile that'd grown narrower since the last time I'd been here, engaging the pillow tires manually to break through a little ridge of waxy snow, methane and ethane not really frozen, but caught up in a sticky mess of organic polymers, pulled around a smoky pool of colorless liquid nitrogen that'd be gone in days.

Ahead of me, on a sloping surface that'd long ago lost its volatile regolith components, Workpoint 31 was looking older than before, the dome habitat baggy in places, bubble airlock drooping a bit. The weather station looked fine though, antennae sticking up just the way I remembered, anemometer turning slowly. I pulled up to the power transformer, extending my electrical probe, docking and parking in one smooth move, cutting the engines, lights, everything that could be cut.

There was a spacesuited figure standing beside a snowmobile with the battery compartment yawning open, motionless, turned toward me. Looking closely, I could see a pale face, barely visible. No radio hail or anything. Fine by me. I got the rest of my suit on, closed myself into the half-track's too-small airlock, and thumbed the depress valve actuator. There was a soft *woof* as the air went out through the burner, igniting, flaring away with a brief blue flash that lit up the lock's teacup-sized porthole.

It seemed dark outside as I walked toward the snowmobile, the sky not quite . . . lowering. Haze coming down and . . . a silver golfball seemed to materialize out of the air, drifting down a shallow glidepath, coming between me and the waiting figure. The workpoint's structures were reflected upside-down in its surface.

Slow. Slow. Almost as if it were decelerating as it approached the ground. Maybe so. The air gets thicker fast down here. It hit the ground and exploded into a brief crater-shape, complete with central peak.

Ploink.

There was a quick, rippling mirror on the snow, then nothing.

The radio voice, a soft woman's voice, said, "Starting to rain. We'd better get inside."

As we struggled out of our suits, the habitat seemed incredibly cluttered. People had been bringing junk here and leaving it for years. Just leaving it. I don't know. Maybe, someday, it would've been thrown out. Now? No.

The inner surface of the pressure envelope, arching blue plastic overhead, was lumping here and there, slowly, more raindrops coming down. In just a little while, if the intensity of the storm increased, it would look like slick blue pudding, gently aboil.

The woman, who was dumpy, androgynous in her longjohns, but had a pretty oval face, dark green eyes, short, straight, straw-colored hair, held out her hand. "Cristie Meitner."

I took the hand, feeling the small warmth of her fingers briefly in mine. "Hoxha Maxwell." Funny, there's less than a hundred people on Titan. You'd think after four years I'd know them all.

She said, "Hoe-jah?" Not smiling, just curious. Something nervous about her, too. Like she was afraid of me or something.

I spelled it for her. "Named after some two-bit Albanian dictator by socialist parents who thought Marxism might get back on its feet someday." 2004? Getting to be a long time ago, these days. I smiled, and said, "Rubbish bin of history, and all that."

She looked away for a moment, then gestured toward the habitat's kitchen module, much of it buried under piles of unrecognizable hardware. "I was about to have dinner. You, ah . . . afterward, if the rain's let up, I guess we could go down to the instrument platform and get started."

Rain never lasts long here. I shook my head. "I've been going almost thirty hours straight. If I don't get some sleep, I'll break everything I touch."

Looking at me, she seemed to swallow. "Don't you, ah, sleep in the 'track?"

"Batteries won't charge if the systems don't stay powered down for at least six hours." You know that. What's the problem here?

There was something like despair in her eyes.

Asleep, she breathed with her mouth hanging open, making a hollow sound that wasn't quite a snore. Slow, soft inhale. Long pause. Quicker exhale, louder, almost like a word.

She'd put me in her bunk, the habitat's only bunk, had then curled up on the floor, snuggled in a spare bunkliner some-body'd left behind, who knows when. The liner on the bunk was her own, permeated with her scent. Nothing perfumy about it, nothing feminine. Just a people smell.

I felt like my eyes were ready to fall out, but I was too exhausted to sleep, too exhausted to do anything but lie there, looking down at her, lit by dim instrument light. When she'd put out the habitat lights, it'd seemed pitch dark, but after a while, this blue glow, that red one, a little green over there . . .

Almost like daylight to me now.

Abruptly, I remembered a night when I'd watched Lisa sleeping naked beside me, streaming gold hair splayed out on the sheets, head thrown back to show the long, soft curve of her neck, mulberry-bright eyes closed, moving back and forth beneath paper-thin lids.

Dreaming.

What were you dreaming, back then, back when we were so young?

I forgot to ask.

Now I'll never know.

Nights like these, I wish I'd never gone to space. But space was the only way an engineering technician could get rich, move us to a lifestyle where we could have that family.

"A million dollars a year," I'd argued, trying to break through her tears. "A million dollars!"

How long?

It's a twelve year contract, Lisa. Think. Think what it'll be like to have twelve million dollars. . . . And I won't be gone the whole time. I mean, a year on the Moon, a couple of years on Mars maybe. I'll be home from time to time.

Home to help you buy our new life, set things up. And when it's all over . . . instead, I signed on for four years out by Saturn. Four years of triple pay. And by the time I got here, somebody, somewhere, already knew what was coming.

Hell.

We could've died together, standing out in the backyard, holding hands, watching the end of the world fall on us from a star-spangled midnight sky.

It was still night the next day, of course, Christie reluctantly feeding me a breakfast of weak tea and algae muffins. No jelly, no butter, startling me when she pressed the teabags flat and hung them up to dry.

Of course. When it's gone, there'll be no more tea. I doubt there's butter and jelly any closer to Mars. I liked Mars, with its red sky and pale blue clouds. Part of the base where I was stationed, Oudemans 4, with its fine view of Ius Chasma, was under a clear dome. There was a little garden where some people were trying to grow oregano and poppies. I used to take my breakfast out there, sit and drink my instant coffee, nibble on my Pop Tarts and dream.

How many cups of weak tea can you get from a single teabag?

After breakfast, we suited up and got into the half-track,

squeezing through the airlock one at a time, undocking, then lurching off along the terminal escarpment to where some old eutectic collapse had made a jumbled, sloping path down to the seashore.

Other than answering the few questions I could think of, techie stuff about her equipment problems, Christie was silent, looking away from me, troubled. Christ. Everyone I know is troubled. As we watched the murky landscape, foggy with nitrogen mist at two bar, roll by, I said, "How long you been here?" I've met people who came in with the first expedition nine years ago, mostly scientists like Christie Meitner, who've been out in the field most of that time. Some of 'em are a little boggy in the head.

Not looking at me, she said, "Three months. Before that I was on Delta Platform."

Delta Platform, on the other side of Titan, where the Waxsea is an endless, landless, featureless expanse of red-tinted silver-gray. "How long on Titan?"

She turned and looked at me with a slightly resentful look. some people don't want to . . . think about it anymore. "A year. I came in with *Oberth*'s last run."

Oberth's last run. She was still on her way home from Saturn, halfway between Earth and Mars when it happened, which is why humanity's under-two-thousand survivors still have an interplanetary vessel. Last time I was back at Alanhold Base, I heard *Oberth*, damaged when she'd had to aerobrake through an ash-clogged stratosphere, was repaired, was on her way to rescue the Venus Orbital Station personnel.

Two thousand. Two thousand out of all those billions. Jesus. But all I feel is that one damned death.

Used to be three fusion shuttles keeping our so-called "space-faring civilization" up and running, running supplies to a few hundred on Mars, a couple of dozen each at Venus, Callisto, Mercury Base, and the Fore Trojans. The four score and ten out here on Titan. Now there's just the one.

Ziolkovskii was caught in LEO, docked to the space station for repair and refit. I can't imagine why the hell people thought she'd be all right, why the station would come through in one piece. *Ziolkovskii*'s crew got real nervous when they saw what was happening. Got their ship undocked and under way. But.

They were transmitting to Moonbase the whole time, which

made for one hell of a newsreel. All the big impacts were on the other side of the Earth from where the ship and station were at the time, but long before they rounded the planetary limb, you could see rocks rising into her forward trajectory.

Commander Boltano kept transmitting, kept talking calmly, deep, slow voice like nothing unusual was going on, panning his hand-held camera out the command-module's docking window, as the rocks got bigger and bigger, until there was nothing else in sight. His voice cut off with a grunt and the camera view made a sudden, rapid excursion, just before the picture turned to static.

Goddard, still a few days out, making all those wonderful timelapse videos of the impact sequence, exploded as she tried to aerobrake. I guess by the time *Oberth* got home a couple of months later, things had settled out a bit.

We got to the seashore, running down a long detritus slope, and pulled up to the research platform, which looked a little bit like those old-style unmanned landers, some of them going all the way back to the 1970s, you find scattered around the surface of Mars.

Beyond it, the flat, empty surface of the Waxsea stretched away like an infinite table, until it was lost in low, dark red mist. Behind us, the delicately folded face of the Terra Noursae terminal towered like cornflower blue curtains, mostly exposed water ice, the beach we stood on cracked icebits strung through with ropes of peach-colored polymer and black strands of asphalt.

Down by the mean datum, Titan's sky really is orange, dull orange even at night, with only invisible Saturn's glory for light, and it seems awfully far away overhead.

Christie was looking for me, face no more than shadowed eyes seen through her suit's visor. "Can we get started? I'd like to get back to work."

"Sure."

Funny thing. There were old snowmobile batteries scattered like a perimeter fence around the instrument package, seated in the beach "sand," tilting at angles like so many silent sentinels. As she showed me what was wrong, she kept looking away, looking out at the beach beyond.

I got to work on her problems, easily fixed, mostly shorted out capacitors and the like, carefully packing each ruined component in my toolkit as I replaced it. We used to throw these things away, but . . . well, maybe somebody can figure out how to fix solid states, one way or another. We sure as hell aren't going to make new ones out here. Not for a long time, even if . . .

Moonbase keeps talking about component fabrication, but it's just pissing in the wind. Watching *that* newsreel, my buddy Jimmy Thornton, who'd come in on the same flight as me, was scheduled to go home with me, commented there must be plenty of good hardware sitting in collapsed, half-melted warehouses on Earth.

Sure. Maybe we *could* repurpose a Venus lander and get it back to LEO. Figure out where to land, get what we needed, get back up.

Later that night, Jimmy cut himself with a utility knife, not leaving a note behind.

Maybe he figured I wouldn't miss him.

Maybe he figured I'd be along shortly.

Christie watched me work for a while, maybe not trusting that I knew what was what. Scientist types are like that. After a while, she wandered off, and, as I worked, I could see her spacesuit drifting about the beach, white against the colored background of Titanscape, out beyond the ring of abandoned hardware sentinels.

Something else we need to rescue. Ruined batteries are easy enough to fix, especially when you've got plenty of chemicals just lying around.

Finished, I buttoned up, turned, and watched her a bit.

She had her back angled toward me, walking around the perimeter, half turned away, watching the ground. Every now and again she'd take a quick step outward, seeming to dance like a child, then stand and watch.

Going nuts already, Dr. Meitner?

Well, maybe so. Most of the scientists have just continued doing their jobs, gathering data, doing interpretations, just like . . . well. Techies keep doing *theirs* because if they don't, we all die right now.

She was standing with her back fully toward me, hands on hips, looking out to sea. There was a hazy layer of mist out there, Waxsea a little bit like Lake Michigan seen from Chicago's Loop on a cold November morning.

I walked toward her in the gloom, wondering which way our shadows would fall, if we'd had shadows. Just beyond her, I thought I saw something, a bit of yellow smudged on the waxy icecrust. Moving? A ripple caused by a thermocline in the dense air? Hard to tell. It . . . she took a quick step forward, stepping right into the puddle of yellow, which vanished like a mirage.

Off to one side, out of her suit-limited peripheral vision perhaps, there was another smudge, red, tinged with a bit of blue. As I watched, it started rippling slowly, moving in the direction of the hardware platform and parked half-track, aiming for a point midway between the two nearest batteries. When I stepped toward it, the thing edged away, following a long curve.

I heard a muffled gasp in my earphones.

Christie rushed past me, bounding toward it in a standard low-gee kangaroo hop. The ripple of red was still for a second, then, just as she got to it, seemed to dissolve into the sand.

"What the hell's going on here? What is that stuff?"

She turned to face me, skin around her eyes pale behind the suit's faceplate, hands behind her back like a naughty child caught in the act.

I stood still, transfixed by the terror in her eyes. Lot of people going crazy these days. No one should be surprised. "Are you all right?"

She nodded inside the suit, eyes going up and down. "Sure. Sure, I . . . they're . . ." Her eyes darted away from mine, scanning the landscape behind me for a second, but I was afraid to turn and look. "They're a kind of . . . a complex waxy polymer construct. They form at the interface between the Waxsea and Terra Noursae, apparently. Just on the beach, though I've found a few beneath the seacrust." She suddenly stopped talking, squeezing her eyes shut hard for a moment, looking away from me when she opened them again.

"What makes them move?"

"Our waste heat." Pause, darting eyes, then, "I've made some cold-soak instrumentation that shows they normally flow along tidal stress cracks in the beach."

Wandering goo. "Why were you . . ." All I could do was gesture. Hiding them from me? How could I ask that and still seem . . . reasonable?

There was a long pause, filled with my heartbeat and the soft groan of a distant wind, then she said, "I'm . . . not ready to publish yet."

I tried to stop myself from speaking, but failed. "*Publish?* Christie, there aren't any . . . I mean . . . uh."

Eyes blazing, she snapped, "*Shut up!*"

I felt cold sweat form briefly inside my suit. "Sure. Sorry, I . . . um. Sure." Inside the half-track, all the way back to Workpoint 31, she was silent, as if I'd ceased to exist.

Coming in along the south approach to Alanhold Base, you arrive at Bonestell Cosmodrome about twelve klicks out. This is where the first piloted landing set down, 20 April 2048, though when the second expedition arrived two years later, they tractored the components of the new base some distance away. Good idea, what with the contamination, the explosion risk, and all.

I skirted the edge of the ragged cryofoam disk that kept launches and landings from slowly digging the base's crater deeper and deeper in the ice, not intending to stop, glancing at the activity out of one side window from time to time.

TL-1, the original lander, almost always down for repair these days, was hidden in its hangar, yellow light glowing through the plastic, casting the gray shadows of workers like puppet-show phantasms. *TL-2* was on its meilerwagen being towed to our only launch gantry.

None of it's necessary, of course. When these things break down, we can use the little ships the way they were designed to be used, wingless lifting bodies setting down feather-light on stubby landing legs, lifting off again in a bowl of blue fire.

Great idea, indigenous propellant nuclear thermal rockets. Wonder how long they'll last? No longer than our last shipment of radionuclides. Then what? No answer.

Briefly, I thought of the talk Jimmy and I'd had about converting *TL-1* to run off one of the base's fusion cores. Could be done, I guess. *TL-1* won't last much longer anyway.

I'd ridden the landers three times in three years. Getting here in the first place. Going out to service hardware on Phoebe. Making emergency repairs at Ringplane Station.

Christ, that was beautiful. Like being a fly on a wall thirty thousand kilometers high, looking straight down to yellow

Saturn's hazy cloudtops, feeling giddy at the thought of some-how falling.

Guess I expected one last flight, climbing up out of Titan's orange soup clouds into a sky true blue indigo, then black and spangled with stars, docking with *Oberth,* then going on home.

Back at Alanhold, I parked my half-track in the base's unpres-surized garage, corrugated arch sort of like a Quonset hut open on both ends, docked to a charging mast, and got out. I always take a quick look up when I roll out through the airlock door, because you can see the last bits of your depress fire boiling around under the ceiling, like a misty, glowing blue cloud.

Out one end of the garage, I could see somebody'd strung a brand new UN flag on the base's pole, woven plastic fabric rolling gently in the breeze. Every now and again, it'd stretch out a bit so you could see the white lines of the map. Maybe they should reconsider the flag? Sooner or later, we'll run out of them.

There was a sparse snow falling, big, shiny white flakes like Ruffles potato chips, tumbling, shrinking visibly as they fell straight down. I don't think any of them reached the ground intact. We put a lot of waste heat into this environment, whether we like it or not.

I turned away, remembering a picnic I'd had with my parents. Just some city park, summer, blue sky with a few wisps of pale white cloud, kids running around, screaming and yelling. Us on a blanket. Ruffles potato chips. Scaltest French Onion dip with so much MSG it made me sleepy afterward. A&W root beer.

Dad was killed in an autohighway pileup back in the twenties. Made the national news, he and thirty or so other poor bastards ground up in the wreckage, media exposure forcing Congress to cancel the project.

Mom . . . I don't know. She and Lisa never really got along so . . .

I went in through the base airlock.

After changing in my cubbyhole, not even enough room to stand fully upright, I went to the cafeteria, passing silent people in the hallways, stepping to my right, turning to face inward each time, men's and women's faces passing centimeters from mine, always with eyes downcast. Nobody in here, tables empty, dusty, chairs jumbled every which way, no one bothering to push them in any more.

I went to the freezer and got a couple of tacos, bemusedly wondering what life would be like when they ran out, now that Taco Hell is no more, picked out a pouch of cherry Hi-C while they were nuking, took my mess and went next door to the day room. More people here, TV on, playing a disk of the latest newsreel.

The screen was showing a gently curved planetary limb, layer of bluish haze hanging in an arc over featureless gray ash clouds. As I watched, light played in the clouds, first one dull spark, then others, propagating around it, then nothing.

Lightning.

I sat down next to Ron Smithfield, slouched in a chair with his legs splayed out on the floor's worn green carpet-tile. Green like grass. Green, the psych manuals said, so we'd feel comforted, when we were far, far from home.

He said, "You missed Durrell. Have to wait for the replay."

On the screen, the limb view was gone, nothing now but the gray clouds, growing steadily closer. There was a line of text, yellow-green letters, deceleration values crawling across the bottom of the image. "What'd the bastard have to say for himself this time?"

Rodrigo Durrell had been Secretary of Space in the second Jolson administration. He and the Undersecretary for Outer System Exploration, a Ms. Rhinehart, had managed an "inspection tour" of Moonbase, complete with their families, just before the asteroid intercept mission was launched.

Ms. Rhinehart, I understood, had a five-year-old daughter. Wonder what it feels like to be the only five-year-old girl in the universe?

Wonder if President Jolson knew? Did she stay on the job out of bravery or ignorance? Did she and her teenaged children huddle together in the White House, or in that old shelter in Virginia, waiting for it to happen? For a while, Moonbase kept trying to raise the National Command Post in Colorado. Nothing. Maybe Cheyenne Mountain took an impact.

Ron sighed. "Mercury Base personnel are dead."

The image on the screen was starting to grow dark now as the ash clouds got close. You could see a bit of pink where the plasma bowshock was starting to form around the probe's aeroshell. "I thought they had another few weeks of air left."

He nodded. "Apparently, once they understood *Oberth* couldn't come get them for another five months, they took a vote. Had the base doctor give them shots of surgical anesthetic. He radioed in their decision, then injected himself."

"Mmh." Nothing you can say about something like that. The image on the screen broke up into jags of colored static, quickly replaced by a colorbar pattern.

"Durrell says they're going to bring us all home in order, Venus, then the Trojan habitats, then Callisto. Then Mars, then us."

Home. I imagined myself on the dead Moon, sitting out the rest of my life looking up at dead Earth. "I guess we're last in case *Oberth* breaks down."

Ron nodded. There was a man on the screen now, some scientist type, talking, but I got up and left the room, not wanting to hear his excuses. Last time, he said it might take a year before a manned landing would be feasible, get a crew down there so we could see what the hell we've got left to work with.

That figure, I imagine, will be revised upward. Then revised upward again.

Nothing to do but go to the showers, then get myself to bed, get a good night's sleep so I could resume work in the morning. I took a towel and shampoo lozenge from the dispenser, got out of my coveralls and hung them on a peg, got under a nozzle in the far corner of the room, hot water sluicing over the back of my neck, cascading over my shoulders, running down my spine like warm, wet hands, making me shiver.

One thing we'll never run out of, here on Titan: hot water. Plenty of ice. Plenty of fuel for the fusion reactors.

A shadowy figure came in, carrying its own towel and lozenge, got out of its coverall and hung it on the hook next to mine, came walking across the room toward me.

"Hoxha," she said. Standing still, looking up at me with her big, dark eyes. Maybe waiting for me to make room for her under my nozzle?

I stood flatfooted, looking down at her, taking in a thousand naked-woman details. "Hello, Jennah."

She looked up for another few seconds, then her eyes fell.

She turned on the nozzle next to mine, cloud of steam rising, making the mist even denser. The floor seemed sticky under my feet, whoever had tub-and-tile duty shirking the job.

I turned to watch her, slim, pretty woman with long, curly black hair turning slowly around under a fine needle spray, maybe showing off for me, maybe not, water streaming over her shoulders, jetting provocatively from her nipples, running down her belly, spattering between her legs.

After a while, she looked up at me again, stretching her arms over her head, arching her back, flashing the red dot of a steropoeic implant. "You used to be interested, Hoxha."

Sure. Used to interest me a lot. Lisa and I talked about this, agreed that four years was just too long, that we'd tell all when it was over and done with, tell all and forgive whatever there was to forgive.

I shrugged. "Sorry."

She looked at me for another few seconds, then nodded, looking away, turned off her shower and walked away.

I stood in the mist for a little while longer, thinking about the failure of my interest in . . . well. Went to my room and went to sleep. Didn't want to dream, but I dreamed anyway.

In the morning, tired after a night's sleep fractured by fragmentary images of things that didn't exist anymore, I stopped by Tony Gualteri's cubby on the way down to the half-track hangar. Tony was a geochemist who'd been on *TL-1* the day it set down on Titan, had been out here ever since, slowly turning into the small, wiry old bald guy I'd first met almost four years ago.

When I told him about the colored wax things I'd seen floating along the beach surface out by Workpoint 31, he looked puzzled and scratched a chin made black by dense beard stubble.

All sorts of crazy things on Titan, he said. Anything's possible.

I stood expectantly, waiting. Well?

He'd shrugged. It's her project. None of my business. Then he turned back to the screen of his little computer, doing whatever it is geochemists do with their data.

Do, even when . . .

My own day's work was up the coast, so I had a fine drive

along the terminal escarpment, going to where one of the
remote automated resource stations had inexplicably gone
silent. Probably no surprise waiting for me there. Things fall
apart. I'm here to fix them.

By the time I got there, the weather was lifting and the Sun
was starting to rise, long streamers of golden light fingering
through the orange-brown sky, diffuse smudge of red-gold
smearing up through the mist hiding the Waxsea horizon.

It'd stay that way for a long time, Sun taking hours to clear
the mist and disappear in the sky, becoming no more than a
diffuse bright region, turning its part of the sky to shades of
orange peel, layered like mother-of-pearl.

The station was on the rim of the escarpment, weather
instruments spinning and nodding away, like nothing was
wrong, sensors on cables hanging down the cliffside all the way
to the beach, far below. I stood looking over the edge for a
few minutes, imagining I could see strange colors shining in
the sand, but . . . right. Imagination. Too far to see anything.
Anything at all.

Problem turned out to be simple but aggravating: Something
had shorted out a sensor head hanging off the end of one of the
cables, sending a power spike back up the line that made the
data recorder shut itself down as a safety measure. Then it
couldn't come back up, because something was still wrong
down at the sensor.

Easy enough to reset the computer, but it took me four hours
to reel in the cable. Somehow, some kind of black, tarry stuff
had gotten inside the instrument, gotten into electronics, and
then acted as a very nice conductor, the exact definition of a
short circuit. Took about a second to clean it out, saving a bit
of sample in a bottle for whoever might be interested, and that
was that.

Back inside the half-track, I sat in the driver's seat, looking out
over the wide, silver-red expanse of the Waxsea, toward the
dark mist of the horizon, smelling the faint odors of Titan that'd
made it through the lock-purge event, accompanying me inside.

They aren't bad smells. Not bad smells at all. Certainly not
the organic rot odors some old writers had imagined, imagination hardly colored by rational thought. Just a faint, crisp smell
like white campstove gas, uncontaminated by oxygenation

compounds. I remember my grandfather talking about the pleasant smell of the gas pump, back when he was a boy, back before they loaded the fuels with ether and alcohol. That and an occasional whiff of creosote, Titan smelling like an old-fashioned telephone pole, weeping black tar in the hot summer sun.

Thinking about black tar, feeling heavy lidded, the Titan-scape seemed to expand in my eyes, filling them up, driving away the insides of the half-track. Like I was outside. Like I could walk around outside, feel the wind in my hair, icy silver golfball raindrops ploinking on my skin, the flutter of waxy snowflakes like butterflies in my face.

What the hell was it about that stuff in the sensor head?

I really haven't learned enough about Titan despite my years here. Too busy being Mr. Fixit. Scientists not caring what I knew or didn't know.

Jennah. Jennah tried to talk to me sometimes, times when we were finished with what we had in common, lying cramped together in her bunk or mine. Tried to talk to me about her specialty, some branch of meteorology, studies on the high-pressure atmospheres of gas giants.

Can't get there from here, she'd said. No trips to Jupiter, to Saturn. Not in my lifetime. Maybe, someday, a bit of work high in the skies of Uranus or Neptune? Maybe in a generation? Too damned late for *me,* she'd said. Titan. Titan is all there'll ever be for me.

Prophetic words?

In all innocence, I guess.

And, talking, she made it sound like nothing more than numbers, reducing a beauty that had the power to mist my eyes into something like math homework. *Cubus plus sext rebus aequalis vigentum.*

Once, staggering under the workload of a powered exoskeleton, I'd looked off the top of Ishtar's Veil, high in the Maxwell Montes of Venus, and seen a colored glory, swirling with the ripples of a Kirlian aura, stood transfixed by it. No numbers there. No numbers at all.

I'd shut Jennah up with renewed kisses, overwhelming her with the demands of innumerate flesh. After a while, she gave up telling me about the arithmetic of her dreams.

In time, I fell asleep, hoping to dream about Jennah, at least.

Dream about the things we'd done together, the simple fun we'd had in those little rooms. Maybe, if I dreamed that dream, I'd awaken in the night to find myself flooded with renewed desire. Maybe in the morning, I'd turn this thing around and drive on back to base. Drive back, look Jennah up and . . . what the hell would they do if I took some extra time off? Fire me?

Instead, sleeping, I dreamed about Christie Meitner, dumpy in her longjohns, barely human in her pressure suit. Christie Meitner and her fields of color. Christie Meitner hopping like a maniac, hopping on puddles of melted crayon stuff, driving the colors away.

I woke up in the morning, looked for a bit at my refrigerated sample, and then set sail for Workpoint 31, calling base to let them know I was sidetracked, that I'd call them again later with a revised schedule.

It's not far out of the way, I thought. A few hours, that's all.

She wasn't at the habitat, blue dome looking baggier than ever, rather seedy by daylight, and didn't respond to my radio hail. Well. Snowmobile's gone, at any rate. Since there was plenty of juice in the batteries, I turned and drove on, following the tracks down to the edge of the escarpment, heading for the rubble fall and her instrumentation site.

For some reason, I stopped a few hundred meters shy of the turn and got out, listening to the soft woof of the vent burner, wondering if she'd see the cloud of blue flame as it dissipated, rising above the cliff's edge.

I walked down that way, waxy surface crackling under my boots, steam rising around me once I got off the beaten track and started disturbing virgin regolith, finally stopping right on the verge, looking out into open space. The beach, silver sugar crystals woven with orange and black thread. The silver-red sea. The red-orange-brown haze farther on. The sky, orange and brown with red clouds and dark, faraway snow, descending blue bands of rain like shadows in the mist.

A soft voice inside whispered, *Alien world*. Truly alien. Moon, Venus, Mars, all just dead rock, whether under black sky, yellow, or pink. This place, though . . . I shivered slightly, though it was hot in my suit, sweat trickling down my ribs, under my arms, trickling down 'til absorbent undergarments wicked it up, fed it to the suit systems, turning it back into drinking water.

Below, stark and alien in the middle of the beach, Christie's instrument cluster was unnaturally motionless, *powered down,* I realized. Christie herself was a tiny, spacesuited white doll figure perched precariously atop the weather station access platform.

Batteries. The dead batteries were gone too. Ah. Over there, piled at the foot of the eutectic fall, where she'd also parked the snowmobile. Maybe she was planning on hauling them back to camp to take away. Good idea. Nice of her to . . .

Beyond her on the beach, right down by the edge of the sea, was a writhing spill of color. Blue. Green. Red. A broad stripe of olive drab, like a foundation between the others, making it almost look like . . . well, no. Only to me. Christie's down by the beach. What was she seeing?

The colors were moving slowly, like swirls of oil in a lavalite.

I released my suit's whip antenna and turned up the transmitter gain, intending . . . the colors suddenly started to jitter and Christie seemed to crouch, as if coiled by tension. Like she was . . . expecting something? Jesus. Imagination run riot.

I said, "Christie?" There was a background hum in my earphones, feedback from the halftrack communication system.

The colors jumped like water splashing away from a thrown rock, but Christie didn't look up, seemed wholly focused on what she was seeing.

"Christie? Can you hear me?" Could she possibly have her suit *radio* turned off? Stupid. Fatally stupid in this place.

And the colors? They broke up into jags and zigzags as I spoke.

Waste heat. Radio waves are a form of heat. Just another sort of electromagnetic radiation, pumping energy into the environment.

Christie stood up straight, looking at her chaotic colors, putting one hand to her helmet, as if trying to scratch her head. She looked down, bending slightly at the waist so she could check to see her suit controls. What? Checking to make sure everything that could be turned off was?

"Christie!" The colors pulverized into hundreds of tiny

globulcs, which started winking out rapidly, one by one, then in
groups.

Christie suddenly stiffened and spun in place, looking up,
first at the clathrate collapse, then scanning along the top of the
cliff. I was just a speck up here, but starkly alien against the
sky, and she saw me in seconds.

Long moment of motionlessness, a quick glance back to
where the colors had been, as if reassuring herself they were
gone, then she waved to me. It took a minute or so before she
remembered to turn on the radio.

By the time I'd gotten the half-track down to the bottom of
the fall, wondering whether I ought to inject any words into the
silence, failing to make any decision, Christie'd turned the
instrument station back on, its weather station spinning and
nodding, my comm system picking up its signal, data relayed
to Workpoint 31, then on back through the microwave link to
Alanhold.

How much energy is there in a microwave beam?

Plenty, I guess. Human science is playing merry hell with the
Titanian   oh, hell. Ecosystem's not the right word, is it?
Not in this dead place. Well. Our science wasn't making nearly
the mess here Mother Nature'd made of Earth.

When we're gone, Titan will get over it.

Interesting to imagine a solar system empty but for our
pitiful few ruins.

I helped her load all the dead batteries into the halftrack's
unpressurized cargo bin, then followed her home in the snowmobile's wake, watching its misty rooster tail gradually grow
smaller as she drew ahead.

By the time I got into the habitat, she was already stripped to
her longjohns, bending over the open refrigerator door, rooting
around among a meager pile of microwave delights. Holding
the red plastic sack of a Quaker meatball sub in one hand, she
half turned, face curiously blank, and said, "You want anything? I got, uh . . ." She twisted, looking back into the fridge.

All sorts of goodies.

God damn it.

I said, "Christie, we need to talk about what you just did. I
mean, turning off your *radio*. . . ?"

She turned her back to me, putting the sub away, slowly

closing the refrigerator door, slowly straightening up, facing the wall. Finally, a whisper, "What did you *see,* Hoxha? How long were you . . ."

How odd. What *did* I see? While I was thinking, she turned and looked at me, startling me with the depth of fear in her eyes. What the hell could I *possibly* have seen, that I . . . "I'm not sure. You were watching . . . colors on the beach, over by the sea shore."

A bit of relief.

"You know, it's funny," I said, watching carefully. "Those colors almost looked like they were . . . I don't know. Making a picture. Swirls. Like abstract art."

The fear spiked.

She said, "Did you . . . mention what happened last time to . . . anyone?"

I told her about Gualteri, watching her swallow before she spoke again.

"What did he say?"

I shrugged. "Said it was none of his business. Said you'd let us know when you were ready to . . . puh—publish." *Publish!* Jesus.

Audible sigh, eyes rolling back a bit. Then she looked up at me, stepping closer, and said, "That's right, Hoxha. My business. Um. I'd like you to promise me you won't . . ."

"Christie, I want to know why you turned the radio off. Now." People willing to violate safety regs for their own purposes could kill us all. And you know that, Dr. Christine Meitner, Ph.D.

The look in her eyes became almost desperate. "Hoxha, I'll give you anything you want to keep your mouth shut."

Laughter made me stutter again. "You're offering me a *bribe?* What the hell did you have in mind, your Swiss bank account?" Scientist like this would get a pretty penny for a trip out here. A lot more than some miserable little engineering tech. "You think there's anything *left* of the fucking Alps?"

That made her flinch for just a second, not quite getting through. Me, I suddenly saw Geneva in flames as the sky burned blue-white with tektite rain.

She looked away, breathing with her mouth open, swaying slightly. When she turned back, I was shocked to see tears in her eyes. She said, "Christ, Hoxha. Please. I'll give you anything you want! Just name it!"

Then she took the zipper ring of her longjohns and pulled it open, open all the way down the front, showing me big, flabby breasts, roll of soft fat around her belly, ratty tuft of reddish brown pubic hair peeking through the vee at the bottom

Standing there then, looking at me, eyes pleading

And I felt my breath catch in my throat, caught by a bolt of unfamiliar feeling.

I put up my hand, palm toward her and, very softly, said, "Christie. Just tell me what's going on, okay?"

She looked down then, face clouded over. Slowly zipped up her longjohns, and I almost didn't catch what she said next.

It was, "I think the melted-crayon things are alive."

I held my laughter, looking at her, mouth hanging open.

It's all a lifetime ago, for all of us.

I remember when I was a little boy, seven years old, I guess, sitting with my grandfather, who must have been in his early sixties then, watching reports from the *Discovery* lander, setting down on Europa, releasing its probe, drilling down and down through pale red ice, down to a sunless sea.

Remember my grandfather telling me how, when he was seven, it'd been *Sputnik* on the TV, dirigible star terrifying on the edge that atom-menaced night, his grandfather a man born when the Wright Brothers flew, man who remembered being a little boy when Bleriot made his fabulous channel crossing.

There was no life under the icy crust of Europa, just a slushy sea of organic, scalding bubbles of water around lifeless black smokers. My grandfather died a few months before the first men got to Mars and proved there was no life there either, probably never had been, just as his grandfather died not long before *Apollo* touched down on the moon.

I figured I'd probably die just before men got to the nearest star, living on in some little boy's memory.

Shows how wrong you can be.

And now here I stood on Titan's lifeless chemical wonderland, facing a woman who'd gone mad, suffocating in a delirium of loss and denial.

Christie didn't argue with me, anger growing in her eyes, displacing the fear, masking her with the familiar scientist ego

I'd seen on so many self-important faces, so often before. Sometimes they say, "Well, you're just a tech," and turn away. More often than not, I guess.

Christie led me outside to the half-track and made me drive her back down to the beach. We parked the vehicle well clear of the instrument station and she told me to stand on top of the cargo bin. "You stay here and watch. Otherwise we'll make too much waste heat and . . ."

On the run then, no more words for me.

Over by the instrument station, she took a pair of utility tongs and fiddled with something I could see sticking out of the beach regolith. Squint . . . yes. The top of a small dewar bottle. When she uncorked it, a hazy mist jetted, like smoke from a genie's bottle, rolling briefly, beachscape beyond made oily looking by the vapor.

"What's that stuff?"

She was panting on the radio link, out of breath, voice loud in my ears as she pulled the bottle from the ice. "Distilled from beach infiltrates. It's . . . what they eat."

She had it clear now and was scurrying toward the rimy area where cracked-ice beach became Waxsea surface.

"What're you . . ."

"Shut up. Watch."

She suddenly dumped the bottle, just a splash of clear liquid that quickly curdled and grew dark, billow of greasy fog momentarily disfiguring the air, then scuttled back toward me, dropping off the tongs and empty bottle as she passed by the station.

And it didn't take long for the colors to bloom.

Before she got to my side, blobs of red and yellow, pink, green, blue, were surfacing by the edge of the beach. Surfacing and then sliding inward, making the beginnings of a ragged vortex around the chemical spill. Around and down, dropping under the surface, not quite disappearing, surfacing again.

The smoking puddle of goo started to shrink.

And Christie, standing beside me now, said, "You see? You *see?*"

I said, "I don't know what I'm seeing. I . . ." I jumped down off the halftrack, bounding slowly in the low-gee, heading across the beach.

Christie said, "*Stop!* Stop it, you'll . . ."

I stopped well short of the slowly writhing conflagration of colors, marveling at how they stayed distinct from one another. You'd think when the blue one touches the yellow, there'd be a bit of green along the interface. Nothing. not even a line. Not even an illusion of green, made by my Earth-grown eyes.

They looked sort of like cartoon amoebas, amoebas as a child imagines them before he's looked through a microscope for the first time and realized "pseudopod" means exactly what it says.

And it really did look like they were eating the goo.

Suddenly, the blue blob nearest where I stood became motionless. Grew a brief speckle of orange dots that seemed to lift above its surface for just a moment, then it was gone, vanished into the beach ice.

All in the twinkling of an eye, too quick to me to know exactly what I'd seen.

The others followed it into nothingness within a second or so, leaving the smoking goo behind, an evaporating puddle less than half its original size.

I think I stood staring, empty-headed, for about thirty seconds, before trying to imagine ways you could account for this without invoking the magic word *life*. "Christie?"

Nothing. But I could hear her rasping breath, made immediate by the radio link, though she could have been kilometers away. "Christie . . ." I turned around.

She was standing right behind me, less than two meters away, eyes enormous through the murky faceplate of her spacesuit. She was holding my ice axe, taken from its mount on the outside of the half-track, clutched in both hands, diagonal across her chest.

I stood as still as I could, looking into her eyes, trying to fathom . . . Finally, I swallowed, and said, "How long have you been standing there?"

"Long enough," she said. Then she let the axe fall, holding it in one hand, head raising a few icechips from the beach. "Long enough, but . . . I couldn't do it."

She turned and started to walk away, back toward the half-track.

The ride back to the habitat was eerie, full of that shocky feeling you get right after a serious injury, when the world seems remote and impossible. I couldn't imagine what would've happened if she'd tried to hit me with the axe.

Like something out of one of those damned stupid old movies.

The one about the first expedition to Mars, movie made almost a hundred years ago. The one where the repair crew is out on the hull when the "meteor storm" comes. There's a bullet-like flicker. The inside of this guy's helmet lights up, showing a stunned face, twisting in agony, then the light goes out and he's dead, faceplate fogged over black.

Just like that.

Our suit pressure's kept just a few millibars over Titan ambient by helium ballast. Maybe if she cut my suit, there'd be a spark and . . . I pictured myself running for the half-track, spouting twists of slow blue flame.

She said, "I guess . . ."

Nothing. Outside, the sky was dull brown and streaked with gold, as well-lit as Titan's sky ever gets. Somewhere up there, Saturn's crescent was growing smaller, deepening shadow cast over her rings. You could tell where the sun was, a small, sparkly patch in the sky, like a bit of pyrite fog.

I said, "I keep trying to think of ways it could just be some fancy chemical reaction. I mean, organic chemistry . . ."

She snickered, making my skin crawl.

Back in the habitat, out of our suits, sitting at the table in our baggy underwear, we ate Caravan Humpburgers so old the meat tasted like filter paper, the buns stiff and plasticky, and mushy french fries that must've been thawed and refrozen at least once in their history.

Too much silence. Christie sat reading the ads on the back of a Humpburger package. Something about a contest where if you saved your wrappers and got four matching Humpy the Camels, you could win a "science vacation" to Moonbase.

I pulled the thing out from under her fingers and looked at the fine print. The trip date had been seven weeks before the impact. Christ. I said, "Maybe whoever won this is still alive."

Or maybe, knowing what was about to happen, they just sent him home to die.

Christie was staring at me, eyes big and unreadable.

"You going to tell me about the crayon things now?"

Silence, then she slowly shook her head.

I found myself thinking about the way she'd looked a couple of hours ago, offering her virtue to me like . . . hell. Like a character in one of those silly romance vids Lisa was always watching when we . . . nothing in my head now but Christie with her suit liner zipped open, titties hanging out, eyes begging me to . . .

I felt my face relax in a brief smile.

Her eyes narrowed. "Who you going to tell?"

"Nobody. I guess I was . . . reconsidering your offer." My own snicker sounded nervous.

Christie's face darkened and her eyes fell, clouding over with anger. Then she said, "I . . . I'm not steropoeic."

Not . . . I suddenly realized the magnitude of her bribe, what it might've cost her to make the offer.

And then I was picturing us together, crammed into the little bunk, maybe sprawled on the habitat floor, having cleared away junk to make a big enough space.

Felt my breathing grow ever so slightly shallow?

Really?

No way to tell.

I said, "Sorry. I was just trying to . . . lighten things up. You know. I mean . . . when I saw you with that axe . . ."

She nodded slowly. "Are you really not going to tell?"

I shrugged. "What difference does it make?"

Eyes hooded. Keeping something to herself.

"You going to tell me?"

Long, shadowy look. Making up her mind about what kind of lie she might want to tell. The silence drew out, then there was that same little headshake.

I said, "Okay," then turned away and started getting into my suit, while she sat and watched. Every time I looked, there was something in her face, like she wanted to spill whatever it was.

Every time she saw me look, her face would shut like a door.

Once my suit was on and pressurized, I went out through the lock and was on my way.

I tried thinking about it rationally, all the long drive back, but I couldn't. All that kept coming into my head was, *What difference can it make now?* and, *Why does she care?*

Care enough to pick up an axe and consider splitting a doomed man's head.

There are fewer than two thousand people left alive in the entire universe. We are all going to die, sooner or later, when the tech starts to fail, when our numbers fall, the spare parts run out . . . when we all go mad and run screaming, bare-ass naked, for the airlocks.

I pictured myself depressing the halftrack, rolling out the lock door, rising to my feet in godawful cold, taking a deep breath of ghastly air and . . . hell. Can't even imagine what it might be like.

Like sitting in the electric chair, heart in your throat, senses magically alert, waiting for the click of the switch, the brief hum of the wires and . . . and then what?

We don't know.

Funny. Just a day ago, just yesterday, I thought I knew. Thought I wouldn't mind when the time came that I . . . yeah. Like Jimmy Thornton and his utility knife. Just like that.

I thought about getting myself a big bowl of nice warm water, sitting down on my bunk, all alone with the bowl between my legs, putting my hands and the knife under water, making those nice, painless cuts, watching the red clouds form.

Probably be a little bit like falling asleep, hm?

Jimmy looked asleep when they found him. Didn't even spill the water when he went under.

I crested the last hill before the base, Bonestell Cosmodrome coming over the horizon, and parked the half-track on a broad, flat ledge at the head of the approach defile, wondering why the hell my skin had begun to crawl.

TL-2 was on the launch pad now, tipped upright, fully fueled, her meilerwagen towed away. On Earth, a rocket like this is always surrounded by a falling mist of condensation. Here, where heating elements are used to keep the fuel from gelling, there's a narrow, rippling plume, mostly thermal distortion, going straight up.

Today, it only went up a few hundred meters, then was chopped off by wind shear.

As I watched, the engines lit, bubble of blue glow swelling between the landing jacks, *TL-2*'s dark cone shape lifting slowly. There was a sudden, snarled blossom of red-orange fire spilling across the plastic as superheated hydrogen started combining with atmospheric components, nitrogen, miscellaneous organics, HCN a major combustion byproduct.

The flame was a long, beautiful tongue of blue-white-yellow-red, swirling like a whirlwind as it climbed against the orange-brown sky, passing through first one layer of diaphanous blue cloud, then another, then disappearing, becoming diffuse light, then nothing.

She was on her way to Enceladus, I knew, where we'd found a few million liters of helium trapped in an old ice-9 cell, the precious gas one of the few things we couldn't make or mine on Titan.

As I put the halftrack in gear, heading on home, I thought about what it would be like to try to live for the rest of my life on the Moon, Earth's moon, the only real Moon, dead old Earth hanging like an ember in the sky.

Maybe we're making a mistake.

Maybe they should all come here.

Driving under a featureless brown sky, surrounded by a blue-misty landscape of red-orange-gold, I tried thinking about Christie's little beasties again, but failed.

I wound up hiding in my room, staring at the bulkhead for a while, then turning on the miniterm, watching with alarm as the screen sparkled, choking with colored static for a moment before the menu system came up.

What will happen when the electronics go?

Will we all die then? Or try lashing up homemade replacements, try flying without guidance, try . . . there was a space program before there were real computers. Men on the Moon, that sort of thing. That technology might have gotten us out here. Maybe not.

Nothing in the base library I hadn't seen a hundred times already, other than those last dozen episodes of *Quel Horreur,* the French-language sitcom that'd been all the rage right before the end. JPL wasted one of its last uplinks on that and . . . well, they knew. They must've known. What were they thinking?

Can't imagine.

I'd watched about thirty seconds of the first one, happy laugh-track, pale blue skies, white clouds, green trees, River Seine and *Tour Eiffel.*

Stayed in my room so I wouldn't have to deal with Jennah, who kept on looking at me as I stopped by the mess to pick up my dinner. Went to my room and then couldn't stop thinking about her, about the last time we'd . . . which led to thinking about Christie with her longjohns hanging open, offering herself up to a fate worse than death, then on to Lisa, sprawled in our marriage bed.

They say you can't really remember pain, remembering only the fact of it, not the precise way it felt. Maybe the same thing's true of happiness.

I hung like a ghost beneath the ceiling of a room that no longer existed, looking down on a naked woman whose touch, taste, feel, laughter I was already losing, grappling with the loss, struggling to reclaim the few bits and pieces I had left.

Sometimes I wonder why I ever left Earth. Maybe we could've been happy without the money. Maybe.

Regret, they say, is the most expensive thing in the world, but it's a lie. Regret is free; you get to have as much regret as you want. And then, when you're done wanting regret, you find it's yours to keep forever.

At some point while I was staring at the base library menu system, the remembered image of Lisa turned to the much fresher image of Jennah, damp and eager in my arms, then, somehow, to Christie, huge eyes beseeching.

The next day, I went on out to Workpoint 17, a drilling platform on the backside of Aerhurst ridge from Alanhold, sitting at the top of a long slope, giving a vista like nothing on Earth, or any other place I'd been, long, flat, fading into the mist dozens of kilometers away, like the greatest ski run you could ever imagine.

When I first got here, the sight of these vistas, wonderful and strange, made me think about all the places I'd been already, made me think about the red crayons of Mars, the rugged orange mountains of Venus, the soft black lava plains of the Moon.

Made me remember my first sight of Earth from space, stark, incredible, white-frosted blue seen from the other side of the sky.

I remembered standing atop the terminal scarp of Terra Noursae, looking out over the Waxsea's unimaginable wasteland, and wondering if I shouldn't tell Lisa I was never coming home, that I'd keep on giving her the money, all the money, but she'd have to find another man to help her spend it, another man with whom to have those children we'd discussed.

Christ, they were talking about the moons of Uranus back then! And me, I started thinking about what it'd be like to stand on a cliff ten kilometers high. Started thinking about the geysers of Triton, dim blue Neptune hanging in the black sky overhead. . . .

It still had the power to make my insides cramp with desire.

Workpoint 17 was manned by two Russian women who'd been brought out from the Fore Trojans about two years back, a pair of stocky, blunt-faced, red-headed petroleum geologists from Kazakhstan, looking like twin sisters, maybe in their forties, maybe a lot older, who'd been knocking around the solar system for something like fifteen years.

They'd always been cut-ups, kind of fun to be around, always ribbing each other, ribald stuff half in English, half not, kidding about who was going to have me first and who'd have to take sloppy seconds, though I always figured them for lesbians.

It was inside their habitat, with its stark, vinegary smell, watching one of them getting out of her suit, broad rump poking up, seam of her longjohns starting to pull apart where the stitching would soon give way, that I made some vulgar remark or another.

Irena, I think it was, looked at Larisa, owl eyed with surprise, then back at me, making a wan smile.

"Uh. Sorry."

Irena stood up, facing me now, spacesuit still cluttered around her ankles, and, very gently I thought, said, "Don't be. We've been worried about you."

Later, I sat in one of my parking places, high atop Aerhurst, on a crag of pure white ice projecting from where the beaten track crosses the low shoulder of a slumping, rounded peak, lights out, engines off, all but powered down, staring out the window.

In the distance, over the lowlands, was a torrential rainstorm, vast, flat, blue-gray cloud hanging under a darkened sky. The rainfall beneath it was like a pointillist fog, freckled with dots too little to see, somehow there nonetheless, an edgeless pillar of silver-blue blotting out the landscape beyond.

Atmospheric cooling.

Somewhere above the clouds, I knew Saturn was all but gone, turned to black, blotting out the sun. I looked up, trying to make out the shadow's edges, make out the ringplane backscatter, but the turbulence was too great today.

Maybe some other time.

Just what I'd thought of saying to Irena and Larisa, anticipating an offer that never came. Still, it was nice to think of them worrying about me. As though I still mattered to anyone at all.

The comm light on the dashboard began to wink, an eye-catching sequence of red-blue-amber-green, one color following the other at quarter-second intervals, colors merging into a brief, bright sparkle. I reached out and touched a button with the tip of my finger, spoke my call sign, and listened.

Christie's voice came out of a rustle of static: "Can you schedule me for a maintenance visit?"

Something about that voice, odd, nervous, reluctant, eager. Or maybe it was just my imagination. How much can you read into a voice turned to whispers by radio interference?

"What's wrong?"

Long pause.

"I'm not sure. Maybe the same as before, only worse."

Nothing much had been wrong before. A few toasted chips; nothing serious, nothing that couldn't have waited if I hadn't been . . . I scrolled my schedule, thinking about Christie, about her colored waxworks beasties, about . . .

I said, "I'm on a routine maintenance run through the automated geophone chain this side of the ridgeline. I can divert to your workpoint between numbers three and four."

"When?"

Urgency?

Nothing's urgent anymore.

I said, "Thirty-one hours."

Much longer pause. "Oh."

The disappointment was stark, bursting right through the static.

She said, "I guess that'll be okay."

"See you then."

I punched the button and sat back to watch the rainstorm build as the sky grew slowly darker above it, taking on the rich colors of mud.

What can have happened? What can she be wanting? Something to do with the melted-crayon things? Certainly not anything to do with *me*. My thoughts strayed again to her zipped-open longjohns, making me smile at myself. I'd never been one for a one-track mind. Not in this lifetime.

But funny things happen when life's reduced to terminal stress.

She was waiting, suited up outside, standing by the powerplant, when I rolled up to the workpoint, scrunching into the airlock, cycling on through. I've seldom been inside a halftrack while someone else is coming aboard; the hollow thumping of knees and feet on metal and plastic, the odd lurchings, were all very unnatural.

The inner hatch popped open, filling the cabin with a faint alcohol and ammonia tang, quickly suppressed when Christie opened her helmet, folded it back, pushed aside by human gastrointestinal smells.

I remembered an old story where that'd been the smell of Titan, because its author was thinking of methane and swamp gas, barnyard smells and all.

Silly.

They put butyl mercaptan in natural gas so you'll smell a leak.

Her face had a damp, suffocated look, as if being in the spacesuit made her claustrophobic. "Let's go," she said.

I unclutched the tracks and set off, lurch of the cabin throwing her against my shoulder, felt her brace herself, keeping what distance she could, not much in this little space. How much of what I'm feeling is fossil emotion, old subroutines frozen in my head?

I don't know what I want because I'm afraid, is that it?

I said, "Christie? When are you going to tell me what's going on?"

When I turned my head to look, her face was no more than a hand's breadth away, but facing forward, eyes not blinking as she watched familiar Titanscape come and go. Overhead, from down in the bottom lands, the eclipsed sky was the color of a fresh bruise, blue and gray, dull purple, tinted with vague streamers of magenta.

Then she turned her head toward me, eyes on mine. That

brought her close enough we were breathing on each other. You
know how that goes. You get in each other's facial space and
there's tension there, because the next move is that forward
craning, that . . .

She looked away again, not outside, just at the inner surface
of the wall, at a circuit breaker panel mounted about eye level.
"Did you tell anyone else?"

I shrugged. "Nothing to tell, I guess."

No answer. Tension in the arch of her neck. I wanted to reach
out and touch her, tell her some nonsense about how it'd be
all right. Then, with my arm around her, with her space
invaded . . . there's something about the vulnerability of fear,
about there being some terrible thing wrong.

She said, "Pull up here. Let's get out."

We'd come to the cliffs by the beach, but were still some
distance from the familiar way down, rolling one at a time out
the lock, then following my earlier tracks to the place where I'd
spied on her before. They'd been joined by numerous other
footprints now, hundreds coming and going.

All hers, I guess.

There was a thin wisp of black smoke rising above the
instrument package, like an elongated drop of india ink in clear
water, rolling with the convection currents, just beginning to
dissipate.

And, all around it on the beach, were swipes and smears of
color, shades and shapes moving round and round, all so very
slowly. As I watched, a dark blue one came close, stretching
out a long, narrow pseudopod. It came within a few centimeters
of one support leg, hesitated for a moment, then touched.

The pseudopod shriveled, shrinking quickly back toward the
main body, which seemed to roll over, turning to a lighter shade
of blue, then sinking into the beach, gone in an instant.

There was another black curl in the air, rising above the
instrument package, drifting slowly away as it dissipated. I
thought of the sample I'd taken of that earlier instrument
contamination, presumably still in the halftrack refrigerator
where I'd left it.

Little beasties investigating the alien machine. Innocent little
beasties getting themselves killed.

Is curiosity just a tropism?

Moths to the flame.

I said, "I guess that makes your case, hmm?"

I don't know what I expected next, but she said, "Turn off your radio now."

"Um . . ."

She turned and put her hand on my arm. I couldn't feel it through the suit material, but those big eyes, begging . . . I switched it off and waited. She just turned away, quickly stepping to the edge of the cliff, dangerously close given the fragility of this chemical ice, and pulsed the carrier wave power setting of her suit's comm system, one, two, three, off.

All very much like in a movie.

Down on the beach, the wax things froze in place, a conscious freezing, just the way a spider will freeze the instant it realizes you're looking. That sudden crouch, alien eyes pointing your way, spider brain filled with unknowable thoughts.

I remembered the way one of these things had grown a speckle of orange dots before and recalled a science film I'd seen as a kid, high speed photography of slime molds in action. Eerie. Not more so than this.

Suddenly, between one frame and the next, the beach was empty.

In all those old movies, old stories, they get the feeling of this moment terribly wrong, don't they? I reached for my comm controls, but Christie, catching my movement from the corner of one eye, raised a restraining hand.

Wait.

I . . .

Down on the beach, a flat, ragged-edged plain of blue formed. Time for a few heartbeats, then a sharp-edged stripe of pink slid across the side of the plain nearest our vantage point.

Then a conical shape slid into view from the other side, visibly falling toward the pink.

Falling.

Just before it hit, there was a reddish-orange swirl under the blunt side of the cone. It slowed to a stop, popping out little landing legs, flame gouting on the surface, then winking out.

Little blue and green dots appeared, embedded in the pink, drawing in toward the motionless cone. As they drew close, one by one, they would turn black and vanish. After a while, you could see they'd learned to keep their distance, hovering around the edge of the picture.

My mouth was dry as I switched on my radio and whispered, "How the hell do they know what our sense of perspective is like?"

Whispered, as though someone might be listening. Something.

Her voice was hardly more than a breath, blowing through my earphones: "They're not really two dimensional creatures."

It's not Flatland. They're not waxy paintings on the surface of the ground.

Fire blossomed under the cone and it lifted off, climbing out of the picture, and all the remaining blue dots turned black before vanishing.

After a while, more of them crept from the edge of the picture, creeping through the pink toward the place where the cone had been. At first, the leaders turned black and died, but only for a little while. In time, they finished their investigations, then went sliding on their way.

The blue plain with its empty pink strip vanished suddenly, and the beach was empty again.

I turned to her and said, "Why'd you show me this?"

Seen through the faceplate, she was nothing but eyes. Big blue eyes. Serious. Frightened. "I won't make this decision by myself. I'm not . . ." Long hesitation. "You know."

Yeah. Not God. That's how that one goes.

Back at the habitat, after a long, silent ride, we sat together in our longjohns, made tea and drank it, made small talk that went nowhere, circling round and round, as if something had changed, or nothing.

We're dead men here, I'd thought on the way back, watching a snowdrift blow across the beaten path before the halftrack, slowing down as if to stop, then suddenly lifting off in the wind like a flock of birds making for the sky, clearing the way for us.

Fewer than two thousand survivors . . .

In the old stories, old movies, that would've been more than enough, two thousand hot, eager Adams and Eves, getting about their delving and spanning, wandering the freshly butchered landscape, pausing by the shores of an infinite, empty sea, being fruitful, multiplying until they'd covered the Earth again.

This star system no longer contains an inhabitable planet.

Bits of memory, snatches of Moonbase newsreel. When

Oberth gets home with the crew of the Venus orbital station, who hadn't had to commit suicide, she'll be bringing a stockpile of hardened probes intended for research on the surface of Venus.

Hardened probes, and, of course, one of the piloted Venus landers.

Then we'll know for sure. Then we'll . . .

Couldn't stop myself from imagining, ever so briefly, myself on that first damned crew, riding the Venus lander down through howling brown muck, down to a soft landing in my own backyard.

I've been on Venus. I'm qualified for Venus EVA ops. I . . .

Read a science article when I was a kid that described the Chicxulub impact at the KT Boundary as being "like taking a blowtorch to western North America."

The image in my head was a double exposure, the image of collapsed and burned out cities, like something from an atomic war fantasy, superimposed over the reality of a cooling lava ejecta blanket.

Just wisps of smoke.

That's all that's left of her.

Christie, face pushed down in the steam from her teacup, was looking at me strangely. God knows what my expression must have been like. Did you have anyone, Christie Meitner, or was it only strangers that died? Billions and billions of strangers.

She said, "I guess we'd better talk about it now." Unsaid, Whether we want to or not.

I nodded, not knowing what I wanted, looking into a face that wasn't all that expressive. A face not so different from my own. I tried to remember what I looked like, call up the man in the mirror, but there was only fog, no way to know what she was looking at now with those big, hollow eyes.

She said, "It's so simple, Hoxha: They're alive, and this is their world. If we stay here, even just the few score of us, Titan's environment will slowly change; until this is no longer an inhabitable world for them."

And then?

Right.

"Does it make a difference now that we know they're intelligent?"

She shook her head. "If we work together to keep it secret, to keep the others from stumbling over this, once we go away, back to Moonbase . . ."

I said, "The Earth's not going to recover and we can't survive forever at Moonbase. The Saturn system's our best bet, otherwise were spread too thin. Even Mars . . ."

She said, "The odds are against us, no matter what."

I nodded.

"So we come here, obliterate the Titanians, and then die out *anyway,* erasing their future as well as ours."

Does this mean anything? What's my next line? I know: Christie, this is proof positive life is common in the universe. Right. Idiot. I remember the way she'd looked, face so pale, eyes so big, standing behind me with the ice axe, willing herself to kill. How many Titanians would've exploded and burned under the beach had my blood been spilled?

I said, "So that's what all this is about? Some good old-fashioned eco . . ." Right. Like the idiots who protested *Cassini*'s launch all those years ago while not doing a damned thing about the world's hundred thousand hydrogen bombs.

Pick your targets. Some are easier than others.

She seemed tired. "It's not just that. If it was just about them being living things, intelligent living things, you wouldn't be sitting here now."

"Dead and buried?" I smiled. "That would've been hard for you to explain."

"I wasn't thinking clearly. I was panicked that you'd . . ."

"What, then? Why am I still here?"

Long, long stare, still trying to fathom if there was a human being behind my face, someone just like her. She said, "Day before yesterday, I found evidence that their life process involves some kind of directed nucleosynthesis."

You could see the relief in her face. There. I've said it. And . . .

Nucleosynthesis?

Talking about details is what we're doing.

In those old stories, old movies, the details are always important, imaginary science chatted up by happy, competent characters until God springs from the machine and utters his funny-elf punchline.

Now?

Not important.

Not anymore.

And yet . . .

I said, "That could tip the scales in our favor. We come here, we learn to exploit them, we survive as a species."

Her face fell.

I don't think she expected me to see it that easily.

Probably there was a scenario in there in which the pedantic teacher explains things to the gaping mechanic in the simplest possible terms. That's the story way, isn't it?

She sat back in her chair and sighed. "I don't know what we should do. Do you?"

People love to pretend they make rational decisions. It's called excuse-seeking behavior. Christie and I sat facing one another for a long time, tension making it seem we were about to speak, but we never did. You want to be the first one to start offering up excuses? No, not me. How about you? If it was important enough to reach for that axe, surely . . .

I wasn't thinking clearly.

Right.

So we talked about the evidence, which she explained to me in the simplest possible terms, until I was able to pick up the thread and begin spooling it into my own knowledge base, understanding it in my own terms. Understanding. That's an important part of making excuses for what you *do*, isn't it?

Or what you fail to do.

Think about the possibilities, Christie.

Think about the technology we could build here. Think of the resource base. And the Titanians? Is it important what happens to them?

In the end, we slept, I curled up on the floor, Christie huddled in her bed, back toward me, curled in on herself, head down in the vague shadows between her body and the wall. I lay awake for a while, trying to think about the whole damned business, trying to convince myself, God damn it, that it *mattered*.

When I awoke, however many hours later, Christie was on the floor beside me, asleep, not touching me, head on one corner of the folded-up blanket I was using for a pillow.

Lisa never did that. Lisa always had to touch me while we slept together, sometimes huddling against my back, other times insisting that I curl myself around her like a protective shell. I remember when we were very young and new to each other, how I used to wake up sometimes to find her breathing right in my face.

Breathing in each other's breath, I used to call it. As intimate a thing as I could possibly imagine.

So, awakening, breakfasted, we got in the halftrack and went back down to Waxsea beach, where the fairy tales of science were waiting after all.

I don't know what made me stop the halftrack up on the terminal scarp. Maybe just some . . . sense of impending something. Maybe just a longing for the view. Christie stared at me for a second or two when I told her to get out, Stirlings vibrating the frame below us, idling down in the track trucks. Then she nodded, folded her helmet over her face, pressurized the suit, wrinkly off-white skin suddenly growing stiff and shiny, obliterating her shape.

When the depress valve had woofed, when I could see her out the cockpit window, I had a sudden memory of an old TV commercial from the retrofad going on when I was in grammar school. Pillsbury Doughboy.

Doughboy. Funny. Wonder if those long-dead copywriters imagined him with a tin-plate helmet and bayoneted Enfield, marching upright and stalwart into the machine-gun fire of no-man's-land.

I think she was relieved when I joined her on the surface, no way to tell through the suit visor, just those same eyes, with their same expression, a pasted-on affect of surprise, fear, resentment. But she followed me to the edge of the cliff, where we stopped, and I let her get behind me, image of the ice axe fresh enough, hardly mattering.

And, of course, there was the cliff. One hard shove and I'd float on down to . . . I don't know. Gravity here's low enough I might survive the fall, given that two bar atmosphere, but . . . would my suit?

I imagined myself exploding like a bomb.

Overhead, the sky stretched away toward the absent horizon like a buckled red blanket, crumpled clouds of coarse wool, dented here, there, everywhere with purple-shadowed hollows, little holes into nothingness.

Down on the silvery beach, the instrument platform was ringed by motionless blobs, each ring a single color, blue, green, red, violet, working their way outward from the hardware.

Christie grunted, "Never saw that before." Radio made it seem like she was inside my suit, pressed up against my back, chin on my shoulder, speaking into my ear.

If you looked closely, you could see the blobs were connected by thin strands, monochrome along the rings, blended between. Slowly, one of the blobs extended a pseudopod toward the platform. That's right. In a minute, it'll blacken and curl, shriveling in on itself until the parent blob goes belly up an sinks out of sight. Will the ring close up then, each soldier in that row taking one easy step, forward into an empty space, like Greeks in a phalanx?

Christie said, "I wonder why they do it?"

Inviting certain death in the pursuit of knowledge?

Good question.

The pseudopod slowed as it came close, flattening, widening, forming a sort of two-dimensional cup on its end, a cup that drifted slowly back and forth, arcing along the surface, a few centimeters out. After a moment, beads of yellow began forming at the cup's focus, detaching, speeding back up the pseudopod to the parent blob. From there, they replicated, spreading around the ring, then outward.

I said, "Think they know we're here?"

The first blob withdrew its pseudopod, while the next one in line extended an identical . . . instrument? Is that the right word? Examining the next section of the platform's heat shield.

Christie said, "I don't know. Their radio sensitivity's not that great. I always have to turn the carrier wave full blast to get their attention."

I turned away, stepping back the way we'd come. "I guess we should just go on down and . . ."

Not sure what I was going to suggest. Christie gasped and put out a hand, gripping my forearm hard enough that my suit was compressed, forcing the liner up against my skin, feeling like cold, damp plastic, making me shiver slightly.

When I looked back, down on the beach, the rings had broken up, blobs perfectly spherical now, appearing and disappearing in the cracked ice, like colored ping-pong balls bobbing in a tub of water. Bobbing in unison.

One, two, three . . .

They exploded like so many silver raindrops, reaching out for one another, merging, spreading like a cartoon tide, until the beach was a solid silver mirror filling the space between the cliff, the sea, the instrument package, reflecting a slightly hazy image of the red sky above, complete with streamers of golden light coming through little rents and tears, picking out the drifting snowbanks like dustmotes on a lazy summer afternoon.

Somewhere overhead, I saw, there was a tiny fragment of rainbow floating in the sky.

The image in the mirror grew dark, dimming slowly, as though night were falling, though the real sky hung above us unchanged, streamers of light tarnishing, red becoming orange then brown, bruise blue, then indigo, almost black.

Almost, for freckles of silver remained.

Freckles of silver in a peculiarly familiar pattern, bits of light clustered here and there, gathering to a diagonal band across the middle and . . .

Christie's gasp made me imagine warmth in my ear as she recognized it a fraction of a second before I did. Well, of course. She'd seen the real thing a lot more recently than I had.

The stars dimmed, Milky Way becoming just a dusty, dusky suggestion of itself.

Christie's voice: "*How?* How could they *see* . . ."

A bright silver light popped up in the center of the starfield, circled by dimmer lights, some brighter than others, most white, some colored, this one blue, that one red.

Tiny bright beads began flying from the blue light, swinging by orange Jupiter, heading for yellow Saturn, some stopping there, others flying on, disappearing from the scene.

In a row across the bottom of the image, bottom being the side facing us, flat, near-schematic representations of space-craft appeared, matching each tiny bead as it flew. Little *Pioneer.* The *Voyagers. Cassini* and *Huygens* . . .

Voice no more than a hushed whisper, Christie said, "I wonder how long they knew? Why they waited so long and . . . why *me?*"

If they knew about *Pioneer,* then they knew about us when

my father was a little boy, my grandfather a young man, reveling in the deeds of space, imagining himself in the future, still young, strong, alive and happy.

Down on the beach, the solar system faded, leaving the hint of starfields behind; then, like a light winking on, blue Earth appeared, oceans covered by rifted clouds, continents picked out in shades of ocher, hard to recognize, circled by a little gray Moon.

I could feel Christie's hand tighten on my shoulder, knowing what was coming.

There. The asteroid. The brilliant violet light of the hydrogen bombs. The spreading of the fragments. The impacts. The red glow of magma. The spreading brown clouds.

I wondered briefly if they'd had something to do with the rock coming our way. No. That's just an old story thing, pale imagination left in my head when I was a child.

One of those damned things we teach our children because we don't know what's real. Don't know and don't care.

Somewhere in my head, a badly fueled story generator supplied images of what would come next. Down on the beach, the image of a tentacled alien would form. Something not human, but within the reach of terrestrial evolution, would stretch out a suckered paw, inviting.

Take me to your leader.

What was I remembering?

"The Gentle Vultures"?

Maybe so.

Down on the beach, the end of the world faded, replaced by a white disk, wrinkled in concentric rings. It tipped around, as if in 3D motion, showing us complex mechanisms, considerable mechanical detail, obvious control systems.

I said, "Fresnel lenses."

Christie said, "They could see through the clouds with that, if they could build it for real. See the sun, the larger planets, the brighter stars, as patches of heat in their sky. But . . ."

The infrared telescope was replaced by an image of Titan, recognizable by the topography of Terra Noursae, Titan stripped of its clouds. The image rotated, showing the Waxsea hemisphere, Waxsea bearing interconnected concentric rings, some gigantic version of the array we'd first come upon here.

Christie said, "Long baseline interferometer. With enough computation . . ."

If they could build it.

Nucleosynthesis?

I said, "How do you distinguish between a life process and a technology?"

Christie said, "Oh," sounding surprised.

Imagination builds nothing. Not even the knowledge of how to build. Not unless you can somehow project it into the real world.

Down on the beach, another image formed, a fantastically detailed portrait of the cosmodrome, showing the two landers upright on their pads. On the ridge above, tiny blue Titanians waited at a safe distance, ominous, like Indians looming above the ambush, foolishly cavalry waiting in the defile.

A blue sphere rolled down, making for the little ships. I waited for them to be spun down, like tenpins before the ball.

It rolled to a stop, not far from the ships. Tiny, spacesuited humans connected a blue thread to the ball, to the ships. The ball shrank away to nothing. The ships took off, unrolling red flame as they climbed through an orange overcast and were gone.

Behind them, the base and cosmodrome disappeared, one component at a time, leaving an empty landscape behind.

Christie sighed in my headphones.

Just one more all-too-familiar fairy tale, that's all.

Below, the silver screen cleared again, reforming as faint stars against velvet dark, surmounted by a slow-moving orrery of the solar system. Beads of light moved from Saturn to blue Earth—*brown,* I thought. They should've made it brown.

The sky stood empty. Christie said, "I guess . . ."

I whispered, "Sending us home to die then?"

Another bead appeared, crossing from Earth to Saturn, then going home again. Then again. Then again. More beads, this time from Saturn to Neptune. After a while, the voyages began a three-way trip, Saturn, Neptune, Earth.

What's at Neptune?

Triton, of course.

I remembered how much I'd always wanted to go there, almost willing to abandon Lisa just so I could see diaphanous geysers against a deep blue world, out on the edge of the infinite.

Christie seemed somehow hollow, as if she were speaking from the depths of a dream. "They send us home to the Moon. Help us to survive with trade and . . . I . . ." She stopped.

What are you thinking about, Christie? That you might see the atmospheres of the gas giants after all? Is that it?

She said, "We could never mine tritium from the atmosphere of Jupiter, where it's free for the taking. Not in that radiation environment. Not anytime soon."

Tritium. Out of the depths of the past, I suddenly remember the *Daedalus* designs, so long forgotten.

She said, "Even out here at Saturn, there's a deep gravity well to contend with. And the collision danger from equatorial ringplane debris spiraling in. Neptune . . ."

Low-density gas giant with all the tritium we might want. And a big icemoon for the Titanians to . . .

A myriad of bright sparks suddenly emerged from the Earth, moving not toward another planet, but receding into the background sky, sky whose stars grew bright again, while the fleet of sparks grew smaller and smaller, until it merged with an unremarkable pattern of stars.

Christie muttered, "Something in Pavo, I think. I was never very good with the lesser constellations."

Delta Pavonis?

Is there a planet there? A planet just like the one we lost?

I said, "You think their technology's *that* good?"

She looked up at me, still nothing more than big eyes looking out through scratched, foggy plastic. "Maybe not. Not out here in the ice and cold. But put together with *ours* . . ."

Maybe so.

I said, "I guess the decision wasn't ours to make after all."

I awoke in the middle of the night, opening my eyes on darkness defiled by blue light from the instrument panels, perched on the edge of the bunk, curled inward, shadow of my head, shadow of tousled hair cast on the habitat wall. Christie was bunched into the space between my body and the wall, curled in on herself, the two of us damp and soft against one another, sharing some soft old blanket.

Somewhere outside, a new day is dawning.

Some time during that day we'll have to make our decision, get in the half-track, go on back to base and . . .

What will happen?

Oh, nonsense. The fantasy we've just been through was no better than one more iteration of White Man's Burden.

The decision's been made. Not by us.

All we have to do is carry out our part, speak our lines according to the script.

Lights. Camera. Action.

Fade to black.

If I held still, paid attention, I could feel Christie's back against my chest, moving slowly in and out as she breathed, pausing briefly before reversing direction. Asleep, I guess. I tried hard to remember what Lisa'd felt like sleeping against me.

Faded and gone, like just about everything else.

I listened for the soft sound of breath coming and going through what I imagined would be an open mouth, hollow breathing like the ghost of a snore, but the sounds of Titan coming through the habitat wall blotted it out. Sighing wind close by. A large wind farther away, moaning in the hills. Tidal creak of the deep crustal ice coming to us through the floor.

Christie seemed to sigh in her sleep, pressing back against me ever so slightly, like something from a dream.

I remembered the lights merging with the stars and found myself dreaming of a new world, of standing on a hillside under a crimson sunset, alien sun in the sky, sun with prominences and corona plain against the sky, something from a remembered astronomical illustration. Something from a children's book.

As in all children's books, there's a woman under my arm, standing close against me, standing close.

Below us, below the hillside, was a rim of dark forest, trees like feathery palms swaying in a tropical breeze, beyond it, a golden sea, stretching out flat to the end of the world.

Us?

Or just a dream?

Christie stirred suddenly, turned half toward me, nuzzling her head against my shoulder, and murmured, "Maybe things will . . . work out after all."

After all that.

It was a moment before I realized what she meant.

Another moment before I felt the burden lift out of my heart, ghosts hurrying away to their graves, one more golden tomorrow awakening from a dream.

PENGUIN PUTNAM INC.
Online

Your Internet gateway to a virtual environment with
hundreds of entertaining and enlightening books from
Penguin Putnam Inc.

*While you're there, get the latest buzz on
the best authors and books around—*

Tom Clancy, Patricia Cornwell, W.E.B. Griffin,
Nora Roberts, William Gibson, Robin Cook,
Brian Jacques, Catherine Coulter, Stephen King,
Jacquelyn Mitchard, and many more!

**Penguin Putnam Online is located at
http://www.penguinputnam.com**

PENGUIN PUTNAM NEWS

Every month you'll get an inside look at our upcoming
books and new features on our site. This is an ongoing
effort to provide you with the most up-to-date
information about our books and authors.

**Subscribe to Penguin Putnam News at
http://www.penguinputnam.com/ClubPPI**